Iain B   ʳst
novel _ _ _ꓑ _ꓥctory_, in 1984. Since then he haᴣ gained
enormous popular and critical acclaim with further works of both
fiction and science fiction, all of which are available in paperback
from either Abacus or Orbit. His novel _The Crow Road_ was a
number one bestseller and was adapted for television. _The Times_
has acclaimed Iain Banks as 'the most imaginative British novelist
of his generation'. His latest novel with Abacus is _Stonemouth_
which was described by _The Times_ as 'Tender, funny and heart-
stoppingly exciting'.

'Banks's clever, tense book gives a good idea of where fiction might
usefully go with this material. Staying away from the media-
described events at Ground Zero, he impressively details the social
aftermath in London: paranoia on underground trains and in high
buildings, suspicion of foreigners, a delirious new edge to political argument and sexual encounters'

Mark Lawson, _Guardian_

'Banks ranks – along with Irvine Welsh and Ian Rankin – as one
of Scotland's most successful writers, and his new novel, _Dead Air_,
will do nothing to diminish his reputation. A thrilling read, it's a
dazzlingly clever, edgy, suspenseful book'

Scotland on Sunday

'A Buchanesque adventure yarn set in 21ˢᵗ-century London'

The Times

'_Dead Air_ is just one of many immediate responses to a shocking
event, the kind of exhausting, careering ride of a novel adored by
speed junkies. Possibly though, it's just what we all need'

Independent

IAIN BANKS

Dead Air

ABACUS

First published in Great Britain in 2002
by Little, Brown
First published by Abacus in 2003
Reprinted 2003 (six times), 2004, 2007, 2009

This edition published by Abacus in 2013

A CIP catalogue record for this book
is available from the British Library.

ISBN 978-0-349-13924-1

Typeset by Palimpsest Book Production Limited,
Falkirk, Stirlingshire
Printed and bound in Great Britain by Clays Ltd, St Ives plc

Papers used by Abacus are from well-managed forests
and other responsible sources.

MIX
Paper from
responsible sources
FSC® C104740

Abacus
An imprint of
Little, Brown Book Group
100 Victoria Embankment
London EC4Y 0DY

An Hachette UK Company
www.hachette.co.uk

www.littlebrown.co.uk

For Roger

With thanks to Mic and Brad

Contents

One

'B' IS FOR APPLE

'You're breaking up.'

'—orry?'

'Never mind.'

'—at?'

'See you later.' I folded the phone.

This was three weeks before the stuff with the Clout club and Raine (sorry; the stuff with the Clout club and 'Raine') and the taxi and the road under the railway bridge and the window and the nose-biffing incident and basically the whole grisly West-to-East-End night experience when I realised some bastard or bastards unknown seriously wanted to harm me, or even – and this was according to their own threats – kill me.

All of which actually happened not far from here (here where we're starting; here where we're picking up our story precisely because it was like the start and the end of something, a time when everyone knew exactly where they were), all of it probably within sight, if not a stone's throw, of this raised *here*. Maybe; there's no going back to check because the place where we're starting's not there any more.

Whatever; I associate what happened in one place with

3

what happened in the other, with things beginning and finishing and – like the first tile in one of those impressive but
irredeemably geeky record-breaking domino-falling displays
that people stage in sports halls, where one tiny event leads
to a whole toppling, fanning, branching cascade of tiny events,
which happen so fast and so together they become one big
event – with just stuff generally being *set in train*, being pinged
from a rest state into restless, reckless, spreading, escalating
motion.

'Who was that?' Jo joined me at the parapet.

'No idea,' I lied. 'Didn't recognise the number.'

She pushed a short glass into my hand. There was ice in the
whisky and an apple squatting on top of the glass like a fat
red-green backside on a crystal toilet. I looked over my shades
at her.

She extracted a strip of celery from her Bloody Mary and
clinked my glass with hers. 'You should eat.'

'I'm not hungry.'

'Yeah. Precisely.'

Jo was small with very thick black hair – cut short – and
very thin white skin – variously pierced. She had a wide, rock-
star's mouth, which was sort of fitting as she did PR for the
Ice House record label. Today she was looking vaguely Drowned
World-era Madonna-ish, with black tights, a short tartan skirt
and an old leather jacket over an artfully ripped T-shirt. People,
not all Americans, had been known to call her cute and feisty,
though not normally twice. She had a temper, which was why
I automatically lied about the phone call even though I had
no reason to. Well, almost no reason.

I hoisted the apple from the glass and took a bite. It looked
shiny and great but tasted of nothing much. Jo was probably
right that I ought to eat something. Breakfast had been some
orange juice and a couple of lines of coke each. I did very little
of that stuff these days, but I had this theory that the last time

4

you want to get coked up is late at night when you just make your body stay up way beyond the time it wants to and you therefore stand a good chance of missing the next day; snort during the hours of daylight instead and sort of slide off into alcohol as the evening descends, so maintaining something remotely like the body's usual rhythms.

As a result we hadn't eaten much of the wedding brunch at all and probably should force ourselves to eat a little, just to keep things on an even keel. On the other hand the apple was pretty unappetising. I put it down on the chest-high brick parapet. It wobbled and started to roll towards the drop. I caught it and steadied it before it could fall the hundred or so feet to the pitted asphalt of the abandoned car park beneath. Which was not, in fact, totally abandoned; my pal Ed had left his gleaming new yellow Porsche at one end, near the gates. Everybody else had parked in the almost unnaturally quiet and empty street on the other side of the old factory.

Kulwinder and Faye had lived here in the not-yet fashionable bit of London's East End north of Canary Wharf for a couple of years, always knowing that the place was likely to be demolished at any time. The red-brick building was over a century old. It had originally made stuff with lead; mostly lead soldiers and lead shot (which apparently needed a big tall tower to drop little spits of molten lead down into a big water pool). Hence the height of the place; eight tall floors, mostly full of artists' studios for the last dozen years or so.

Kulwinder and Faye had leased half the top floor and turned it into a big New York style loft; spare, echoing and vast. It was as white as an art gallery and it didn't really have many readily identifiable rooms; instead it had what stage people would call spaces. Mainly one big space, full of minimalism, but very expensive and artfully arranged minimalism.

However, some developer had finally got their planning permission and so the place was getting knocked down in a week or two. Kul and Faye had already bought a place in Shoreditch. Buying seemed to encourage the need for further commitment so they'd got married this morning and Jo and I were two of the fifty or so guests invited to the wedding (I couldn't make it; show to do) and the subsequent feast back at the loft. Not, like I say, that we'd eaten much.

I frowned and dug into my glass to hook out the ice, dropping the glistening blocks on the wide brick parapet.

Jo shrugged. 'That's the way it came, hon,' she said.

I sipped cold whisky and looked out towards the unseen river. The roof terrace faced south and east, producing shadowed views beneath the scattered clouds floating over the towers of Canary Wharf and the unending cluttered flatness of Essex. A cool wind chilled my wet fingers.

I didn't like it when Jo said 'hon'. Thought it sounded like an affectation. She said 'daunce' sometimes, too, when she meant 'dance'. She'd grown up in a posh bit of Manchester but she sounded like she was from somewhere between Manhattan and Mayfair.

I looked at the slowly melting ice cubes puddling on the brickwork and wondered if there were similar little things about me that were starting to annoy her.

I flicked the lozenges of ice overboard, down to the cratered asphalt of the car park.

'Ken; Jo. How you two doing?' Kulwinder joined us.

'Fine, Kul,' I told him. He was wearing a cool black suit with a white shirt and Nehru collar. Skin as rich and glistening as dark honey; big liquid eyes, currently shielded by some silver-framed Oakleys. Kulwinder was a gig promoter and one of those annoying people who was effortlessly stylish, never more so than when they went back to some old fashion people had half forgotten but which – when picked up again by somebody like Kulwinder – everybody suddenly realises actually looks pretty good. 'Married life still suiting you?'

He smiled. 'So far so good.'

'Nice suit,' Jo said, touching his sleeve.

'Yeah,' Kul said, holding out one arm and inspecting it. 'Wedding present from Faye.'

Faye was a journalist/newsreader on the radio station I work for; she and Kul met at one of our after-show pub afternoons. I think I'm on record on air describing Faye as 'comely'.

'When do you head for NYC?' I asked. They were honeymooning in the States; New York and Yosemite. Just for six days due to Kul's gig work and the move to Shoreditch next week.

'Tomorrow.'

'Whereabouts are you staying?'

'Plaza,' Kul said. He shrugged. 'Faye always wanted to stay there.' He took a drink from the bottle of Hobec he was holding.

'You going on Concorde?' Jo asked. Kul liked to travel in style; drove a restored Citroën DS.

He shook his head. 'No. Hasn't started flying again yet.'

Jo looked at me accusingly. 'Ken won't take me to the States,' she told Kul. He raised his eyebrows at me.

I shrugged. 'I was thinking I might wait until democracy had been restored.'

Kulwinder snorted. 'You really don't like Dubya, do you?'

'No, I don't, but that's not the point. I have this old-fashioned belief that if you lose the race you shouldn't be given the prize. Getting it handed to you because of electoral roll manipulation, the police in your brother's state stopping the black folks from voting, a right-wing mob storming a counting station and the Supreme Court being stuffed with Republican fucks is called . . . gosh, what's the technical term? Oh, yeah; a coup d'état.'

Kul shook his head and looked at me with his big, dark eyes. 'Oh, Ken,' he said sadly. 'Do you ever get down off that high horse?'

'Got a whole stable full of them, Kul,' I told him.

'Shit,' Jo said, staring at her mobile's display. I hadn't heard it ring; she usually had it set on vibrate (which about six months ago gave me the idea for one of the show's more long-running and successful items. Well, long-running in the sense I still went back to it now and again, and successful by the perverse standards of me and my producer in that we'd had dozens of complaints about our crudity and obscenity rather than the more common handful). Jo thumbed a button, scowled heroically and said, with a totally insincere brightness, 'Todd! How are you? What can I do for you?'

She shook her head and sneered down at the phone while Todd – one of her bosses at Ice House and allegedly deeply inadequate in every way – talked. She held the phone away from her and clenched her jaw for a moment, then turned and put the phone back to her ear. 'I see. Can't you deal with it?' she said as she walked slowly along the broad terrace. 'Right. No. I see. Yeah. Yeah. No, of course . . .'

'So, what about you, Ken?' Kul asked, leaning on the parapet and glancing at Jo, who was a few paces away now and giving the finger to her phone while still making noises into it. 'Jo going to make an honest man of you?'

I looked at him. 'Marriage?' I asked softly, also glancing at Jo. 'Are you talking about marriage?' He just grinned. I leaned on the parapet too, looking down at the gradually browning flesh of the apple. 'I don't think so. Once was enough.'

'How is Jude?'

'All right, last I heard.' My ex was currently shacked up with a cop in sunny Luton.

'Still in touch?' Kul asked.

'Very occasionally.' I shrugged. Slightly dodgy territory here, as Jude and I did meet up now and again and on a few of those occasions had – despite all the bitterness and recriminations and other usual failed-marriage stuff – ended up falling

8

into bed. Not something I wanted Jo to know about, or Judith's boy in blue. Not something I'd talked about with any of my friends in fact. Also not something that had happened for over half a year, so maybe that was over at last. Probably just as well.

'You must have been seeing Jo since about when Faye and I met up,' Kul said. Jo was on the other edge of the terrace, leaning on the parapet facing south, still on the phone and shaking her head.

'That long?'

'Yeah; about eighteen months.' He drank again, looking past me at Jo. 'I guessed you'd either be settling down or splitting up,' he said quietly.

I showed the surprise I felt. 'Why?'

'Ken, your relationships rarely make it past the year-and-a-half mark. A year is probably the average.'

'Jesus, Kul, do you keep notes on this sort of thing?'

He shook his head. 'No, I just remember stuff, and I can see patterns.'

'Well,' I began, and would maybe have half admitted that perhaps Jo and I weren't going anywhere, except she shut her phone and came marching over to us. 'Trouble?' I asked.

'Yeah,' she said, almost spitting. 'Those fucking Addicta wankers again.' Addicta were Ice House's latest hot band. Happening; their time was very definitely now. I kind of liked their music – melodic English grunge with oases of surprising wistfulness – but had come to hate them in a vicarious, solidarity-inspired way because they were, according to the usually reliable source that was Jo, such total and complete arseholes to deal with. 'That fucking useless *cunt* needs me to go and hold their fucking hands while some fucking precious snapper drapes them across a fucking Bentley or something. Supposed to happen yesterday but the fucking dickhead forgot to let me know.' She kicked the parapet with one Doc Marten. 'Cunt.'

'You're upset,' I said. 'I can tell.'

'Oh, fuck off, Ken,' she breathed, heading for the flat's interior.

I watched her go. Chase after and try to smooth things, or let her go, not make a bad thing worse? I hesitated.

Jo stopped briefly to talk to Faye, who was heading in the opposite direction with some people, then she was gone. In a moment Faye was smiling at me and introducing these people and the possibility of pursuit and attempted mollification had gone.

'Ken. Thought you were avoiding me.'

'Emma. As if,' I said, sitting beside her on one of the main space's two chrome and black-suede couches. I chinked glasses. 'You look great,' I told her. Just jeans and a soft silk shirt, an Alice band in her hair, but she did look good. It's a few drinks later here, but it definitely wasn't the drink talking or looking. She just raised her eyebrows.

Emma was married to my best pal from school days in Glasgow, Craig Verrin; Craig and I were our own little two-guy gang for fifth and sixth year, before he left for University College London and within a year was settled down with Emma and a baby girl. Meanwhile I – viciously scapegoated by my teachers and examiners on some trumped-up charge of not having done the necessary work to pass my exams – left to make tea and score drugs for the more lazy and dissolute DJs on StrathClyde Sound.

Emma was smart and funny and attractive in a delicately blond way and I'd always loved her to bits, but things had become a little spoiled between us because we shared the guilty secret that, just the once, we'd slept together. She and Craig had been going through a bad patch when it had happened after Craig had strayed and been found out, and they were split-up again now – had been for a couple of years – so it somehow seemed not quite as bad as it could have been

10

. . . but still. My best pal's girl; what the hell had I been think-ing of? The next morning had been probably the most embar-rassing of my life; Emma and I had both been so ashamed it had been pointless trying to pretend to the other that what had happened had been anything other than a colossal mistake.

Well, it was just one of those things you wished you could delete from reality. I supposed we'd both done our best to forget about it, and just the passing of time made the guilt less sharp, but sometimes, when Emma and I looked each other in the eye, it was like it had been only yesterday, and we both just had to look away. I lived in intermittent terror that Craig would find out.

I suppose it was sort of similar to but different from when Jude and I fell into bed. And it was another relationship I couldn't talk to anyone about. Come to think of it I couldn't talk about most of my relationships/liaisons/whatever you wanted to call them, for one reason or another. I certainly couldn't talk about the other big one; the one with Celia – Celia the svelte, Celia the sexy, Celia the slinky as a seal – either. Jeez, a shallow person could come away from a review of my private life with some sort of idea that I liked a frisson of danger in my dalliances, but that particular one was not just dangerous, that one could get me very seriously hurt, or worse.

In my darker moments it sometimes occurred to me that these entanglements – or one of them – would be the death of me.

'Haven't seen you for a while.' Emma was leaning towards me, talking quietly, voice nearly lost in the party's hubbub.

'Things have been hectic.'

'I bet. I saw Jo storming out.'

'Well, no; that wasn't quite a storm. It wasn't a common walk, either, granted. Somewhere in between; more of a flounce.'

'Something you said?'

11

'Remarkably, no. No, that was a work-related flounce, or storm. Where's Craig?'

'Picking up Nikki.' She glanced at her watch. 'Should be here soon.'

'And how is the gorgeous—?'

'So,' Emma broke in. 'How's your programme going?'

'You have to ask?' I pretended to be hurt. 'Don't you listen any more?'

'You lost me when you were banging on about how only criminals should have guns.'

'That's not quite what we were saying.'

'Maybe you should have been more clear. What were you saying?'

'I can't remember,' I lied.

'Yes you can. You were saying criminals should have guns.'

'I was not! I was saying the idea that if you took hand-guns away from ordinary law-abiding people then only criminals would have guns was a crap argument for keeping guns.'

'Because?'

'Because it's the ordinary law-abiding people who go crazy and walk into primary schools and open fire on a class of kids; compared to *that*, crims use guns responsibly. To them a gun's just a tool, and something they tend to use on other crims, I might add, not a gym full of under-eights.'

'You said criminals should have guns; that's a quote. I heard you.'

'Well, if I did, I was just exaggerating for comic effect.'

'I don't think it's anything—'

'You probably missed the way we developed that,' I told her. 'We decided only extroverts and nutters should get guns, crims or not. Because it's always the quiet ones that go mad. Ever noticed that? The shocked neighbours always say the same things: he was very quiet, he always kept himself to himself . . . So; guns for nutters only. Makes sense.'

12

'You're not even consistent; you used to argue everybody should have guns.'

'Emma, I'm a professional contrarian. That's my job. Anyway, I changed my mind. I realised I was on the same side as people who argued that the States and Israel were havens of peace and security because everybody was tooled up.'

Emma snorted.

'Well,' I said, waggling the hand that wasn't holding my drink, 'the statistics aren't that clear-cut. They have a lot of guns in Switzerland, too, and not much gun crime.'

Emma watched her drink as she swirled it in her glass. 'You wouldn't last in the States,' she muttered.

'What?' I said, mystified.

'Somebody would shoot you.'

'What?' I laughed. 'Nobody's shot Howard Stern.'

'I was thinking more of jealous husbands, boyfriends, that sort of thing.'

'Ah.' I knocked back my Scotch. 'Now that's a different argument entirely.' I stood up. 'Can I get you another drink?'

In the long, gleaming gallery that was the kitchen, Faye was sweeping up a smashed glass from the slate floor. The caterers were unpacking more food from cool boxes. I squeezed through a group of people I vaguely knew via my pals in advertising, saying Hi and Hello and How are you?, smiling and patting, shaking offered hands.

Kul was leaning against the puce-coloured SMEG fridge while a suit with a flushed face and holding a slim briefcase tapped him on the chest.

'. . . us have to go to work this afternoon you know,' the suit was saying. 'We have meetings.'

Kul shrugged. 'I put on gigs, man. I work at weekends. This was the first day we could both manage.'

'Well, okay, let you off this time,' the flushed suit said,

swaying. 'But don't let it happen again.' He laughed loudly.

'Ha ha,' Kul said.

'Yeah, don't let it happen again,' the suit repeated, heading for the front door. 'Na; it was great. Great. Thanks. Thanks for the invite. Been brilliant. Hope you're both very happy.'

'Thanks for coming. Take care,' Kul told him.

'Yeah, thanks. Thanks.' The suit bumped into somebody, spilling a drink. 'Sorry, sorry.' He lurched round to wave to Kul, who had already turned away and was headed for the loft's main space. I poured myself some more Glen Generic then saw that somebody had brought a bottle of cask-strength Laphroaig, so abandoned my first glass and poured another of the Leapfrog and went to the fridge for some water.

'Hey, Ken.'

I closed the fridge door and saw Craig, official best pal (Scottish). Usual faintly diffident grin and sloppy-looking, thrown-on clothes; wee round glasses beneath a shaven head. When Craig still had visible hair it was black like mine; maybe a little curlier. We've both always had the same medium-slim build and since third year in High School I've been a couple of inches taller. We used to get mistaken for brothers, which both of us thought unfairly flattered the other. Our eyes are different; his are brown and mine are blue. Alongside Craig was his daughter Nikki, balanced on a pair of crutches. A few seconds were required to take in this vision.

I hadn't seen Nikki for over a year, when she was still at school, all gawky, awkward and blushing. Now she was as tall as her father and as beautiful as her mother. She had long glossy auburn hair half hiding a slim, pale face that just shone with youth and health.

'Craig! Nikki!' I said. 'Kid, you look fabulous.' I looked down at the freshly plastered leg hanging at an angle from her boot-legged jeans. 'But you've broken your leg.'

'Football,' she said, shrugging as best she could. Craig and I

14

hugged and slapped backs in full-on hail-fellow-Caledonian-well-met style. I embraced Nikki rather more tentatively. She sort of leaned into the cuddle and nodded against my cheek. She smelled of the open air, of somewhere fresh and perfect a long way from London.

'Heard you're about to start at Oxford, yeah?' I said, shaking my head as I looked at her. She was nodding.

'Uh-huh,' she said, then, 'Yeah, just a water or something,' to her dad.

'Chinese, wasn't it?' I asked.

'Yup.' She nodded.

'Brilliant. Good for you. You can teach me how to swear in Mandarin.'

She giggled, suddenly, briefly a child again. 'Only if you promise to do it on air. Uncle.'

I sucked air through my teeth. 'Favour; don't call me Uncle, okay? Make an old man happy while we're together and pretend you just might be a trophy waif I've picked up.'

'*Ken!*' She kicked out at me with one crutch.

'Hey,' I said, rubbing my shin. 'I've a reputation to keep up. Or down-hold. Whatever.'

'You're *terrible*!'

'Come on,' I said, offering my arm. 'Let's get you a seat. Craig; we're through here,' I told him. He waved. Nikki nodded me to go ahead of her. 'Hobble this way,' I said and pushed through the pack of people towards the main space while Nikki clumped after me. I looked at her again as we got clear of the kitchen crowd, and sighed. 'Oh dear, Nikki.'

'What?'

'You are going to break *so* many hearts at Oxford, youngster.'

'Organs, rather than bones. Good idea.'

'Mm-hmm. Football, you said?'

'Girls do play it nowadays, you know.'

15

'Golly, you don't say. Don't you find the long skirts get in the way? Ow! Will you stop *doing* that?'

'Well . . .'

'What position?'

'Striker; I was scythed down in the penalty box. On a hat-trick, too.'

'Disgraceful.'

'Nikki, Nikki; here. Oh, Nikki!' Emma had jumped up. She hugged her daughter tightly, eyes closed. I hovered for a bit, but there was no room on the sofa once they'd got settled, and Emma seemed to be deliberately ignoring me. I waved to Nikki and wandered off. Time for another line or two, and/or one more quick session on Kul's PlayStation 2 (if that last bit makes me sound like some kid whose parents won't or can't buy him a games machine of his own, I have to plead half guilty to the childishness charge; I did have a PS2 of my own but I got annoyed at it one drunken night back in the summer and threw it overboard. I live on a houseboat so I can do that sort of thing).

A drink or two later, a couple of lines and various conversations to the better, I was standing on the terrace again, admiring the view and breathing in the fresh autumnal air. With Jo gone I felt a sense of freedom and even opportunity and promise, the afternoon and evening stretching ahead invitingly. I had a couple of Evo 8s with me and pondered taking one. Loved up for the rest of the day. This would mean, though, that I'd be out of synch with Jo, assuming we reconnected before the day was over. With Addicta involved, probably we wouldn't, but then you never knew.

An arm slipped round my waist. A body against mine, a kiss on my cheek and a voice purring, 'Herr-lerrr.'

'Amy. Well, hello indeed.'

Amy was a friend. One of Jo's friends, originally, though I

suspected she and I got on better these days than she and Jo, who seemed to have cooled towards her. Amy was nearly my height; she had fine, shoulder-length dark-blond hair with a natural curl. She also had very long legs and a *figure*. There was something slightly time-warped about Amy altogether; she was actually younger than Jo by a year but she dressed and acted five or ten years older. PA to a lobbying firm.

'You look well, Ken.' Amy leaned back against the parapet, arms along the stone. She wore pearls, a blue blouse, a mid-length skirt and a long jacket; court shoes.

'And you look delectable as ever,' I told her, smiling. Amy and I met up for lunch every now and again. We'd been flirting and joking about having a torrid affair for a year or so but we both knew it wasn't going to happen. Well, probably. It was Amy I'd been on the phone to earlier when we'd got cut off.

She smiled slowly and looked around. 'Jo here?'

'Was. Had to go. Work.'

'Was it her Addictive Band lot again?'

'The same.'

She held a glass of white wine and took a delicate sip. 'What was the wedding like?' The wind produced a tiny gust, moving her hair across her face. She blew it away.

'Don't know,' I said. 'Couldn't make it; show to do.'

'Ah-hah. Ken, do you have any drugs?'

'Some coke; couple of Es.'

'Think I might have some of the Charlie? I don't know why. Just feel like it.' She wrinkled her nose. 'Do you ever get that?'

'Every day with a "Y" in it.'

There were a couple of children at the party and at least two print journalists I didn't trust, so we found a room off the loft's only corridor. It had been Faye's office but now it was full of packing cases, ready for the move.

17

Back on the terrace a little later, the two of us talking up a storm, she picked up the part-eaten apple still lying on the parapet, twirling it in her hand.

'It's all right,' I told her. 'It's one of ours.'

She threw it to me. It looked pretty unappetising, all brown around where I'd taken my single bite out of it. I leaned on the brickwork and held it over the drop to the car park. Amy leaned beside me. I let the apple go. It tumbled very slowly, almost disappearing.

It hit the asphalt and exploded in a highly satisfactory manner, all little lumps of whiteness bursting out across the dark surface.

'Excellent!' Amy clapped her hands. We looked at each other, our chins just off the brick parapet. I felt, suddenly, like I was a schoolboy again.

'Hey,' I said.

'What?'

'Let's drop more stuff.'

'That's just what I was thinking.'

'I know.'

Which is how it came to pass that we ended up chucking what seemed like half the contents of Faye and Kul's loft over the parapet. We started with more fruit. 'They've got far too much food in anyway,' Amy said as we loaded up on oranges, bananas, a melon and more apples.

We stared at the asphalt a hundred feet below. 'That was disappointing.'

'Was a bit, wasn't it?' I said, looking down at the squishy mess produced by a couple of oranges. 'I don't think citrus fruits are the way to go. They just don't fragment in a satisfying manner.'

'Or bananas.'

'Agreed. Let's go back to apples.'

'Then the melon. That might be good.'

'Yes. I have high hopes for the melon.'

'Let's do two apples at once; one each.'

'Good idea. On three. One, two, three . . . Oh yes. Very good.'

'Well synchronised. Let's do four this time. Two each.'

'We've only got three apples.'

'I'll get another one. No dropping the melon while I'm gone.'

'Wouldn't dream of it.'

'Ere, wot are you two up to?'

'Ed; hi. Hope you don't mind. Dropping fruit onto the car park. S'okay; nowhere near your car.'

'Fucking ell, mate, I hope not. Only got it last week. Cost me seventy grand.' Ed was my official best pal (English). Slight of build with a face that always reminded me of a black Mark E. Smith; hard and soft at the same time, the phizog of a pliable bantam-weight bruiser. Club DJ; sort of in-demand guy does two gigs a night and catches a helicopter in between. The Porsche probably constituted a week's wages.

'It's a beautiful car,' I told him. 'But *yellow*?'

'That's a fuckin traditional Porsche colour, that is.'

'Traditional? How can yellow be traditional? Blue, or green; those are traditional colours. Even red, but not yellow. Yellow is traditional for JCBs and Tonka toys. Even lime green at a pinch; Kawasakis. But not yellow.'

'Wot a load of shit,' Ed laughed. 'Wot are you on?'

'Hi, Ed,' Amy said, returning with another apple. 'Here.'

'Thanks. Fibre,' I said to Ed, holding the apple up to him. 'I'm on lots of fibre.'

'Ready?'

'Read— hey,' I said indignantly, 'there's a bite out of this apple.'

Amy nodded. 'Ya. Somebody was eating it.'

I looked at her. 'What are you loik?' I said in my best Dublin accent.

19

She just shrugged and got ready with her two apples, poised to drop. 'Ready?'

'Ready,' I said.

'Wot you doin this for?' Ed asked as we let the apples go. 'Eh? Ken?' Ed said, while Amy and I concentrated on the fruit falling to its doom. 'What's the—?' The apples duly splattered. 'Aow, yeah!' Ed said.

'See?'

'That's why,' I said.

'Cool, man.'

'Melon?' said Amy.

'Melon, definitely,' I agreed, hefting it.

'Let me!' said Ed. 'I want to drop the melon!' Amy and I exchanged looks. 'Come on!' said Ed. 'I haven't got to drop nuffink yet.'

'That's the test,' Amy said, sternly. 'You have to bring something worth dropping to the party, or it's no entry.'

I nodded. 'You haven't been initiated.'

'I'll get sumfing!' Ed started towards the apartment, then stopped. 'Old on; let's see the melon go first.'

I held it out over the drop with both hands and then let it go.

Amy whooped and we high-fived. 'Outstanding!'

'Fucking yeah, man!'

'Fine sport.'

'We need more fruit.'

'I'll find some, I'll find some.'

'You'll be lucky.'

'Yeah, something of a short-fall situation on the fruit front.'

'I'll find sumfing else.'

'What?'

'I dunno; rubbish, junk.'

'Have you seen this place? Their living-room's like an operating theatre; they don't have junk.'

'They're movin, man. They must have stuff they're frowin out.'

'Good point. See what you can find.'

'Let's all see what we can find.'

'Even better.'

'What's going on out here?' Kul asked.

'The very man!' I said. Kul had a bit of a sheen on him; looked a little glassy-eyed. It never did take much to get him drunk. 'Kul; you must have *loads* of stuff you were going to throw out, haven't you?'

'Umm, well . . .'

Most of the people at the party were taking turns to throw things over the parapet. For a dedicatedly minimalist couple, Faye and Kul had a surprising amount of stuff they weren't going to miss when they quit the loft: quite a lot of old kitchen bits and pieces, like bowls, plates, jars, a broken juicer, a defunct Thermos flask, some outdated goblets, a bilious green fondue set . . . then a handful of ornaments they'd been given by Faye's parents, which they'd never liked or ever displayed but had kept in case the old couple ever came to visit (the ornaments were, like Faye's parents, pretty hideous), followed by bigger stuff as Faye and Kul got into it and people started to camcord what was happening: an old hi-fi system, a bust TV, a misbehaving radio, and bottles; lots of bottles.

'Me fuckin car!' Ed wailed as half a dozen carefully released wine bottles plummeted to their destruction. A big cheer went up as they shattered, more or less simultaneously.

'The wreckage is going nowhere near the damn car, Ed,' I told him.

'You can't be fuckin sure, man. What about me tyres? Those are fuckin brand new tyres. They cost a bleedin fortune. Plob'ly.'

'*Bean* bags?' Amy laughed as one of Kul's promoter chums

21

heaved through the crowd clutching two of the things over his head like giant brown scrotums.

'You have – you ever *had* bean bags?' I said to Kul.

He shrugged. 'Promise you won't tell.'

'What's the point?' somebody shouted. '*They're* not going to shatter.'

'Now,' the promoter chum said (he meant 'No', but, like Ed, he was from Sarf Landin). 'But I was finking that if you, like, dropped eavier stuff on top of them . . .'

'Brilliant!' I yelled, deeply impressed at such forethought.

'Kul?' Faye said, laughing but sounding a little unsure. 'I thought you *liked* that chair.'

'Yeah, well, not that much,' Kul said. 'Give me a hand here . . .'

We got the big metal and wood chair up onto the parapet, a whole bunch of us positioned it where it looked like it would drop onto one or both of the bean bags, then we let it go.

Very big cheer for the chair; direct hit on one of the bean bags resulting in an explosive spray of white polystyrene beads splashing out across the now fabulously wreckage-strewn car park like a giant snowy feather pointing towards the chain-link fence.

'Hey, if we dropped this fish tank, would the fish experience weightlessness? I mean, like, double weightlessness? Just kidding.'

'Faye, do you want this old table?'

'I found more bottles!'

Faye looked at Kul, her eyes wide. She clicked her fingers. 'That case of awful Cava my uncle got cheap from Tesco! Remember?'

Kul took her face in his hands and kissed her. 'Knew it would come in useful for something. You certainly can't drink the stuff.' He set off towards the interior. An unsteady stream of bottles of various sizes whistled to the asphalt, each getting a small cheer as it hit. People were calling out marks for technical merit and artistic achievement.

'I bet you started this, didn't you, Ken?' I turned to find Nikki perched on her crutches, all grumpy glare.

I held up my hands. 'Guilty,' I said, surprised at her expression. 'Why? What's wrong?'

'Throwing perfectly good food away is wrong, Ken,' she said, shaking her head as though at a child who needed to be told that scrawling on the walls with crayons was bad.

'It was only a few bits of fruit,' I said. 'It would probably have been—'

'Oh, Ken,' she said. She shook her head and stumped away.

Kul came back with a cardboard box full of bottles of Cava and started handing them out to the many grasping hands. 'Just for dropping,' he told people seriously. 'I beg of you; whatever you do, don't drink it.'

I half-heartedly considered trying to get to within bottle-handing-out range of him, but the press of people was too great.

I turned to Amy and held up my hands.

'Never mind,' she said.

We leaned back against the east-facing parapet. She put out her hand to shake. 'Good new game, Ken.' She looked flushed, excited.

'I don't know,' I said, keeping hold of her hand. 'I liked it more in the old days.'

'Really?'

More big cheers as the full Cava bottles hit with satisfyingly loud thuds and booms. 'Shake them first! Shake them up first!' somebody was shouting.

'Yeah,' I said. 'Call me a purist, but I feel the soul kind of went out of it when we switched from fruit and lost our amateur status.'

23

'You can't live in the past, Ken.'

'I suppose.'

'We should be proud we were there at the start.'

'You're right. Was it my idea or yours?' I asked.

'Maybe we had it together.'

'Indeed.'

'Absolutely.'

'Great minds.'

'Idea; time had come.'

'Not about ownership; about result.'

'Destiny.'

'–'s Child.'

'Synchronicity.'

'The Police,' I said, just as my mobile went (I keep mine on vibrate, too). As I pulled it out of my jacket, Amy's ring-tone sounded; something classical I knew but couldn't name.

'Ha-ha,' she said. 'Synchronicity indeed.'

I laughed and looked at the display on my phone; my producer, calling from the office. I heard one or two other phones going off around the place and thought I could hear the landline in the apartment too and wondered hazily whether for some bizarre reason everybody here had something urgent they had set alarms for, a little after two o'clock on a Tuesday in September.

'Yo, Phil,' I said. Amy answered her call too.

'What?'

'*What?*'

'New York?'

'The what?'

'Where?'

'The World Trade Center? Isn't that—?'

'A plane? What, a big plane, like a Jumbo or something?'

'You mean, like, the two big, um, skyscrapers?'

Kulwinder was walking back through the crowd of people

24

as more phones went off and faces started to look puzzled and the atmosphere began to change and chill around us. He was heading for the loft's main space again, talking to somebody on his phone. 'Yeah, yeah, I'll put the TV on . . .'

Two

DRESS-DOWN
WEDNESDAY

'Half Man Half Limp Bizkit there. Their *Mission Impossible* theme-ette. Hasn't been on the play list for a while, Phil. You attempting to make some sort of point with that title?'

'Not me, boss.'

'You sure, Phil?' I looked across the desk at him. We were in our usual studio at Capital Live!. I sat surrounded by screens, buttons and keyboards like some sort of commodities dealer, because that's the way studios have gone, even in the relatively short time that I've been in the wonderful world of radio broadcasting; you had to search for the two CD players – in this studio, up to my right between the e-mail screen and the callers' details screen – to reassure yourself that you weren't some suit playing the futures market. Only the microphone, angle-poised out from the main console, gave the game away.

'Positive,' Phil said, blinking behind his glasses. Phil's glasses had thick black frames, like Michael Caine as Harry Palmer, or Woody Allen as himself. Phil Ashby was a big, gentle, rumpled-looking guy with thick, unruly, prematurely salt-and-pepper hair (the grey entirely down to me, he said, though I had photographic evidence to the contrary) and a slight West-country burr to his voice; he had a relatively slow, drawly, almost sleepy delivery, which, though I'd never admit it to him, complemented my own voice. A running joke we've used is that he's on permanent Valium while I'm forever speeding, and one day we'll swap drugs and just both sound normal. Phil had been my producer for the last year here at Capital Live!. Another two months and I would have established a new on-air employment record. I rarely last more than a year before I get sacked for saying something that somebody somewhere thinks I shouldn't have. 'Lalo.'

'What?' It was my turn to blink.

'Lalo,' Phil repeated. I could only see his head above the various screens and electronic gear between us. Sometimes I couldn't even see that if he'd got his head buried in a newspaper.

'Isn't that one of the Teletubbies? I only ask because I know you are an expert.'

'No; Lalo Schifrin.' He fell silent, shrugged.

'Good radio shrug there, Phil.' I had sound effects for many of the silent syllables that made up Phil's fractured body language, but I was still working on one for a shrug.

He raised his eyebrows.

'Right.' I picked up an old-fashioned mechanical stopwatch from the green baize of the desk. I clicked it. 'Okay, I'm putting the dead air stopwatch on you until you explain yourself, Ashby.' I glanced up at the big studio clock above the door. Another ninety seconds and we were off air. Through the triple glazing, in the production suite where producers used to be decently confined, in the good old days, our assistants appeared to be conducting a low-level conflict, which consisted of throwing paper planes at each other. Bill the newsreader wandered in on them, waving his script and shouting.

'Lalo Schifrin,' Phil said patiently into the silence on our

30

side of the glass. 'He wrote the original theme for *Mission Impossible.*'

I clicked the stopwatch off. 'Four seconds; you're not even trying. So; Lalo. You mean for the TV series, I take it.'

'Yes.'

'Bully for him. And your point would be, caller?'

Phil knitted his brows. 'Vaguely pop-related people with names that sound like they were given them by babies.'

I snorted. 'Just people? So "Ob-La-Di, Ob-La-Da", by the Fabs, wouldn't count? Or "In-A-Gadda-Da-Vida"? Or "Gaba-Gaba Hey"?'

'Hardly target audience, Ken.'

'Is *Lalo*?'

'Jay-Lo.'

'Jay-Lo.'

'Jennifer Lopez.'

'I know who Jay-Lo is.'

'P. Diddy, for that matter.'

'Lulu? Kajagoogoo? Bubba without the Sparxx? Iio? Aaliyah?'

'Gawd rest the poor girl's soul.'

I shook my head. 'It's only Tuesday and we're at the Friday bottom-of-the-barrel stage already?'

Phil scratched his head. I pressed a Function button on my FX keyboard; an exaggerated, wooden, head-scratching noise of dubious comedic value sounded in my headphones. It was either that or the dead air watch again, and you can over-do these things. Our listeners, whom we knew – thanks to some very expensive, pro-active and robust market research – to be statistically stoutly loyal and containing a major proportion of ad-agency prime-target As and Bs with a lofty disposable income profile, would be familiar with the array of assertedly wacky and indeed even zany sound effects I used to give them an idea of Phil's silent on-air actions. They also knew about dead air, which is the terrifically technical term us radio boffins

31

use for silence. I took a breath. 'Can we talk about what we haven't talked about yet?'

'Must we?' Phil looked pained.

'Phil, I was held off the air for three days last week; we played the pop equivalent of martial music through the whole show yesterday—'

'What, is that what you get from Marshall amps, yeah?'

'—and yet we're told the world changed for ever seven days ago. Shouldn't a purportedly topical show reflect that?'

'I didn't even know you knew the word "purportedly".'

I leaned closer to the mike, lowering my voice. Phil closed his eyes. 'Thought for today, listener. For our American cousins . . .' Phil groaned. 'If you do find and kill Bin Laden, assuming he is the piece of scum behind this, or even if you just find his body . . .' I paused, watching the hands on the studio clock flick silently towards the top of the hour. Phil had taken his glasses off. 'Wrap him in pigskin and bury him under Fort Knox. I can even tell you how deep: thirteen hundred and fifty feet. That's one hundred and ten storeys.' Another pause. 'Don't worry about that noise, listeners, it's just the sound of my producer's head gently thumping on the desk. Oh, one last thing: as it stands, what happened last week wasn't an attack on democracy; if it was they'd have crashed a plane into Al Gore's house. That's it for today. Talk to you tomorrow, if I'm still here. News next after these vital pieces of consumerist propaganda.'

'I was in Bond Street this morning. DKNY had no normal stock that I could see at all. Do you know what they had instead, Kenneth?'

'No, I don't know, Ceel. Why don't you tell me?'

'They had five thousand red T-shirts with the twin towers on them. Five thousand. Red. That was all. In the whole shop. It was like an art gallery, not a shop. I thought, Hey, that's really touching, really artistic. I also thought, They'll never sell

32

all those, but somehow it didn't matter.' She turned in the bed and looked at me. 'Everything seems so quiet, so spooky, don't you think?' She turned back again.

I stroked away a rope of her long brown hair and licked at the valley between her shoulder blades. That hollow was the colour of milk chocolate and tasted of salt. I breathed in the warm scent of her skin, senses swimming, losing myself in the sweet, heady microclimate of her long, slim body.

'It's the planes,' I said at last, smoothing a hand down her flank, over waist and hip to thigh. Her body, so light for some-body so definitely black, looked dark as old mahogany against the startling whiteness of the hotel sheets.

'The planes?' she asked, taking my hand and holding it in hers.

'They've stopped them flying over the city on the way into Heathrow. So another Mr Atta can't crash-dive into the Canary Wharf tower or the Houses of Parliament. Makes the whole place seem quieter.'

(That day, sitting in the ruins of the abandoned party at Faye and Kulwinder's, while it slowly dawned on those two that they would not be going to NYC for their honeymoon, at least not the following day and probably for many days, we kept going out onto the terrace to look at the Canary Wharf towers, tall against the skyline less than a mile away, half expecting to see them hit by a plane and crumble with the same awful grandeur as the first tower. 'It's Pearl Harbor II,' we said. 'They'll fucking nuke Baghdad.' 'I can't believe this. I just can't believe I'm seeing this.' 'Where's Superman? Where's Batman? Where's Spiderman?' 'Where's Bruce Willis, or Tom Cruise, or Arnie, or Stallone?' 'The barbarians have seized the narrative.' 'Fuck, the bad guys are re-writing the scripts . . . !' '*Challenger* and Chernobyl were SF, Aum Shinrikyo and the Tokyo Underground was manga; this is a disaster movie directed by Satan.'

33

Switching channels, some man on the Beeb was saying that when people claimed they'd seen people jumping from the towers they were really only seeing cladding falling off. Then you switched back and saw the bits of cladding holding hands as they jumped together, skirts blowing up around their bodies. Then the second tower collapsed, and there was no more jumping or falling to be done, just the catching up with the additional fragments of atrocity popping up and ploughing in elsewhere in America.)

'I see,' Celia said softly, turning away again. 'You're right.' She stroked my hand. 'But I mean it's really quieter, too, Kenneth.' Ceel was the only person apart from my mother who ever called me Kenneth. (Well, also apart from Ed, who sometimes called me Kennif, and Ed's mum, who's been known to call me Kennit, but that doesn't count.) 'Less . . . fewer people. Especially in places like Mayfair and Knightsbridge, and Chelsea, too.'

'Ah; the posh places; the hedonistic 'hoods. You reckon they're quieter?'

'Yes. I think they're all staying in their places in the country.'

'You're probably right. So why are you still here?'

'I hate Gladbrook.'

Gladbrook was Ceel's place in the country, or rather her husband's. Deepest Surrey. Disliked it the instant I heard of it, even before Ceel told me her husband only really used it for business meetings and impressing people. She said she could never feel at home there and hated staying so much as a single night. I mean, Gladbrook; it even *sounded* wrong, like the name of an off-the-shelf company some well-smarmy City type would buy to front a dodgy tax-shy scam. Never actually been there, but I saw the estate agent's details for the place once; basically a coffee-table book, it should have had its own ISBN number. Ran to a good forty pages including all the glossy photographs, but all anyone needed to know was that the main

34

house had a heated driveway. You know; for all those blizzards they get in Surrey.

'Is that where Mr M is?'

'No, John is in Amsterdam again.'

'Hmm.' John. Mr M. Mr Merrial. In the import-export business. Drugs, to begin with; people, largely, these days. Plus fingers in more pies than he has fingers. Some of Mr M's business interests were even legal these days; impressive property portfolio, apparently. A man a little older than me; maybe about forty. A quiet, even diffident guy, by all accounts, with a half-posh, vaguely south-east accent, pale skin and black hair, usually dressed in an unshowy Savile Row suit and not at all the sort of chap who looks like a multi-millionaire crime lord who could have people much more important than me rubbed out as quietly and efficiently – or as painfully and messily – as he wants, any day of the week. And I'm screwing his wife. I must be fucking mad.

(But then when we fuck, and I am lost in her, surrendered to those depths beyond mere flesh, nothing could be better, nothing ever has been better, nothing ever will be better. There is no one like her, no one so calm and studied and child-like and innocent and wanton and wise all at once. She thinks I am mad, too, but only for wanting her so much in the first place, not for risking whatever her husband would do to me if he ever found out about us.

For herself she says she has no fear because she feels she is half dead already. I have to try to explain this. She doesn't mean half dead in any trivial sense of being tired-out or tired of life or anything like that, but half dead in a way unique to – and only capable of definition by – her own bizarre, self-made religion, a belief system without name, ceremony or teachings, which she cleaves to with the airy casualness of the truly convinced, not the fundamentalist intensity of those who secretly guess they may well be wrong. It's a mad, bastard concoction of Voodoo spirituality and cosmologically intense

35

physics, like something Stephen Hawking might have dreamed up on a really bad acid trip.

Me, I was a Humanist, an Evangelical Atheist, a fucking card-carrying member of the Rationalist Inquisition, and Ceel's totally barking but utterly unrufflable beliefs just drove me crazy, but the truth was neither of us really cared and the only time we discussed stuff like that was in bed; she enjoyed being told she was nuts and she loved the way it got me worked up.

What it boiled down to was Ceel sincerely believed herself to be half dead in the sense of existing in this world while in a deeply soul-entangled state with a twin Ceel in another reality who was dead, a Ceel who died almost exactly half her life ago, when she was fourteen.

It's all to do with lightning, with the lightning . . . We'll come back to this.)

'And have you seen, Kenneth, how everybody's become so suspicious?'

'Suspicious?'

'Yes; looking at each other like everybody they meet might be a terrorist.'

'You want to take the Underground, kid. People have started eyeing each other; especially anybody carrying anything that might be big enough to be a bomb, even more so if they put it down on the floor and could even conceivably leave it there when they get off.'

'I get claustrophobic on the Underground.'

'I know.'

'I take buses sometimes,' she said in a small voice, as though to apologise for having a chauffeur-driven Bentley on call and an unlimited taxi account.

'So you've told me. And may I express, on behalf of the struggling masses, our gratitude that you deign to descend amongst us and grace our mean and surly lives with your radiant presence, ma'am.'

She slapped my hand gently and made a tutting sound. I took my hand away and brought it down over her flat belly, through the soft spring of curls and dipping to the cleft beneath.

Her upper thighs tensed, closing fractionally. 'I'm a little sore there, from before,' she said, taking my hand again. She held it as she rolled over on the snow-white sheets and settled on her front.

(On her left side there is a strange patterning of dark shadows, exactly as though somebody had traced a henna tattoo of forest ferns upon her light-brown skin. It stretches from one shoulder, skirting her breast, and continuing down to the honeyed swell of her hip. This is from the lightning.

'What *is* that?' I remembered breathing, on the night of the day that I first saw it, nearly four months ago in the alloyed sheen of golden street and silver moon light, in another room across the city. It was like something from an iffy Science Fiction series, from budget *Star Trek* or *Alien Nation* or something; thinking it really was some sort of weird fern/henna tattoo I even tried to lick and rub it off. She just lay there, watching me, great dark eyes unblinking.

'That is from when I half died,' she said matter-of-factly.

'What?'

'From the lightning, Kenneth.'

'*Lightning?*'

'Yes, lightning.'

'Lightning as in thunder and—?'

'Yes.'

She had stood on a cliff in Martinique once, when she was barely more than a child, watching a storm, and had been hit by lightning.

Her heart stopped. She could feel it had stopped, and when she fell down it was pure luck that she fell back into the grass and not forward off the cliff towards the rocks thirty metres below. She had felt very calm and had known as she lay there

37

– waiting for her heart to start again and the smell of burning hair to disappear – that she was most definitely going to live, but she was also absolutely certain that the world had gone in two different directions at exactly the point when the lightning bolt struck her, and that in another world, right alongside this one and identical until that point in every respect, she had died, either killed by the bolt itself or fallen to her death on the rocks below.

'There is still a small mark on my head, too,' she'd told me, in the dark-brown heat of that first remembered room. She'd smoothed back her hair above her forehead, revealing a thin, wavy brown line that ran, barely more than the thickness of a single hair itself, from the edge of her scalp back into the tangled wilds of her long, light-dark hair.

I stared at it for a while. 'Jesus Christ. I'm fucking Harry Potter.' She'd smiled.)

I traced the frond-lines with my gaze as she guided my hand down to the cheeks of her perfect behind. 'If you like,' she said, 'perhaps you may go here, instead?'

'I'm on it, babe.'

'. . . Ah yes, so you are. Gently, now.'

Somewhere beyond and beneath the layers of thick, dark curtains, London growled quietly to itself.

'What's that?'

'Ah.' I sighed happily, staring at the framed note. 'Yes; my very first complaint letter. I was sort of locum DJ at Strath-Clyde Sound, sitting in on the nightly *Rock Show* while our resident Tommy Vance wannabe was attending to his customary mid-January drying-out regime.'

'I can't read it.'

'Yeah; I used to think the smudges were the result of tears, but then I realised it was probably just drool. Least it's not written in green ink.'

'What did you do?'

'Suggested Lynyrd Skynyrd and Mountain should appear on a double bill.'

Nikki looked at me blankly.

'Well, you had to be there,' I sighed. 'Before your time anyway, child.'

'Lynyrd Skynyrd were a band from the States whose plane flew into a hillside,' Phil supplied, looking up briefly from his *Guardian*. 'They wrote a song called "Sweet Home Alabama", seen as a Confederate reply to Neil Young's "Southern Man", which was an indictment of Southern racism.'

'Ah-hah,' Nikki said. I had the strong impression we might as well have been talking about ancient Greece.

'Phil has all the annoying attributes of Encarta without the ease-of-turning-off facility,' I told her.

'Start talking about your sex life, Ken; that usually does the trick,' Phil said, reaching for another piece of chewing gum.

'Oh yeah, and he smokes,' I said. 'Phil, isn't it time for your next nicotine patch?'

He glanced at his watch. 'Nope. Eighteen minutes, forty seconds to go. Not that I'm counting.'

We were in the show's office in the Soho Square Headquarters of Capital Live!, part of The Fabulous Mouth Corporation complex in what used to be the United Film Producers building. Afternoon; Phil – who trawls the press assiduously for material before the show – then goes on to read the broadsheets afterwards. Unforgivable.

Assistant Kayla – a droopy-eyed über-fem-geek forever in graded shades and camo baggies – was on standard afternoon perpetual phone duty, hitting and hitted, scribbling notes and talking in a quietly intense monotone.

Nikki shook her head and hobbled towards the next frame on the office wall. She was down to one crutch now, but still lame. Her plaster had been covered in a variety of multi-coloured messages. She was here because I knew she was a Radiohead fan and Thom Yorke had been coming in to talk on our lunchtime show. Only now, we'd just heard, he wasn't, so the best I could offer the girl was a tour round the place, culminating here in the narrow, much partitioned and generally broken-up space where Phil, myself, our two assistants and the occasional back-up researcher put the show together each day. From here we had a fine view of the rain-stained, white-glazed bricks of the light-well, though if you squatted down by the windows and looked up, you could see the sky.

The office walls were mostly covered in posters for Indie bands I had never heard of – I suspected Phil only hired assistants who heartily despised all the music we played; it was one of his little rebellions against the system – however, we did have (as well as the office-equipment mandatory portrait of our Dear Owner, Sir Jamie) a few Sony awards, donated gold and platinum discs from artists and bands who'd been cruelly deceived by their record companies into thinking we'd helped them with their careers, and – what I was genuinely by far the most proud of – a modest but high-quality collection of framed landmark hate mail.

'This one's a lawyer's letter,' Nikki said, frowning.

'Just a sample,' muttered Phil.

'Yes,' I said. 'I'd suggested that if you speeded up "You Are The Sunshine of My Life" by Stevie Wonder, you got the main riff from "Layla" by your man Clapton. There was talk of legal action, but it passed.'

'Duane Allman,' Phil said.

'What?' I asked him.

'Came up with the riff; not Clapton. Allegedly.'

'You know, the lips are particularly rich in blood vessels, Philip; you could usefully stick that nicotine patch there.'

Nikki nudged me hard with one elbow and nodded at the next Frame of Shame. 'That one?'

'Ah, my first death threat,' I said with what I hoped sounded like undue modesty. 'A particularly proud moment.'

'*Death* threat?' Nikki asked, wide eyes twinkling.

'Yes, my dear, from funny, sleepy old Northern Ireland, where time stands still. I'd said *let* the Orangemen walk through Catholic areas, but for every march they got to take part in, a similar-size one had to be allowed through Loyalist areas, with tricolours, posters of Bobby Sands—'

'Seventies hunger-striker and Republican martyr,' Phil squeezed in.

'—lots of hearty singing of Republican songs; that sort of thing,' I continued. 'Which sort of developed into my patent three-word solution for the Troubles: "United, federal, secular. Now get on with it."'

'That's eight words,' Phil mumbled.

'I was allowing for subsequent editing,' I said, looking brightly at Nikki. 'Anyway, exception was duly taken; they're awfully touchy over there.'

Phil cleared his throat. 'I think your humorous observation about the Red Hand of Ulster being a symbol of a land won by a loser prepared to mutilate himself to claim a scraggy patch of rain-lashed bog may have contributed to your healthy fanbase in the Shankhill, too.'

'See? You try to bring out the local colour in some quaint little part of the Provinces and these silly people insist on taking it all the wrong way.'

'I'm sure your Nobel Peace Prize is in the post, Uncle Ken,' Nikki said. 'This one?'

'First international death threat,' I said. 'All due to our then spanking-new web-feed. Back to the old gun control debate again. I was arguing for, if memory serves. But I was making the point that in the US it was all too late; they'd made their bed and they damn well had to lie in it. In the States I was for no gun control laws at all. In fact in the States I reckoned guns should be made *compulsory* for all teenagers. Might produce a grand kill-off, of course, but who's to say that was such a bad thing in the end? That way there'd be less of the little bastards to bother the rest of the world. And why stop at just hand-guns and automatic weapons? Let's get with grenade launchers, pull down some mortar and mines action, get jiggy with some surface to air ordnance and serious-calibre heavy weaponry. Chemical and biological weapons, too; they're kind of the green option, in a wacky sort of way. Long-range missiles. Nukes too. And if some dickhead with a grudge decides to waste Manhattan or Washington with one of these, well, too bad. That's the price you pay for freedom.'

Nikki looked at me. 'And they pay you for this, Ken?'

'Young lady, for this they don't just pay me, they compete for me.'

'He's a hot DJ,' Phil said.

'There you are,' I told her.

'Yup, hot like a potato,' Phil said.

I smiled at Nikki. 'He's going to say, "Always getting dropped . . ."'

'Always getting dropped.'

'. . . Told you.'

'Now, Nikki. Are you sure I can't take you for lunch?'

'Yeah, I'm fine, thanks.'

'But you must be hungry.'

'No, I'd better get back. Books to order, stuff to read, you know.'

'Flying start at the Chinese course.'

'That's the idea.'

We were sitting in my ancient Land Rover in the office's underground car park, waiting for the engine's plugs to warm up.

'Are you *sure* I can't take you for something to eat? Come

42

on; it'll make up for not meeting Lord Thom of Yorke. I was all set to deliver this great treat and then I was thwarted. I really feel I need closure here. Seriously; I know some great places. We may well see some celebs.'

'No, thanks.'

'Is that your final answer?'

'Yep.'

'Would you like to call a friend?'

'No, really. Look, you don't have to drive me back to Craig's, Ken. I can jump in a taxi.'

'Jump?'

'Well; hobble, fall in. Honest. I don't mind.'

'Not at all. I promised your dad I'd get you home safely.'

'I can look after myself, you know, Ken,' Nikki said, smiling indulgently at me.

'Never doubted it. But taking you back is the least I can do. Rain check on lunch? Some other time? Say yes.'

'Some other time,' she agreed, sighing.

'Brilliant.' The little coil-warming lamp on the fascia went out; I started the engine and it settled down into an alarming percussive rattle. 'Hey,' I said, heaving on the bus-sized wheel to pull us out of the parking bay, 'I don't know if I've said, but I think it's really cool you getting into Oxford.'

She shrugged, looked almost embarrassed.

'You're absolutely certain you don't want to celebrate your ascension to the dreaming spires with some slap-up nosh?'

She just looked at me.

I laughed, turning for the exit ramp. 'Oh well. Come on then; let's get you home.' I swung the Land Rover out of the Mouth Corp car park; we went bouncing and rattling and squeaking into Dean Street. I looked over at her. 'What's so funny?'

Nikki laughed to herself for a moment, then glanced over at me through her long red hair. 'I wasn't expecting a Land Rover,' she said. 'I thought you'd have a Harley Davidson, or a limo, or maybe a Smart or one of those Audis that looks like a bar of soap or something.'

'I was never into Harleys,' I said. 'Suzis and Kwaks were my kind of bikes, back in my courier days. But this old thing –' I slapped the dark grey plastic fascia under the narrow slab of the Landy's windscreen '– despite, I'll grant, looking like the sort of transport that would be infinitely more at home hauling a brace of sodden sheep from one field to another on a failing hill farm in darkest Wales, is almost the ideal car for London.'

'You reckon?' Nikki sounded like she was humouring me.

'Think about it,' I said. 'It's old, slow and a bit battered, so nobody's going to want to nick it. Even the wheels don't fit anything else. Look; comedy wipers.' I turned on the windscreen wipers. On a Land Rover of this vintage they're about seven inches long and just sort of flop about in a disheartened kind of way, looking more like they're waving at the rain to welcome it onto the glass than undertaking to do anything so strenuous as actually clear the drops off the windscreen. 'Look at that; pathetic. No self-respecting vandal's even going to bother bending those. Wouldn't be sporting.'

'They are a bit pathetic,' Nikki agreed as I turned them off and let them slump with what looked like exhausted gratitude to the base of the screen again.

'You're high up – as you may have noticed clambering awkwardly in here with your gammy leg – so you can see over most other traffic, the better to take advantage of what overtaking opportunities do arise in the hurly-burly of metropolitan motoring. Then there is the fact this is a Series Three of the diesel persuasion, so when people hear you coming they think you're a taxi and often mistakenly treat you with the respect due to your standard Hackney Carriage. The ancient design means that the vehicle is narrow as well as having a short wheel-base for squeezing through gaps and into restricted parking spaces, and, lastly, driving one of these, no kerb in

London holds any terror for you whatsoever. If a brief expedition onto the pavement or over a minor traffic island is required to facilitate progress, you just happily bump onto and over it without a second thought. Now, thanks to the appalling noise levels and seats patently constructed from low-grade friable concrete it would, certainly, be utterly hellish on long journeys or at any speed above a brisk jog, but then when the hell do you get to do either of those in London?' I glanced over at her. 'So, for an agricultural device only one automotive chromosome removed from a tractor, this is a surprisingly suitable urban runabout. And I commend the vehicle to the house.'

I waggled my eyebrows at her as we inched along Old Compton Street. I'd been developing this Why-a-Landy's-great-for-London speech, and variations thereof, for nearly a year and this was, IMHO, a particularly fine and well-delivered example of the breed, which I thought might have elicited a pained grin if nothing else from the lovely Nikki, but it drew only a woundingly blank Oh-yeah, ho-hum look across her glowing features.

'Could do with power steering, couldn't it?' she suggested.

'And a better turning circle. But glad you spotted that,' I said. 'The chance to maintain upper body strength through in-car exercise is a truly valuable no-cost option.'

'Yeah, right,' she said. She was silent for a few moments, then nodded at the radio. 'That's not your station playing, is it?'

'Ah, no; that'll be Mark and Lard on Radio One.'

'Isn't that disloyal?'

'Deeply. Can I let you in on a terrible secret?'

'What?'

'I'm only half joking about it being secret,' I said first. 'The press haven't heard this yet and on a quiet news day with a following wind it could just make it into print and conceivably cause me problems in a straw-that-breaks-the-camel's-back kinda stylee.'

'Guide's honour,' she said, saluting ironically.

'Thanks. Okay; here it is . . . hold on . . .' I'd been gradually nudging the Land Rover's much-dented front further and further into the traffic stream for the past few vehicle-gaps, and somebody in a nice car had finally got the message. I waved cheerfully at the silver Merc that let us out of Old Compton Street, as we swung onto Wardour Street to start heading north in a vaguely Highgate-ish direction. I looked at Nikki. 'Yeah. It's this: I cannot fucking *stand* commercial radio.' I nodded. 'There; it's out now and I feel better for it.'

'Including the station you work for, obviously.'

'Obviously.'

'So you listen to Radio One.'

'It'll get turned off promptly at three, but for large parts of the day, yes. And I have a definite weakness for Mark and Lard. There; listen.' In fact, all we were listening to was the Landy's rattling engine and ambient outside traffic noises until the Boy Lard squeaked, 'Carry on,' and the programme resumed. 'See?' I said. 'Dead air, there; silence. Used to be anathema for DJs and radio people in general. Nowdays, well, nobody's much bothered about leaving pauses any more, but these guys have made it into a feature. Repeat until funny, as they'd say themselves. Genius.' I glanced at Nikki, who was looking sceptically at me from beneath her mass of red hair. 'But the point,' I insisted, 'is that the Beeb has minimal advertising. I mean, they carry trailers for their own shows and those can get wearing enough, but what they *don't* have is relentless high-rotation drivel every fifteen minutes from fucking loan companies, ambulance-chasing shyster legal firms and Chipboard Warehouse's owner shouting at you from too near the mike to come on down and feel the cut of his special offers. I hate adverts. I prefer the licence fee. That's how I want to pay; up front, efficiently, then get to listen to what I want to listen to and nothing else, whether it's pop-clones or Beethoven or the sort of crap all-day talk shows that taxi drivers listen to.'

'I suppose that guy Phil points out that the adverts are what pay your wages.'

'Phil?' I laughed. 'He's a Radio Three and Four man. Hates adverts even more than I do.' I glanced at her again as we troubled the usually little-used upper regions of the Landy's gearbox in a miraculous void in the traffic, which gave us an almost clear run to the lights at Oxford Street. 'Don't get me wrong; he's a good producer and he's a real muso – goes to see a band practically every night, whether it's at Wembley Arena or a pub in Hackney – but he can't stand Capital Live! either. No, it's our friendly local Station Manager to whom it falls to bring the realities of commercial radio regularly to our attention.'

We crossed Oxford Street and started to head up Cleveland Street, following a motorcycle courier on a Honda VFR. Perhaps, I thought, a little reminiscing about my days as a fearless gonzo courier – only a few years ago, after all – would impress Nikki. It started raining and I turned on the wipers, to hilarious effect. I looked at Nikki. 'Well, do *you* listen to Capital Live!?'

'Mmm . . . sometimes,' she said, not looking at me.

'Yeah, well, exactly. You're eighteen; you should be part of our target audience. What *do* you listen to, anyway?'

'Umm, well, they sort of come and go? But I think they're all illegal black stations from south of the river.'

'What? K-BLAK? X-Men? Chillharbour Lane?'

'Yeah, and Rough House, Precinct 17.'

'Radio Free Peckham . . . is that still going?'

'No, it was closed down.'

'Well, frankly, good for you for ignoring the usual commercial tat.' I was snatching glances at Nikki to see if she was impressed that I knew all these cool illegal stations, but she didn't seem to be. 'Not,' I added, 'that many of them play much Radiohead, as I recall.'

'Sadly, no.'

'Never mind. Radiohead are local where you're going; bound to get loads of air time in Oxford.'

'Hmm.' She sounded distracted and when I glanced over she was looking at a clothes shop window. I looked ahead again.

'Shit!'

'Oh—!'

A blue car swept out of a side street right into the path of the courier in front of us. I caught a brief glimpse of the car driver, looking the wrong way and talking on his mobile. The bike rider didn't have time to bail or brake, just went *whump* into the BMW Compact's wing; the bike stood on its front wheel then clattered back to the rain-greased street just in front of us, files spilling from one pannier and skidding papers over the street and into the gutter. The rider went sailing over the Beemer's bonnet as it braked and skidded to a stop. He landed heavily on the road ahead, sliding on his back a metre to hit the kerb hard with his helmet.

'Oh! Oh!' Nikki was saying.

I'd pulled up. 'He'll probably be okay,' I told her quickly. 'You just stay here.'

She nodded. She cleared some hair from her face with a trembling hand and pulled a mobile from her jacket as I opened the door. 'Should I phone for an ambulance?' she asked.

'Good idea.' I jumped out and ran past the white-faced car driver, just getting out, still holding his mobile. It crossed my mind to tell him what a fuckwit he was, but I didn't. A couple of people were already standing looking down at the black figure lying in the road. He wasn't moving. Some kid in a puffa jacket was squatting by him, doing something to his helmet.

'Just leave the helmet on, yeah?' I said to the kid, kneeling on the courier's other side and carefully lifting up his visor.

Behind me, somebody had the sense to turn off the fallen bike's engine, which was more than I'd thought to do.

The courier was older than me; grey beard, glasses, face

pinched by the helmet's foam padding. He blinked. 'Fuck,' he said weakly.

'How you doing there, pal?' I asked him.

'Bit sore,' he croaked. The rain was making little spots on his glasses. He put his gloved hand up towards the helmet's fastening. I held on to it.

'Hold on, hold on,' I said. 'Can you feel everything? Waggle your toes and stuff?'

'Ah . . . yeah, yeah, I think . . . yeah. I'm all right. I think I'm all right. Breathing's a bit . . . What about the bike?'

'Think you're going to need new forks.'

'Shit. Fuck. Ah, rats. You a biker too, eh?'

'Yeah. Used to be.'

He looked away to one side, where I sensed more people standing, and somebody approaching. I turned round and saw the car driver. The biker coughed and said wheezily, 'If this cunt says, "Sorry, mate, I didn't see you," deck him for me, will you?'

Nikki was beautifully bedraggled by the rain.

'You didn't need to get out, kid,' I told her. She was trying to dry her hair with a small chamois leather. The Landy's interior was trying to mist up.

'The operator was asking me where the incident had taken place, and I couldn't see the street names,' she explained. 'Then I thought I'd better stop the bike's engine.'

'Well, I think the guy's going to be all right. We did good. We make a fine emergency team; triples all round.'

I'd left our details with the cops, and the biker had been persuaded to take the ambulance; he was still dazed and might have some broken ribs. Nikki had handed him the VFR's keys, though the cops had taken them away again because they wanted them left with the machine.

She gave me back the chamois leather. 'Thanks.'

'You're welcome.' I used it on the windscreen. 'Blimey. Welcome to London, eh? Oh; do just say if you need a stiff drink or anything.'

She shook her head. 'No, thanks.'

'Yeah, just straight home, I think.' We continued north, through the rain, for Highgate.

'This is about what I think it's about, isn't it?'

'Think so.'

'So, what do you think?'

'That we're going to get carpeted, old son.'

'Cripes, Biffo. A rocket from the WingCo, eh what?'

'Severe dressing down. After you.'

'Tally-fucking-ho.'

'". . . Well here is an alternative fatwa: women of Islam, judge your men, and if they are bad, kill them. They oppress you and scorn you and yet they are frightened of you; why else would they keep you from power and the sight of other men? But you have power. You have the power to judge whether your man is good or not. Ask yourself this: would your husband kill another person just because they are Jewish or American or something else people are simply born to be? Allah has let people be born these things; would your man kill them for no other reason than the faith or the country they were born into, by the will of Allah? If he would then he is a bad person and deserves death, for he brings shame upon your faith and the name of Allah. When next he comes to you, have a kitchen knife concealed beneath your bedclothes, or a pair of scissors, or even a penknife or a carton-cutter, and slit his unworthy throat. If you have no knife, bite out his throat. If you wish only to mutilate him, use a knife or your teeth on his manhood." But *do* we actually say—'

Debbie Cottee, our Station Manager, used the remote to

50

click off the DAT machine on the other side of her light, airy office. She slid her glasses down her nose and looked at me with weary, bleary blue eyes. 'Well?'

'Hmm, I don't know,' I said. 'Do you think we're using too much compression on my voice?'

'Ken . . .'

'But nobody,' Phil said, 'was actually saying that. I mean, there was a bit just before that where Ken was saying that we didn't force Muslim women in this country to wear mini-skirts or bikinis, whereas a Western woman going to Saudi has no choice but to conform to their dress-code. The whole point is about toleration and intolerance, and about public figures like religious leaders being allowed to pass what is in effect a death sentence, without any sort of trial or defence, on nationals of another country. That was the whole point of putting the bit at the start pointing out that nobody in a position of responsibility in the West *would* say something like that—'

'Is fucking irrelevant, Phil,' Debbie said, putting her glasses down on the surface of her desk, which covered about the same area as our whole office. Her view, from near the top of the Mouth Corp building, was out over the Square and the cluttered rooftops of Soho, towards the blunt, pitted blade of Centrepoint. Debbie was thirty but looked older; she was fit in a chunky sort of way, her hair was mousy brown and she had tired, puckered eyes.

'I'm not sure I see it as irrelevant at all, really,' Phil said with the air of an academic discussing some fine point of ancient Etruscan property law, or the historical basis of estimates for the Yellow River's silt-deposition rate during the Hang dynasty. 'The whole point is that you put a disclaimer at the beginning and the end. You're not saying, "Go and kill these people." You're saying, "No one here is *saying*, 'Go and kill these people.'"'

Debbie glared at him. 'That's just semantics.'

'No, it's . . . grammar,' Phil said, appearing baffled that any-body could possibly think otherwise. He looked briefly at me. Of course it *was* semantics rather than grammar (I was almost positive), but Debbie, who was certainly one of the more human execs in the Mouth organisation in general and Capital Live! in particular, and not an ignoramus, wasn't quite smart enough to feel confident arguing the toss over that. At such moments I loved my producer.

'Phil!' Debbie said, slapping the surface of her desk. Her flat-screen monitor wobbled. 'What if somebody, what if a Muslim person switches on just after your so-called disclaimer at the start of this, this . . . diatribe, and then switches off, totally fucking incensed – as well they fucking might be, if they can even believe their ears – just before the end? What the fuck are *they* going to think they just heard?'

'Oh, come on,' Phil said. 'That's like asking what if some-body hears the word "country" but switches off before the "—ry" bit. I mean, it's just one of those things.' He held his hands out.

'That's one word; this is a whole speech.'

'Yes, but it's the principle,' Phil insisted stubbornly.

Debbie switched from Phil to me. 'Ken,' she said, 'even for you . . .'

'Debbie,' I said, holding up both hands as though in sur-render. 'We're proving our own point here.'

'What?'

'About prejudice, about bigotry.'

'How does insulting people do that? How does the Islamic Council of Churches screaming down the phone at me do any-thing to defeat bigotry? You're just—'

'Because we had the Head Rabbi screaming down the phone last month,' I pointed out.

'The Israel-as-a-rogue-state rant,' Phil said, nodding.

'So fucking what?' Debbie said loudly. 'Are you trying to claim that insulting two religions is somehow better than insulting one?'

'It's being even-handed,' I agreed.

'It's being bigoted towards ethno-religious groupings!' she shouted. 'It is, arguably, inciting religious and even racial hatred towards Jews and Muslims!'

'That's not fair,' I protested. 'We insult Christians too whenever we possibly can. We did that whole week of Christ as Certifiable Nutter.'

'But he was a Jew!' Debbie yelled. '*And* sacred to Islam as well!'

'One stone; three birds!' I yelled back. 'What's the problem?'

'All Abrahamic religions have been selectively targeted, over time, for trenchant, robust, but above all fair criticism,' Phil put in. 'I have the relevant records.'

Debbie looked from Phil to me. 'This isn't a fucking joke, guys. There are mosques, synagogues being fire-bombed—'

'You sure?' Phil said.

'—people being attacked because they're "Middle Eastern" in appearance—'

'Yeah, I know,' I said, shaking my head. 'Jesus; *Sikhs* have been attacked for being Islamic terrorist sympathisers.' I spread my arms. 'So proving the essential point here; bigots are fuck-wits.'

'The point,' Debbie said exasperatedly, 'is that some nasty little dickhead from the National Front or the British National Party could listen in to a programme of yours where you lay into the Jewish people or the Muslims and *fucking cheer you on*, Ken.' Debbie slapped the desk again, but softer this time. She put her glasses back on and fixed her gaze on me. 'Now is that what you want?'

This was actually a pretty good point, and one that Phil and I had worried over ourselves. 'That's why we have to attack bigotry and stupidity everywhere!' I blustered. 'If we stop now they'll be left thinking the last lot we went after were the definitive bad guys.'

'*What?*' Debbie said, looking over her glasses at me again. (Fair enough; this last assertion didn't make much sense even to me.)

'I think that is a fair point,' Phil said, nodding.

'Well, here are another two points, gentlemen,' Debbie said, sticking her glasses back up her face and pulling herself closer in towards her desk. 'There's such a thing as this station's licence and the Broadcasting Standards Authority. There are also such things as our advertisers. They pay all the fucking bills and they can pull their ads even faster than the BSA can pull our licence. Several already have.'

'But they've been replaced,' Phil said, looking just a little red in the face now. He took his glasses off.

'For now, at lesser rates,' Debbie said steelily.

'Rates have been going down everywhere for the whole year!' Phil protested. He started polishing his glasses with a clean hanky. 'New ones are always going to be lower than old ones in the current climate! It's—'

'Some very important people, some very vital advertisers, have been having words with Sir Jamie,' Debbie said through clenched teeth. (To our credit, I thought, at this point not one of the three of us even glanced towards the Dear Owner's portrait on the wall.) 'At cocktail parties. In his club. At board meetings. On the grouse moors. At charity events. Over his mobile and his home phone. He is not happy. He is not happy to the extent that he is seriously weighing up which he needs most: your show or his good name. Which do you think he will choose?' She sat back, letting this sink in. 'Guys, you run a reasonably successful programme for us, but in the end it's only ten hours of air time per week out of one hundred and sixty-eight. Sir Jamie's backed you until now, Ken, Phil, but he can't let you jeopardise the station, let alone the reputation of the Mouth Corporation or the goodwill he's built up from nothing over the last thirty years.'

Phil and I looked at each other.

'Jesus Christ, Debs,' Phil said shakily. 'Are you telling us to tone it down, or are we sacked? I mean, what?' He put his glasses back on.

'You're not sacked. But it's not just tone it down, it's make amends.'

'Make *amends*?' I squawked.

'This attacking Islam and Judaism, in particular, has to be reversed.'

'So we *can* attack Christianity?' I suggested. Debbie glared at me. 'What?' I said, holding out both hands.

'We've got the perfect thing,' Phil announced, just like that.

I did probably the first genuine double-take I'd ever done in my entire life. 'We have?'

Phil nodded. 'Ken doesn't know about this yet,' he told Debbie.

'I don't?'

'Suggestion came in just yesterday from the *Breaking News* people.'

(I *just* managed to prevent myself saying, 'It did?')

'The new Channel Four thing?' Debbie asked, eyes narrowed.

'Yeah; their competitor for *Newsnight*,' Phil said.

'Weren't they trying to poach Paxman for that?'

'I think so, but he wasn't having it. Last rumour I heard was their main presenters would be Cavan Lutton-James and Beth Laing.'

'She's on Sky, isn't she?'

'Contract coming up for renewal.'

'Anyway,' Debbie said, waving one hand.

'Anyway,' Phil said. 'They're still doing dummy programmes at the moment but they start for real on Monday and they want something hard-hitting and controversial; something that'll get them headlines.'

'I thought they just wanted me to practise on in one of these dummy programmes,' I said. (Stupidly, I realised, as soon as I'd closed my mouth again; it was entirely possible Phil was winging it here.)

'They did, at first,' Phil said. 'I persuaded them otherwise.'

'They want Ken for the Monday programme?' Debbie asked.

'If we can get the terms right,' Phil said.

Debbie could probably see the surprise on my face. 'You're not Ken's fucking agent, Phil.'

(This was true, though he sometimes acted like one. My real agent, the long-suffering Paul, complained that thanks to my – to him incomprehensibly bizarre – political fastidiousness, what I needed was an anti-agent; somebody who would look for brilliantly remunerative work I could then cheerfully turn down. In fact, he said, aside from contract negotiation time at the station, all I really needed was an answering machine that shouted 'No!')

'I mean the terms of control over content and the people involved,' Phil explained patiently. 'I didn't want Ken going in there thinking he was about to do a short piece of light relief about mike technique or something and then being confronted with half a dozen swivel-eyed fanatics representing all the different brands of fundamentalists we've upset over the last year. That's the sort of thing that can happen and I just wanted to make sure it wouldn't.'

'Why is Ken looking like . . . well, like that?' She gestured at me. *Like what?* I thought. I tried to look business-like and unperturbed.

Phil glanced my way then said, 'Look, this is something Ken and I talked about. We've had too many dodgy, manipulative offers for TV appearances for him in the past. Either they're too trashy to be worth considering in the first place, or they

56

sound really interesting and we get all fired up about it then it falls through, or they change their mind, or it turns out there was some hidden agenda. We agreed that I'd handle these proposals until there was something worth taking to Ken, then we'd talk about it.' Phil glanced at his watch. 'If it hadn't been for this meeting we'd be doing just that right now,' he said. (Happily he didn't add 'in the pub'.) He looked at me. 'Sorry to land this on you like this, Ken.' I waved a hand.

'So . . .' Debbie said, still sounding and looking suspicious. 'What are you proposing?'

'That we give them something hard-hitting and controversial,' Phil said.

Debbie still looked deeply dubious, but I could see she was interested. 'Which would be what?'

'One of their ideas is to get Ken to debate with a genuine Holocaust denier; a guy from the extreme-right Aryan Christian Movement who claims the Allies built the death camps after the War,' Phil said. All three of us exchanged looks. 'I wasn't so sure about that,' he added. 'But, well, maybe – given what you've been saying about the perceived if mistaken bias against the Jewish and Muslim faiths – that would be the way to go after all.' He turned from Debbie to me. 'Obviously, only if you feel comfortable with the idea, Ken. I'm still not sure about it, frankly.'

'Oh, I'm comfortable with it,' I said. A fucking Holocaust denier? Somebody from the extreme Christian right prepared to put themselves up for a tongue-lashing? What self-respecting militant liberal wouldn't want to get their teeth into one of those fucks?

Debbie's eyes were so narrow they were almost closed. 'Why do I feel that this might just be a good idea,' she asked slowly, 'and yet we seem to have come back to the original, totally facile and childish proposal that the way out of all this was to insult Christians some more?'

'Oh, come on,' Phil said with a laugh in his voice. 'This guy's Christian like Satan is Christian. The point is he's wildly anti-Semitic and he's mad. Articulate, but mad. Ken'll be seen defending—'

'You sure this guy's mad?' Debbie asked.

'Well, he agrees with the idea currently gaining ground in sections of Arab society,' Phil said, in the sort of slow, considered voice that told me he felt back in control here, 'that the September eleventh attacks were organised by the International Zionist Conspiracy to discredit Islam and give Sharon carte blanche against the Palestinians. But it's okay; he hates the Arabs too. This guy has a consistent belief system totally based around race, religion and sexuality; Nordic/Aryan/Christian/straight equals good . . . everything else is just shades of evil.'

'Who is he? What's his name?'

'His name is Lawson, umm . . . Briarley or something.'

I was only half listening. It was while Phil was talking about this that I thought of it; my big idea. I knew what I was going to do. If they did let me onto the show with that anti-Semitic fuck, I knew exactly what I was going to do to him.

It was perfect! Mad, bad and dangerous to contemplate and it probably meant I was a bit mad, too, but hey; fire with fire. My mouth went dry and my palms felt suddenly pin-pricked with sweat. Oh, fuck, I thought. What a sweet, beautiful, terrifying idea. Did I really dare?

'Okay, I'm going to have to consult on this,' Debbie announced.

I clicked back to reality. Debs was going to kick it upstairs. Sensible woman.

'Fine by me,' Phil said. He looked at me and I nodded. 'But we need a decision by Friday at the very latest; tomorrow would be better.'

'We'll have one,' Debbie said. She pushed back on her desk,

her big, black, leather executive chair rolling over the wooden floor. We were excused, obviously.

'Debbie?' I said, getting up.

'What?'

'I want you to make it very clear to whoever else you talk to about this that I really want to do it. I mean, *really* want to do it. I think it's important.' Phil looked at me with a frown, then smiled at Debbie.

'I'll let you know,' she said. 'In the meantime, I think we'd all really appreciate it if you avoided offending any major ethnic or religious groups. Could you do that for us?'

'We can certainly try,' Phil said merrily.

'Fuck.'

'No, it's okay,' Phil said as we walked away down a broad corridor lined with framed plaques, discs, awards and letters of thanks and endorsement, none of which were mine. 'This is a feature, not a bug.'

'You weren't making any of that up in there, were you?'

Phil grinned. 'Course not, you silly sod.' 'Sod', which I was under the impression had dropped off most people's List Of Plausible Invective around about the early seventies, was Phil's most powerful expletive. 'I'll call the *Breaking News* people before we hit the pub.' He frowned at me as we stepped into the lift. 'Didn't realise you'd be *quite* so keen.'

I wasn't going to tell him about my idea. Best if he didn't know for his own sake, apart from anything else. 'Yeah, well,' I said. 'Keen Ken; that's what they call me.'

'No they don't.'

Three

DOWNRIVER,
UPTOWN

'What I said was, these namby-pamby Holocaust revision people didn't go *remotely* far enough. It wasn't just the Holocaust that didn't happen, it wasn't just the death camps that were faked; the whole of the Second World War is a myth. Occupation of Paris? Battle of Britain? North African Campaign? Convoys and U-Boats? Barbarossa? Stalingrad? Kursk? Thousand-bomber raids? D-Day? Fall of Berlin? Singapore? Pearl Harbor? Midway? Hiroshima and Nagasaki? *None* of it happened! All special effects and lying. Guys of a certain age; you remember thinking how close those Airfix Spitfires and Lancasters looked to the real thing you saw in the film footage? That's because *they* were just models *too*! All the old airfields, the concrete tank traps, a few so-called bomb-sites; they were built after the war.'

The girl looked uncertain, then she laughed. 'That's insane.'

I clinked her glass. 'That's the point. And besides, I said, what sort of chicken-shit Neo-Nazis are these people anyway? They should be saying, "Sure we killed six million; wish it had been more", not splitting hairs about whether it was one million or two million and whining about the fucking Führer being misunderstood.'

'You don't actually believe *any* of this, do you, though?'

'Are you mad?' I cackled. 'Of course not! I'm taking the piss out of fascist fuckwits!'

'So is this what this TV thing's about?'

'Yeah. They're going to get one of these nutters for me to "debate" with.'

'Should people like that really be allowed to say that sort of stuff on national TV, though?'

'Ask Channel Four that, not me,' I said, drinking up. 'But, yes, I think they should. You can't hide that poisonous shit away for ever; it'll come out somewhere. Better to face it and squash it. I want it out in the open. I want to know who these people are, I want to know where they live.' I finished my drink. 'That's why these cowardly little shits love the Internet. They can post any sort of hate-filled drivel they want with no comeback because on-line they can hide. It's the perfect medium for bullies, liars and cowards.'

We were in the Golden Bough, our usual after-show drinking hole, in Hollen Street. The Bough was a basic central London pub; one of those places neither flattered nor insulted to be called a boozer. Not fashionable, rarely crowded to the point of standing-room only (save on a Friday evening and Saturday night), reasonable juke box, basic, unpretentious food, only one gaming machine – tucked out of the way under the stairs to the small first-floor function bar – and a solid, unadventurous choice of drink.

There was no particular crowd associated with the place. Instead you got a smattering of all sorts in the Bough: workmen in dusty boots and paint-specked overalls, advertising creatives, theatre types, tourists, office workers, music people, film people, homeless guys nursing a half and keeping warm, waiting staff from restaurants and posher bars, one or two girls from the sex shows, and us. There was one dealer who used the place, though for a quiet drink, not for dealing.

A couple of cops stuck their heads round the door about once a month or so.

The manageress was Clara, a brusquely rotund, no-nonsense, half-Portuguese grandmother with a dry, wheezy laugh and sixty-a-day habit. Nobody we know has ever seen her without one of two turban-like things on her head – one green, one yellow – and there was a long-standing, variable-odds pot-bet, which has allegedly been running with a rolling roster of regulars for over twenty years concerning whether she was bald underneath there or not. Last time I'd checked it had been 65/35 for slap-headedness and I'd stood to make a fiver if it turned out she wasn't.

'Can I get you a drink? What'll it be?'

'Oh, thanks. WKD blue. Cheers.'

'I haven't asked you your name,' I said to the girl as I signalled to Clara.

'Tanya.' She stuck her hand out.

'Ken. Pleased to meet you, Tanya.'

Tanya had overheard Phil and me talking about the *Breaking News* thing earlier. I'd seen her staring, brows pinched, at us and she hadn't looked away when I'd stared back. I'd guessed she'd picked up an alarming selection of race-hate-associated buzzwords and was thinking about either walking out or throwing her drink at us and then running.

'It's okay,' I'd said to her, past Phil's shoulder. 'We're both nice liberals really and this is genuinely one of those rare occasions when it honestly isn't as bad as it sounds.'

Tanya was quarter Jewish, which was one reason she had been taking offence at what she'd thought she'd been overhearing. She worked for a film company in Wardour Street. I could be pretty sure of this because Phil had grilled her about the film industry, albeit subtly, for a few minutes. Phil had this paranoid theory that unscrupulous tabloid journalists had realised we drank in the Bough, that they thought we were

65

worth exposing in some way and were likely to send somebody here to coax me into saying something I might regret, thinking I was talking off the record to a civilian when in fact it was an undercover journo and I was very much on the record.

Given what I say when I know I'm on record and on air, this seems a fairly bizarre fear, but there you are.

Anyway, Tanya seemed to pass Phil's hostile-journo filter and he lost interest in her when our production team and assistant gaggle walked in.

Tanya was short and slim and dark and always moving; sort of half dancing, swaying to and fro, seemingly without really knowing she was doing it, rhythmic and slow like an underwater plant in a meandering river's languorous undercurrent. I'd seen girls doing this before in situations like this and it often meant they were loved up, but I didn't think she was. She had wide grey-green eyes and hair in little black spikes.

We ended up with the others from our show and a couple of people from Timmy Mann's, the one after ours, though not the boy Mann himself. It turned into a moderately serious drinking session, all sat round our favourite circular table in one end corner of the Bough. I was getting on, I thought, awfully well with Tanya, who laughed at all my jokes and touched me on the forearm a couple of times.

I'd been supposed to meet up with Jo that night and take in a film but Jo had to cancel – yet another Addicta crisis – and I'd started thinking that maybe I should see how things progressed with Tanya instead.

Tanya was drinking her blue WKDs very slowly and I had moved on to whiskies after a couple of pints of Fuller's, but for the past two Scotches I'd been cheating. When nobody was looking I'd lower the short glass towards the floor and upend it, letting the drink fall onto the ancient and already pretty tacky carpet underneath. Jeez; they were single twenty-five mill measures with no water; probably evaporated before they made it to the floor, but the point was they weren't getting me drunk. If anything did develop with the lovely Tanya, I'd be in a fit state to appreciate it.

All in vain; Tanya had to go at six to meet some friends, and would not be dissuaded. I even followed her to the door of the pub and out onto the street. She gave me her mobile number and disappeared into the twilight, heading for Tottenham Court Road Underground station. I sighed as I watched her go, looking at the display on my Motorola where her number still glowed.

The phone's screen went dark and I went back inside.

Our drinking party started to break up as people went off to catch trains, tubes and buses. Phil and I decided on takeaways from the Taj, our local curry house round the corner from the Bough, then went our separate ways. I felt sober enough to drive, but I knew I wasn't, so I left the Landy in the Mouth Corp car park and got a mini-cab home, suffering a lecture on the superior qualities of wholesome Caribbean soul food compared to this highly suspect Indo-Pakistani fare from Geoff, the Jamaican driver I always seemed to end up with whenever I was clutching a carrier bag full of curry or a leaking parcel stuffed with doner kebab.

'Me car gonna stink now, mon!'

'Here's an extra fiver, my good fellow; wave it around and it should help disperse the ghastly sub-continental pong.'

Geoff thought this was so funny he lit a big spliff as he drove off down Lots Road, cackling and trailing clouds of ganja smoke.

Sometimes I told people I lived in a tied cottage. The houseboat at Chelsea Wharf used to be one of Sir Jamie's pads in the city, back when he was basically trying to be Richard Branson (Sir Jamie even had a supposedly trademark beard back then, too, though he switched to a pony-tail and earring shortly afterwards, surrendering the high ground of facial fuzz to the Bearded One). The *Temple Belle* was an old and much-converted coaster. It still belonged to Mouth Corp but it was rented to me at an extremely reasonable rate. I was on a pretty good contract since I'd shifted to the late-morning show and I could probably have afforded the rent or mortgage if I'd had to pay the market rate for the tub, but getting it cheap certainly made an appreciable and very pleasant difference, though it did, as Phil had been the first to point out, give Sir Jamie an extra hold over me; if I lost the day job I lost the cool houseboat and Chelsea address too.

The *Temple Belle* was riding high on the flood tide as I walked down the jetty past the other houseboats; music and light came from a couple of them. Upriver, where the breeze was coming from, seeded with light rain, a train grumbled across Battersea railway bridge. Nearer, the towering façade of the Chelsea Reach development glittered with a cheesy opulence. The river was silent and traffic pretty much inaudible. The high tide meant there was no awful smell; the main drawback of living on the boat was that at low tide, especially on a hot summer's day, the revealed mud smelled of ancient shit and things long dead. Probably because that was exactly what it was.

Despite the rain and my empty belly, I hesitated by the old wheelhouse with the door keys in one hand and the slowly cooling curry in the other, looking out at the dark water for what turned into a minute or two, feeling a little lonely all of a sudden, and then – in my defence, almost immediately – a bit ashamed for feeling sorry for myself. The gentle background roar of the unsleeping city filled the sodium-stained skies and I stood listening for the river's dark, liquidic music in vain.

From my parents' house, in Helensburgh, thirty kilometres down the north bank of the Clyde from Glasgow, I could see the river from my bedroom. I grew up watching the distant cranes of Greenock gradually disappear as the shipyards closed, to be replaced, later, by offices, shops, housing developments and leisure facilities. By then we'd moved to Glasgow itself to be near my father's new dental practice in the city centre. Our first-floor flat in the leafy South Side was big – my brother Iain and I had rooms easily twice the size of those we'd had in the bungalow in Helensburgh – but the outlook was to the broad, tree-lined street, the parked cars and the tall red sandstone tenements like ours on the far side. I missed the view of river and hill more than I'd expected.

I met Jo on a river cruise one sticky summer night, Ceel in Sir Jamie's glittering new penthouse at Limehouse Tower, during a storm.

'You're the guy did that Cat Stevens cover. Didn't you get sued?'

Late summer, 2000. I was still doing the Capital Live! pre-midnight programme at the time and had been talking to my then producer near the stern of the little river cruise boat. We had been watching the metallic shells of the Thames Barrier pass – each one like a sinking ship, up-ended, the last of the sunset's ruby light flaring from their summits – when this crop-haired, blond semi-goth with lots of facial metalwork barged in between us.

Producer Vic stepped back to give her room, looked the girl up and down, decided I probably didn't mind being interrupted by her, raised his eyebrows at me and wandered off.

I did a bit of entirely justifiable sizing-up myself – the girl was all in black: DMs, jeans, scoop-necked vest, battered-looking biker's jacket off one shoulder. About mid-twenties. 'I wasn't exactly sued,' I said warily, wondering if I was talking to a journalist. 'There was an exchange of lawyers' letters that seemed to cost as much as serious litigation, but we managed to avoid an actual writ.'

'Right.' The girl nodded vigorously. 'Oh. Jo LePage,' she said, holding out a hand to shake while nodding back towards the glass superstructure of the boat, where music thudded and impressive-ten-years-ago disco lights flashed. 'I'm with Ice House,' she explained. 'The record company. You're Ken Nott, the DJ, right?'

'Right.' I shook her hand.

'Right. What was that song? "Rushdie and Son"?'

'Uh-huh. But the tune was mostly "Moonshadow".'

'Ha. Right. What was it? "I'm being shadowed by a fundamentalist . . . ?"' she sang, huskily but in tune.

'Nearly,' I said. 'It was, "I'm being stalked by a fundamentalist. I think I'm being shadowed."' I spoke rather than sang the lyrics. I was still feeling wary of the girl. Just because she said she was from the record company didn't mean she really was. I had already given at least one interview without knowing it, one drunken, loved-up night to a girl in a club who turned out to be a reporter for a tabloid with a dreadfully unreconstructed attitude to drugs and drug-taking. The resulting interview had nearly got me fired and started an argument between Capital Live! and the paper about whether she'd told me she was a reporter at the start of our conversation or not. I'd claimed she hadn't but it was just possible she had and I'd not been listening because I was too busy grinding my teeth and staring at her tits.

Jo had rather impressive breasts, too; not large, but high and bra-less beneath her top. The deck lights strung above us showed her nipples as little sharply defined bumps raising the thin black cotton.

'Yeah,' she said. 'I heard it at a party once. Never did get hold of a copy.'

'Well, I'd love to, ah, provide you with one,' I said, grinning, 'but I don't even have a copy myself any more.'

'Sorry,' she said, smiling. 'I wasn't trying to blag one.' She pushed her hand through her spiky blond hair, exposing ink-dark roots in an unselfconsciously endearing gesture and looked back briefly at the main party.

'What do you do at Ice House?' I asked her.

She shrugged. 'Bit of A&R, bit of what my boss calls asset management. Looking after bands.'

'Anyone I might have heard of?'

'Hope so. Addicta? Heard of them?'

'Yeah. Heard the hype, certainly.'

She shook her head emphatically. 'Not hype. They are really good.'

'Right. I saw an interview with them. The lead singer seemed a bit full of himself.'

She grinned. 'And your point would be?'

I smiled. 'Yeah, I guess it kind of comes with the territory.'

'They're okay,' she said. 'The band. Brad can sound arrogant but he's just being honest in a way; he's good and he knows it and he isn't into false modesty.'

'Woh-no,' I agreed. 'I don't think he'll ever be accused of that.'

She looked around. 'So. Enjoying the cruise?'

'No.' I sighed. 'I hate these things,' I said to her quizzical expression. 'Well, apart from what happened to the *Marchioness* . . . I always feel trapped. You can't get off. A normal party or gig or do, you can always bale out and head for the door. One of these things, you're along for the whole ride, whether you're totally bored or . . . well, the opposite of bored. A couple of times I've met somebody and, ah, you know, been getting on exceptionally well with them—'

'Ah. A female somebody.'

'A female somebody of the complementary gender of choice, indeed, and we've suddenly found ourselves in an ungregarious mood and wanted to be somewhere together, just the two of us, and . . . well, we've had a very frustrating wait for the end of the cruise.'

She smiled widely and took a bottle of beer from one jacket pocket. 'You make a habit of picking up women on these cruises?'

71

'Just twice so far.'

'Of course you could always have joined the metre-under club, or whatever you'd call it, fucking in the loos in the boat.'

'You know,' I said, frowning as though this had just occurred to me, 'I've never known a relationship that started in a toilet last very long. Odd that. Hmm.'

'Why are you looking at me like that?'

'Beg your pardon. Counting your piercings.'

'Uh-huh?'

'Uh-huh. Seven, that I can see.'

'Ha,' she said, and hoisted her T-shirt to show a belly button neatly cinched with a little bone-shaped metal rod.

'Eight,' I said.

She drank and wiped her lips with the back of one hand, left her mouth hanging open, her tongue running along the inside of her lower teeth as she nodded and made an obvious job of measuring me up. 'Nine, altogether,' she said, and performed a little movement that made me think at first she was taking a bow, then I realised she was making as though to look down at herself.

'My,' I said. 'Must be fun going through airport metal detectors.'

Her brows furled a little. 'Everybody says that.' She shrugged. 'Not a problem.'

'Well, that's airport security's loss.'

'You're not into piercings?'

'What can I say? I'm a fully paid-up hetero male.' I grinned.

A hoisted eyebrow made it look like she took the second meaning. She glanced back at the lights of the boat again, her facial metalwork glinting. 'Hey,' she said, 'you want to dance?'

'Gee, I thought you'd never ask.'

We didn't join the metre-under club, or whatever she'd called it. We waited a whole extra hour and had boisterous, energetic sex back on another boat, my new home, the *Temple Belle*. I found the ninth piercing.

'Whoo! Rock the fucking boat, man.'

I woke in the depths of the night, my arm gone to sleep beneath her. The *Temple Belle* rested on some not-quite-perfectly-level mud at the bottom of the tide, so that you could, to that minimal extent, tell what the state of the tide was even at night, down in the main bedroom with the skylight curtains closed, by the presence or absence of a faint sensation of being tipped towards the head of the bed. I had that feeling now. I took a deep breath, testing for the smell of decay that sometimes infected the air on summer nights like this, born of the mud and capable, on really warm, still nights like this, of insinuating its way even down here. Nothing. Just her perfume.

The girl slept on, sprawled half across me, muttering quietly in her sleep. She liked to talk during sex, too, and she liked being bitten. Well, nipped, really, but fairly hard. She professed herself amazed that I didn't share this predilection. She made a strange little exhaling noise in her sleep, like an exasperated sigh, then snuggled up closer to me and fell still and silent, breathing slowly and regularly.

Just visible in the glow from the radio alarm, a little plastic canister rested on the bedside table; her party contacts. Jo wore fashion contact lenses that made her eyes seem to fluoresce under ultraviolet light. Dancing with her on the cruise boat with its dated lighting rig had been . . . interesting.

Looking carefully at her face, I could just make out the soft reflections from some of the surgical steel piercings that punctuated her skin. I didn't mind in the least if people wanted to get tattoos or prick their bodies with bits of metal – was it better, worse, or no different from having a face-lift, or collagen implants, or liposuction, or Botox injections? I didn't know. But the more you thought about it, the more shoving lumps of metal through your skin did seem a slightly odd thing to do. The lengths we go to to differentiate ourselves, I thought. But then people had earrings and metal fillings in their teeth, and there were much weirder things, like the tribe that put more and more rings round the girls' necks as they grew, until they were extended to such a length that if the rings were taken off, their necks just collapsed, and they died.

Jo was fun, UV contacts and all. We'd already established we were both between serious relationships (which kind of implied we were both ready to start a new one).

We'd see.

'—guest in your country, sir, and I could not believe that which I was hearing here in the city of London was not really coming out of Kabul, or Baghdad. I could not believe my ears. I had to look around and reassure myself I was in a London cab, not—'

'Mr Hecht—'

'Where the hell do you people get off? Dear God, man, we lost four thousand people in a morning. Every one of them innocent civilians. This is war. Don't you understand that? It's time to wake up. It's time to choose sides. When the President said that you're either for us or against us, he spoke for all decent Americans. Your Mr Blair's chosen which side he's on and we'd like to think he speaks for all decent English people, but I don't know what side you think you're on. It sure doesn't sound like ours.'

'Mr Hecht, if the choice is between American democracy and murderous misogynists and a state governed by diktat and sharia, believe me I *am* on your side. I'd shop – I'd turn in my own brother if I knew he'd had anything to do with the attacks on September the eleventh. Mr Hecht, I know it doesn't sound like it usually, and I'm sure it didn't sound like it to you when you heard me yesterday, but there's a lot about America I love. I love its freedoms, its celebration of free speech, its love of . . . *betterment*. It is still the land of opportunity, I know that; there's no greater place on Earth to be young and smart and healthy and ambitious. A lot of us Brits affect to be appalled so few Americans have passports, but I've been to the States, I've travelled all over it and I know why they don't; America is a world in itself. The states *are* like countries, the sheer scale of the place, its variety of climate and landscape; it's stunning, it is truly beautiful. And is there any nation and ethnic group in the world *not* represented in the States? Americans don't have to go out into the world; the world's already come to them, and you can understand why.

'I still have a *lot* of issues – I have a problem with anybody who voted for the man claiming to be your president, for example . . . but then as not all Americans are eligible to vote, and half of those who were eligible to vote didn't bother to vote, and less than half of those who did vote voted for Dubya, that means I guess I'm probably only appalled by about twenty per cent or less of the population, which is not so terrible. But these are like the issues you have with a family member you love; they only matter so much because you're so close to them in the first place. My point is that in your anger and your pain, you're – your government is making a series of awful mistakes, mistakes that will damage America, damage all of us in the future. And I do not want to see that.'

'Well, this is like listening to two different people, sir, I don't know how you square what you're saying now with what you said yesterday.'

'Mr Hecht, I'm saying that there's a kind of madness built up about this already, a denial that benefits nobody. No, that's not true; it will benefit the sort of people who did this. Your denial will benefit your enemies. If you don't understand this, if you don't understand them, you'll never defeat them. So believing that America was attacked out of jealousy is not just ludicrous and self-deluding, it's self-defeating as well. This was not an act of grossly over-developed petulance, for God's sake. Twenty highly motivated men do not train for months to kill themselves in a meticulously planned and executed operation that the biggest, best-funded security services in the world don't get the faintest whiff of – even though it's happening right under their noses – because *you've* got more domestic appliances than *they* do. What was the phrase? "It's the economy, stupid"? Well, in this case, it's the foreign policy. It's that damn simple.

'It doesn't even matter if you or I don't see it this way, Mr Hecht, but to them it's every corrupt, undemocratic regime the United States has poured money and arms into since the last world war, propping up dictators because they're sitting on a desert full of oil and helping them crush dissent; it's the infidel occupying their holy places, and it's the unending oppression of the Palestinian people by America's fifty-first state. That's the way they see it. You can argue with their analysis, but don't kid yourself any of this happened because they're just jealous of your shopping malls.'

'Damn right I'd argue with their analysis. So are you now trying to say you are on our side?'

'May I refer my honourable friend to the answer given above?'

'I'm sorry?'

'No, I'm sorry, Mr Hecht; a piece of British Parliamentary phraseology we use on the show sometimes. Look, Mr Hecht. Do I think you should invade Afghanistan? For what it's worth – and it's worth almost nothing, I realise that – no. But, when you do, it couldn't happen to a nicer regime. I've been banging on about the Taliban for years. But don't forget you helped put them there; you funded the Mujahidin and you armed Bin Laden and supported the Pakistani security service, like you once supported the dictator Saddam Hussein because you

76

needed him and like you're supporting the dictator General Musharraf and the grotesque mediaeval despotism of the Saudis now, because you need them . . . Meanwhile, New Missile Defense, which destroys arms limitation treaties with pinpoint precision but is utterly guaranteed to have no discernible effect on any enemy missile whatsoever, which needs a homing beacon in the nose of its target to miss it in the same hemisphere, and which, after September the eleventh, has been proved to be an even more wilful and irrelevant waste of money, is a hundred per cent certain to happen. I mean . . . this is madness, Mr Hecht. It's national psychosis.'

'We have a right to defend ourselves, sir. We had that right before nine-eleven. Now we have the right to demand it. And we're going to have it whether it suits people like you or not. If you want to be part of it, fine. But if you're not part of the solution, you're part of the problem.'

'You know something, Mr Hecht? Back when I was a teenager, just starting to think for myself, I came up with a very basic formulation. I decided that whenever somebody says, You're either for us or against us, you *had* to be against them. Because only moral simpletons and outright conniving rogues see, or even claim to see, the world in such preposterously black and white terms. I am deeply dubious about being on the same side as anybody that stupid or that disingenuous, and certainly will not be led by them. Evil always starts with a good excuse, Mr Hecht. George W. Bush may be, in effect, President by acclaim now, and, compared to the people who attacked America, he's personally almost blameless, but the fact remains he got where he is by chicanery and deceit and – not even very deep down – he's a sad, inadequate little man.'

'Go to hell, sir, as you surely will.' Mr Hecht hung up.

'Think we lost him, Notty.'

I took a deep breath. 'That is your single deployment of that word for this year . . . Philly-Willy.'

'US Embassy on line one!'

'Oh, stop it, you're killing me.'

'Ken, great to meet you. Come in, come in. Ah, yes, let this delightful young lady take your coat . . .'

'Nice to meet you, ah . . .'

'Jamie. Call me Jamie. No standing on ceremony here. Come on in to the body of the kirk, as they say. I have Scotch blood too, you know. Us Heelanders have to stick together against these Sassenachs, eh? Listen, we're all really excited about you joining us at Capital Live!. I hear you're doing incredibly well. Caught you a few times myself; wish it was more. Schedules, meetings, business; you know, but I've heard you. I have heard you. Very good, very good. Very near the bone, very near the bone, but I like that. That's my style, too. Edge work. Nothing like it, is there? The danger, the risk. Risk-taking; that's what it's all about, isn't it? Don't you think? So, how are you set-tling into the old *Temple Belle*?'

'Ah, very nicely,' I said. I hesitated, wondering whether to point out that I'd been settled in there for over a year.

'Brill. Superb, superb! Ah. Helena. Like you to meet Ken. Ken Nott. Ken; this is my wife, the lovely Helena. Ah; drinks. Excellent, excellent. Ken. Champagne?'

'Lady Werthamley,' I said, nodding to her. 'Thank you.'

Sir Jamie Werthamley, our Dear Owner, had a penthouse in the top two storeys of his own newest office building, Lime-house Tower, overlooking the river at Limehouse Reach. This was April 2001 and I'd been working for him for nearly a year by then – three months of that on the relatively prestigious late-morning show – but this, one of his birthday parties, was my first chance to meet him (strictly no presents, the invita-tion had said, which might have seemed superfluous for a man who owned several gold mines, a bank, a Caribbean archipelago and his own airline. Anyway, I'd happily complied).

Sir Jamie was a young-looking fifty; ginger going grey. The trademark pony-tail was long gone but the single diamond stud in his ear was still there. He was dressed casually in designer jeans, a white T-shirt and a blue jacket that looked glossily fine and very expensive. I'd dressed in my best smart-but-casual but I felt like a tyke next to him.

There were maybe a hundred people in the sunken space of the main room, which, famously, had been fashioned by a film-set designer. The room held the crowd easily. I had my coat whisked away by what looked like one supermodel and a glass of dark gold champagne slipped into my fist by another before I'd really had a chance to draw breath. Sir Jamie was the touchy-feely sort; taking your hand, cradling your elbow, patting your back, gentle-punching upper arm, all that stuff. And all the time talking in that intense, breathily enthusiastic manner, words only just getting out of each other's way in time. In that respect he was exactly the same as when he was interviewed on TV.

His wife sat, upright and poised, in a tall, high-tech wheelchair. Lady W had suffered a bad fall horse-riding ten years earlier, not long after they were married. She wore something blue and gauzy, and a few shimmering pieces of diamond and platinum jewellery. She was maybe ten years younger than her husband and had raven black hair and violet eyes.

'Call me Helena, please,' she said, letting go of my hand.

'Thank you, Helena.'

She turned the wheelchair round using a little joystick at her right hand and moved it towards the steps down into the sunken part of the room. 'I listen to your show, Ken,' she said over her shoulder as I walked after her.

'Thank you.'

'You are terribly outspoken, aren't you?'

'That's my job, Helena,' I said as Lady W's chair got to the top of the steps and stopped.

'You do upset a lot of people.'

'I'm afraid I do.'

'A lot of important people, in fact.'

'Guilty as charged, ma'am,' I agreed.

'I know quite a lot of those people.'

'I . . . I'd be surprised if you didn't,' I said evenly.

She snorted in a very English public schoolgirl way and looked up at me, winking. 'Yes, well, keep up the good work. Now, who shall we find for you to talk to?' She surveyed the room. I did, too. The space itself was very swoopy and primary coloured. It did look like a film set; actually it looked like the bad guy's lair in an Austin Powers film, which was a funny thing to spend a couple of million quid on, but there you were. The windows, facing south and west, were three metres tall and easily fifteen long; great slabs of darkness sprinkled with the lights of London.

There were a lot of famous faces, from, I guessed at the time, pretty much every walk of life that led to people getting their faces into the papers or onto TV apart from crime. (Actually I was wrong about the crime bit.) I imagined that the people I didn't recognise were just plain rich, or powerful in a low-profile way, or both, and realised there was a decent chance that I was the least important person in the whole apartment, with the not-a-given exception of the supermodel-resembling serving staff.

'Ah,' said Mrs W decisively. 'You might be interested to meet Ann and David Schuyler. She teaches Political Philosophy at the LSE and he's a Tribune Group stalwart. Come on.' The wheelchair lurched forward and – using a rotating three-wheel set-up at each corner – descended slowly, motors whirring, to the dark red carpet below.

The Schuylers were charming and fascinating and interesting to talk to and I chatted to various other people who were all or most of those things during the course of the evening and passed some pleasant time with a Formula One driver, a Junior Minister who was about fifteen years older than me but still amazingly attractive (and who had an even more amazing, eye-watering contempt for her Minister) and a beautiful young actress whose name I could still recall weeks later but whose personality entirely escaped me. I drank the champagne and sampled some of the melt-in-the-mouth food circulating on silver salvers borne high by the catwalk-grade serving staff.

And fascinating as all this felt at the time, the only thing that came to mean anything, eventually, was meeting Celia, later.

I had already seen her, as I made my way back from the loo ('Head for the Monet and then hang a right at the Picasso,' as Sir Jamie himself had instructed me). She was standing with a smallish, pale man who was dressed in a severely tailored black suit, listening while he talked quietly to a rotund Lord who owned a national daily and a few regional titles.

She wore short heels that brought her nearly up to his height of about 170 centimetres, and a long, black, high-necked dress. A single string of large grey-black pearls; skin like milky coffee. She looked mixed-race, a combination of white and black and maybe South-East Asian too. Pushed, I'd have guessed she was in her mid-twenties, but her face was extraordinary; it gave the impression that it belonged to either a teenager who had seen some terrible things in her short existence or a sixty-year-old who'd never had a day's trauma or a single ageing event in her entire life. There was a sort of intense calmness to her features, an almost wilful innocence that I couldn't recall ever having seen before. It seemed almost identical to the poised serenity of a secure, untroubled child, and yet profoundly different; something struggled for and arrived at rather than inherited, rather than bestowed. Her eyes were amber beneath fine sculpts of dark brows and a forehead like a smooth and perfect bowl, and there was a roundness to her mouth and eyes that swept into elongated lines at the outside edges, contributing to that expression of thousand-yard tranquillity. Her hair was gathered up, full and shining, immaculate. It was the colour of heroin.

Her gaze slid straight over me as I passed a few metres away, in pursuit of some more of that very pleasant champagne. I didn't recognise her or the man at her side – who looked a bit like Bernie Ecclestone with no glasses and better hair – though I did see him leaving, an hour later, without her, but with a blond guy so wide and tall he just had to be a bodyguard.

A storm had been advancing on London from the west since the vividly bloody sunset hours earlier. The party was in full swing by the time it hit but aside from a distant roar if you stood near the windows, and the swirling patterns of rain whirling over the west-facing glass, it was easy to miss.

I headed towards the Monet again, ready to turn right at the Picasso, but there was already somebody in the bathroom. Sir Jamie, clutching a thin-necked bottle of Krug and in the company of a pair of giggling young soap stars, stopped and said, 'Ken! Queue? Walk this way; show you another pissoir. *Mi casa*, and all that. Oh! Fancy a game of snooker afterwards? We're missing – oh, I tell a lie, no, we're not,' he said as a sort of vapidly handsome young man I recognised from a boy band came clumsily down some spiral stairs to our right. 'Beg your pardon, Ken; offer suddenly and embarrassingly withdrawn. Hiya, Sammy,' Sir Jamie said, grinning, and slapped the young man on the arm. He turned to me and nodded to the spiral stairs. 'Ken; up there. Or there's a lift, of course. Either way, follow your nose. Ha ha! See you later. Have fun.' Then to the girls and the young man, 'Right!' And off they went.

I walked up the stairs then along a broad, deeply carpeted corridor lined with Art. Windows at the far end gave out onto a view east to the Millennium Dome, crowned with a circlet of red high-building lights. I couldn't find any open doors, so I shrugged and chose, adventurously, the one double-set I could see. A suitably large bedroom the size of a tennis court presented itself and I crossed to where I guessed the en suite might be. It was a gym, but far away, on the other side of the room, was the bathroom. It really did have a little lidded ceramic pissoir fastened to the wall, as well as an ordinary loo, two sinks the size of small baths, a vast sunken bath studded with nozzles, lights and underwater speakers, a colossal shower cabinet with marginally more nozzles than the bath, and a sauna the size of a log cabin.

It felt slightly pathetic only to do a pee in this palace of evacuation, exfoliation and immersion, like using a McLaren F1 as a golf cart. I stood there looking around and realised that this was probably just Sir Jamie's bathroom; there was no special facility to help a disabled person use the place. It was all immaculate save for a poorly wiped-clean area on a glass shelf where a few tiny white crystals lay scattered. I lifted some to my tongue with a fingertip and tasted cocaine. Moderately heavily cut, so surely not Sir Jamie's. Probably Sammy, the clumsy boy bandee.

About to quit the bedroom, I saw the curtains that filled one wall move at the edge, and felt a hint of a draught brush my face. I hesitated, then tentatively pulled the curtains back.

The view was to the north-east over a terrace cut diagonally across the tower's summit. Shrubs and small trees in giant pots swayed in the wind and the surfaces of ornamental pools ruffled as the gusts stroked and struck them. The sliding pane at this edge of the giant window had been left open a finger-width. I wondered if I ought to close it. If the wind changed . . . but so what? Sir Jamie probably had a butler or a major-domo or whatever the hell to do this sort of stuff. I was going to let the curtain fall back and just leave things as they were when I caught a glimpse of a figure in the shadows near one edge of the terrace where thin, straight railings segmented the view.

Lightning. Much later I thought it ought to have been lightning that lit the scene, that it had been that sort of storm and when I first saw her standing there it was courtesy of a flash of lightning, which lit up the Mysterious Figure in the Shadows. But it wasn't. Just the lights of the storm-pressed city. Sometimes reality isn't Gothic enough.

I could see it was a woman, standing about four metres away in the lee of the building under a roof projecting over part of the garden. The shelter was only partial; I could see her being buffeted by the swirling gusts. She looked thin and frail and dark. Her arms were crossed under her breasts. The wind tugged at the hem of her long dress and as my eyes adjusted I could see little strands of her hair whipping about her face and flickering up about her head like quick, attenuated flames.

I realised she was probably aware that somebody was watching her – a sliver of light had fallen across the paving stones at her feet when I'd pulled the curtains back – just as she turned her head to look straight at me. She stood like that for a moment, then her head tipped to one side. I recognised the woman in the narrow black dress with the extraordinary face. I couldn't see her eyes.

Even then, in theory, I could just have let the drapes fall back and toddled off downstairs, tipsily descending to the party. But, you come upon opportunities, little chance set-ups like this, too seldom. Even without having read about scenes like this, or watched them in films and on TV, even if you'd never read anything or watched anything in your life, there would be a kind of imperative of the moment that required you to behave in a certain way, take advantage of the presented chance, because to do anything else was just to declare yourself terminally sad. Or maybe I had swallowed Sir Jamie's chummy bullshit about being a fellow risk-taker. In any event, what I did was slide my hand into the gap between the windows and their frames and push the heavy glass panel aside.

'Hello?' she said, her voice barely audible over the roar of the wind.

84

'You'll catch your death, you know.'

'I beg your pardon?'

I raised my voice. 'Your death,' I said, almost shouting. I was already feeling foolish, the grand gesture of the occasion evaporating, shredded by the noise and force of the wind. 'You'll catch it.'

'Yes?' she said, as though this was new and important information I'd presented her with.

Gawd, I thought, she's some sort of simpleton. 'Look,' I said, 'will I just . . . ?' I gestured back into the bedroom, meaning to suggest I'd leave her to whatever solitary communing with rooftop nature she'd been indulging in.

She tipped and lowered her head, holding one hand to an ear. She shook her head.

'Shit,' I said under my breath, and stepped out onto the stones. Well, what else was I going to do? She was beautiful, the guy she'd been with had left the hoo-ha without her, I was thirty-five and starting to watch my weight and check my hair for grey each morning, and I wasn't so entangled elsewhere that I couldn't handle the potential extra complication of getting tangled up with a woman who looked as good as she did. Providing she wasn't simple, and unlikely as it probably was anyway. Rain sprinkled itself across my face and the wind uncombed my hair.

'Ken Nott. Pleased to meet you.' I held out my hand.

She looked at it for a moment, then took it in hers. 'Celia. Merrial,' she said. 'How do you do.'

Her voice was soft, with a faint accent that was probably French.

'You okay out here?' I asked.

'Yes. Is it all right?'

'Sorry?'

'For me to be here? Is it all right? It is permitted?'

With a sinking feeling, I realised that she hadn't recognised

85

me from earlier, down in the party. It sounded like she thought I was a security guard for Mouth Corp come to shoo her back to the properly appointed fun-having territory down below.

'Haven't the faintest idea,' I admitted. 'Civilian here myself.' This wasn't leading anywhere. Make excuses and leave. This was preposterously early to be baling out of a potential situation, but some sort of instinct I would usually ignore was telling me to forget it. 'Listen,' I said. 'If you're okay, I'll just leave you to it. I just . . . you know, I saw you out here and . . .' I wasn't even handling my withdrawal gracefully.

She ignored this. Her head was canted to one side again, quizzical. She frowned and said, 'Ah. I know your name.'

'Do you now?'

'You are on the radio,' she said, brushing away a strand of hair sticking to her mouth. She had a small mouth and full lips. 'Someone said you would be here.' Her teeth were very white as she gave a little, tentative smile. 'I listen to you.'

That was me hooked. As far as my ego was concerned she might as well have claimed to be my biggest fan. At the same time, a tiny crease of disappointment ruffled my contentment. Intelligent, rich, over-achieving and wildly influential though I naturally assumed all my listeners to be, there was something insufficiently exotic for a woman like this to be listening to my pop-raddled, commercial-choked show on daytime radio. Between the hours of ten and midday this woman ought to be perfecting her technique playing Bach fugues on her grand piano, or wandering the galleries clutching a draft of her thesis, standing in front of vast canvases, nodding wisely. She should be a Radio Three type, I told myself; certainly not listening to any radio station with an exclamation mark in its title.

I'm sorry, you fall beneath the acceptable standards of intriguingness that my over-heated and deeply wretched romantic sensibilities demand. Very Groucho altogether. Sad git.

'I'm very flattered,' I told her.

'Are you? Why?'

I gave a small laugh. A gust of wind thudded into us, showering us with rain and making us sway together, as if dancing to the pummelling music of the storm. 'Oh, I'm just always flattered when I meet somebody who admits to listening to my terminally facile and disposable show. And you—'

'Is it really so?' she said. 'Do you really think it is facile and disposable?'

I had been going to say something on the lines of, And you are the most stunningly beautiful creature at this party largely composed of stunningly beautiful creatures, which makes your interest in me especially gratifying . . . but instead she was having the temerity to interrupt a professional talker, and taking my small talk seriously. Didn't know which was worse.

'Well, it can certainly be facile,' I said. 'And when it comes down to it, it is just local radio, even if it's local radio for London. Noam Chomsky it ain't.'

'You admire Noam Chomsky,' she said, nodding and stroking away another strand of hair from her mouth. The wind was howling round the building, scattering rain drops over the two of us. It was April, and not too cold, but there was still a fair amount of wind-chill factor happening here. 'You have mentioned him a few times, I think.'

I held up my hands. 'Closest thing to a hero I have.' I folded my arms. 'You really do listen to the show, don't you?'

'Sometimes. You say such things. I am always amazed that you get away with what you do. So often I think, They won't let him get away with that, and yet, next time I switch on, there you are.'

'We do call the studio the—'

'Departure Lounge,' she said, smiling. 'I know.' She nodded. The wind hit her in the back, making her take a step forwards, towards me. I put a hand out but she adjusted her stance, straightening again. She didn't seem to notice the gale blowing round her. 'You must make many enemies.'

'The more the better,' I agreed airily. 'There are so many people deserving of utter contempt, don't you think?'

'You really don't care?'

'That I might make enemies of my elders and betters?'

'Yes.'

'Not enough to stop.'

'You really don't worry that somebody might take such offence at what you say they try to harm you?'

'I refuse to worry,' I told her. 'I wouldn't hand people like that even the partial victory of knowing I was concerned.'

'So, then, are you brave?' she asked with a small smile.

'No, I'm not brave. I just don't give a fuck.'

She seemed to find this amusing, lowering her head and smiling at the paving stones.

I sighed. 'Life's too short to spend it worrying, Celia. *Carpe diem.*'

'Yes, life is short,' she agreed, not looking at me. Then she did. 'But you might risk making it shorter.'

I held her gaze. I said, 'I don't care,' and, just then, there on the roof in the loud midst of the storm, I meant it.

She lifted her face up a little, as another gust shook her and me in sudden succession. I really wanted to take hold of that perfect little chin and kiss her.

'Look,' I said, 'apart from anything else, like I say, it's just radio. And it's a reputation I have, that I've developed. Mostly by getting sacked from other radio stations, admittedly, but it's what I'm known for. I kind of get a special discount because of that. People know I'm paid to be controversial, or just plain rude. I'm a shock jock. The Shock Jock, Jock the Shock, if you prefer your definitions in tabloid form. If Jimmy Young or one of the Radio One DJs or even Nicky Campbell said the things I do there'd be some sort of outcry, but because it's me people

88

just dismiss it. To really make an impression these days I'd have to say something actually slanderous, and that would get me fired. Though that'll probably happen soon enough anyway.'

'Still, it seems strange to approach what you do the way you do. Most people want to be liked. Or even loved.' She presented this as though it was something that might not have occurred to my sorry, cynical ass before.

'Oh, I'm always ready for my fair share of both,' I told her.

'But you insult people, and their ideas. Even their faiths. The things they love.'

'People don't have to listen.' I sighed. 'But, yes, I do insult things people hold dear. This is what I do.' She was frowning. I put my hands to my cheeks. 'Look, I don't mean I insult people or their beliefs because I want to hurt those people, because I get some sort of sadistic kick out of it, I mean that what I find I need and want to say – and which is what I do, sincerely believe, which is what I think is the truth as exactly as I can tell it – is stuff that happens to hurt other people. Does that make sense?'

'Yes, I think so,' she said in a measured, sceptical tone.

'What I'm trying to say is, I have my own beliefs. I . . . oh, shit, this is like so not post-ironic or post-modern and so insufficiently cynical for our knowing, you know . . . cynical . . . sorry, repetition of cynical . . . Jeez.' I took a deep breath of the storm's air. 'I believe in truth,' I told her. She was smiling a little now. I was making a complete idiot of myself but I didn't care any more. 'There; I said it. I believe there is something pretty damn close to objective truth more or less all the time and I'm not accepting this shite about everybody having their own truths or respecting somebody's opinions just because they're sincerely held. The Nazis sincerely hated the Jews; they weren't just kidding. I'm not respecting their fucking ideas just because they were deeply held. I believe in science, in the scientific method, in doubt, in questioning, in facing truths, not hiding from them. I don't believe in God but I admit I could be wrong. I don't believe in faith at all because faith is belief without reason, and reason is the only thing we have, the only thing I do believe in. I think people have every right to believe in anything they want, no matter how ridiculous it might be, but I don't accept their right to coerce others into the same views. And I certainly don't accept any right they might think they have not to have their views challenged just because they're going to feel peeved in the process.'

'You have faith in reason,' she said calmly, tucking some strands of hair back into place. 'Don't you?'

I laughed out loud, waving my arms about. 'This is crazy!' I yelled. 'We're standing here on top of a tower block in the middle of a fucking hurricane getting soaked to the skin and we're talking about *philosophy*?' I left my arms spread. 'Does the essential absurdity of this situation not strike you, too? Celia?' (I added, in case she thought I'd forgotten her name).

She put her head to one side again. Another staggering gust of wind, another adjustment of stance. 'I'm sorry. Are you cold?' she asked, sounding concerned. 'We could go in.'

'No, no,' I told her. 'I'm fine out here if you are. I'm a Scotsman; we're legally and morally bound not to admit to feeling cold, certainly not in the presence of thinly clad females and especially not heart-stoppingly beautiful thinly clad females we might legitimately assume are used to balmier climes. The penalties are actually quite severe. They endorse your passport and—'

She was nodding, a tiny frown creasing her brows. 'Yes. You only become inarticulate when you are being especially sincere,' she said, concluding.

That took the wind out of my sails. My hands dropped; I'd been talking with them as well. 'What *are* you?' I demanded. 'Celia, come clean; are you some sort of flying squad critic-come-philosophical psychoanalyst?'

'I am a married woman, a housewife, a listener.'

'Married?'

'Married.'

'Do you give your husband this hard a time?'

'I would not dare.' She looked quite serious. Then she shook her head. 'Well, I might, but he would not understand.'

Fuck this; I was getting cold. This was the most interesting, even unusual woman I'd met in a long, long time, but there comes a point.

I held her gaze and, after a breath, said, 'And are you a faithful wife, Celia?'

She didn't say anything for a while. We just stood there looking at each other. I could see little drops of rain on her face like sweat or tears and her hair was coming undone in the tearing wind. She shook in those gusts, as though shivering.

'I have been,' she said eventually.

'Well, I—'

She stopped me, holding up one hand towards my mouth, shaking her head. She glanced behind me, to the still open window.

'My husband is . . .' she began, then stopped. She tutted, looked down and to one side, and pinched her lower lip briefly with the fingers of her right hand. She looked up at me. 'Once,' she said, 'I thought that if I really, really hated somebody, I would make love to them, and have my husband find out. But only if I really hated the person, and wanted them dead, or perhaps thought that they wished they were dead.'

I let my eyebrows rise. 'Holy shit,' I said, reasonably. She did not look like she was joking. 'He is, ah, of the jealous persuasion, then.'

'You do not know his name.'

'Ah,' I said, embarrassed. I tapped my temple. 'Was it Merry—?'

'Merrial,' she said. 'He is John Merrial.'

I shook my head. 'I'm sorry,' I said. 'Not ringing any bells.'

'It should, perhaps, I think.'

'Well, you have the advantage over me,' I said.

She nodded slowly, solemnly. She said, 'I would like to see you again, if you would like.' Her voice was nearly drowned by the wind.

'Yes, I'd like,' I said. I was thinking, *I haven't touched her, kissed her, anything, yet. Nothing.*

'However you must know that if I were to see you,' she said, 'it would have to be seldom, and secretly. It might seem, sound . . . casual,' she said, frowning again, as though she wasn't putting this just as she would like. 'But it would not be. It could not be. It would be . . .' she shook her head '. . . of significance. Not something to be entered into lightly.' She smiled. 'I make it sound all very formal, do I not?'

'I've suffered more romantic propositions.'

I moved slowly forwards and reached for her. She came up on her toes, raising her head and tipping it, bringing her hands to either side of my face and opening her mouth to mine, while the wind tugged and pushed and jostled us and the rain sowed the gusts like a soft, cold shrapnel of the storm.

Jo had been at a big Ice House bash that night. She rolled in drunk half an hour after me, staggering down the steps into the *Temple Belle*, grinning and smelling of smoke. She laughed and started tickling me, then kissing me, then we fell into bed.

She had a way she preferred to be fucked sometimes when she was drunk like this; on her back, naked but for her T-shirt lifted up over her head and caught round her neck with her arms folded up inside it, making a sort of square around her head, her face hidden in the black cotton as she yelled and whooped, a horny, swearing wild-child in the carnal negative of a burka.

'*John* Merrial? *Mr* Merrial?' Ed said. 'He's a gangsta, mate.'

'He's *what*?'

'He's a fuckin gangsta, I'm telling you. Crime boss. Whatever you want to call it. Yeah; boss is better. Mind you, I'm saying that, but could be he's not much involved in actual villainy these days. Gone legit, inne? Like in *The Godfather Part Two*, when they talk about in a while they'll be totally legit by the end of the year or whatever it is, you know? That sorta fing. Course, on the *uvver* uvver hand, there's better profits in stuff like drugs and refugees an cars an computah crime an stuff.'

'Computah crime?'

'Yeah. You know; fraud. Must be hard to give up on that sorta action an let uvvers in. Pride involved, even, I should fink. Plob'ly. Why?' Ed's eyes went wide. 'Fuckin ell, Ken, you ain't finking of sayin sumfink orrible about *him*, are you? Fuckin say it ain't true. I'm serious, mate. Fuckin bargepole, know what I'm sayin?'

'I wasn't thinking of saying anything about him,' I said truthfully. 'I just saw him at a party the other night and somebody said who he was but not what he was and I thought I'd ask. I had no idea he was a cross between the Kray brothers and Al fucking Capone.'

'Well, he is. Leave well alone, know what I mean?'

'I *am* leaving him well alone.'

We were in Ed's then new car; a black Hummer with darkened windows. It made my Land Rover feel like a 2CV. We were driving through the streets of south London on the way to a gig in an old cinema in Beckenham. Ed was determined to make me some sort of club DJ, or at least teach me the intricacies of getting two bits of plastic to revolve at different rates so that the tunes contained sounded like they had the same bpm.

'Wot sort of party was this you was boaf at, anyway?'

'The Dear Owner's. Sir Jamie. One of his birthday parties.'

'What? Does he have more than one, like the Queen? An official birthday and a real one? What's that about, then?'

'Just the one birthday, but several parties. I think I was at the second most exclusive soirée.' We drew up, obstructed by a bus loading people at a stop on one side, and the oncoming stream of traffic on the other. There was, in fact, a sizable gap between the two, one you could have got any normal car, or even a Transit van, through quite comfortably (the Landy could have made it with both doors wide open), but Ed was probably right in erring on the side of caution, especially as the machine was left-hand drive. Behind us, a horn sounded. 'Jesus Christ, Ed,' I said, looking at the rear end of the bus to our left, and the Hummer's expanse of bonnet, 'I do believe this thing is literally wider than a London bus.'

'Yeah, it's rough, innit?' Ed grinned, teeth like a snow field.

'Rough?'

'Yeah; wicked, innit?'

I slapped the transmission tunnel. This was a tall, black-fur-lined box between Ed and me about the size of a big fridge-freezer combo; you could have believed the thing had a spare Mini hidden underneath. If Ed had been any shorter I'd have had to rise out of my seat to make sure he was really there. 'What the fuck is it with this fucking black patois shit?'

'What?' Ed said innocently. We still weren't going anywhere. The horn from behind sounded again. I didn't know who was leaning on it, but they were brave. If I'd been stuck behind a blacked-out Hummer I wouldn't have done that; I'd have been too scared the fucker would get slung into reverse and just roll right over me.

'Rough means good,' I said indignantly, 'wicked means good, fucking hell, *bad* means good. I mean, I realise there are issues about slavery and centuries of oppression here, but do you have to take it out on the language?'

'Na, mate,' Ed said, finally making slow forward progress as the bus rolled off ahead of us. 'It's like you go so far into the concept, right, the meaning, that you come out the far side. Know what I mean?'

I looked at him.

'What?' he asked.

'My mistake,' I said, waving one hand and looking away. 'Silly old me. I didn't even realise that meanings had sides you could come out of. Serves me right for passing up a university education. That'll learn me. Or not, as is in fact the case.'

'It's what language is about, innit? Communication.'

'You don't say. But if people make words mean the opposite of—'

'But everybody knows what they really mean, don't they?'

'Do they?'

'Course they do. It's about context, innit?'

'But hold on, the first time somebody said bad when they meant good, how did anybody know what the hell they really meant?'

Ed thought about this. 'Right,' he said. 'Way I see it, it was like this. Some bloke was trying to cop off wif this bird, right? An she was a bit coy, right, a bit not wantin to seem too eager, but still wantin it, yeah? An she says, Oh, you wicked man. Or somefing. Like, maybe he'd been telling her all the fings what he wanted to do wif her and she was pretendin to be modest but actually she was gettin really wet, right? He was gettin her juices flowin. But she calls him wicked, an smiles, an they boaf know what she means, see? So that's the first time that somebody says wicked an means good, brilliant, bring it on. So then, like, by extension, know what I mean, people start using uvver words what are the opposite of what they seem to mean, like rough for cool and bad for good, cause it's not, like, really much of a leap from usin wicked that first time, an the reason that all this is happenin in the black community, right, here or in the States, is precisely because the bruvvers haven't got much else that is theirs. We could be boxers or

95

musicians an that, but all these uvver, like, modes of expression is closed off to us artistically, and so we fuck wif your language. An that's what I fink happened. Plob'ly.'

I stared at him. 'There could actually be a grain of truth in that silo of gibberish,' I said. (Ed went, 'Hee hee hee', in a wheezy voice.) 'But this still doesn't explain how you can come out the other side of an accepted lexicological meaning for a perfectly clear and unambiguous term such as "bad".'

'It's like Klein bottles, innit?'

'It's like *what*?'

'Klein bottles. They're like four-dimensional bottles what can only exist in fuckin hyperspace, man.'

'What the fuck has *that* got to do with anything?'

'My old mum knitted me a Klein bottle hat when I was a nipper.'

'Are you on drugs?'

'Hee hee hee. Na, but listen, like, the spout of a Klein bottle sorta curves round and goes back into the bottle, doesn't it?'

'It may astonish you to know – and it certainly appals me to admit – that I do sort of know what you're talking about.'

'So that's like the meaning I was talking about earlier, innit? Goin out beyond itself an then coming back in. Bleedin obvious, I should fink. Fuckin pay attention, Ken.'

I was actually lost for words. Eventually I recovered enough to say, 'And you seriously had a hat that resembled a Klein bottle, you mad fuck? Or was that the bit I hallucinated?'

'Me mum was doing this Open University course, wasn't she? Geometry an that. So she decided to knit a Klein bottle, and then it sorta turned into a Bob Marley hat. Fuckin orrible it was. She made me wear it to school once, too, cos she was so proud of it; came to the school gates wif me an everyfin so I couldn't accidentally lose it.'

'I do trust that your pals did the decent thing and kicked the living shit out of you.'

'Ha! They did, too.' Ed shook his head, a happy, nostalgic expression on his face. 'Never liked mafs, ever since.'

We were silent for a minute or so. Then I said, 'Hey, we just went past a cop car without you getting pulled over.'

'That's cause they fink you're driving the fucker.'

'Of course; white man in the right-hand seat. Easily enough to confuse the average plod, I'll grant you.'

'Zactly. Why else do you fink I offered you a lift?'

'You fuck! You're exploiting me!'

'Hee hee hee.'

Four

LACKING THAT SMALL MATCH TEMPERAMENT

'No, no, I'm for *lots more* CCTV cameras. I think they should be everywhere, and especially in *police stations*.'

Craig, rolling a joint on the kitchen table, sniggered.

'I'm serious,' I told him. 'Canteen culture? Sounds interesting. Let's see it. Total coverage; even the toilets. No more of these black or Asian guys beating themselves up, throttling themselves and stamping on their own heads, and then blaming our stout-hearted defenders of decency!'

'The stairs,' Craig suggested. 'Don't forget the stairs.'

'Oh, Christ, yeah, the stairs; you'd want serious Sky Premier League coverage on the stairs; top and bottom at the very least. With the important Player Cam option, naturally.'

'Prisoner Cam.'

'Sus Cam. Con Cam.' I nodded vigorously, with the intense concentration on total trivia of the truly stoned. 'Crim Cam.'

'Shplim shplam bim bam,' Craig wheezed, laughing.

'What?' I said.

'You still not got Sky yet?' Craig said, raising the joint to lick the Rizlas.

'Did you really say . . . ? But, moving on. What, Sky? No

101

fucking way,' I said vehemently. 'I'm not giving that shite Murdoch any of my . . . soft-earned dosh.' I'd moved into the *Temple Belle* a year earlier. It hadn't been lived in for many years so it only had terrestrial; Craig had been trying to persuade me to have Sky fitted ever since.

'Mind you,' Craig mused, 'for a Clydebank supporter, what's the point? I suppose.'

'Fuck off. Hun.'

Craig and I had this unpleasant though also comforting habit of reverting to our West Coast Male Scottish cultural stereotype when we met up, talking about football. Craig was a bluenose, a Rangers supporter. Almost his only failing, really, unless you were going to count his part in a long-term-struggling marriage (and in a spirit of male solidarity and the above-mentioned cultural stereotype, I was duty-bound to blame that mostly on Emma, regardless of anything else).

It was early May 2001, a couple of weeks after the party at Sir Jamie's groovy pad at the top of Limehouse Tower. We were sitting in the kitchen of the family home in Highgate, an elegant three-storey terraced house with a large conservatory and lots of decking in the garden. Emma had her own place these days, a garden flat a couple of streets away. Nikki lived with Craig but spent occasional nights at Emma's. Those tended to be the nights I came along and Craig and I got the chance to relive an adolescence that he – a father and effectively a husband at eighteen – had quit maybe too abruptly and I – arguably dissolute, still alone but variously entangled at thirty-five – had never quite shaken off.

So we listened to some music, smoked joints, drank beer – or wine, more often these days – and talked about women and, of course, fitba. It was my misfortune to be, nominally at least, a Clydebank supporter (could have been worse; I might have decided to support Dumbarton). Clydebank were the closest team of any note to where I grew up, in the prim grid of sunny, south-aspected Helensburgh, a town far too middle class to have anything as proletarian as a decent football team of its own. The Rugby Club, on the other hand, was a social centre almost on a par with the Golf Club. Clydebank is one of those teams at least one level beneath the big Scottish clubs that are themselves a level beneath the big two, the Old Firm of Celtic and Rangers. Craig had inherited his Rangers scarf from his dad. They were posh Hun; not bigoted or anti-Catholic, but unswervingly committed to the team.

'Supporting a team like Clydebank has its compensations,' I told Craig as he lit the spliff, blowing smoke into the darkened kitchen. I had a sudden vision of Nikki the next day, sniffing the air and flying round opening windows here and in the adjoining conservatory. '*Da-ad!*' Though actually these days she would say, '*Crai-aig!*'

'Compensations?' Craig said, cupping his free hand to his ear. 'Hark! Do I hear the sound of a straw being grasped at? Why, I do believe I can!' I just looked at him. In fact what he could hear was Moby sounding soulful and interesting on the kitchen mini system. 'What compensations?' he demanded. 'Having to travel to Cappielow for your home games, or visiting East Fife?'

'No,' I said, ignoring the insults. 'I mean that it prepares you more comprehensively for life as a supporter of the national team.'

'You what?' Craig said, sounding very London for a moment.

'Think about it,' I told him, accepting the joint. 'Ta. If you support a team like Clydebank you get used to disappointment . . .' I paused to pull on the number, then talked out through the smoke. 'The grossly truncated cup run, the good players – the very rare good players – sold on before they have a chance to do much for the club beyond show up the rest of the team for the sorry plodders they really are, the mid-season nervousness as they sink towards the lower reaches of the league, even, in the long term, the occasional promotion you know will probably end in demotion the following year; the just plain boring, inept displays of football where you sit in the cold for two hours realising you've doled out twenty quid to watch two gangs of intellectually challenged bampots running around a muddy field hacking away at each other's legs and seemingly competing to see who can punt the ball the furthest up the park, while your fellow men around you hurl abuse and insults at their own team and the other supporters.' I took another deep toke and handed the J back.

'Ah, the beautiful game,' Craig said, affecting misty-eyedness.

'And so,' I said, 'when it comes to supporting Scotland as a national team, you're fully prepared for the resulting failures, disillusion, frustrations, let-downs and general all-encompassing despair, which is the natural result of following our plucky but generally rather undistinguished Bravehearts. You've been inoculated against such disenchantment throughout your supporting life; this is the sort of rubbish you're used to watching and coping with every week or every fortnight of the three seasons where it rains. You just scale up your already pre-battered, ready-deflated expectations a little and you're there. You, on the other hand,' I said, taking the number back. 'You,' I repeated after a deep pull, 'with your fancy nine league championships in a row and your players with Ferraris and your forty-five thousand fans through the turnstiles every home game and your European experience . . . you get used to success. You feel cheated if there's no new silverware in the trophy . . . yeah, you have a trophy *room*; we have a trophy cabinet.'

'Currently empty, if memory serves. Thanks.'

'Fuck off. You start whining when you don't finish top of something at the end of the season. We're just glad our teams still exist and some fucker hasn't sold the ground out from under us for a new B&Q. The point is that you get totally conditioned to winning, to victory, so when *you* support Bonnie

Scotland, as you're genetically programmed and constitutionally bound to, you can't cope with the fact we're basically crap.'

'We're not *crap*,' Craig said defensively.

'Well, not *total* crap, but just not much better than a team from a country of only six million people ought to be. So suddenly you're in a position of inferiority, of having to deal with—'

'All right, all right,' Craig said, kicking off his moccasins and putting his feet up on the farmhouse table. 'I take the fucking point. You end up taking refuge in peripheral stuff, like having nice supporters.'

'Nicer than those nasty, yobbish, xenophobic English supporters, certainly, which is the unspoken subtext of this aren't-we-great Caledonian self-congratulation.'

'Drunk but amiable.'

'Harmless.'

'Pretty much like the team.'

'Exactly.'

'Just going for the spectacle,' Craig said with a trace of sadness, stretching to hand me back the spliff.

'It's the national equivalent of the straws you clutch at league level with teams like Clydebank: people around you applauding sportsman-like behaviour, the fleeting glimpse of skill when somebody on the park accidentally does what they meant to do, the combined pride and resentment when a player sold to the big boys three seasons ago scores a hat-trick in the English Premier.'

I pulled on the J until it was finished and then mashed it into the ashtray with the one we'd had before Craig's home-made chilli. I reached for my wine.

'Yeah, but when you do win . . .' Craig said, leaning back in his seat and putting his hands behind his neck. 'It's worth it. Even as a supporter of the Bankies you must have at least heard of this, you know, from supporters of other teams.'

I ignored this too. 'Is it? I'm starting to question that, frankly.'

Behind his Trotsky glasses, he blinked. 'What? Winning isn't fun?'

'Na, I mean I'm getting fed up with football in general.'

Craig gave a stagy gasp and said, 'Wash your mouth out with half-time Bovril, you blasphemous bastard.'

'Do you not think so?' I asked. 'Seriously. I'm just getting super-saturated with the damn game, and that's without having fucking Sky. There's too much football.'

Craig put his hands over his ears. 'Now you're starting to scare me. I'm going to pretend you're not here until you stop saying bad, scary things.'

'I had this idea.'

'Can't hear you.'

'World Cup.'

Craig started to hum. I raised my voice above this and Moby, still being moody somewhere inside the Sony system's jewel-like mechanisms.

'World Cup,' I repeated. 'Takes far too long,' I shouted. 'My idea would get the whole overblown rigmarole over with in one day. Same with any cup competition, actually.'

'La, la, la-la-la.'

'What's the best, most exciting, most intense and nail-biting part of many a final?' I yelled. I spread my arms. 'The penalty shoot-out!'

Craig looked incensed. He took his hands down from his ears and said, 'You're not suggesting—'

'Yes! Scrap the ninety minutes of the actual game, ditch the half-hour of extra time and go straight for the penalty shoot-out without all the running around and panting and diving beforehand. Total intensity from the first whistle of the first game through to the last fall-on-your-knees-with-your-face-in-your-hands, goalie-jumping-up-and-air-punching moment that sends the Jules Rimet trophy back to Luxembourg where it belongs!'

'You are such a fucking heathen even to have thought of that.'

'The Yanks would love it,' I told him. 'The networks would finally have a soccer format they could get ads into every three or four minutes. The attention span of your average Peorian would not be taxed.'

'The penalty shoot-out is a disgraceful travesty of the world's best game,' Craig said solemnly. 'Tossing a coin is more honourable; at least it's admitting it's just luck.'

'Spoken like a member of the SFA. I'm talking about the future, you reactionary bluenose bastard. Get with the programme or start following shinty, Luddite.'

Craig did a very good impression of not listening. He was gazing, frowning at the mini system, where Moby's *Play* was about to Stop.

'Moby,' he said, looking at me.

'What about him?'

'D'you not think he looks a bit like Fabien Barthes?'

Later in the lounge, sitting side by side on the couch, waiting for my taxi to arrive, sharing one last joint and a final couple of glasses of Bin 128: 'Emma says we never talk about important stuff.'

'Oh?' I said.

'Yeah. It's about number three hundred and seven on her list of Reasons Why Craig's Crap.'

'Well, if she wants to talk to you about so-called important things—'

'No no no, not her and me; *you* and me. You and I.'

I looked at him. 'What's she talking about?'

'I think she means we don't gossip.'

'Oh, you mean we talk about things that we think are important, like football, sex and politics, not, like, relationships?'

'Something like that,' Craig said, scratching his head. 'Whenever I've seen you she asks after your mum and dad and your brother and Jo, and I end up shrugging and saying, I don't know.'

'Ah, right.'

'So, how are your mum and dad and your brother Iain and girlfriend Jo then, Ken?'

'They are all fine, thank you, Craig.'

'Thank you. I shall inform my currently estranged first wife when next I encounter her.'

'How is Em, anyway? How are you two these days?'

Why did I feel so guilty whenever I asked after Emma? She was a friend, she'd always meant a lot to Craig and no doubt always would, and we'd only spent one drunken night together, which we both severely regretted and wished hadn't happened, so why did I feel so like a traitor when I mentioned her to Craig?

'Ah, we're bumping along,' Craig sighed. 'The bottom, I think, but bumping along. Yourself? Still seeing Jo?'

'Yup.'

'Anybody else?'

'Not really. Well . . .' I grimaced.

'So, still playing the field, then?' Craig said, with an easy smile.

I squirmed a little, acknowledging awkwardness. 'Not so much actually playing the field; more darting out from under the cover of the hedgerows every now and again, to—'

'Retrieve your ball.'

'I was thinking more of ploughing and seed-scattering analogies, but you could put it that way,' I conceded.

Craig looked away, thoughtful. 'I think I should have done more of that.'

'Jeez, man, you're thirty-five. You're in your prime. You're not at the baffies and pipe stage yet, for Christ's sake.'

'Yeah, but I have friends who're mostly married. And I work from home; no flirting over the coffee point or the photocopier for me.'

'How's your work going?' I asked him. 'Designed any good webs recently?'

He groaned. 'Don't ask. Spent the whole day flushing out the PCs with Anti-Virus. Probably some little shit from Outer Khazaktavia with a fucking Sinclair Spectrum. What about you?'

'You're not supposed to ask a radio DJ how things are going,' I told him tiredly. 'You're supposed to tell me how each successive show of mine that you listen to every day is even better than the one before.' I looked at him. 'You're not really totally up to speed with this "friendship" thing yet, are you?'

'What the hell do I want to listen to you for?' Craig demanded. Ruby light from a second-generation, post-ironic lava lamp on a shelf behind him reflected off his glasses and his shaven head. 'If I was desperate enough to listen to you tomorrow—'

'What do you mean "if", you disloyal ex-so-called best friend brackets Scottish close brackets?'

'—all I'd hear,' Craig went on, 'would be what I just heard tonight.'

'What?' I screeched.

'Look me in the eye, you devious, lying toe-rag, and tell me you won't be regurgitating that drivel about supporting rubbish league teams being a better preparation for supporting rubbish national teams than supporting successful ones, or that gob-shite nonsense about the World Cup composed entirely of a series of penalty shoot-outs, you shocking, shocking man.'

I stared at him for a while. 'It's a fair cop,' I said huskily.

'I should demand royalties,' Craig said. 'A wage.'

'Do you really never listen to me?'

Craig guffawed. 'Course I do. Until the adverts drive me nuts. But you do recycle stuff we've been talking about.'

'I know. Should I start mentioning you? Crediting you? Enrol you in the Crapital Live! BUPA scheme?'

'I told you; a regular cheque would suffice.'

'Fuck off.'

He sighed. 'Anyway.'

'Anyway, don't fucking sit here feeling sorry for yourself; get—'

'I'm not feeling sorry for myself.'

'Neither you should. You've got a good, satisfying, successful career, you've helped raise a smart, beautiful daughter, and you're the lucky friend of at least one really great dead famous person; me. I mean, what more can you ask for?'

'More sex?'

'Would have been nice. Look, get out there and start social-ising. Meet some women. Come out with me. We'll go club-bing.'

'Yeah, maybe.'

'No, not maybe; definitely. Let's do it.'

'Call me. Persuade me when I'm sober and not morose.'

'Are you morose now?'

'A little. I do love my job, but sometimes I think it's just electronic wallpaper and what's the point in it all? And Nikki is totally brilliant but then I think she's probably going to get hurt by some worthless bastard . . . I mean, I know it's caveman stuff, but I don't even like to think of her having sex.'

'You don't? Shit, I do.'

'Oh, Ken,' Craig said, shaking his head. 'Even for you . . .'

'Sorry, sorry,' I said, sincerely.

The doorbell chimed.

'Good,' Craig said. 'Now get tae fuck out of my house, you vemonous—'

'Vemonous?'

'—you venomous cake of shite that you are.'

'Okey-dokey,' I said, jumping up and slapping him on one knee. 'Same time next week?'

'Probably. Safe journey back to the gin palace.'

110

On the doorstep, I stopped, clicked my fingers and said, 'Oh; I didn't mention.'

'What?' Craig said warily.

'About my torrid homosexual affair with Lachlan Murdoch.'

'Uh-huh?'

'Yeah, and funnily enough I've started writing for one of his dad's tabloids, too.'

Craig closed his eyes. 'Let's just get it over with, okay?' he sighed.

'Just thought you should know; I've got a column in the Son.'

'Oh, fuck.'

'See ya!'

'Yeah, try telling that on the fucking radio, Mr Funny.'

'That was just for you, baby. Til next week.'

'Yeah, yeah . . .'

When I first kissed Celia, on the night of the storm, that was as far as it went. It was a fabulous kiss, with her warm, taut body against mine and her soft mouth and hard little tongue flickering inside my mouth like a tiny flame of moist muscle, but that was all. She wouldn't even give me her address or phone number or mobile or anything. At the time, of course, I still didn't know who her husband was, just that he sounded somewhat on the psycho side (which, goodness knows, should have been enough). I worried that, despite all the solemnity a few moments earlier, she was kidding me on, that this was all just a bizarrely serious tease. But she would be in touch, she said. Now she had to get back to the party, for soon a car would be coming for her to take her away.

Another long, unbearably sexy kiss, when she let me run my hands all over her, then she slipped inside the bedroom. I stood there in the wind and rain, hard-on like a giant redwood, waiting for a decent interval and wishing, for once, that I smoked, because now felt like the right sort of time to do just that.

Then – via the mega-bathroom again, to dry my face and comb my hair – I went back down to the party.

Celia had already left.

Nothing, for weeks. Life went on, all the usual nonsense happened (dental appointments, run-ins with management, a couple of boozy, flirtatious lunches with the lovely Amy, a gig in Brighton with Ed, which ended in some chilly dawn skinny dipping with a couple of girls from Argentina). Jo and I went out to parties and films, got loved up and went clubbing, had good, fun sex every now and again, and I decided that Celia was just one of those never-quite things; a little oasis of high-grade strangeness, charm and drama in an existence not normally all that short of them in the first place. Anyway, the woman was a gangster's moll. Worse; his wife, for God's sake. Edge work and risk-taking and all that crap was all very well, and I hadn't been entirely lying when I'd told her I didn't give a fuck, but I wasn't actually suicidal. Life was too short not to seize the day but she'd been right about behaviour that might shorten that life, dramatically.

Then, one overcast Wednesday in mid-May, over a month later, a courier arrived with a slim, padded envelope, immediately after I'd finished the show. The envelope was light, so light it felt empty. There was a grey plastic hotel key card inside. I was in the corridor from the studio to our office at the time; I looked inside the envelope but there was nothing else in there; I tipped it up and tapped it but still nada. I looked back down the corridor as I walked, in case I'd missed something else inside falling out. Nothing there, either. The key card didn't say what room it was for, or what hotel. They never do. I put it in my pocket and inspected the envelope, looking for a sender's name, wondering if I could trace it back to whomever had sent it.

My mobile sounded as soon as I switched it back on. The phone's display said Anonymous.

'Hello?' I answered.

'Is that Kenneth?' said a female voice.

'Ken Nott, yes.'

'May we talk?'

'Yes,' I said. I stopped by the office door. Inside, I could hear Phil and Andi, his assistant, talking and laughing. 'Who is this?'

'We met on the roof, about five weeks ago, do you remember? Please don't say my name, but do you remember me?'

'Ah. Well, ah, yes. Yes, of course I do. How are you?'

'Do you still . . . I am not sure what to say. Wish to proceed? This is very unromantic, I am sorry.'

'Ah,' I said, staring at the carpet beneath my feet. 'I found out who, ah, who your other half is.'

'So you do not. I see. I'm sorry. I have been stupid. Please dispose of—'

'Well, no, hold on.'

'You received what I sent?'

'Size of a credit card? Nothing else?'

'That's right.'

'Yes. Where is it for?'

'The Dorchester. Six zero seven. It's just that . . . I would have liked to have seen you again.'

I don't know. It was just something about the way she said it. I swallowed and asked, 'You there now?'

'Yes.'

I glanced at my watch. 'I have a few things to tidy up here. Half an hour?'

'We have all afternoon, until about six.'

'So, I'll see you.'

'Two things.'

'What?'

'You must not leave any mark on me. Nothing.'

'Of course, I understand.'

'Also . . .'

113

'What?'

'Just this time, would you be silent?'

'Silent?'

'Completely. From when you arrive to when you go.'

'That's a little weird.'

'It is a private . . . superstition, you would probably say. I know it makes no sense to you. But I would like you to indulge me in this.'

'Hold on,' I said, nearly laughing, 'is this place bugged?'

'No.' I could hear her smile. A pause. 'Will you do this for me? Just this one time?'

'What if I say no?'

'Then I will not have been indulged, and because of that, if we go ahead, I will believe that this will end badly for us. I do not know what you will believe, Kenneth.'

I thought about this. 'All right.'

'Half an hour, then. I will wait for you.'

'See you soon.'

'Yes.'

The phone clicked off.

At the Dorchester, number 607 was a suite. I hesitated at the door. I was sweating. Mostly this was because I had walked from Capital Live!. The stuff I thought I might have to tidy up had proved utterly trivial or just entirely fit for putting off until tomorrow or later, and so I'd made my excuses – the following day's show was pretty much prepared already – and left. I'd walked the streets under the low grey sky. It was warm and the air felt thick and humid for May.

Walking gave me time to think. Was I doing the sensible thing here? Well, that was hardly worth answering. Objectively, knowing whose wife I was, hopefully, about to fuck, I was behaving like a masochist with a death wish. Or not, of course; maybe she'd been exaggerating that night on the terrace outside

Sir Jamie's bedroom. Perhaps she'd been dramatising the whole thing because doing so fulfilled some appetite for mystery, and her husband didn't give a damn what she did or who she did it with.

I fingered the little sliver of plastic in my pocket. The whole cloak-and-dagger set-up with the key card was either faintly amusing and reassuring, or deeply worrying. What was I doing? *He's a gangsta, mate.* We reassure ourselves that we're all special, but was anybody *that* special, was anybody so extraordinary they were worth taking the sort of risk I might be taking?

Of course, people had been taking mad risks for sex, lust, love, for as long as we'd been people. Wars had been fought for what you could, if you were being uncharitable, charac-terise as basically a bit of slap and tickle. Holy books had been rewritten, the laws of God changed to facilitate the having of some desperately yearned-for piece of ass. Desire was the back-handed compliment humanity had no choice but to pay itself. It was just the way we were, it was what we did. We couldn't help ourselves.

Seen one, seen 'em all, I reminded myself. But then that, of course, was such shit. Sexists said that the way racists claimed, They all look the same to me. Both were confessions of per-sonal inadequacy, of the inability to really see.

I used the key card and stepped into a dark hallway, illu-minated only, once I'd closed the door, by light spilling from a small loo on the other side of the hall. The air was very warm; I had to take my jacket off. On a small table opposite, a huge display of flowers filled the air with a thick, sweet scent. There were two large doors, left and right, both ajar, both rooms dark beyond. Just ambient sound of the city in both directions, heavily muffled. The first door led to a sitting-room, darkly curtained, the afternoon sunshine held at bay by drapes thick as carpets, tall as the distant ceiling. All a bit Edwardian, but suitably sumptuous. The other door led to the bedroom.

115

There had been a light on in here all the time. Celia was sitting at a roll-top desk on the far side of the room, reading by a desk lamp. She was wrapped in a white robe that was too big for her. Her golden brown hair was down, spreading and reaching almost to the seat of the chair. She turned round when she heard the door open. She wore little round glasses. It felt even warmer in the bedroom; a vent thundered quietly over-head, producing a draught of tropical heat that was already drying the sweat on the back of my neck and uncombing my hair.

She raised one finger to her lips. My heart was thudding; I was half expecting muscled goons with eighteen-inch collars to burst out of the wardrobe, whack me on the back of the head, gaffer-tape my mouth and zip me into a body-bag . . . though, from the impression I had of the room from the desk lamp's weak light, this place was too posh for wardrobes; it had a dressing-room, instead. I stood there in the heat, won-dering how much initiative she wanted me to take; how much, indeed, I wanted me to take. This whole silent running deal – or at least me agreeing to it – had put that ball pretty firmly in her court. The dome of an elegantly gleaming trolley sat in one shadowy corner of the bedroom. A champagne bucket and two glasses sat on a low table in front of a towering display of lilies. The flowers' scent saturated the blood-warm air.

Celia closed her hardback, took off her glasses, got up and walked over to me, raising herself on her toes with her last step and kissing me just as she had on the night of the storm. She smelled of musk and roses. I used both hands to undo the rope-thick belt, then pulled her robe open. Her skin was smooth and warm, warmer even than the over-heated air of the room. I held her away a little to look at her. She let the white robe fall.

My eyes went wide and I breathed in, seeing the strange, curled imprint of her lightning scar for the first time. I was about, I think, to say, 'Good God,' but she anticipated me, and gently put her cupped hand over my mouth, silencing me as I stared at the tracery of dark brown lines. She stood still in the glowing white whorl of the fallen robe, letting me inspect the fern-mark, raising her arms and gathering up her hair to let me see better, displaying herself quietly.

On, not in, a vast bed beneath a swooping canopy, we fell to our shared cause. I let her undress me, an urgency in her hands and expression I could not comment on. I stroked her hair while she did this, ploughing its rich thickness with my fingers. Her body was the most sensuous thing I had ever seen in my life, limbs slim but muscled enough to curve, waist tiny. Her areolae and nipples were unexpectedly pink for her caramel skin, whose tone – save for the lightning-intaglioed print descending her left flank – didn't vary anywhere except faintly on the palms of her hands and the soles of her feet. Her pubic hair was darker than that on her head, surprisingly soft but tightly curled. She skinned my jeans off. The head of my cock was already protruding out the top of my Calvins, purple and positively polished-looking between the grey cotton and the pasty flesh of my irredeemably pale Scots skin. I had always thought this looked a bit gross – erections usually did, regardless of the circumstances – but she smiled when she saw it, as though it was already an old friend, and peeled off my briefs.

I mimed putting on a condom and pointed at my jacket, which she'd hung over a chair. She shook her head. I raised my eyebrows and shook my head slightly in what I hoped looked like a suitable translation of, You sure? She nodded emphatically.

Well, okay, I thought, as she kissed me again.

I wanted her so much, so immediately, but I decided to take charge a bit, and got her down on her back. I wanted to see her, to experience every part of her with as many senses as I could bring to bear. I knelt between her legs, clutching her perfect little buttocks in my hands and lifting her up. Her vagina

117

was pink as her nipples, parenthesised by the full, rosy-grey folds of her labia, fronded and frilled and rising to the little puckered lip of hood hiding the glistening stubby button of her clitoris. Her cunt smelled of talc, tasted of sweetened salt. I buried tongue and lips in her, pressing and nosing her like some truffling hound while rubbing and pressing the tiny rosette of her anus with one thumb, listening to her breath quicken, feeling as though my mouth would burn with the engulfing heat of her.

Entering her was a slow, gradual, almost tentative process, just the opposite of what I think we'd both expected. I found myself quivering, shaking like some adolescent getting laid for the first time, my mouth suddenly dry, tears – tears! – welling in my eyes. She lay on her hair, head to one side, facing the darkness, the tendon on the side of her neck a taut, deeply shadowed column, her arms thrown out across the bed, fingers clutching, caging fistfuls of plump white pillows, her legs in a tensed V, toes pointing, then, finally, when at last I was fully in her, she gasped and threw herself around me, arms and legs wrapping and squeezing me with an astonishing power, as though my whole body was one huge cock and her body a hand, limbs fingers.

I even managed to come quietly, but then, afterwards, lying there, chests heaving, limbs trembling, she rolled over to me, slick with sweat, and put two fingers delicately to my lips. 'It's all right,' she said softly. These were the first articulate sounds she had made. 'We can talk now, Kenneth.'

It did cross my mind to shake my head, or just ignore her, or pretend to fall asleep; in other words, or their lack, tease her, but instead I said, 'You've changed your mind?' She had said to remain silent throughout.

She nodded slowly. Her long, thick hair fell spooled, tangled, heavy on my chest. 'Just the beginning was enough. And that you were prepared to.'

'Uh-huh?'

'Uh-huh?' she said, mimicking me.

I took a handful of her hair, rolling my fist around in it, taking up all slack. Her head tipped towards my hand. Her large, darkly amber eyes gazed down. 'You are a very singular woman, Celia.'

'Will we do this again?'

I raised my head and made a show of looking downwards. 'In about five minutes, I'd guess.'

She smiled. 'You will meet me again?'

'Oh, I should think so.'

'Good. We won't be able to go out, to meet in public. It will have to be like this.'

'This is okay. I can handle this.'

'Handle me,' she whispered, lowering herself into my arms.

So began my erratic, erotic tour of the luxury hotels of London. Every few weeks – apart from once when holidays got in the way – a courier would deliver a slim package holding only a hotel key or key card. The accompanying phone call got shorter and shorter each time until all I would hear was, 'The Connaught, three one six,' or 'The Landmark, eight one eight,' or 'The Howard, five zero three.'

In a succession of tall-ceilinged, feverishly hot, darkened suites, on top of a series of King- or Emperor-size beds, Celia and I pursued our sporadic affair.

That first time, in the Dorchester, it turned out we had longer than she'd first said; not until six but until ten, when she really had to go. I'd nodded off at one point, into sharply sultry dreams of swimming in thick red perfume beneath a fiery lilac sun, then woke to find all the lights out but the room illuminated from outside and below and her standing by the windows, looking out between the drawn-back curtains, the silvery lustre of a full moon combining on her skin with the glow of the hotel's floodlights reflecting from the ceiling and framing her slim, dark form with gold.

I padded up behind her, held her, and she put her hands on mine at her shoulder as I nuzzled her neck and hair. That was when I asked her about the long, swirling mark on her left flank, and she told me about the lightning strike.

The dark bodies of Kensington Gardens and Hyde Park lay strung with pinprick cords of light. Below us, cradled in the scoop of the building's forecourt facing Park Lane, a great dark tree rustled in a freshening breeze, new growth all green and black and full of life and movement and promise.

'Who are you, Celia? Tell me about yourself,' I said into the darkness, later. 'If you want.'

'What do you want to know?'

'Everything about you.'

'Everything would be boring, Kenneth. Don't you know that? Knowing everything about anybody would be boring.'

'Not you, I suspect.'

'I told you; I am a married woman, a housewife, a listener.'

'Perhaps you could start a little closer to the beginning.'

'I am from Martinique. You know where that is?'

'I know.'

'My father was a fisherman, my mother a waitress. I have four brothers, five sisters.'

'My, your parents were busy. Sexual athleticism runs in the family, then.'

'I studied languages, I became a model, I moved to Paris, then London. I met a man who I thought loved me.' She hesitated. 'Perhaps that's not fair to him. He thought he did love me. We both did, then.'

'What about you loving him?'

Her body tensed fractionally against mine, then relaxed again. 'Love,' she said, as if saying, tasting the word for the first time, getting the measure of its meaning in her mouth and

120

mind. 'I don't know.' I felt her turn her head to stare off into the shadowy heights of the room. Eyelashes flitted against the skin of my shoulder. 'I felt fondness for him. He was kind to me. He helped me. Helped me considerably. I don't mean to say that I married him out of gratitude, but I felt that I knew him and that he would be a good husband.'

'And is he?'

She was silent for a while. 'He treats me well. He has never struck me. He became cold towards me about the time when it was found I could not have children.'

'I'm sorry.'

'The point is more that it does not matter that he is a good husband to me; what matters is that he is a bad man to others. He would say they always deserved it, but . . .'

'Did you know he was like that when you married him?'

She was silent for a moment. 'Yes and no. I knew a little. I did not want to know it all. I should have.'

'Do you mean to stay with him?'

'I would be afraid to tell him I was leaving him. Also, practically my whole family works for one of his businesses now, on the island.'

'Ah.'

'Ah, indeed. What about you, Kenneth?'

'What don't you know from my many exciting and unfailingly accurate profiles in top media outlets?'

'Your marriage? Your wife?'

'I married a nurse called Jude. Judith. Met in a club when I was between jobs, not long after I moved down to London. Great sex, similar interests, robust cross-platform political beliefs with only a few troublesome legacy systems – she believed in astrology – compatible groups of friends . . . and we certainly thought we were in love. She didn't really want to get married but I insisted. I knew what I was like; I knew I was very likely to stray, or certainly to want to stray, to be

121

unfaithful, and I came up with this bizarre concept that if I got married then the fact I'd made a solemn promise to her to forsake all others, made a legally binding commitment, would stop me.' I paused. 'Probably the single most barmy idea I've ever entertained in my entire adult life, and that when, by common assent, the field of other contenders is both wide and deep.' I shrugged gently, so as not to jar her head where it lay against my shoulder and chest. 'However. I cheated, she found out, confronted me with it, and I swore it wouldn't happen again. I meant it, too. I always meant it. Repeat until no longer funny.' I breathed deeply. 'She's okay now; in a stable relationship. I still see her now and again.'

'Do you still love her?'

'No, ma'am.'

'You still sleep with her.'

I felt my body jerk. She must have felt it too. 'You guessing, Celia?' I asked. 'Or are we in some creepy *Play Misty For Me* vibe here?'

'Guessing, you would call it. I am good at it.'

'Well, as you guessed.' I shrugged again. 'We never mean to, it just happens . . . Old times' sake, I suppose. Lame, but true. But anyway not for a while.'

'And you have a regular girlfriend?'

'Yes. Nice girl. Bit mad. Works for a record company.'

'She doesn't know, I hope. About you and me. I hope nobody does.'

'Nobody.'

'You don't mind? Some men like to boast.'

'Not me. And no, I don't mind.'

Usually we met on a Friday, but not every time. Never at the weekends. She said this was because she liked to listen to me on the radio beforehand. Soon, with every show I did, I'd start to wonder, was she listening? More to the point, was she listening in an eight-hundred-quid-a-night suite, slowly undressing in the darkness while a cranked-up heating system wound round to maximum gradually toasted every molecule of air in the place?

On several occasions, especially on Fridays, I had to stand people up. Jo, a couple of times. I claimed a commiserating, men-only drinking party with a just-dumped colleague on the first occasion, and plain alcohol-induced forgetfulness in a mobile-reception-free dive bar the second time. Jo shouted at me on both occasions, then wanted to have sex, which was awkward. I just about managed it the first time, though I felt a) sore, and b) guilty that I was still thinking about Ceel. The second time I faked incapability through drunkenness. I began to make Friday night engagements tentative rather than firm.

Wherever it was I met Ceel, she was always there, always waiting, almost always reading a book – usually something recent I'd heard of: *White Teeth*, *Man and Boy*, *Bridget Jones's Diary*. Once it was *The Prince*, once *Madame Bovary*, and once the *Kama Sutra*, which she was reading for ideas we didn't really need. Twice it was *A Brief History of Time*. The room – suite – was always dark, always hot. There would be something light to eat if we wanted, and vintage champagne. It was a while before I realised the glasses we drank from were always the same ones, and that there would always be a different, spare glass present. She brought the crystal flutes herself; they belonged to her. She seemed pleased that I'd noticed.

'You were a model, you said?'

'Yes.'

'What, like, clothes?'

She gave a one-breath laugh into the warm dark. 'Those are what one usually models, Kenneth.'

'Swim-wear, lingerie?'

'Sometimes. I began in swim-wear, when a magazine came to the island to shoot a feature and two of their models were hurt in a car crash. That's how I got my break.'

123

'What about them?'

'How do you mean?'

'Did they break anything?' I shook my head, already feeling foolish. 'Sorry, I—'

'The two models? Yes, one broke an arm and both had facial injuries. I don't think either ever worked as a model again. It was very upsetting. Not how I'd have chosen to get into such a career.'

'Sorry. I shouldn't have said anything.'

'That's all right.'

'Did you appear mostly in French magazines?'

'Yes. I'm afraid I have no portfolio to show you.'

'What was your modelling name?'

'Celia McFadden.'

'McFadden?' I said, laughing. 'What possessed you to take a Scottish name?'

'It was my maiden name,' she said, sounding surprised.

'You're a McFadden, from Martinique?'

'My great-great-grandfather was a slave on Barbados. He was given the name of his slave master, who may have been his biological father. He escaped, and ended up in Martinique.'

'Woh. Sorry.'

'That's all right,' Celia said, shrugging. 'You changed your name, didn't you?'

'Yeah. Not officially, just for the radio. It still says McNutt on my passport.'

'McNutt?' She smiled.

'Yes, with two "t"s. So, this,' I said, changing the subject and stroking the lightning scar, 'has appeared in public, has it? It wasn't a problem?'

'Perhaps it was a small problem. I always had enough work but I'm sure I lost some jobs because of it. But no, I don't think it ever appeared.'

'What did they do, cover it with make-up?'

'No. They shot from the other side.'

'So all your model shots are from the right?'

'Mostly. Though they don't all appear so once they're printed. You just reverse the neg.'

'Oh, right. Of course.'

'Sometimes, when the light or the background meant we had to, they would shoot from my left side and I would hold my arm in a certain way and if there was anything of the scar visible it would be air-brushed out later. It is not a problem.' She shrugged. 'Covering things up is easy.'

The latest she ever stayed was ten p.m. I was welcome to stay longer if I wanted, but I never did, and I knew she preferred me to leave first. She would arrive and depart with her hair tightly compressed under a wig – usually blond – and wore large dark glasses and baggy, undistinguished clothes.

In Claridge's, she'd stripped the bed to its bottom sheet and covered the surface and a dozen extra pillows in red rose petals. The lights mostly stayed on for that one. This was where she finally explained her insane theory about having half died when the lightning struck her.

'*What?*'

'There are two mes. Two of me. In different, parallel worlds.'

'Hold on. I think I know this theory. Simple idea but the complexities are hideous.'

'Mine is quite simple.'

'Yeah, but the real one is confusing to a bonkers degree; according to it there are an infinity of yous. A pleasing prospect, I might add, except there is also, are also . . . anyway, an infinity of mes, too, and your husband. Husbands. Whatever. See how confusing it is?'

'Yes, well,' she said, waving one dismissive hand. 'But for me it is very simple. I half died then, when the lightning struck me. In that other world I am half dead, too.'

'But also half alive.'

'Just as in this one.'

'So did you fall off this cliff in the other world, or not?' I asked, deciding to humour this matter-of-fact madness of hers.

'Yes and no. I did, but I also fell back onto the grass, just as I did here.'

'So in this world, here, you fell off the cliff too?'

'Yes.'

'And yet you woke up on the grass.'

'That part of me did. This part of me did.'

'So in the other world? What? If you woke up on the grass in this one, she must have not woken up, because she was lying dead at the bottom of the cliff.'

'No, she woke up too, on the grass.'

'So who the hell fell off the bleedin cliff?'

'I did.'

'You did? But—'

'Both of I.'

'I and I? What, now you're a Rastafarian?'

She laughed. 'We both fell off the cliff. I remember it happening. I remember seeing myself fall, and the noise the air made, and how my legs made a useless running motion and how I could not scream because the air had been knocked out of my lungs and how the rocks looked as I fell towards them.'

'So did the lightning kill . . . half kill you, or was it the fall?'

'Does it matter?'

'I don't know. Does it?'

'Perhaps both did. Or half did.'

'I think we've gone on to quarters by this stage.'

'Perhaps either would have been enough. All that matters is that it happened.'

'It would be useless to suggest, I suppose, that this might all really only have happened in your head, the result of having ninety thousand volts zapped through your brain pan and down your body?'

126

'But of course it is not useless to suggest it! If that is what you need to believe to make sense of what happened to me by your way of thinking, then of course that is what you must believe.'

'That's not quite what I meant.'

'Yes, I know. But, you see, when it happened, I was there, and you, my dear, were not.'

I let out a long breath. 'Right. So . . . so what are the symptoms of you being only half alive in this world . . . and the other one? You do seem wholly and, I would risk saying, even vibrantly alive in this world, to me. Especially about ten minutes ago. Oh, though there is that thing about the French calling it the little death, of course. Though that's not what you're talking about, is it? But back to the symptoms. What makes you feel this?'

'That I feel it.'

'Right. No, no, not right. I'm not getting it.'

'It feels obvious to me. In a way I always knew it. Reading about parallel universes simply made sense of that feeling. I didn't feel any more certain of what I felt, and it did not really alter what I felt, or what I believed, but it made it more possible for me to explain it to others.'

I laughed. 'So all we've been talking about in the last five minutes is *after* it became easier to explain?'

'Yes. Easier. Not easy. Perhaps "less difficult" would be a better formulation.'

'Right.'

'I think it might all change on my next birthday,' she said, nodding seriously.

'Why?'

'Because the lightning hit me on the day of my fourteenth birthday, and on my next birthday I will be twenty-eight. You see?'

'Yes, I do. My God, your aberrant personal belief system is actually contagious. I suppose they all are.' I sat up in the bed.

'You mean that on the day of your twenty-eighth birthday, in April next year . . .'

'The fifth.'

'. . . What?'

She shrugged. 'I don't know. Perhaps nothing. Perhaps I die. Perhaps the other one of me dies.'

'And if the other one dies?'

'I will become fully alive.'

'Which will manifest itself . . . ?'

She smiled. 'Well, perhaps I will decide that I love you.'

I stared into those amber eyes. It seemed to me then that she had the most direct, clearly honest gaze of anybody I had ever met. No humour there just now, no irony. Not even doubt. Puzzlement, perhaps, but no doubt. She really believed all this.

'There,' I said, 'is that big little word that neither of us have spoken until now.'

'Why should we speak it?'

I wondered what *that* meant. I might have pursued the matter, but then she shrugged again, and her immaculate breasts moved in just such a way that in this world and surely any other all I could say was, 'Oh, come here.'

In the Meridien Piccadilly, finding she had a suite with a kitchen attached, she had already been across to Fortnum and Mason and bought the ingredients to make an omelette, flavoured with saffron. She was trying out different types of underwear on that occasion, so that I came, bizarrely, to associate the smell of eggs cooking in olive oil with a basque and stockings.

I laughed as she presented the tray to me in bed.

'What?' she asked.

'You spoil me,' I said as she jumped up onto the bed, her stockinged legs folded neatly beneath her. She took up a fork. I gestured at the food, at her. 'This is . . . pretty much most guys' fantasy.'

128

'Good,' she said. She looked round the dark bedroom, then at me, and smiled. 'No complaints here, either.'

'Think you might let me pay for one of these conjugal visits one day? Or even take you away for a weekend?'

She shook her head quickly. 'It's better this way.' She put the fork down. 'This has to be outside of real life, Kenneth. That way we can get away with it. We expose ourselves less. Less of a risk is taken. And, because this happens outside of our normal lives, it feels less connected to what we might talk about to other people. It is like a dream, no? So we are both less likely to say something that might give us away. Do you understand?'

'Yeah, sure. Just a residual scrap of old-school male pride, wishing to pay for something. But it's all right; being an intermittently kept man rather appeals to me.'

'I wish you could take me out,' she said, smiling at the thought of it. 'I would love to sit in a café with you, watching people go by. Go to lunch with you, sitting on a terrace by a river, in the sunlight. Be taken to a play or a film or to dance. Sit on a beach with you, under a palm tree, perhaps. Just the two of us crossing a street, holding hands. I find myself dreaming of these things sometimes, when I am low.' She looked away, then back. 'Then I think of this. The next time we shall meet. That makes everything well.'

I gazed into her eyes again, lost for a thing to say.

She smiled, winked. 'It will get cold. Eat up.'

In the Lanesborough we spent hours in a cavernous bath, experimenting with various lotions and creams; she emptied a bottle of No. 5 into the oiled foam and I smelled of it for three days.

'What do you *do*, Ceel?'

'What do you mean?'

'How do you pass your days? What is your life like?'

'I'm not sure I should tell you. This is supposed to be separate, not attached to our real lives, don't you remember?'

'I remember, but telling me what a more normal day is like isn't going to make that big a difference.'

'I do what the women of rich men are supposed to do; I shop and lunch.'

'Friends?'

'Some. Different friends for different things. Some for shopping and lunching, some at my health club, some for ice skating—'

'You skate?'

'A little. Not well. There are a couple of friends I have from my modelling days who are also married now, or settled down, with rich men. Just two who live in London. I visit Paris to see friends there, and one of my brothers. It is so easy now, with the train.'

'You go to Paris a lot?'

'A few times a year. Sometimes I go there with John. Usually he travels alone. He's away often; Europe, South America. I go to Paris more than anywhere else. John doesn't like me to spend nights away unless he knows the people I stay with well. In Paris it's all right because I stay with my brother, who works for John and lives in a company apartment.'

'What does your brother do?'

She looked at me. It was one of the few occasions she'd ever looked even slightly angry. 'Nothing bad,' she said sharply.

'Okay.' I held up my hands. 'Do you have any really close friends?'

She turned away. 'Most of the women my age have children, and that separates us.' She shrugged. 'I spend time on the phone each day, calling my family back on the island. And they come to visit sometimes.' She paused. 'Not as often as I'd like.'

(Later, while she was in the bathroom, I noticed her Bridge shoulder bag lying on a chair, and her mobile phone inside its little brown leather cave, a green light blinking slowly. She

130

usually switched her phone off while we were together. This must be the phone my mobile knew only as Anonymous. I watched the faint green light for a few more beats of its tiny silicon heart.

Looking straight at it, it almost disappeared. I could see it better from the corner of my eye.

I swallowed a little pride, not to mention some principles, and quickly rolled over and dug the dainty Nokia out. I'd had a similar, if chunkier, model to this, two mobiles back, and knew how to access the phone's own number. I scribbled it on a piece of hotel paper and stuffed the note in a jacket pocket after I'd returned the phone to her bag, long before she reappeared. This was a safety precaution, I told myself. In case I ever needed to warn her of something; like a terrorist threat we'd heard about via the newsroom but couldn't broadcast because it would cause mass panic . . . Yes, something like that, say.)

In the Berkeley she had brought drugs and we had time to have frenetic coked-up sex and make slow, stoned love.

'I didn't know you smoked.'

'*Mais non!* But I don't!' she giggled, coughing.

A little later, lying there in a stunned haze of drugged satiation, limbs spread where they'd fallen on our uncoupling, I watched a small patch of sunlight – the product of a sunbeam penetrating the tall sweep of the drawn-over curtains from the very centre of their summit – move slowly across the white sheets towards her left arm. Half asleep, I kept staring at the molten coin of yellow as Ceel drifted into a quiet, smiling doze. The egg-sized blob of buttery light slid gently up her coffee skin, slow as the hour hand on a clock, and revealed the tiny, years-old scars spattered on the flesh above the veins on her upper arm and the inside of her elbow.

A flurry of them, like pale, minutely puckered tear-shaped freckles on that smooth surface of golden brown.

131

I gazed at her face, lying half averted on the pillow, her blissful smile directed into the darkness of the suite, and then I looked down again at her arm. I thought about her time in Paris, and about Merrial and the bad situation he'd helped her out of. I decided I would never say anything, if she didn't.

Beneath the light, beneath the skin, her blood pulsed slow and strong, and I imagined it, minutely warmed by that small fall of light, coursing through her body while she stared, unconscious and blind, back to the memory of a poisoned chemical rapture.

A few times I tried to follow her, to see where she lived, or just what she did next after one of these trysts. There was a bar in the Landmark with a view of reception. I sat there pretending to read. I'd peeked in her bag earlier to check which wig she was wearing that day, and in the wardrobe to see what clothes she'd arrived in; it was a grey suit, hanging neatly above some Harvey Nics' bags. I sat there and I watched really carefully but I still didn't see her. I don't know if she had more than one wig, or if I just glanced down at the wrong moment and she'd walked quickly through, the bill already paid, or what, but I sat there for an hour and a half, drinking whisky and nibbling rice crackers until my bladder drove me from my look-out post.

A month later I tried again, sitting in a café across from the Connaught. Again, I didn't see her, but after about an hour I got a call on my mobile.

Anonymous, said the screen. Oh-oh.

'Hello?'

'I live in Belgravia. Usually I go straight home. Sometimes I do a little more shopping. Bookshops, often . . . Are you still there?'

'Yup. Still here,' I said. I took a deep breath. 'I'm sorry.'

'You would make a very poor spy.'

'Yeah.' I sighed. 'It's not . . .'

'It's not what?'

'It's not some weird, obsessive thing. I mean, it's not something to worry about. It's not like I'm stalking you or anything like that. I'm interested. You intrigue me. We're so . . . intimate and yet, you know, so . . . strange to each other. Strangers, still.'

'I'm sorry it has to be that way. But it does. You do accept that?'

'Yes, of course.'

'You won't do this again, will you? Please.'

'No, I won't. You're not angry with me?'

'More flattered than angry. But more alarmed than either. It's not worth the risk.'

'It won't happen again. But . . .'

'What?'

'It was worth it for this phone call.'

She was silent for a moment. 'You are very sweet,' she said. 'I have to go now.'

In the Ritz, I'd brought some E. We knocked the pills back with champagne, listened to some white-label chill-out sounds I'd been given by one of Ed's DJ pals, and drifted into some sublimely blissful, loved-up fucking until my balls ached with the emptying.

'You never ask me about John.'

'That's right.'

'Do you hate him?'

'No. I don't know him. I don't hate him just because he's your husband. If he's some sort of crime boss, I suppose I ought to hate him on principle for being what he is, but I can't work up any enthusiasm for the subject. Maybe I've taken to heart your idea of keeping this compartmentalised from real life. Or maybe I just don't want to think about your husband in the first place.'

'Do you ever hate me?'

'Hate *you*? Are you mad?'

'I stay with him. I married him.'

'I'll give you the benefit of the doubt there, I think.'

That was the time I swallowed more pride and checked her purse. I think I was half expecting to find a fat roll of bank notes, but there was barely a hundred in there. It had occurred to me that she would not want to pay all these hotel bills by credit card, not if she was trying to keep all this as secret as possible. Finding no thick Swiss-roll of grubby twenties kind of stumped me. It was only later I thought that maybe she paid in cash all right, but before rather than after.

(That was the longest interval, after the Ritz. Her husband was taking her to Oz and New Zealand on a month-long holiday, and there was a week-long overlap while Jo and I spent a fortnight doing the tombs on the Nile and snorkelling in the Red Sea. While she was away I made the mistake of going to see a film called *Intimacy* about a couple who meet up every now and again in a filthy flat for sex, and remain strangers to each other. It was probably a good film in a British art-house kind of way but I hated it and walked out halfway through, something I'd never done in my life. Sometimes I'd take out my mobile and cursor through to Ceel's number, and just sit and stare at it for a few moments, until the phone's back-lighting clicked off. Infected by Celia's caution, I hadn't even entered her name in the mobile's own memory, or the SIM card's, just put the number in by itself. As far as my phone was concerned, she was just Location 96.)

In the Savoy one night, amongst mirrors and acres of cream and gilt, in a suite looking out across the dark river to the floodlit bulk of the Festival Hall, she had turned off all the lights and drawn the curtains right back. She placed a small seat in front of the tall, open windows. She had me sit there, bollocks to the chintz, already licked sweetly, achingly erect, then she straddled me, facing the same way, both of us gazing

134

out to the light-browned clouds and the few bright stars between, while the sounds and smells of the summer city rolled in through the opened doors of glass.

'Like this,' she said, placing my hands just so, so that I was, in effect, holding her in a head lock. 'Ah, yes.'

'Lordy fucking mama.'

'So what's the problem? Basically you're having the perfect affair. Perfect sex.'

'I don't know. Well, the actual sex . . . fuck, yeah. But . . . I don't know.'

Craig and I were sitting in his lounge, watching football on the telly. It was half-time; time for Men To Talk. After peeing, anyway. Nikki was in her room, two floors up, listening to music and reading. I'd told Craig the absolute minimum about my very occasional affair with Celia.

Normally I might have shared this sort of thing with Ed, who possessed the merit of pursuing – with extravagant success – a lifestyle that made mine look restrained to the point of celibacy in comparison, but the trouble was I'd asked him about Mr Merrial that day in the Hummer, and I wasn't absolutely sure that I hadn't mentioned seeing Mr M's wife at the time, too, and – paranoid though I knew it was really – I felt it would be just possible that Ed would put two and two together and, well, faint, probably.

Maybe Celia guessing about the fact Jude and I still fell into bed together every now and again had spooked me a little.

'Look at it objectively,' Craig said. 'You meet up with this mystery female whom you describe as the most beautiful woman you've ever slept with. You always meet in circumstances, surroundings, that you describe as somewhere between "very nice" and "sybaritic", where you proceed to fuck the arse off her and . . .'

'Yeah, but the fact remains I'm in a relationship where the

best thing that can happen is that it just fizzles slowly, sadly out . . . What?'

'Oh fuck.'

'What?'

'Just there.'

'*What?*'

'When I said "you fuck the arse off her", right?'

'. . . Yeah.'

'You winced. Well, your cheek winced. Like a facial tic.'

'Never . . . Did I? Really? Oh. Okay. Right. So?'

'That means you're falling in love with her. *Now* you have a problem.'

The big *Breaking News* thing was stuttering. It got all rather hyper and frenetic over the next day or two after our meeting with Debbie the Station Manager, the way sometimes these relatively trivial things tend to, with urgent, all-hours, weekend-long phone calls, texts and voice mails flying back and forth between Channel Four, Capital Live!, the production company, Winsome, assorted producers, assistants, secretaries, PAs, agents, lawyers and people whose job it seemed to be purely to ring up and say they needed to speak to somebody urgently, all tying up a significant proportion of the capital's mobile and fixed-line telephony capacity trying to get this incredibly vital piece of exciting, epoch-making, edgy, challenging, confronta-tional television arranged for the Monday evening. Even Sir Jamie himself got involved, because according to my contract he needed to give personal permission for me to appear on another not pre-agreed media outlet. This turned out not to be a problem as he was a good friend of the owner of Winsome Productions, and even had shares in the company.

Then, of course, just as everybody concerned had whipped themselves up into a high, teetering, effervescent froth of wild-eyed expectation and teeth-chattering frenzy, it all fell apart.

Even I'd got myself all worked up, and I'm Joe Totally Cynical about these things after years of people telling me they have this great project for getting me on telly and how they're really excited about bringing a new dimension to my work, and then nothing happening.

'You're telling me it's not fucking going ahead.'

'It's being postponed,' Phil said tiredly, putting his mobile down on the scratched wooden table. We were in the Capital Live! canteen on the floor beneath Debbie's office, having an early breakfast. It was just after seven o'clock. We'd come in early to do a special recorded edition of the show so that I could get to the Channel Four studios in time for the recording of *Breaking News* (they'd backed off the original idea of doing it live).

My mobile vibrated on my belt. I checked the display. My agent. 'Yes, Paul?' I said. Then, 'Yes, I just heard.' Then, 'Yeah, I know. Me too. Par for the fucking course. Yeah . . . yada and then yada, raised to the power of yada. Yeah, when I see it. In fact probably not until I see it when it's number thirty-seven on TV's One Hundred Most Embarrassing Moments. Yeah, we'll see. Okay. You too. Bye.'

I sat back in the creaking flexibility of the brown plastic seat and drummed my fingers on the table top, looking at my toast and marmalade and my cup of milky tea.

'Look on the bright side,' Phil said. 'They'd just have wanted you there about four hours early, and then they'd have wanted to do another of those pre-interview interviews where some breathless researcher with a famous name just out of chalet school asks you lots of questions so they can find out which ones are the good ones and you give really good, fresh answers and then they ask you those same questions in the actual programme and you sound all stale and talked out because you've already answered them once and got bored with them, and during the recording you'll have to answer the same questions

137

a third or a fourth time because somebody knocks over a bit of the set and they have to start again from the top, so you'll sound even more stale and talked out, then they'll record more than three hours and use less than two minutes and you'll forget to take your make-up off and workmen will give you funny looks in the street and afterwards people whose opinion you respect will say they missed it, or go all cagey when you ask them what they thought, and people you don't like will call up and tell you they loved it and the papers you hate will either dismiss it or say how you should stick to what you're good at, not that you're very good at that either, and you'll be all depressed and grumpy for weeks.'

Probably Phil's longest diatribe; it was too laid-back to be called a rant. I looked at him. 'So, when did they tell you it might happen now?'

'Oh, tomorrow,' he grinned.

'Fuck off.'

'Na,' he said, leaning back too and stretching and yawning. 'Lucky to be this year, now, according to my new close friend at Winsome, Moselle. Major rethink on format after the events of September the eleventh.' He scratched his head. 'What a brilliant excuse that's turned out to be, for so many things.'

'Yeah,' I breathed. I toyed with my toast and stirred my already well-stirred tea. Part of me was deeply relieved. I'd come up with this great idea for what I was going to do on the programme if they put me on with the Holocaust denier guy, and it still excited me and scared me in equally intense proportions. Now I wouldn't have to either do it and let fuck knows what happen, or chicken out and not do it and curse myself for evermore for being a sad, pathetic, hypocritical, lily-livered crap-out merchant. In fact, just the sort of sad, pathetic (etc.) who would feel as relieved as I now did that I wouldn't have to make that choice, at least not for a while and maybe, the way I knew these things tended to work, ever.

I threw the teaspoon down and stood up. 'Ah, come on, let's go and do the fucking show.'

Phil glanced at his watch. 'We can't. Judy T's using the studio till half past.'

I sat back down again, heavily. 'Fuck,' I said eloquently, putting my head in my hands. 'Fuck fuck fuck fuck fuck.'

Five

MISSION STATEMENT

'Yeah, I'd just like to say that don't you think these Eurosceptic people should be called Europhobes, yeah?'

Phil and I rolled our eyes. I leaned right up to the microphone. This has the pretty universally automatic effect of making people lower their voices, and I was no exception. It should sound like I was talking personally just to the caller. 'Actually, Steve, we went through all this two years ago, on the evening show, and, if you recall, we did a sort of rolling Greatest Hits of the Evening Show for the first week of the daytime slot when that very point came up, oh, a few times. Kind of guessing here you're new to the programme, Steve.'

'Oh. Sorry. Yeah.' Steve seized up, audibly. 'It's great,' he managed. 'Keep it up.'

'Practically my personal motto, Steve,' I said with a smile, sitting back again. 'Thanks for calling.' I clicked on to the next caller, which the screen said was a Mr Willis, from Barnet. Subject: Eurp & poound (Kayla may have put the ass in assistant, but her typing owed more to the carpet-bombing approach than any concept of precision targeting).

Mr Willis. Not a first name. That told you something

immediately, without even saying Hello to the guy.

'Mr Willis,' I said crisply. 'Mr Nott. Your point, sir.'

'Yes, I just wondered why an apparently intelligent fellow like yourself was in such a hurry to get rid of the pound and throw in our lot with a currency that's dropped so much value since it was launched.'

'I'm not in a hurry, Mr Willis. Like most people in Britain I think it's going to happen sooner or later, so it becomes a question of which is best, when is best, but I don't claim to know. My point is that it's all about economics and politics, and it shouldn't be about sentiment, because the pound sterling is just money, like any currency. If the Germans can give up the Deutschmark, we can surely stop using bits of paper with the monarch's head on them.'

'But, Mr Nott, why should we? A lot of us happen to think the pound is important. We love the pound.'

'Look, Mr Willis, you lost the pound . . . whatever it was, thirty years ago. I can just about remember this; the pound – the real pound – had two hundred and forty pennies; a third of a pound was six and eightpence—'

'Yes, but—'

'—there were thrupenny bits, sixpences, shillings, florins, half-crowns, half-pennies, ten-bob notes, and—'

'I know—'

'—if you were being fancy, guineas. That all went in the sixties and *that* was the end of the pound. What you've got now is a British dollar, basically, so why all the belly-aching about it?'

'It's not belly-aching to wish to preserve a vital part of our proud British culture. I am a member of an organisation—'

I looked at Phil on the other side of the desk and spread my hands. He did the throat-cutting thing. I nodded. 'Mr Willis,' I said, fading his voice down, 'here's a handy hint; attack the Euro via the interest rate. A single interest rate barely makes sense throughout the UK, let alone all twenty-five members of an expanded EU, unless you want – in fact to impose – absurd levels of worker mobility or a vastly increased centralised regional compensation fund.'

'Look, we didn't fight and win the Second World War—'

'It's been interesting talking to you, Mr Willis. Goodbye.' I looked at Phil as I cut Mr Willis off. 'We getting crossed lines with the *Daily Mail* letters page or something?'

'I think it's encouraging that we have a spread of listeners of various ages, views and ethnic and cultural backgrounds, Ken,' Phil said, leaning towards his mike.

'Phil Ashby, listeners. Voice of Reason. Singing in harmony from the hymnal of Corporate Mission Statements.'

'That'll be me, then. Hi,' Phil said, right up to the mike. 'Who's our next caller?'

'It's another Steve, from Streatham.' According to the screen he wanted to talk about Scotz && Erop & U.

'Streatham Steve, hello.'

'Awright, Ken? Ma *man*!' a deep voice shouted. I looked at Phil and crossed my eyes.

'Steve, you're doing some violence to the mike on that mobile. I'm sure if you return it promptly to its owner they may not press charges.'

'Wot? Agh, ha-ha-ha! Na, mate, it's mine.'

'Well, bully for you. And the exact flavour of your beef would be what?'

'Wot?'

'What is it you want to say, Steve?'

'Yeah, I don't want to be a European!'

'You don't? Right. Which continent should we tow the British Isles to lie off then?'

'Na, you know what I mean.'

'Indeed I do. Well, so vote against it whenever you have the chance.'

'Yeah, but it's still gonna happen, innit?'

'Fraid so. It's called democracy.' I hit the FX for Hollow Laughter.

'Yeah, but the fing is, I blame you Scots, don't I?'

'Ah-*hah*,' I said. 'Any particular reason, Steve, or is this just some generalised anti-Caledonian prejudice?'

'Yeah, the government's all Scotch, innit? The Labour Party. They're all Jocks, aren't they?'

'Very high proportion of the top jobs, yes, Steve. The Dear Leader himself, our prudent Chancellor is a Scot—'

'Worse, he's a Fifer,' Phil cut in.

'Na, Phil, sorry,' I said.

'What?' Phil asked.

'Yeah,' Steve said, 'That's what—'

'Hold on, Steve, pal,' I said. 'Come back to you in two seconds, but I just need to straighten something out with Producer Phil. Okay?'

'Ah,' Steve said. 'Yeah . . .'

'What?' Phil repeated innocently, blinking behind his glasses.

'Sorry, Phil, pal,' I said. 'But you can't do that.'

'Can't do what?'

'Bring up divisions or petty squabbles between different bits of Scotland. Our internal prejudices and micro-management bigotries are our own affair. We're allowed to indulge in that but you're not. It's like black people can call each other nigger but us white folks can't. And rightly so, I might add.'

Phil nodded. 'Things don't mean what the sayer says, they mean what the listener hears.'

I hit the FX key for a quiet, minute-long sample of the 'Hallelujah Chorus', and over it said, voice raised, 'Still our most elegant formulation of what really would be one of our mission statements if we didn't spit on such foul aberrations from a great height and grind the ordure-jammed cleats of our Jockboots into their snivelling faces.'

146

'Along with,' Phil said, 'If you don't give people justice, they'll take revenge.'

'And, Never underestimate the greed of the rich.'

'Not forgetting, Ditto the ability of people to take exactly the wrong lesson from a disaster.'

'NMD? Come on down!' I was laughing again. 'Or our emission statement: I'm coming! I'm coming!'

'Or the posh version: I'm arriving! I'm arriving!'

'Indeed.' I un-clicked the sample.

'But anyway,' Phil said, still grinning.

'But anyway indeed, Philip.'

'What it boils down to is,' he said slowly, 'that I can't say the things about the Scots that you say all the time.'

'Of course not! You're English. A few of us clever Jocks still blame you for the whole Glasgow–Edinburgh antipathy thing. The good citizens of each very-much-equally-worthy conurbation just loved each other to bits until you guys came along. And frankly the utterly preposterous idea that if we hadn't had the English to unite us in hate we'd still be a bunch of bare-arsed hill tribes marrying our sisters and murdering each other in caves holds no water with us whatsoever, no sirree. We reckon you were just dividing and conquering. So, like I say, just don't start, okay?'

'It's a good job you've got us to blame,' Phil said.

'It most certainly is,' I agreed emphatically. 'Just don't for a nanosecond expect the least scintilla of gratitude.'

'As if,' Phil said, smiling. 'As apparently the young folk say, these days.'

'Yeah, you'll prise that copy of *Clueless* out of the video one day, Phil.' Phil laughed silently and I went back to Steve. 'Steve. Yeah. All these Scots in Westminster? Hear what you're saying, but don't forget: if you think the Scots are crap, and they're the ones who've clawed their way to the top of this particular greasy pole, what does that say about the English politicians?'

'I fink it's a conspiracy, mate.'

'Brilliant! Phil; a conspiracy form.' I picked the paper copy of the running order from the desk in front of me and rustled it near the mike. 'Thank you. Steve? Ready; shoot.'

'Cos, like, you want to get us into Europe, don't you?'

'We do?' I smiled widely at Phil. 'Yeah! We do! You're right. Steve, I think you're on to something here. Possibly a rehab programme. But listen, this makes sense. It's a Scottish conspiracy to get revenge for three hundred years of oppression, which we secretly feel we never did resist strongly enough.'

'I fink it's cos you're jealous.'

'Of course we are. Our invasions of you lot never worked. Same with yours of us, though obviously our impression is very much that you were always much better at killing lots of us than we were at killing lots of you. *Then* you guys realised where our weak spot is and just bought us. That was smart. Except we've never forgiven you for being cleverer than us; we're supposed to be the canny ones in this relationship.'

'Yeah, cos you lot *do* want to be in Europe, dontcha?'

'Naturally. Scots'll make great Europeans. When we hear the English say, We don't want to be ruled from a distant capital where they speak differently from us and impose an alien currency on us, we think: hold on, we've had that for three centuries. We've been there, we've had the conditioning, we've done the apprenticeship. London, Brussels, what's to choose? Better to be wee and ignored in a potential superpower than wee and ignored in a post-imperial backwater where the only things that arrive on time are the corporate bonuses.'

'Yeah, well,' Steve said.

'Excellent work there, Steve. Fine contribution. Breaks my heart we don't pay anything.'

'Sawright.'

'Of course this does mean, though, Steve, that having started to uncover the conspiracy, the people who really run the

148

country are now going to be after you. Basically you're on the run from here on in, chum. Sorry. And I'd get moving now, frankly, because these people don't hang around. They've been known to collar somebody while they're still making the phone call that alerted what little remains of our so-called free society to the threat in the first place. I'm not kidding, mate, while they're still—' I'd clicked Steve's line off. 'Steve? Hello? Steve? Steve? *Steve!* Are you . . . Dear God, Phil,' I said in hushed, strangled tones. 'They've got the poor beggar. My *God* they're fast.'

'That was quick,' Phil agreed.

'He's probably already trussed into a head-to-toe strait-kilt and being bundled into an unmarked Irn Bru van even as we speak.'

'Ayee,' Phil said, in what was already recognisable as his incurably atrocious Scots accent. 'He'll be languishing in a pibrock on the Isle of Ocktermuckty before the day is oot, Ken.'

'Och, Phil,' I sighed happily, 'when you speak, it's like being home again.'

'Shplendid. Sho, who'sh our nexsht caller?'

'Well, we're obviously shunted onto a deeply Scottish vibe here, Phil, as that spookily accurate Sean Pertwee impression of yours so powerfully testifies. Let's have . . .' I scanned the call-monitoring screen, paging down to where the new calls were still appearing. 'Ah; Angus. Now there's a fine choochter name.' I clicked on his line. 'Angus. Are you Scottish? Say yes.'

'Aye, man, ah am. Hullo. How're ye doin?'

'Fine and dandy. Yourself?'

'Magic, aye.'

'And what have you and your magic eye been looking at, then?'

'Aye, ah was jus listenin to what yur man there was saying about us an the English, an ah jus thought he wiz talkin a lod a shite.'

149

Beep. 'Shite' was a beepable word; Phil did the business this time, though we all had a button. Beepable words were: cunt, fuck (and variations thereof), shit (and variations thereof), shite (but not crap), bastard (but not, apparently, the Scotified versions I kept getting away with), prick (in context) and cock (in context). We could do this because the show went out with a three-second delay. This meant that, in theory, Phil could beep me if I said anything slanderous or likely to bring Capital Live! into disrepute, or court. Ha, ha.

'So cogently put, Angus,' I said.

'Aw, sorry, man.'

I looked across the desk. 'Beep count today, Phil?'

'That's the first.'

'Thought it was. Seventy minutes in. Dear me. Standards are slipping. So, Angus, is that all you want to say? We do allegedly have a national reputation for cogent intellectual discourse we ought to be maintaining here, Angy, and frankly you're not coming up to the mark. Or pound, or groat.'

'Na, but it's just, if the English don't want to be part of Europe, fine. But why should we have to no be a part of it too, like? Let them go their own way. We'll go ours. We don't need them. Man, they're just an embarrassment sometimes.'

This made me laugh. Phil took umbrage. 'From the nation that gave us the Krankies?' he said, voice rising indignantly. 'And the deep-fried Mars bar? *We* embarrass *you*?'

I was still laughing. 'Yeah, well, Angus,' I said. 'I know what you're saying, but then we've always wanted it both ways, haven't we? Us Scots, I mean. When the Empire was still commonly held something to be proud of we were like, Aye, an dinny forget who really built it fur ye; we wur yer best sodjers an engineers an aw sorts, and we built yer ships fur ye too, an mined the coal tae make them go. Aye, when ye were takin civilisation tae the fuzzy-wuzzies it might a been the Inglish general an is foppish chums on their horses on the ridge sayin

150

charge an tally-ho chaps, but it wiz the bams wi the kilts an the bagpipes that stormed in tae dae the real bayonet work. Oh, an did we mention we inventit the steam engine an the telly?

'Right? But then, like, soon as imperialism became a dirty word we were giving it, Aye, solidarity there, black brother; ken exactly whit ye've went through by the way; those Inglish bastirts invaded our country before anybody else's, so they did; under the imperialist yoke fur three hunner years, us. Totally exploited. Stole that steam engine an the telly frae us, too, by the way.'

Angus's mobile feed had crackled, broken up and gone back to the dial tone about halfway through this.

Phil said, 'Angus has left the airwaves.'

'Indeed he has,' I said, glancing at the studio clock and using my pencil to cross off another segment on the running order. 'Well, that's the end of the Looney Tunes section of the show, where all you brave, brave people ring up to be insulted by a professional. We've got some vitally important information about stuff you didn't know you wanted coming up right here, and then, after that, talking about insults, it'll be Shaggy. Take it away, Shaggy. Take it very, very, far, away . . .'

'What on earth are you doing?'

'I've changed me mind. I want a gin and juice.'

'So you're phoning Craig to change your order.'

'Yep.'

'He's about eight fucking metres away,' I protested, pointing into the bar. 'I can *see* his slap-headed cranium.' We were sitting on some aluminium chairs on the pavement outside a bar on Frith Street. This was back in August, I think. It was a Saturday evening, one of those warm summer nights in Soho when the whole place feels like it's inside, like it's a vast, warren-like room, when the people throng the streets between the low-rise buildings and turn it all into a single space, and the cars,

151

edging slowly, slowly up the narrow streets, often slower than the people walking, seem to bloom to the same size they look in a showroom; big, ungainly things, all that hot, fast metal trapped by the press of soft, summer-stripped bodies. Music came whumping out of the bar's open doors and windows, seeped from a club down some steps across the road, and pulsed from the vehicles crawling their way up the street, sounding dull if the windows were closed and sharp if the windows were open. I smelled cigars, blow, exhaust, perfume, curry, kebabs, beer, sweat and tar. Plus, every now and again, there came the faint, almost subliminal smell of drains, of sewage, like something decaying and noxious seeping up from underneath.

Ed twisted briefly in his seat, glancing back towards the crowded, noisy bar, where Craig had, it seemed, finally got to the counter. 'Yeah, maybe he is,' he said, thumbing the phone. 'But *you* try gettin froo to im or attractin is attention.'

It occurred to me that Ed had a point. It also occurred to me that a well-aimed ice cube might do the trick, but I looked at my bottle of Budvar and Ed's bottle of Beck's, and thought, No. Even with a reliable ice cube supply (which we didn't have), and my fabulous lobbing abilities (which it was highly unlikely had been in any way compromised by the three or four hours of drinking accomplished until this point), such behaviour could, just conceivably, result in a miss, a misunderstanding and a fracas. Even a mêlée.

'Ullo, Craig? Yeah. Hee hee hee. Best way, mate. Na, a gin and juice. You know; wif orange. Yeah, cheers, mate.'

'Make it a double!' I yelled at the phone. Some passing people looked at me.

'Yeah, that was im,' Ed said into the mobile. 'See you.'

'You're so decadent,' I told him.

'I'm so pissed off.'

'Don't take it personally.'

Ed should not have been here. He'd been just about to start

a gig in Luton when it had been cancelled due to a series of bomb alerts. With nothing to do, he'd joined Craig and me on our Night Out. This was supposed to end up with Craig and I going clubbing but somehow we'd kind of side-tracked ourselves down a Serious Drinking route. Loved-up dancing on the prowl for luvverly laydeez was now almost certainly out of the question. Of course we might convince ourselves otherwise in the interim, but in that case the night would almost certainly end in abject humiliation.

'Why would somebody bomb a club, anyway?' I asked Ed. 'Or threaten to.'

'Turf war, mate. Settin these fings up, doin the security, providin the pills; lot a dosh involved.' Ed finished his Beck's. 'Course it usually all runs nice an smoov cos that's in everybody's inarest so that the money keeps comin slidin froo, but every now an again there'll be some sort a disagreement where neevir side'll back down an some cunt feels the need to make a point. This evenin patently being one of them.' He nodded at me. 'Sorta fing that Merrial guy might be involved in.'

'Really?'

'Possibly.' Ed shrugged. 'I don't know an I don't want to neevir. Just a bastard when these geezers can't get their fuckin acts togevver. Leaves a onist jobbin DJ out of pocket, dunnit?'

'Wait here; I'll organise a whip-round.'

'Fack orfft.'

I have no idea where this happened.

'Ere.'

'What?'

'D'you unnerstand everyfin your mate's sayin?'

'What? Craig?'

'Yeah, oo else, ya nutter.'

'Course I do.'

'Bit of a accent though, asn't he? Dontya fink?'

153

'What the hell are you talking about?'

'I mean, I can just about cope wif your Highlan brogue, but I almost need a interpretor wif im.'

'Are you trying to be funny?'

'Na, I'm serious, mate. Hee hee hee.'

'You're talking nonsense. Craig hasn't got a Scottish accent any more. Well, virtually none; he goes back to Glasgow and they think he's a Londoner.'

'Na, but really.'

'And what the hell's this about *my* accent too, ya bastard?'

'What? D'you really fink you speak BBC English or somefing, do you?'

'Better than that!' I roared. I think people looked round again. 'I don't *have* an accent!'

'Ha! You got an accent, man! I'm telling you!'

'Naw ah dinny!' I said. I meant it to be ironic.

'Hee hee hee. All right, then; what nationality am I?'

'You're British.'

Ed rolled his eyes. 'All right, which *bit* of Britain?'

'Brixton.'

'You is just being deliberately obtuse here, man.'

'All right! You're English!'

'See? I'm not; I'm Inglish.'

'"Inglish"? What d'you mean "Inglish"? There's a fucking "E" at the start there!'

'Yeah, but it's pronounced "Inglish", innit?'

'I beg to differ.'

'Say "film".'

'Fim.'

'Na! Come on; say it like you always say it.'

'That is how I always say it.'

'Fuck off! You say "fillum"! You always do.'

'I do not. Film. There.'

'See?'

154

'See what?'

'You said "fillum"!'

'I did not!'

'Yes you did. Here's your mate; let's see how he pronounces it. Ere, Craig, mate; say "film".'

Craig sat down, put the drinks on the table and, smirking, said, 'Movie.'

Oh how we laughed.

'Na, it's just, like, realising there's the powerful and the power-less, the strong and the weak, the rich and the poor, the winners and the losers, and which lot do you identify with? If it's with the winners, then you're basically saying, Right, fuck the poor or the dispossessed or the oppressed or the whatever; I'm just out for me; I want to be one of them winners and I don't care who I hurt or what I do getting there and staying there. If you identify with the losers—'

'You're a loser,' Ed said.

'No, no; no, you're not.'

'Anyway, you got money.'

'I'm not *saying* having money at all is immoral. Though I'm not so sure about having shares . . .'

'Lissen to you, man! Wot's wrong wif havin shares?'

'The legal precedence you're automatically accorded over workers and consumers, that's what,' I said. At this point, even I was aware I was sounding a bit pompous.

'Yeah, right. I bet you got shares anyway, man, wevvir you know it or not.'

'No I don't!' I protested.

'No?' Ed said. 'You got a pension?'

'No!' I exclaimed triumphantly.

Ed looked amazed. 'Wot? No pension plan?'

'Nope. Opted out of the company's and never opted into another.'

'You're mad.'

'I'm not! I'm principled, you bastard.'

'Self-righteousness is easily worth a few percentage points to a man like Ken,' Craig told Ed. At the time, I thought in support.

'Still fink you've got shares somewhere. Where do you keep your dosh, then?'

'Building society. Nationwide; the last big mutual. All *my* money goes to provide loans to people buying houses, not into the rest of the capital market and certainly not into lining the pockets of fucking fat cat directors.'

'Yeah,' Ed snorted. 'An wot you gettin? Four per cent?'

'A clear conscience,' I said. Oops; skirting the perimeter of the pomposity precipice again. 'Anyway, my point is that you can still have ambition and want to do well and want your friends and family to do well, but you're keeping your, keeping your . . . what am I trying to say here, Craig?'

'You're tryin to say "I am drunk."' Ed laughed. 'Loud and clear.'

'I think,' Craig said, 'you're trying to explain what determines whether you're right- or left-wing. Or liberal or not. Something like that.' He waved one long arm. 'I don't know.'

Craig sat looking gangly and overhanging his seat, limbs on a very low state of readiness, light reflecting from his shaven head. We had moved on to the Soho House after the bar had shut. There might have been somewhere in between (see above). Whatever; we had all been very sorry to leave the bar because all these stunningly beautiful women had kept walking by us, going up and down the pavement and the street, and we'd all observed that they'd got more and more beautiful as the evening had gone on, remarkably.

Anyway, now we were here in the House and it was crowded and hot and when I thought about it I couldn't remember what floor we were on or which room we were in or where the loo would be from here. At least we'd got a table somehow, but sitting down in the midst of all these standing bodies meant you were situated kind of low to spot any natural landmarks and so get the old bearings. I had no idea how we'd got onto this stuff about belief but if I'd stopped to think about it, it would probably have been me who'd brought the subject up.

'Something like that,' I said, feeling I was agreeing with an important point, though not quite able to recall exactly what it might be. 'It's a fucking mission statement, man. One that actually has some point. It's about where your sympathies lie; with yourself or with your fellow man. Women. Human beings. This is what it's all about; this.'

'What?'

'This, what I'm going to explain, right here, right now.'

'Well?'

'Go on then.'

'It's about, do you see somebody having a really tough time of things and think, Tough shit, loser? Or do you see somebody having a really tough time and think, Hmm, too bad, or, Oh, that's a shame, or, Oh, poor person, I wonder how I can help? That's the choice. Choices. Choice. It's all about how nasty or nice you are.'

'Wow, you really *must* be nice,' Craig said. 'You missed out the one that's worse than, Tough shit, loser.'

'I did? There is one?'

'Yes; it's, Hmm, how can I exploit this already down-and-out and therefore usefully vulnerable person for my own ends?'

'Fuck,' I breathed, abashed by my own lack of sufficient cynicism. 'So I did.' I shook my head. 'God, there are some *real* bastards around.'

'Never more than ten feet from a rat,' Ed said. He raised his eyebrows. 'Specially round ere.'

'Ten feet?' I said. 'I thought it was ten metres.'

'Twenty feet,' Craig offered, possibly as a compromise.

157

'Wotever.'

'Yeah,' I said. 'Soho. I suppose there just might be the odd tad of exploitation going on here.'

Ed made a show of spluttering into his drink. 'Fuckin Exploitation City here, mate.'

'The girls are all slaves,' Craig said, nodding wisely.

'Who? What girls?'

'The prossies,' Craig said.

'The girls wif their cards in the phone boxes,' Ed said.

'Oh. Yeah. Of course.'

'Yeah, *you* try findin a ho wot can speak English round ere.'

'Right,' I said. 'Yeah; they're all from Eastern Europe or somewhere now, aren't they?'

'Slaves,' Craig repeated. 'Take their passports, tell them they've got to work off some ludicrous amount of debt. The girls think once they've done that they can start earning some for themselves and sending money back home but of course they never do.' He nodded. 'Read about it. *Observer*, I think.'

'And the police are out, I suppose,' I said, 'because then they'll just get deported, or slung into a detention centre or something.'

'Not to mention what'll appen to their family back ome.' Ed clicked his fingers. 'Nuvvir fing your Mr Merrial's involved in, come to fink of it. Im an is Albanian chums.'

'Who?' Craig said, looking mystified.

I had a sudden fit of hull-breach-category paranoia, and waved one hand with what I hoped looked like airily casual dismissiveness.

'Woops!' Ed said, catching the glass before it fell all the way to the floor. 'Nuffing in it anyway.'

'Sorry, sorry,' I said. 'Um, ah, yeah; too complicated,' I told the still mystified-looking Craig. I turned to Ed.

'Ed,' I said. 'What do you believe in?'

'I believe it's time for anuvver drink, mate.'

* * *

158

'I wasn't. I didn't. I didn't say half the things I was supposed to have said.'

'Ya. So, like, what did you say?'

'Three things. Two of them simple, unarguable road safety points. One: estimable and thoroughly civilised city though it is, it was something close to criminal neglect on the part of the Parisian authorities that a piece of road like that had massive, square concrete pillars unprotected by crash barriers. It couldn't have been much more intrinsically dangerous if they'd attached giant iron spikes angled to face into the traffic stream. Two: this is supposed to be a mature, responsible adult, mother of two, beloved by millions, so she might have done the first thing that any rational human being does when they get into a car, especially one that might be going to travel quickly and even if you haven't guessed the driver is quietly pissed, and *put on a fucking seat belt*. Three, and this is the one that really caused the trouble: my conscience was clear. But a lot of the people who turned up to watch the procession and throw flowers onto the hearse, *if* they blamed the photographers chasing the Merc on their motorbikes – which a lot of people did – then they were hypocrites, because by their own logic they'd helped kill her.'

'Ya. Right. Ya. How?'

'Because why were the snappers bothering to stay up late outside a flash Parisian hotel in the first place? Because the photographs they might get could be worth something. Why might the photographs be worth something? Because the papers would pay good money for them. Why would the papers pay good money for them? Because those photos sold newspapers and magazines.

'My point was that *if* any of the people that blamed the photographers – a profession I have no great love for, believe me – ever bought newspapers that regularly featured the royals in general and Princess Di in particular, and *especially* if they had ever changed from whichever newspaper they usually bought, or bought an extra one, because it contained or might contain a photograph of Diana, then they should blame themselves for her death, too, because their interest, their worship, their need for celebrity gossip, their money, had put those snappers at the door of the Ritz that night and set them off on the chase that ended with a black Merc totalled round an underground chunk of reinforced concrete and three people dead.

'Me, I'm a republican; nothing—'

'What, like the IRA? Right.'

'No, not the fucking IRA. I mean I'm a republican rather than a monarchist. Nothing against her madge or the rest personally . . . well, anyway . . . but as an institution I want the monarchy dumped. I wouldn't buy a piece of shit like the *Sun* or the *Mail* or the *Express* in the first place, but even if for some bizarre reason I'd ever been tempted, I'd have been less, not more likely to do so if there had been a photo of Princess Di on the cover. So I hadn't helped kill her. My question to whoever might have been listening was, How about you?'

'Right, I see.'

'Right. Do you?'

'So they sacked you. Bummer.'

I shrugged. 'The papers got a little upset. Personally I think the *Express* and the *Mail* just didn't like being called tabloids.'

'But you found something else, right, ya?'

'Oh, ya.'

'Oh, you're making fun of me. You're terrible.'

'Am I?'

'Yes, I'm a big fan. You shouldn't insult me. I thought I was doing quite well.'

'What? You thought *you* were doing quite well?'

'Amn't I?'

I looked her down and up. 'You're funny.'

'You think?'

160

'Definitely. Another drink?'

'Okay. No; you sit. I'll get them. You haven't let me buy anything yet. Please.'

'If you insist, Raine.'

'I do. Same again?'

'Yeah.'

'Don't go away,' Raine said, touching me on the arm again. She'd done this a lot over the last hour or so. I liked it.

'Oh, okay then,' I said.

Raine slid out from behind our table and insinuated her lithe, size six body into the crowd, towards the bar. Phil leaned over. 'I think you're in there, mate.'

'Yeah, I think I might be, too,' I agreed. 'Who'd a thunk it?' Shit, I was a bit drunk. I'd actually knocked back that last whisky. Mistake. I turned to Phil. 'Can I have some of your water?'

'Yep. There you go.'

I drank from his bottle of Evian.

We were in Clout on Shaftesbury Avenue, a big, coolly swish, third-generation pleasure complex designed for the discerning older clubber who might equally favour Home or be found in FOBAR (Fucking Old Beyond All Recognition, age-profile successor to FUBAR: Fucked Up Beyond All Recognition).

Phil and I were sitting in a booth in the Retox Bar, on Level Tepid. If you listened carefully you could just make out the thud-thud-thud from the main dance area on the floor above. From downstairs, where the main chill spaces were and quiet, relaxing sounds were the ambient noisescape, there was what sounded like silence. Well, maybe just the occasional quiet pop of yet another fried brain cell departing this world.

Above, you could hardly hear the person next to you if you hollered in their ear. Below, it felt wrong to do much more than whisper. Here, music played but normal conversation was perfectly possible. I must be getting old, because I preferred it here. Fucking right I did! Here was where you obviously got to meet pieces of class ass like Raine! Fucking yee-ha!

Calm down, calm down, I told myself. I tried breathing deeply. 'I've been on a real fucking roll recently,' I told Phil, shaking my head. Jo, Ceel – ah, Ceel, who was really in another category altogether, who was a whole world in herself, but who I saw so horribly seldom – . . . I'd lost track. Start again: Jo, Ceel . . . that Argentinian girl in Brighton, one or two others, Tanya – well, not Tanya, who'd baled out on me – but I still reckoned I was green-light with Amy if I wanted to take things further down that next-on-personal-playlist route, and . . . and now this Raine girl. A total fucking stunner with a Sloane accent and *she* seemed to be after *my* body! I loved London. I loved even the modest morsel of fame that I had. 'I have, haven't I?'

'Yeah,' Phil said, nodding wisely. 'Don't know what they see in you, myself.'

'Me either,' I agreed. I drank some more water and studied the floor at my feet. The floor of the Retox was some blond Scandinavian-looking wood. Pouring a whisky away straight onto it might cause unseemly dribbling, splashing noises, like you'd pissed yourself or something. Ah-hah; Phil had put his jacket down on the floor when Raine had slipped in beside us. Perfect. I hooked his jacket closer underneath me with one foot while he wasn't looking.

'Here you go,' Raine said, setting my whisky down in front of me. It was a double. 'Here; I got you some more water, ah, Paul.'

'Phil,' said Phil.

'Ya. Sorry. Phil.' Raine smiled at me and raised her glass; it looked like a G&T. I raised mine. 'Down the hatch,' Raine said, and drank deep. I put my glass to my lips and made a big show of drinking, but didn't, keeping my lips tightly closed. I sniffed it, instead. I was getting paranoid about this, thinking that Raine was watching me drink. I made my Adam's apple bob, like I

162

was swallowing. I put the glass down on the table, keeping it covered by my fingers so the level wasn't obvious.

'Nice. Bit peaty. Is it an Islay?'

'Ah, ya,' Raine said. 'Ya, that's right.' She wore tight leather pants, a couple of layers of pink and white chiffon blouse, and shades with a faint yellow-tint that made her look a bit like Anastacia. Mid-twenties, like her waist. Awfully good cheek-bones and a jaw line like David Coulthard's, except smoother, obviously. Her nipples were kind of obvious through the chiffon – was it fashionable again? Looked good on her, anyway – and something about her bare shoulders reminded me of Ceel. Raine's hair was blond and thick and she kept flicking it back off her face.

'So, Raine,' Phil said. 'Ever sky-dived in La Mancha?' He grinned inanely at her, then at me. I got the impression he was at least as drunk as me. We'd started mob-handed in the pub, gone on to the Groucho, then the Soho House, and ended up here, losing co-workers en route to pathetic excuses like food, prior engagements, life-partners, children; that sort of thing. I had the vague impression we'd had a good talk about the show during some part of this and come up with some new ideas and stuff for me to rant about, but I couldn't recall any of the details at all. Luckily Phil usually did, and he normally took notes in tiny writing in the Useful Diary he always carried with him.

It was a Friday, so we didn't have a show tomorrow; we were allowed to go out to play, dammit. Jo was absent for the weekend, with the Addicta boys in Stockholm and Helsinki. Also, it had been three weeks since I'd seen Celia and I'd been hoping there would be a couriered package for me immedi-ately after the show and an Anonymous call on my mobile; in fact I'd spent the show, the day since I woke up, even the week, if I was being honest, looking forward to signing my name on a dispatch rider's acknowledgment form; received in good condition, sign here, print here, insert time here . . . But there had been nothing, just an empty feeling.

I'd decided it was time for a jolly good drink.

'Sorry?' the girl said.

Phil waved a hand woozily. 'Nothing. Ignore me.'

'Ya.' Raine looked rather meanly at my producer, I thought. Bit cheeky, I thought. This man was one of my best friends and a very fine producer, too. Who did she think she was, looking at him with a just-fuck-off expression? How dare she? This man deserved respect, for Christ's sake. While she was distracted, I took the opportunity to pour about half my whisky over Phil's jacket, then brought the whisky glass up and did the pretend drinking thing again, just as Raine switched her attention back to me, and a smile reappeared on her face. She clinked glasses once more. I thought I could smell the whisky fumes evaporating from the dark surface of Phil's old but still serviceably stylish Paul Smith. I swirled my whisky round in the glass. Raine was watching.

'You trying to get me drunk?' I asked her in a sort of kooky, role-reversal kinda stylee.

She lowered her eyelids a little and slid up to me on the seat until I could feel the warmth of her through my shirt. 'I'm trying to get you to come home with me,' she murmured.

'Ha!' I laughed. I slapped my thigh. 'You *shall* go to the ball, Cinders!'

Phil was snorting with laughter on the other side of me. Raine gave him a dirty look. I took her chin in my hand and brought her mouth towards mine, but she put her hand on my forearm and gently pushed my hand down. 'Finish your drink and let's go, okay?'

I'd already disposed of most of the rest of the whisky and could happily have slugged the rest because it wasn't enough to make any real difference, but by now it had become something between a game and a point of honour to dispose of the whole lot without a drop passing my lips, so I looked over Raine's shiningly blond head and said, 'Okay . . . Shit, is that Madders and Guy Ritchie?'

She looked. I dumped the last of the whisky onto Phil's jacket and stood up, lowering the whisky glass from my mouth as Raine turned back again. 'Guess not,' I said. I felt fine, I thought. The prospect of sex with somebody new, especially somebody new who looked as good as Raine, was a profoundly sobering influence all by itself. Still, I felt myself sway as we edged out of the booth.

'Phil, got to go.'

'Fine. Have fun,' he said.

'That's the intention. You take care.'

'And you precautions.' He sniggered.

'See you Monday.'

'I just have to visit the loo,' Raine said as we crossed through the crowds.

'I'll see you at the cloakroom.'

I spent a couple of minutes nattering to the cloakroom girl on the ground floor. Unlike Phil I usually checked my jacket in, but then I didn't use mine as a wearable handbag.

'Ready?' Raine asked, passing her receipt to the girl.

'Very,' I said.

Raine let me help her on with her coat. It was an Afghan, which I interpreted as a retro-fashion-driven coincidence rather than some subtle geopolitical statement. She turned and looked me in the eye, gaze switching from one pupil to the other. It felt good, very sexy, to be inspected so closely. She hadn't tipped the cloakroom girl but I didn't care. I kind of fell against her and she let me kiss her, though not deeply. She pushed me away and glanced at the girl. 'Come on,' she said.

It was raining as we left. I nodded at the bouncers, who smiled and nodded back. I was moderately certain I knew their names, but I wasn't absolutely sure, and getting bouncers' names

165

wrong was a lot worse than not calling them anything. I stared at the rain and the traffic sizzling up and down the Avenue, lights bright in the drop-jewelled darkness. 'It's rain, Raine,' I said.

'Right, ya,' she said, gazing down the street. Yes, Kenneth, I thought to myself, like she'll never have heard that one in her life before.

'Friday night in the rain,' I said authoritatively. 'Our best chance is a taxi dropping somebody off. I'll bravely volunteer to make a dash for one if it pulls up.'

'Right.'

'Or I could just phone a mini-cab,' I said, taking my mobile out after a struggle with the little holster at my hip. 'I'll tell them there's an even more exorbitant tip in it than usual.' I squinted down at the little Motorola as I flipped it open. 'Just don't say anything about curry,' I muttered, closing one eye to see the display properly.

Raine looked round. She put her hand over mine, over the phone. 'No, it's all right. Here's a taxi now.'

A black cab had just pulled up at the kerb. 'Glory be,' I said, putting the mobile away again. 'Na, its light's off . . .'

But Raine was already pulling me across the pavement towards the cab. 'Ya, I flagged it.'

'*Fine* work, Raine,' I said, grabbing for the door handle and missing. She opened the door but I insisted on holding it open for her. I then hit my head getting in. 'Ouch.'

'You all right?'

'Fine.' I started searching for my seat belt. 'This is a really good omen, you know, Raine,' I told her, raising my backside off the seat to grab at the belt.

'Ya, it is, isn't it.'

'Getting a taxi that quickly on a rainy Friday?' I said. 'You're a miracle worker. Or, as a combination, we're just blessed.'

'Right, ya.'

The cab pulled out into the traffic, heading north-east. I finally got my seat belt on. Raine hadn't bothered with hers. I started lecturing her on the extreme inadvisability of this, given what had happened to Princess Di, but she just looked at me strangely and I realised that as well as preventing you from being flung forward, limbs flailing, in a bad crash, seat belts also stopped you from snogging. They made you Safe In Taxis. I was appalled with myself. I was sure I'd known this before but I seemed to have forgotten.

'You're right,' I said, though she hadn't said anything. I undid my belt. 'Solidarity, sister.' I slid along the seat towards her. I caught the driver glancing up at us in his mirror. Raine let me slip my arms round her, pressed up against the seat corner. I covered her mouth with mine. She opened up a little more this time. I fumbled to get my hands inside the Afghan coat.

'Maybe you should put your seat belts on, eh?' the driver said. It was an oldish cab so he had to talk through the gap in the perspex screen between us, rather than use the intercom set-up the more modern cabs have.

Raine pushed me away. 'Ya, I suppose we should, ya,' she said, with what I took to be obvious reluctance.

'Ha. See?' I said, wagging a finger at her. I felt for my belt again. She watched me, then put hers on.

'Here,' she said, helping me with one end.

'Thanks.' I sat back, closing my eyes.

'Have a snooze, why not?' Raine said.

I opened my eyes, looked at her. 'I'm not tired,' I told her. 'Is it far?'

'Ya, fair bit to go yet.' She glanced at the driver, then leaned over to me and said quietly, 'Get some rest. You're going to need it.' She gave me one of those heavy-lidded looks again and stroked my hand in a manner I decided was distinctly carnal.

I grinned in what I hoped was not too lecherous a fashion and sat back, closing my eyes. 'If I start snoring, I'm only pretending in a sorta post-modern ironic way, okay?'

'Ya, right, sure.'

The taxi drove on, grumbling and clattering through the late-night traffic. It sounded a lot like my old Landy. Very relaxing. The rain swishing beneath the tyres and against the wheel wells sounded calming and soothing. It was quite warm here in the back. It made me think of darkened hotel suites. I took a deep breath and let it out. A little while to rest the eyes. Why not? A snooze would do no harm. On the other hand, I didn't really want to drop off and start snoring or drooling or looking gross, so maybe it wasn't such a great idea.

Some time passed. A male voice said quietly, 'Is that him gone?'

'Yeah, I think so,' said Raine. At least I thought it was her. Her voice sounded different. 'We nearly there yet then?'

'Nuvver five minutes.'

That was weird, I thought, behind my closed eyes, with my chin somewhere near my chest. Had I dropped off? Just a little. But why was Raine asking the driver if they were nearly there yet? Didn't she know the way home? Maybe she'd just moved in.

But what did the driver mean when he asked her, Is that him gone?

'Just check he's out, will ya, doll?'

Check he's out? What the fuck was that about? I felt a hand stroke mine, then pinch the skin. I didn't react. 'Ken? *Ken?*' Raine said, quite loud. I stayed just as I was. My heart had started to speed up. Then she said, 'Yeah, he's gone.'

'Roight.'

What was going on here? What the fuck was going on? Where were we going, anyway? Had she given the driver an address as we got in? I'd kind of assumed she'd told him her home address while I was getting in and smacking my head off the top of the door frame, but had there been time?

Wouldn't I have heard something? I couldn't remember. Shit, I was drunk; of course I wasn't going to remember stuff like that. But then the taxi had appeared really fortuitously, too. Just rolled up, in the damp midst of a wet Friday some time between theatre and bar chucking out time. On Shaftesbury Avenue. Just appeared, its yellow For Hire light already off, if my hazy memory served me right, ready and waiting at the kerb, just like that. And it had seemed as if she'd been looking for it. But then she would have been; looking for a taxi, any taxi. But then we came back to this Check he's out/Yeah, he's gone shit. What the fuck was all that about? He'd *expected* me to be out, to be gone, to be unconscious . . .

Sweet Jesus H. Christ; the whisky. There had been something in the whisky. What was that date-rape drug? I couldn't remember. But something like that. The drink she'd insisted she'd get, then watched me drink, or thought that was what she was watching while I suppressed a giggle and played my silly game and anointed Phil's jacket with the stuff instead, distracting her, making my Adam's apple go up and down, smacking my lips and doing everything but wipe my mouth on my sleeve; look, I'm drinking it! See? It's gone! She'd put something in it. She must have. What was that date-rape stuff? Euthymol? No, that was a toothpaste, wasn't it? A fucking Micky fucking Finn in this fucking day and fucking age and I'd fucking fallen for it! Or would have, if I hadn't been determined to salvage some dregs of sobriety from my drunken stupor for the purposes of, hopefully, fucking.

Oh shit.

I'd sniffed it. The whisky with the date-rape drug or whatever it was; I'd breathed it in. How powerful was that stuff? Some must have stuck to my lips when I pretended to drink it. Was I falling into a drugged sleep now? No. No definitely not me, no-how, no-way. Very awake and horribly, edgily, tensely sober with my heart hammering so hard I'm astonished that

Raine, if that's really her name, can't hear it, that she can't see my entire body shaking with each thudding, crashing, flailing tremor of it.

'You aw-wight?' the driver asks. For one idiotic moment I think he's talking to me, and for a totally deranged micro-moment I'm actually about to answer him.

Then the girl says, 'Yeah,' quite casually, as though she's bored.

I open one eye very slightly, the left one, away from her. Where are we? I have a vague feeling we're somewhere in the East End but I don't know. My head is down and I can't see much without raising it. How long did the driver say? Five minutes? Yes, it was five minutes. But how long ago was that? One minute ago? Two? *Four?*

I can see the little red tell-tale light on the door at my side, near the handle. Of course; cab doors lock while the vehicle is in motion. Safety device, allegedly. Stop you doing a runner, more like. Doesn't matter. I can't just make a break for it when we slow down. Have to wait for a complete stop. Shit. We slow down here, and I start to get sweaty palms, thinking about grabbing the door handle and sprinting off . . . but then we speed up again.

I use the acceleration as a plausible excuse to let my head fall back, my neck over the back of the seat now and my view through my half-closed eye a bit better. I sense Raine looking at me. I start snoring. Through the trembling blur of eyelashes, I can see a lightly trafficked road and low-rise buildings. I must really have dropped off. We're well away from the West End here. We take a left into a darker, quieter road. What look like low warehouses and light industrial units line the road. I see plentiful graffiti and billboards with old, torn, rain-sodden posters flapping in the cold wind. We go under a bridge, engine echoing off the rivet-studded undersides of massive black girders.

'Nearly there,' the driver says.

'Mm-hmm,' says Raine.

We slow. There's a brighter, noisier road ahead. And traffic lights.

'Just over these lights.'

Turning amber.

'Right.'

Thank fuck.

'Yeah, I fink that's Danny there I can see.'

Turning red.

'Uh-huh.'

Oh yes. Oh yes, just stop right here on the far side of the busy traffic from wherever it is we're going, from whoever the fuck Danny is.

The cab stops, engine idling noisily. The little red light by the door handle should click and go off now. Now. There's a click. I wait for the little red light to go off. It doesn't.

Something in my bowels makes a terrible trembling course through me, squeezing cold sweat from every pore. The driver; taxi drivers can override the door-locks' stationary off-switch, keeping it on. He's locked us in.

I'm fucked. These people can do whatever they want to me. I may be about to die. The lights are still red but the traffic crossing our path has just stopped. The driver is reaching for the gear stick.

I sit up suddenly. Raine looks at me and her mouth starts to open as her eyes finish widening. I click my seat belt unlocked and swing my right leg as hard as I can at the window to my left. It shatters first time. It feels like my leg does too, but the window's gone in an almighty bang, falling spraying to the street outside and the rubber-matted floor of the cab in a thousand square-edged little jewels glinting sodium in the street-light.

The driver's shocked face turns towards me. Raine grabs my arm and I do something I've never done before, ever; I hit a

171

woman. Punch her square in the nose and send her head whacking back against the door window on her side.

Then I'm out of the smashed window on my side so fucking fast John Woo would be proud of me, turning on my back, hands to the top of the frame and levering myself out with just some kicking, flailing footwork to spoil the balletic beauty of it.

I land with a wind-expelling whumpf on the road, just as the taxi jerks forward and then screeches to a stop again, nose dipping. I'm rolling on the broken glass and bouncing to my feet, starting to run. There's shouting behind me and a door slamming. More shouting from further away. These both male. Female screaming now. The road ahead is broad and almost deserted. Some parked cars, one or two Transits and Lutons. I angle for the pavement, to put some of the parked stuff between me and them. More shouting and screaming.

The wind roars in my ears as I run. Engine noise back there now. I'm near the end of the street. The engine behind me whines, caught in the low gear of reverse, then the engine seems to cut out, there's a squeal of tyres, a moment of silence, and the engine screams. Handbrake turn.

I run out onto the street ahead at right-angles and pelt across a sudden burst of traffic, horns blaring right and left as I leap a traffic island in one stride and spot a chip shop with a queue of people outside, a hundred metres away. I make the pavement, just dodging a Royal Mail van, which skids to a stop so close I have my arm stuck out and the grille nudges the flesh of my palm. I run for the chip shop queue, dodging between a few slowly walking people like gates on a downhill slalom course. The Royal Mail van races past to my left, the driver leaning out of the window, shouting that I'm a fucking wanker and backing this up with a gesture. There are two cars at the kerb just beyond the queue at the chip shop. I splash through a puddle. The rain is off, I notice. The cars beyond the chip

172

shop are parked outside a little lit doorway and window with a cheap-looking sign above, glaring yellow-white above the pitted brickwork and spelling out the two most beautiful words in the most beautiful language in the universe: Mini-Cabs.

I slow and look back just as I get to the queue but there's no taxi anywhere to be seen, and nobody running. I straighten my jacket, run fingers through my hair and by the time I get to the first cab in the rank, nodding first to the guy in the doorway and then at the car, I'm actually whistling.

'Well, do *you* ever look at the number of a cab when you get into one?'

'Na,' Craig admitted. 'Who does?'

'Phil, probably,' I said. I'd called him on his mobile and home number but only got answer machines.

'I still think,' Craig said, 'you should have gone to the police.'

'Christ, man, I just wanted to get away.'

'Yeah, but.'

'Yeah but what? It was half eleven on a Friday night. The cops are going to be busy enough with fights and brawls and the usual weekend nonsense. And what exactly would I be ringing up to report, anyway? I *think* I was being kidnapped, I *think* somebody tried to spike my drink, but if you want any proof you'll have to get another guy's jacket and test it for the drug, if it's still detectable. I *think* some violence was planned for me but I don't know. I'm fairly sure I was chased but that's not even illegal. Fucking hell, the only definitely criminal things that actually happened were the things *I* did; I smashed a cab window and I punched a woman in the face. I fucking hit a woman, man! Jesus Christ, *that* was something I had hoped to get through my whole life without doing, like breaking a major bone or changing a nappy.' I sucked very hard on the J. I'd wanted a brandy or something but Craig had reckoned what I needed was a nice, mellow smoke.

My very first thought, once I'd got into the cab and told the guy to head for Basildon (this had to be east of wherever we were, so it meant we didn't need to chuck a U-ey and go past the end of the road I'd been chased down), was to call Amy. She lived in Greenwich, which was feasibly in the area, and turning to her – and up on her doorstep – in an hour of need, on the run from heavies, might be just the sort of romantic ice-breaker required to shift our relationship onto whatever next phase might be on the cards (the last time I'd seen her had been on 11 September, when we'd all sat together in Kulwinder and Faye's loft, watching the unbelievable unfold, until she'd been called away by her boss).

Then I thought of Celia. Christ; Merrial. Maybe he was behind whatever had almost happened back there.

I don't know who I'd imagined might want to have me kidnapped and whisked off to the East End for . . . whatever, but of course Celia's husband had to be a prime suspect. Why the hell hadn't that been the *first* thing I'd thought of? Could this be anything to do with Celia and me? Had we been discovered? We thought we'd been so careful, but who really knew?

Oh shit. Should I use the mobile number she didn't know I had, try to warn her?

But if it wasn't anything to do with her, with us, and she discovered I'd taken her number without asking, without telling her . . .

Yeah, but if all this *was* about us then it was entirely possible a phone call could save her life.

'I'm Ken, by the way,' I said to the guy driving the minicab. He was a strapping white lad with a shock of red-dyed hair. I'd sat beside him rather than in the back. We shook hands.

'Dave.'

'Dave, I've a bit of a funny request.'

'Yeah? Wossat?'

'Can I use your mobile? I've got one of my own but I need

174

to use a different one. Please? Add a fiver to the fare. It's important.'

'Here you go.'

'You are a saint, sir.' I pulled out my own mobile, cursored through to Ceel's entered but never used number, and clicked it into Dave's Sony.

'The mobile phone you are calling is switched off . . .'

Another couple of tries got the same response. No voice mail or message service available. 'Thanks,' I said to Dave the driver, handing him back his phone. 'Never got through.' I hesitated. 'Listen, Dave; what I said about a fiver? Call it a tenner, but in the unlikely event a woman . . . anybody ever phones about a call made, like, now, just say you dialled the same wrong number or something.'

'"You never saw me, I wasn't here,"' the lad quoted, grinning. 'Used to work in a boozer, mate; lying to people on the phone looking for somebody they fink's there is like second nature.'

'Yeah, well, cheers,' I said. I tried Amy next, on my own phone, but her mobile was switched to message and the landline to her place in Greenwich was on answer, with a long beep-time of stacked messages before the tone. I sighed and rang Craig. He was in, sitting watching TV, about to go to bed.

'Okay, Dave,' I said. 'Change of destination . . .'

I tried Celia's mobile again from a phone box near Craig's place in Highgate. Still nothing.

'You should still go to the cops,' Craig said again, looking down at the big old Geographia London Street Plan he'd spread on the kitchen table, to see if we could work out where it had all happened. Idiotically, I hadn't thought to get the number or the name of the mini-cab company. The first thing I remembered from the drive was seeing a sign for Stratford station, off to our left as we'd headed in the general direction of Essex. 'Report what happened,' Craig insisted. 'Because of what might happen.'

'Because of what *might* happen?' I echoed.

'Supposing something else does, and it has to be something the cops get involved in; if what happened tonight comes out they're going to want to know why you didn't mention anything about it. You've got to report it, man. The cops might be able to find out if an old taxi gets its left window repaired over the next couple of days.'

'I doubt that a kidnap that never really happened will be far up their list of priorities just now, plus I have said one or two unflattering things about the boys in blue, over the years,' I observed. Dryly, I hoped. I was still shaking, and my leg hurt where I'd kicked the window out; I was going to have a splendid bruise in a day or two. There were various other mysterious aches, pains, grazes and likely bruises I couldn't recall picking up in all the excitement, plus my hands and fingers were a little cut where I'd grabbed the window. Craig had handed me a bottle of TCP and some kitchen towel and told me to get on with it.

'I know,' he said. 'But you still have to report it.'

'What exactly is this stuff that might happen? What were you thinking of?'

'I don't know.' Craig stretched his lanky frame back in the kitchen chair and put his hands behind his head. 'You don't have any idea who these people were?'

'They were both white, south-east England, maybe London. There was somebody I didn't see called Danny. The place I was being taken to was in the East End and the driver seemed to know the area. I'd guess he's a proper taxi driver, done the Knowledge. It was . . .' I gestured at the map in front of us. 'There, somewhere.'

'Suspects? Motives?' Craig asked, grinning.

'Stop enjoying this, you bastard.'

'No, I'm being serious. Can you think of any suspects and what their motives might be?'

'Oh, Jesus, do you want them alphabetically or in order of appearance? The world is basically composed of people who want me dead, and my close friends.'

'I'm not sure those are mutually exclusive categories.'

'Fuck off.'

'That's a tad paranoid, even for you.'

'Craig, I've lost count of the death threats I've had over the years. We have to report each one to the local nick. They have a photocopied report form with my details already filled in. The people who open my mail get danger money. I'm not joking.'

'You told me it was dirty money.'

'Okay, it's mostly shit, not bombs, but still. The point is lots of people have claimed to want me dead, and that's just the ones who feel a burning desire to tell me. This could be fundamentalists of any persuasion, a corporate hit-job—'

Craig sniggered. 'Oh, come on.'

'Excuse me? I have affected the share price of large corporations. That's a capital offence.'

'Yeah, ha ha. Colour me chortle. But no, you haven't. Not alone,' Craig said. 'You're not an investigative reporter or anything, Ken. You're a commentator. You comment on what others have dug up. If you didn't, somebody else would, people who do dig stuff up. *Private Eye*, Mark Thomas . . . I don't know; Rory Bremner, I mean . . . Shit, people have been trying to close down the *Eye* for decades. If Maxwell couldn't and Jimmy Goldsmith couldn't . . . I mean, why would anyone bother trying to kill *you*?'

'Did any of that make sense even to you?' I asked him.

'I'm tired,' Craig flapped one hand. 'Mr Penfold and I have been in deep discussion most of the evening.'

'Have you heard some of the things I've *said* about people? About fundamentalists in par-fucking-*ticular*?'

'Fundamentalists don't listen to your show.'

'Khomeini didn't read *The Satanic Verses*. So fucking what?'

'Well, they don't sound like fundamentalists, do they? White, man and woman, somebody called Danny.'

'That I'll give you.' I put the dead joint into the ashtray. 'They don't sound like fundamentalist Muslims, anyway. Could be fundamentalist Christians; Aryan Nation militia types or something. They can't all be wanking over pictures of Ayn Rand and polishing their Desert Eagles in South Dakota.' My hand was still shaking. 'Man, I really need a drink.'

'I've got a box of red. Banrock okay?'

'If it's red and it has lots of alcohol in it, that's all that matters.'

Craig rose. 'Sounds like your blood, pal.'

'You ruddy sod. My jacket stank of whisky.'

'I'm sorry. I didn't see it lying there,' I lied. 'D'you still have it? I mean, you haven't washed it or anything, have you?'

'Exhibit A is in a bin-bag in my kitchen,' Phil said. He paused. He shook his head. 'I still can't believe you punched a woman.'

'For the last time! I didn't have a fucking choice!'

'Well,' Craig said. 'As long as you didn't enjoy it.'

'About as much as I'm enjoying this,' I muttered.

Phil had picked Craig and me up on Saturday morning and taken us to the *Temple Belle*. I'd been worried what I might find there; I'd wanted reinforcements. Phil and Craig knew each other so well they frequently had great sport with my insecurities, telling me they were actually better friends with each other than they were with me. This time they didn't do that but they ganged up and made me swear that if they helped me here, I'd report what had happened to the police on the Monday morning.

The houseboat was fine. Nothing had been disturbed, no horses' heads in the bed, nothing. There was a tool box in the cupboard under the stairs; I'd rummaged around in it until I

178

found a hammer, which I suggested we took with us in case we were attacked, but the guys just stood there and shook their heads in unison, like they'd been rehearsing. I put the hammer back.

We went for a pint and a light lunch, then set off for the East End in search of the site of the previous evening's fun.

I found the place eventually. Haggersley Street, off Bow Road, which was where the chip shop and the cab firm were. It all looked very different in the fresh, pale light of an October afternoon. Just past the rail bridge, by the traffic lights, there was still window glass on the road. I took a handful.

We mooched warily around the cul-de-sac on the far side of the lights, where Haggersley Street ended in a dead end off Devons Road.

'I think your birds have flown, chum,' Phil said, kicking at an old lager can. 'If they were ever here.'

'Yeah, thanks, Phil; cheers,' I said. Phil was, compared to Craig, rather more sceptical about my account of what had happened the night before. Probably because he had seen how drunk I was. And maybe because of the jacket.

We were in a place of old, crooked kerb stones, peeling tarmac laid over ancient cobbles, windscreen glass that crunched under foot like gravel, burnt-out and abandoned cars with rusted panels and sagging plastic trim, and – framing it all on three sides – tilted lengths of desultorily graffitied corrugated iron topped by rusting angle iron strung with thin strands of barbed wire, jagged strands of sharp, spaced knots decorated by the greyed-out tatters of ruined black bin-liners, fluttering in a damp wind like the prayer flags of a half-hearted monochrome hell.

Some of the corrugated iron sections were crude gates, all strung with ancient padlocks and grimy chains.

I took a stirrup-step up – Craig made me take my shoe off, which would have made running away interesting – and looked over the corrugated iron walls. Concrete aprons in front of

179

abandoned-looking light industrial units. Freight containers. Sheds. Puddles. Piles of wooden pallets. Waste ground. Weeds. More puddles. There was nobody about; not even any guard dogs came bounding out to greet me. The rain was coming on again.

'I hate this place utterly,' said Phil.

'Seen enough?' Craig asked me.

'I can feel my life-force draining out through my soles,' Phil muttered.

'Nobody wears grey socks any more, Ken.'

'Yeah, you're right,' I said, tutting and detaching one sleeve from a snag in the barbed wire. 'Let us to fuck get.'

'That's you off the German beer until your grammar gets back to normal, pal.'

I tried calling Ceel at least twice a day from a variety of phone boxes throughout central London.

I now knew her number by heart.

She never answered.

Instead, on the Thursday, just after I'd finished my show, a package arrived, by courier. The package was slim and light, like Celia herself, but I didn't dare hope. I signed for it, opened it, and there, glory be, was a key card.

My mobile rang. Something inside me melted and went south for the winter.

From the mobile's tiny speaker, Ceel's voice said, 'One Aldwych. Dome suite.'

'Are you—?' I started to ask, but the line had clicked off. I let my head drop.

My phone burred again.

'What?' Ceel said.

'Are you okay?' I asked, almost choking.

'Yes,' she said, sounding puzzled. 'Of course.'

I smiled into the middle distance. 'I'll see you soon.'

* * *

180

I couldn't fuck. I just wanted to cuddle. Fully clothed. Ceel seemed more confused than annoyed, but also more confused than sympathetic.

'No, I didn't get the taxi's number,' I said. 'Who ever does?'

'I do.'

'Oh yeah? What was the number of the last taxi you—?'

'Four four one seven.'

'Oh, Ceel, you're kidding.'

'No. I used always to leave gloves, scarves, bags, umbrellas and so on in taxis. Strangely, it was always easier to remember the taxi's number than to—'

'All right, all right,' I breathed.

'Kenneth, don't you want to take your clothes off?'

'Aah . . .'

'Or mine?'

'Well, ah . . .'

'I think we need drugs,' Ceel said decisively. 'Luckily I have contacts.'

She was right.

'Do you know what John does when he is not with me, or away on one of his trips overseas?'

'No.'

'Do you want to know?'

'Not particularly.'

'He goes caving.'

'He does what?'

'He goes caving. He spelunks. He descends into caverns under the ground. Mostly in England and Wales, but also abroad.'

'That,' I breathed, 'is so *not* a gangster thing to do.'

We were lying on a giant circular table in one of the rooms in the Dome suite. The Dome itself, in fact, at the very top of the whole hotel. We had made it comfortable with sheets and pillows from the bedroom, two rooms away through the sitting area. The Dome room had numerous small, high windows that looked straight down Waterloo Bridge, part-way up the Aldwych and down most of Drury Lane. If we'd stood up we'd also have had a view to part of the Strand. There were twelve severe, formal-looking seats spaced round the giant table. Even all the soft accoutrements hadn't made the solid surface all that comfortable. The bed would have been more forgiving, but this was how, and where, Ceel had wanted it.

'Mobile phones do not work in caves,' she said after a long time.

I thought. I thought twice, in fact. 'Don't suppose he goes scuba-diving, too, does he?'

'Yes.'

I thought some more. 'Why would he need that excuse?'

'I don't know. That is why I think perhaps it is not an excuse.'

There was silence for a while. Ceel cuddled up to me. She hadn't quite managed to get the suite up to what she considered to be full operating temperature yet, so perhaps she was cold. I lay there, perspiring gently, and thought about what Craig had said, about love.

Some time passed, then she murmured into my shoulder, 'You have my mobile number, don't you?'

I closed my eyes. Holding her had never felt more precious. 'Yes,' I admitted.

She said nothing for a while, but I felt her give what might have been a small nod. 'You have been careful,' she said. 'I appreciate that. I understand now why you were concerned. I'm touched. But please; be even more careful. You have the number committed to memory?'

'I know it by heart.'

'Remove it from your phone.'

'All right.'

'Thank you.'

*　　*　　*

182

'This girl. Was she very beautiful?'

'Very attractive, in a sort of obvious, blond way.'

Ceel was silent for a while. Then she said, 'I feel jealous. I know I should not, but I do.'

'I'm sorry.'

'Me too.'

'Well, I feel jealous of your husband.'

'And yet there are times you and I meet up when the last person to make love to me was you.'

I thought. 'I don't know what's the more pathetic,' I said quietly. 'The fact that that does actually make me feel a little better, or the fact that we are clutching at this straw in the first place. It's not just about sex, Ceel. I mean that I'm jealous he gets to be with you more than I do, that you two can have something like a normal life together.'

'It is not very normal. He is away so much.'

'No, but you can walk across a street together, holding hands.'

Another pause. 'He never holds my hand.'

'You're admitting you assaulted this woman, Mr McNutt?'

'It was self-defence, but yes.'

'I see.'

'Oh, shit,' I breathed.

There was no comeback. Nobody was going to press charges, after all, and, of course, as I'd expected, the cops did nothing. At least nothing they ever told me about. They couldn't even test Phil's jacket for traces of rohypnol; a visiting friend had assumed the jacket in the bag was to be taken to a dry cleaners, and done just that.

Never mind. I'd fulfilled my part of the bargain and reported the incident to the police like a good little citizen.

'Well, maybe, like, we should leak it to the press. Yuh?'

The speaker was Nina Boysert, Mouth Corp Group PR chief

and Special Adviser to Sir Jamie, whatever the fuck that was supposed to mean. She didn't say 'Ya', like Raine – sorry, 'Raine'; hers was more of a 'Yuh'.

Meant the same thing.

We all looked at her. This was her office, an even more spacious one than Station Manager Debbie's. Not high up, but wide and deep and airy and with a pleasant view over Soho Square. Also present were Debbie, Phil and the Group's chief in-house legal mind, Guy Boulen.

'Ah, the police did say not to,' Boulen pointed out. We'd covered this point about a minute ago. Boulen was an oddly rugged man to be a lawyer; about my age, tall and fit-looking and with a face that appeared wind-burnt. Strapping, would be the word; looked like he belonged halfway up a fell in the rain and cloud, manfully scrutinising a compass and leading a bunch of deprived kids on a character-building hike. Softly spoken, though; Home Counties accent.

'Yuh, but, like, they've got their job to do and we've got ours, right? We have to think what's best for the Group.' Nina was business-suit posh; long, not inelegant face, perfect teeth and silky skin; black hair, bobbed. Deep voice. She'd been head-hunted for the Mouth Corp from an internationally renowned management consultancy firm. Still under thirty.

'May I call you Nina?' I asked her with a smile.

'Ah, yuh. Yuh, sure.'

'Ms Boysert,' I said, not smiling. 'My life might be in danger. I'm not entirely sure from what you've been saying whether you've fully grasped that fact. I'm asking for help from my professional colleagues, and from the firm that employs me. Now—'

It was the 'Now' that did it. Phil jumped in after that.

Of course what I'd *wanted* to say was, Listen, bitch, fuck the Group, fuck the shareholders and fuck Sir Jamie, too; *I* was the one being bundled off into the depths of the East End in the middle of the night to have fuck knows what done to me, let's focus on what's best for *me* . . . but I'd reined myself in and come out with a little speech that I thought was far more polite, even with the sarky and probably unnecessary bit at the start about not using the woman's first name.

'I think Phil's right,' Boulen said, to whatever Phil had said (I'd kind of missed it, still glaring at Ms Corporate Good). 'This is a legal matter and we have to take our lead from the police.'

'Yuh, but I'm thinking, like, what about the publicity? I mean, this would be quite big news, yuh? I'm seeing the front page of the *Standard*; Top DJ's Death Threat Hell. And a photograph, of course. Something like that, yuh? I mean, that's big. We can't ignore that; you almost can't buy that.'

There was an awkward silence.

I said, 'Are you for fucking real?'

'Look, Ken!' Phil said quickly, rising and clapping me on the shoulder. 'You've had a tough couple of days; you don't really need to be here. I can look after things. Why don't I meet you in the Bough, half an hour, say? Yeah?' He waggled his eyebrows at me. Guy Boulen was nodding fractionally, his expression somewhere between a grin and a grimace. Debbie was looking at the floor.

'What a splendid idea.' I got up, looked round them. 'Excuse me.'

As I got to the door I heard a deep female voice say, 'Was it something one of us said, yuh?'

'Well done,' Phil said, clinking glasses in the Groucho that evening. We were in the wee nook with the blue plaque, up in the snooker level. 'You told the police what happened and, to my utter astonishment, you didn't tell Nina Boysert exactly what you think of her. Proud of you.'

'Thank you so fucking much. Do I get a badge or something?'

'I'm having a special commemorative medal struck tomorrow.'

'Did she shut the fuck up about leaking the story eventually or did you just throw her out the fucking window?'

'That would be Option A there.' Phil nodded. 'Though it did take Boulen and I threatening to resign if she insisted on going ahead. I did also somewhat talk up your acquaintanceship with Sir Jamie; she might have got the impression that if anything happened you didn't like, you'd take it up with the Dear Owner the next time you're playing polo together.'

I shook my head, drank. 'I bet she leaks it anyway.'

'I don't know.' Phil thought. 'Wouldn't like to hazard a guess. But I wouldn't be at all surprised. I've never met anybody who thought quite so much like a spreadsheet.'

'Well, never mind. Fuck it. Fuck her.'

'Hmm. Well, after you.'

'Hey, look, Phil, can I stay at your place tonight?'

'Jo's away again, is she?'

'Yeah. I hate sleeping alone on the boat.'

'Well, no, you can't. Sorry.'

'Oh, come on.'

'No.'

'I'm vulnerable! Don't abandon me!'

'Stay with Craig.'

'He's got Nikki staying for the weekend.'

'So?'

'They don't want me there.'

'So get a hotel.'

'*I* don't want me there. I . . .'

'What?'

'Nothing. Let me stay at yours, Phil. Come on. Please.'

'No. You're probably safe now; they know you'll be wary.'

'I'm *trying* to be fucking wary! That's why I'm asking you to let me stay with you.'

186

'No.'

'Please.'

'No.'

'Why not?'

'I have a friend staying.'

'What, the compulsively tidy jacket-cleaner?'

'What about Ed?'

'He's away.'

'Oh. Forgot to tell you; those Winsome people rang again, just before we left.'

'The *Breaking News* company?'

'Yes. The thing with this Holocaust denial bloke is back on. Second or third week in December, though that's still tentative.'

'Tentative. Really. Right. But don't go changing the subject. Come on; let me stay over. You'll never know I'm there.'

'No. Stay in a hotel, or go back to the boat.'

'Look, man, I'm fucking *frightened*, don't you understand?'

'You have to face it sometime.'

'I don't want to fucking *face* it! I want to fucking *live*!'

'Even so.'

'I'm thinking about asking Ed to get me a gun.'

'Oh, for goodness' sake.'

Six

LONDON EYE

'Nah, mate. Sorry, no.'

'Ed! Come on!'

'Na. Now, that's wrong, Ken. You shouldn't even have asked me. Let's forget you did. Look at the view instead.'

I sighed and leaned back against the curve of glass. We were on the London Eye, riding one of the big, bulbous cars on its grand forty-minute rotation through the air. We were about two-thirds of the way round now, slowly descending. It was a bright end-of-November day and the air was clear. Most of Ed's extended family were here, laughing and pointing and generally having a fun time. Ed had reserved the car for us. The blazered attendant and I were the only white people on board.

I'd become quite worried on the way up; it had suddenly struck me that the Eye would be a perfect terrorist target. The supporting legs stretched out behind it – looking, I thought, a lot like the marching hammers in *The Wall* – splaying down to the ground by the side of the old GLC building . . . they and their supporting wires and cables suddenly appeared terribly vulnerable. Jesus, I'd thought; a big enough bomb there, blowing the whole structure forward to fall into the river just a bridge away from Westminster . . . but we were on the way down now, my atypical paranoia subsiding along with the gradually flattening view. Downriver, the tall white support towers of the new works on the Hungerford Bridge seemed to echo the architecture of the Eye itself.

Ed had just come back from DJing in Japan and this was the first chance I'd had to catch up with him. It had taken a good twenty-five minutes – and the passing of the best of the view at the top of the circle – for me to get him alone.

'Would you get me a gun if I was black?'

'*Wot?*' Ed said loudly, incredulous. A few of his family turned and looked at us. I guess we'd made it obvious this was meant to be a private word. He lowered his voice. 'Listen to youself, man. Ken! I mean, fuckin ell.'

I shook my head, patted his forearm and sat forward, my head in my hands. 'I'm sorry,' I said, sighing. 'I'm sorry, Ed. That was, that was truly, truly shit. I . . .'

'Look, mate, I can see you're really shaken up wif this. Don't blame you.' Ed leaned down so that he was level with me and he could say even more quietly, 'But a shooter is not going to solve your problems. It'll just add to them. Plob'ly.'

'It's only for self-defence,' I said lamely. But I'd given up. I knew I wasn't going to convince him. Worse, I knew he was probably right.

'Yeah, that's what they all say, chummy.'

'You're not denying you know people who could get me one though, are you?'

'Course not. But come on, Ken,' Ed said. He gestured at the mass of people in the car. 'Look at this lot.' I looked at them. They were a colourful, happy, mostly female bunch, all bright dresses and laughter and flashing smiles. You'd rarely see so many smiles in the one place these days. At least not without a bottle of pills. Ed's mother saw me looking at her and waved, her smile as wide as the view of London. I returned the wave, and could not help but smile back at her. I was well in her good books because I'd remembered to tell her as we boarded the car that her hair looked wonderful. I mean, it did look good, but it wasn't the sort of thing I'd usually comment on because, well, I'm a man . . . but Ed had given me the tip years ago that, with black women in particular, complimenting them on their hair was a bigger step into their affections than anything else he could think of, certainly than anything else he could think of that was free. At the time I'd told him this was appallingly cynical and accused him of belonging to that vast and mostly black movement: Sexists Against Racism, but of course I'd used it ruthlessly ever since.

'I'm not some fuckin Yardie nutter,' Ed told me, nodding at his family. 'I got all them to fink of, an a career. I'm a bleedin businessman these days, know what I mean? I don't need the sorta people who never leave the ouse wifout a Uzi. I've seen what that leads to, Ken, an it's shit. It just does the job the cops an the racists want done for them. Fuckin ell; look at the States. Amount of black-on-black is fuckin heart-breakin, man. The amount of bruvvers in jail an on def row is fuckin obscene.'

'I know.' I sighed. 'I've mentioned this on the show.'

'Yeah, well a lot of that is down to fuckin ordnance, mate, an unless you got no uvver choices – which you ave – an you know zactly wot you're doin – which you don't – you just don't want to get involved.'

'I'm not asking you to hand me a piece, I just want a name, a number, a place to go. What was that pal of yours that did the time? Robe? Couldn't he—?'

'Na. Not Robe. Loss contact, aven't I?'

'Just a *number*, Ed.'

'I can't do that, Ken.'

'You mean you won't.'

'I can't wif a clear conscience. You know what I mean.'

'Yeah,' I said. 'I know what you mean.'

'If you feel freatened in London, take a holiday; go back to Scotland maybe.'

'I've got commitments, Ed, a show to do. I've got a contract.'

'Yeah, well, but maybe somebody's got one out on you.'

'That's why I thought a means to defend myself—'

'Look, either they're so crap you won't need a gun to get one over on them – like you already ave – or they're so good avin a Glock down the back of your 501s ain't gonna make a blind bit a difference. You ever see *Leon?*'

I looked at him. 'You know, I think you were right earlier; we should just admire the view.'

I didn't want to leave London. I liked it here. Part of it was pride; not wanting to run. Part of it was fatalism; depending who might or might not be after me, maybe they could get me anywhere, so I was better off where I had the most friends (even if the bastards wouldn't provide sanctuary or the means to defend myself). Part of it was I had a living to make and a job to do, which I happened to enjoy.

I bought a big, long Mag-Lite torch, a six-cell job even longer than the ones I'd seen security people carrying. A good, strong beam, but – at half a metre long – an even better club. It fitted neatly into the angle between the headboard of the bed and the mattress and sometimes if I woke up during the night, especially if Jo was away, I'd reach out and feel its smooth, massy, diamond-cut coldness, and be reassured, and fall asleep again.

One thing I hadn't told Ed was that Capital Live! and Mouth Corp were in on it now. Phil had insisted, and when I checked with Paul, my agent, he'd confirmed that there was a clause in my contract that meant I had to report any material threat to my life, my well-being or my potential ability to fulfil my contract to present the show. I should have felt outraged but actually I felt relieved.

Sir Jamie himself had phoned me from LA, assuring me that I'd be looked after. Mouth Corp's Head of Security, a grizzled, tough-looking ex-SAS geezer called Mick Beezley, had the alarm system on the *Temple Belle* replaced, a new CCTV monitor added on the quayside linked to Mouth Corp's own 24/7 Security Monitoring Centre, and an X-ray machine installed in the post room (we were, these days, already looking out for anthrax). A satellite tracking system was added to the Land Rover, also feeding in to the Monitoring Centre. Something called a Category Four Thatcham alarm system apparently made the Landy virtually impossible to interfere with or nick except by stealth helicopter. I didn't dare point out that adding all this electronic wizardry to something that was basically diesel, clockwork and string had probably increased its value – and presumably therefore its attraction to those of a thieving disposition – by about two thousand per cent.

I was told I could even have a bodyguard for times when I felt I might be especially vulnerable, though from past experience I suspected I was most vulnerable when I was being led by the dick by some flirtatious floozy and didn't want anybody else around in the first place (with the possible exception of her twin sister).

I said I'd think about the bodyguard idea.

'This is from the boss,' Mick Beezley growled, handing me a chunky box. 'The boss' was how he referred to Sir Jamie.

It was a watch. A very chunky watch with dials within dials and a rotating bezel with lots of marks and notches and tiny figures on it for working out when you might dream of making your last payment on it and it finally becoming yours and a variety of buttons and knobs including one very big one that looked like you could attach Big Ben to it and have a fair stab at winding the bastard. It looked like the sort of watch small boys used to think looked really cool (not nowadays; now they covet the sort of smooth, highly post-modern Spoon I was wearing). The thing looked like it was probably waterproof to the bottom of the Marianas Trench, but it also looked like the sort of watch there would be no point waterproofing because it was so fucking heavy it would drag you straight to the bottom the instant you dived into the briny. I stared at it, then at the piece of simply elegant sculpture on my wrist and then at the scarcely-less-chunky-than-the-watch features of Mick Beezley. 'What is this?' I asked him. 'Fucking James Bond?'

'That is a Breitling Explorer, that is,' Beezley rumbled. 'Instructions included, but basically if you pull this big button here, hard, a wire comes out and a signal goes out to a satellite. Only for use in genuine emergencies, otherwise you're left with a watch with a big long wire sticking out of it and no way of getting it back in again, and a very expensive repair bill. After a real emergency they repair it for free.'

'Does it work indoors?'

'Not so well.'

'Right. How much does it cost?'

'Three and a half grand. So don't lose it.'

'Bloody hell.'

'And it's not James Bond; you've been able to buy these over the counter for years.'

I studied it. 'I've obviously been shopping in the wrong jewellers.' I lifted it up. It wasn't as heavy as I'd anticipated, but it was heavy enough. 'Jesus. It does tell the time, too, I take it.'

Beezley looked at me. I looked at him. After a bit I scratched my head and said, 'Do they teach you that look in the SAS?'

'Okay, we're back to that phone/vibrator thing. For those of you new to the show, this is our long-running project to get somebody to build a mobile phone of the correct dimensions and degree of, ah, proofness to be used, by ladies, as . . . an intimate comfort device – I think that was the euphemism we settled on, wasn't it, Phil?'

'I recall so,' Phil agreed from the other side of the desk.

'So we're trying to get somebody to make it. Come on; there must be some enterprising manufacturer out there. They can make the damn things waterproof these days; what's the problem? Not new technology. Okay, so there might have to be a thin sort of aerial thingy hanging down . . . again . . .'

'There's a precedent,' Phil supplied.

'It has to be safe, it has to be shaped, it has to be comfortable and it has to work. Phone sex will take on a new meaning. When a woman says, Call me, you'll know she really means it, even though you also know you'll probably never get an answer.'

'Till home them cows does come.'

'Thank you, Phil.' I paused. 'Phil; you're looking smug. I realise you labour under the pathetic delusion that you deserve to look like that all the time because you're just so intrinsically fabulous, but why do you look so particularly smug right at this point in time?'

'That was a song lyric.'

'What? "Till home them cows does come"?'

'Yes.'

'Fascinating.'

'Joni Mitchell,' he said quietly, smiling. 'Or was it Melanie Safka?' Then he frowned.

I couldn't help it; I burst out laughing. 'You don't say? Again, not precisely on the button in terms of our target audience, Philip.'

'Permit a middle-aged man his little foibles.'

'Right. Foible away. Anyway. Come on,' I said. 'We're talking to one of the most vibrant cities in the world out there.' (Phil guffawed.) 'It can't be beyond the wit of human kind to invent a phone it'd be an utter pleasure for a woman to use.'

'And men,' Phil chipped in. I raised my eyebrows at him. 'Some men,' he said, shrugging. 'Just a thought.'

197

'Well, we do know you are of that persuasion yourself, Phil, but—'

'Well,' Phil said, taking off his glasses and starting to clean them with his hanky, 'being gay doesn't *automatically* mean you feel a desire, you might even say a burning desire, to put electronic vibratey type things anywhere near your sit-upon area.'

'Give the words "ring tone" a new resonance though, wouldn't it?' I said, laughing despite myself.

Phil grinned. 'Anyway . . .' he said lazily. 'Maybe this isn't really perfect morning-show material.'

I glanced at the call-monitoring screen. 'Phil, from the screen here I can see there are literally integers of people ringing in to disagree with you.'

'Let's hear what the people have to say, shall we?'

'Let's,' I agreed. 'But, listeners, be warned; any more calls consisting primarily of a buzzing noise and the sounds of human passion will be dealt with ruthlessly.'

'Or recorded and used later on a premium-rate line,' Phil added, up close.

'Jimmy,' I said. 'First-time caller from Lambeth. Wants to make a point about the show. What would that be, James?'

I clicked the line open. A quiet, even, male voice with no real accent said, 'They're going to need a new presenter for it, dead man.' Then the line went dead.

Phil could see the expression on my face. He bleeped the lot. I made a cut-off gesture and said, 'Woh! Serious bleep-work there. Mother, I've told you not to call me at work. Hopefully we'll find somebody with a civil tongue in their head on line five. Marissa, that's you. What have you got for us?'

'Ullo, Ken! Yeah! I'd like to place an order for one of them phones! But not too little a one!'

I clicked her off. 'Now *that* is more like the calibre of call

198

we need and want on this show! More, after – hey; some good music! How did that get in? – the Spooks.'

I hit Play and sat back, shaking.

Phil looked at me. 'You all right?'

'I'm fine,' I said, though I didn't feel it.

'Want to take a break? We can go back-to-back with the next few tunes.'

I took a deep breath. 'No. Fuck them. Proceed as normal.'

'Well, okay. But think we should maybe zoo it up a little?' Phil suggested. 'Get Kayla and Andi in too?' I knew what he was thinking of; have all four of us chattering on air, just one big squabbling family, and no more risky phone calls.

I glanced into the control room, where both our assistants were sitting looking serious and nodding through the glass at us. 'Yeah,' I said, 'why not?'

'I thought we weren't taking any more anonymous calls,' Debbie the Station Manager said. We were in a small meeting room in the middle of the building; her office was being redecorated. Phil and I were there, also Kayla and Andi, and Trish Eaton, station Human Resources manager (I was still trying to work out what Personnel had done to fall out of favour).

'We never!' Kayla protested. Andi, who'd also been taking caller details over the phones, nodded supportively.

'The number came up on the auto 1471 screen as normal,' Phil told Debbie. 'It was a mobile. I've passed the number on to the police, but they think it's almost certainly stolen. Or maybe a pay-as-you-go with no record of who bought it.'

Kayla sat back looking justified.

'Well, then, maybe you just shouldn't take any more phone calls at all, what do we think?' Trish suggested. She was a plumpish, matronly type with youthfully smooth facial skin and finely drawn eyebrows.

'Well, it's not our unique selling point, certainly,' I said. 'But it's an important part of the show. I'm loathe to lose it.' I looked round them all. 'So far these people haven't repeated trying to kidnap me, so maybe they won't repeat this, either. And we do still have the three-second delay.'

'This is even assuming the two things are linked,' Phil said, looking from me to Debbie. 'The thing in the taxi and the call this morning.'

'Yes,' I said. 'Let's look on the bright side; maybe this is just a *normal* death threat!' I looked round them, trying to appear reassuring and reassured. They were all looking at me. 'What?'

'Do you need to take some leave?' Debbie asked. Trish was nodding.

Oh shit, I'd misjudged it. 'No!' I said. I lowered my voice, both in volume and tone. 'And I don't believe in giving in to what is basically personal terrorism, either,' I said firmly. 'I say we carry on as normal. Otherwise the bad guys win. I don't think any of us –' I glanced meaningfully up at the portrait of the Dear Owner looking down at us from the wall. '– want to be a party to that, especially in the current climate. There is a war on, after all.' I looked at Trish and Debbie. Now they were both nodding, and I knew I'd won. *That* was the sort of bullshit they understood.

'Oh-kay,' Debbie said slowly. 'But any more calls like that and we pull the phone lines. Agreed?'

We all looked around, nodding.

'Maybe you should get another job,' Jo suggested.

'Why? I love my job!' I protested.

'Do you?' Jo stopped and turned to me. We were walking down Bond Street on the second Sunday in December. 'Ken, you hate most of what you do and what you're involved in.'

'What are you talking about?'

'Think about it. Would you listen to Capital Live! if you didn't have to?'

'Are you mad? Of course not!'

'The music you play; like that?'

'Don't be ridiculous! It's almost all shite during the day. Fucking Westlife and Hear'say. Things have come to a pretty grisly pass when you play Jamiroquai and they sound like a breath of fresh air.'

'What about the people who phone in?'

'With a few honourable exceptions, they're dullards, deadbeats, opinionated dingbats and bigoted fuckwits.'

'The adverts?'

'Don't even get me started on the fucking ads.'

'Fellow DJs?'

'Vapid cretins. Offer them a straight choice between opening another supermarket for a fat fee and sucking Sir Jamie's cock for nothing and their single brain cell would fuse.'

'The Tories? New Labour? American Republicans? The CIA? The IMF? The WTO? Rupert Murdoch? Conrad Black? The Barclay Brothers? What-d'you-call-him Berlusconi? George Dubya Bush? Ariel Sharon? Saddam Hussein? Thingy Farrakhan? Osama Bin Laden? The entire Saudi royal family? Muslim fundamentalists? The Christian Right? Zionist settlers? The UVF? Continuity IRA? Exxon? Enron? Microsoft? Tobacco companies? Private Finance Initiatives? The War Against Drugs? The Cult of the Shareholder?'

She only stopped, I assumed, because she ran out of breath. I stared at her for a moment, then shook my head. 'How *could* you leave out Thatcher?'

She spread her arms. 'There is just so much you hate, Ken. Your life, your working life; it's, like, full of stuff and people and things and organisations you just can't stand.'

'You're trying to make some sort of point here, aren't you?'

'In fact, forget your working life; your leisure life, too. Can we go to the States on holiday?'

'I've told you; not until—'

'Democracy is restored. Okay. Venice? Rome?'

'With that corrupt fuck in charge, surrounded by his fascist—'

'Australia?'

'With *their* racist immigration policy? No fucking—'

'China?'

'Not while the butchers of Tiananmen Square are still—'

'I rest my case. Is there anywhere—?'

'Iceland.'

'Iceland?'

'I'd love to go to Iceland, so long as they don't start whaling, obviously. Plus we have been to Egypt, and then there's France. I feel cool about going to France. I've finally more or less forgiven them for sinking the *Rainbow Warrior*. I've even started buying French wine again.'

'You've always bought French wine.'

'No, I haven't. It was embargoed; I had personal sanctions against it until about six months ago.'

'So what the hell is champagne?'

'Ah. Champagne is different. Though admittedly I ought to despise it on principle as a sort of geographical closed-shop. I look forward to the day when a workers' cooperative in New Zealand can produce the equivalent of a '75 Krug.'

'Jesus. Is there *anything* you really like, without qualification?'

'There's loads of things I like!'

'Like what?'

'Apart from the usual suspects?'

'I'm not talking about films.'

I laughed. 'Me neither. I mean apart from friends and family and world peace and little babies and Nelson bleedin Mandela.'

'Yeah. Exactly. What?'

'Students.'

'Students?'

'Yeah, it seems to be fashionable to be horrible about the little fuckers, but I think they're okay. If anything they're a bit too studious these days, not rebellious enough, but basically they're all right.'

'What else?'

'Cricket. I honestly believe cricket may well be the greatest game in the world. It is total heresy for a Scotsman to admit to this, and I entirely see the point of the American who said that only the English could invent a game that lasts for five days and can still end in a draw, but I just can't help it; I love it. I don't completely understand it and I still don't know all the rules, but there's something about its bizarrely erratic pace, its sheer complexity, its . . . psychology that just lifts it above any other sport. Even including golf, which is full of grotesquely over-paid reactionary bastards but is still a thing of skill and craft and beauty, and was, of course, invented in Scotland, like so much other truly neat stuff.'

'That's still only two things.'

I clicked my fingers. 'Liberals. The chattering classes. Political correctness. Basically I'm for 'em. Again, they get a bad press from veracity-challenged moral midgets employed by greedy zillionaires to wank-off bigots, but not me; I stand right by them. They're my kind of people. Liberals want niceness. What the hell is wrong with that? And, bless them, they do it in the teeth of such adversity! The world, people, are disappointing them all the time, constantly throwing up examples of what total shites human beings can be, but liberals just take it all, they hunker down, they grit their sandals and they keep on going; thinking well of people, reading the *Guardian*, sending cheques to good causes, turning up at marches, getting politely embarrassed by working-class oafism and just generally getting all hot under the collar when they see people being treated badly. That's the great thing about liberals; they care for people, not institutions, not nations, not religions, not classes, just people. A good liberal doesn't care whether it's their own nation or their own religion or their own class or their own anything that's being beastly to some other bunch of people; it's still wrong and they'll protest about it. I'm telling you, it's a sick, sick nation that turned the word "liberal" into an expletive. But there you are; the Yanks think basketball is a sport and that there's nothing cruel and unusual about taking four minutes to kill a man by putting thirty thousand volts through him.'

'Did you say you liked political correctness? News to me.'

'Political correctness is what right-wing bigots call what everybody else calls Being polite, or what everybody else calls Not being a right-wing bigot.'

Jo looked at me through narrowed eyes. 'I bet I could find tapes of you banging on about how political correctness was something else to hate.'

'Like everybody else, I have my own definitions of what is what, and I would never seek to deny that a few stupid people can take a perfectly good idea too far, but I stand by my contention that political correctness is more sinned against than sinning. Besides, a chap can change his mind. Oh, and journalists. I like them.'

'*What?*' Jo said, incredulous. 'You *hate* journalists!'

'No I don't, I just hate the ones who make up quotes, subsidise criminals, hound the innocent, collude with the truly talentless and otherwise squander their undoubted gifts on tat. A disgrace they assuredly are. But a journalist determined to get to the truth of a story, expose lies and corruption, to tell people what's really going on, to make one lot of humanity care for another lot, or even just start thinking about them? Weight-in-gold, they are. In fact, weight-in-microchips. Guardians of liberty. Mean more to democracy than most politicians. Fucking secular saints. Course, it helps if they're liberal, too. Don't shake your head at me, young lady. I'm being serious.'

'Now I know you're taking the piss.'

'I swear, I'm not!' I said, waving my arms. 'And I just thought of something else I like.'

'Yeah? What?'

I nodded. 'This city.'

'London?'

'Yep.'

'But you're always going on about how the tube is dirty, smelly and dangerous, and the traffic is awful, and the air stinks, and the people aren't as friendly as they are in Glasgow, and the drinks are too small and expensive, and it's not as exciting as New York or as civilised as Paris or as clean as Stockholm or as cool as Amsterdam or as groovy as San Francisco or—'

'Yeah yeah yeah, but just turn and look behind you. Look.'

Jo turned round and looked at the shop window she'd had her back to while we'd being going through all this stuff. We'd included Bond Street in our Sunday after-lunch stroll because I'd wanted to look in some posh jewellers and see if they had my excessive new watch. The shop we'd happened to stop outside was a jewellers. And its window was full of fish slices, suspended in the space behind the glass like a surreal hail of twinkling trowels. It was The Rabinovich Collection of Antique and Modern Silver Fish Slices, to quote the elegant sign in the window (we were a few doors down from a shop called Zilli, which seemed somehow appropriate). 'How the fuck,' I asked, 'can you not love a city that throws up stuff like that?'

Jo was shaking her head. She was blond again, and had taken to teasing her short hair into little meringue-like spikes. She stuck her arm through mine. She was wearing a silver puffa jacket. I wore an old RAF greatcoat an uncle had given me when I was seventeen. 'Come on,' she said. 'I'm getting cold.' We started walking again, heading south, back towards the river.

'And music, of course,' I said. 'I love music.'

'But you just said you hated the stuff you have to play.'

'Yeah, because it's commercial effluent. It's the sonic equivalent of a Coke or a McDonald's; it fills you up but it's just production-line shit and there's precious little in there that's really any good for you. The music I love is the music people make because they have to, because they need to, from their souls, not their wallets.'

'You don't believe in souls.'

'I don't believe in immortal souls. I just mean the kernel of who you are, not anything superstitious.'

'Yeah, well, be thankful you just have to play the stuff and don't need to get involved in the process of making it.'

'You make it sound like pies.'

'Pies?'

'Yeah. You know; that thing about it being a good idea – if you like eating pies – never, ever to see how they were made and what goes into them.'

'Yeah, well,' Jo said, hoisting one steel-studded eyebrow, 'believe me; there are a lot of pie bands out there.'

'I believe the same applies to sausages.'

'Ditto.'

I looked over to the far side of the street, at the DKNY shop. I remembered Ceel telling me about its five thousand red twin-towers T-shirts, nearly three months ago. In the December cold I shivered for the dark, baking heat of that hotel room. That had been another, solitary feature of today's walk, one I couldn't share with Jo. Our route had taken us past a few of the hotels I'd been in with Ceel. We had passed Claridge's just ten minutes earlier, and I'd almost suggested that we went in for a drink, or a pot of tea, or just the chance to pretend we were guests and get to ride in a lift that actually had a uniformed lift-operator, but in the end some prophylactic instinct, some grudgingly acknowledged requirement to obey Celia's stricture about keeping our affair as separate as possible from the rest of our lives, prevented me.

'Is *that* your watch?' Jo said, stopping at another jewellers' window and nodding at a display of chunkily sparkling Breitlings on a background of piled yellow cloth.

I glanced at the arm-lengthening bracelet of heavy metal-work on my left wrist. 'No,' I said. 'Not nearly expensive or complicated enough.'

Jo looked at my new watch and shook her head as we walked on. 'That thing makes you look ten years older, you know.'

'Don't diss my timepiece, ho.'

'It makes you look like you should be driving a Roller and shopping for – fucking hell; those.'

We both stared at and then walked quickly past a window containing two large thrones – mere chairs they were not – made of cut crystal and red velour.

'Holy shit.'

'Did we really see those?'

'I feel ill.'

We walked to the Embankment via St James's Park, through similarly sauntering locals and clumps of tourists, amongst coots, storks, black swans and panhandling squirrels. Ahead, the top of the London Eye stood out against sky, revolving almost imperceptibly over the departmental buildings of Whitehall like an ironic, skeletal halo.

'Hey! Skating. Cool.'

'Almost by definition,' I muttered. 'Look, can we head back after this? My feet are sore.'

'Yeah, okay.'

Jo guided me into the great courtyard of Somerset House, where a temporary ice rink had been set up for the winter holidays. Strings of lights articulated the wide quad. Tall windows, columns, arches and chimneys looked down upon the scene, where hundreds of people ambled about, sat swaddled in thick clothes outside little cafés, or stood watching the skaters, who circulated above the inscribed white ice like a slow, flat sweep of leaves caught in a stirring wind. I could smell coffee, fried onions and mulled wine.

Above us was a water-colour sky, hues bleeding and feeding and fading into each other as the light started to wane above the skeins of slowly drifting cloud.

On the ice, people laughed and shrieked, holding on to each other or the sides of the rink, doubled over, feet skidding. Squeals echoed off the courtyard's imposing architecture as people fell thumping to the cold, scarred surface of the rink. A gap opened in the crowds on the ice, there was a blur of rising blue as somebody jumped, and that was when I saw it was Celia.

She was dressed in a powder-blue skating outfit: tights, a short, flared skirt and a sort of tight tunic with a high neck and long sleeves. She wore brown gloves and white skates. Her hair was gathered up. Rising to the top of the jump that had first caught my attention, she twisted sleekly in the air, spinning once, then landed square on her right blade, knee bent, her left leg held out straight behind her. The quiet smack of her blade landing sounded across the ice between the circulating bodies; she sliced away, arms out to balance herself, sizzing across the ice in a wide, slowly tightening spiral. She skilfully avoided a couple of other skaters and then, with an elegant little skip, turned to skate backwards into a clearing space near the centre of the rink, stooping and tensing her body for another jump.

People got in the way, and I lost sight of her. I moved to the metal fencing describing the edges of the rink, putting my hands on the cold tube of rail, trying to see her again. Lengths of blue plasticised canvas were tied to the fencing and I could feel one of the plastic ties under my left hand. My mouth felt cold and dry and a swirl of wind made me feel the tears in the corners of my eyes. I saw her once more as the crowds on the ice parted again and her skimming, sinuous course brought her gliding on a metal hiss towards me like a fabulously exotic alien creature fallen into our mundane world from a higher reality.

I suddenly realised two things. The first was that I had never really seen this woman in daylight before. The second was that she was the most beautiful thing I had ever beheld.

She swivelled, poised, jumped and landed, and then swung into a neat spin, perfectly centred, not ten metres away. She brought her arms in and raised them above her head. The spin speeded up and her slim body became a tall blurred pillar of light blue above a spray of white, reflected light strobing off the glittering blades of her boots. She came out of it and pushed away again, edges aslant across the rasping surface. A smattering of applause from people on and off the ice followed her, and she smiled but didn't otherwise acknowledge the acclaim or look anybody in the eye. She passed only a couple of metres away from me and I swivelled to watch her. Her expression was diffident, almost embarrassed. A blush of rose glowed beneath the light-brown skin of her face.

A body leaned alongside me, rubbing against my side. 'She's good,' Jo said, putting her arm through mine again.

'Yes,' was all I could find to say. Celia went with the circulating people for a while, serene and smooth and steady.

'Huh. Got all the gear, too,' Jo said. 'Looks okay on her.'

'Yeah.'

'Fancy a glühwein?'

'Hmm?' I said. 'Oh, yeah. Yeah. Good idea.'

'My round. You going to stay here?'

'Ah . . . yeah, okay.'

'Back in a mo.'

When she came round the next time Celia was looking at the spectators, as if watching out for somebody. She saw me and did a brief double-take, but her expression barely wavered. She skated past me, not looking at me, scanning the crowds further round the boundary, then waved to somebody there and came to a stop at the edge of the ice about twenty metres away round the perimeter.

Mr Merrial was standing there.

The giant blond guy I'd assumed was his bodyguard when I'd seen them leaving Sir Jamie's party back in April stood at his side. I was amazed I hadn't noticed him.

Mr Merrial was talking to his wife. He looked right at me for a moment and nodded, though not in a way that meant Hello. I felt like an ice sculpture; frozen, fragile, ultimately doomed. Celia took the briefest of looks in my direction. My mouth had gone very dry, as if the saliva had frozen to my gums and teeth. The ground, the whole huge courtyard, seemed to tip beneath my feet. I gripped the metal rail tighter. In front of me a girl, almost doubled-over on the ice, felt her way past me, laughing, creasing the plastic canvas as she pulled herself along.

Mr Merrial was still looking at me, his pale, pinched face looking very white above the thick black coat he wore. His face was all there was to see; he wore gloves, a thick scarf and a Politburo hat. Celia was shaking her head. The big blond guy was looking at me too, now.

Oh shit. I looked away, trying to appear relaxed. I watched the other skaters. Some other people were quite good, too, doing jumps and spins where they could find the space. I brought my right elbow in, just reassuring myself that my mobile was still on my belt. Had I turned it on this morning? I didn't always, on a Sunday. I couldn't remember for sure. I suspected I hadn't.

I shook my left wrist, feeling the suddenly reassuring weight of the big watch.

I risked a sideways glance. Celia was still shaking her head, looking, from her body language, as if she was arguing or pleading with her husband. He was nodding, then shaking his head. Celia spread her arms in what looked like a gesture of defeat, tipped her head to one side, was greeted with a nod, and then skated quickly away, pushing towards the far side of the rink.

I quickly looked back at the other skaters. Oh fuck, we hadn't been discovered, had we? He didn't know, did he? Oh fuck, why did we have to come here? Why couldn't we have caught a bus or a taxi back home from the Embankment? Why hadn't I thought that of course Celia skated, so she might be here, I might see her, and of course if she was here she would probably be with her husband? Why hadn't I just slunk away the instant I'd noticed her? Why did I have to stand like a love-struck adolescent staring at her? Why did she have to see me and do that tiny, fatal double-take? Why did Merrial have to be so fucking observant? Oh shit, why the *fuck* wasn't life a computer game where you could go back and re-live the last few minutes and make a different choice?

I looked back again. The big blond guy had disappeared. I looked round as frantically as anyone can without actually moving their head. I couldn't see him anywhere. How the hell could I miss him? Jesus, they wouldn't try anything here, would they? Too many people. And there were cops around; I'd seen two lots at least. Merrial had gone, too. He—

'Mr Nott?' said a voice at my back.

I froze, staring down at the ice. A pale flash of blue, some-where out there. I turned.

'John Merrial.' The man put his hand out. I shook it.

His face was slim, almost delicate, close up. He looked slightly sad and infinitely wise. His eyebrows were thin and very black, lips thin and very pale. Eyes bright blue. Contained by the coat, the scarf and the fur hat, his face looked unreal somehow, like something two-dimensional seen upon a screen.

'Hello,' I said. My voice sounded very small.

'That was my wife there; in blue,' he said. His voice was

211

quiet. Almost accentless. I saw a massive blond head over the crowds behind him.

'Very good,' I said, gulping the words. 'Isn't she?'

'Thank you, yes, she is.' He narrowed his eyes. 'I think we were both at a party Jamie Werthamley threw, weren't we? Back in the spring. Limehouse Tower. We were never introduced, but I think I saw you, now you've been pointed out to me.'

'I believe we were,' I said. I'm fucking your wife, I'm fucking your wife, I'm fucking your wife, I kept thinking, some suicidally insane bit of my brain wanting to blurt it out, to just say it, to get this over with, to make the worst that could happen actually happen and not have to keep imagining it.

'How is Jamie?' He smiled.

'Fine. Last time I saw him.' Which was at that same party, come to think of it; the party where I met your wife and snogged her and felt her up and agreed to this patently suicidal affair in the first place.

'Good. Pass on my regards, will you?'

Oh, you mean you're not going to kill me right now? 'Ah, happily. Certainly. Yes.'

He looked past me, out to the ice. 'My wife listens to you on the radio,' he said.

Yes. And that hand you just shook has been inside her sweet cunt. See this tongue, these lips? Think of her ears, her nipples, her clitoris. 'Really? I'm, I'm very flattered.'

He gave a thin smile. 'She doesn't want me to ask you this, but I know she'd be very happy if you played a request for her sometime.'

'Well, we don't really do requests,' I heard some fuckwit part of my brain say.

What?

'Oh,' he said, looking down for a moment.

Was I fucking *crazy*?

His coat looked thick and very dark and glossy.

Did I really want to die that fucking *much*?

He wore narrow, black, highly polished brogues and very fine black leather gloves, though he'd taken off the right one to shake my hand.

'But,' I said, clapping my hands together and smiling. 'For . . . for . . .' For somebody I'm shagging the fucking arse off for hours on end whenever I get the opportunity. 'For a friend of Sir Jamie's, and . . . and for such a beautiful, ah, ice-skater . . . I think we can make an exception.' I nodded. Merrial was smiling now. 'In fact I'm certain we can,' I told him. Because you see I have absolutely no principles whatsoever, when it comes right down to it, and I'll do anything – anything at all – to save my miserable, lying, hypocritical hide.

'That's very kind, Mr Nott,' he said evenly. 'I appreciate it.'

'Oh, ah, not at all.' I *love* doing favours for people I hate.

He twisted from the waist about two degrees as he said, 'Here's my card.' And the big blond guy with the metre-wide shoulders was suddenly there at Merrial's side and presenting me with a plain white business card, which I took quickly so they wouldn't see my trembling fingers. 'Call me if I can ever do you a favour.'

'Ah, right.' Well, you could die conveniently. How about that? I put the card in a pocket. 'Thank you.'

Mr Merrial nodded slowly. 'Well, we have to go now. Good to meet you.'

'And you.' You fucking nasty murdering gangster bastard.

Mr Merrial turned to go, then stopped. 'Oh,' he said. He smiled his blade-thin smile again. Fucking hell, you crime lord cunt, I was just about getting my jangling nerves back into some sort of order and now you're giving me a fucking *Colombo* moment? 'I should tell you her name, shouldn't I?' Of course you shouldn't, you dickhead, there's no fucking need; it's Celia. Ceel. Babe babe babe sometimes when I'm coming deep inside her.

213

'Oh! Well, yes, it might help.'

'It's Celia Jane.'

'Celia *Jane?*' I blurted. Well done, Kenneth, put plenty of emphasis in there. Clearly you do still want to die.

He nodded. 'Celia Jane.' He reached out and patted my elbow once before turning away.

They moved off through the crowd, the blond dude leaving a spacious wake. Celia – sorry; Celia Jane – left the ice at one of the rink's access points and they met her there. The blond guy produced a coat and a pair of shoes for her. She didn't look at me and she held on to her husband's arm while she changed from the skates to the shoes. I wiped my eyes with my hands. When I opened my eyes again, Mr and Mrs Merrial and their bulky minder had gone.

I was still shivering when Jo arrived back with two little polystyrene cups of steaming mulled wine.

'Here. Look like you need it, too. You're very pale. You okay?'

'Just fine. Thanks.'

'You fuckin *spoke* to the guy? He shook *hands* wif you?'

'His wife's a fan.'

'What of? Knee-cappings?'

'Of mine, you buffoon.'

'You're fuckin kiddin me, man!' Ed's voice went very high; the speaker in my mobile struggled to cope.

I filled in the details of meeting Mr M at Somerset House.

'Aow yeah; they used to register stuff there, didn't they? Burfs and marriages. An defs.'

'Yeah, well, now it's got an artificially cold heart and that's where I bumped into him.'

'An you're goin to play his missus a record?'

'Damn right I am.'

'Sweet, man! An he says now he owes you a favour?'

'Well, that's what he implied, but—'

214

'Ask him to find out who's got it in for you, then. Fuckin ell, dedicate a whole show to his bitch an he'll fuckin rub them out for you as well.'

'I think that might be a little excessive.'

'He's an excessive geezer, mate.'

'Yeah, well, I think I'll keep him well away from whatever messes I'm already in.'

'Wisdom, Kennif.'

I drummed the fingers of my left hand on my right arm. I was standing on the deck of the *Temple Belle*, looking out at the dark waters. Jo was below, opening some Korean take-away containers just delivered from a restaurant in Chelsea. I'd felt I just had to tell somebody at least something of what had happened that afternoon, and Ed had been the obvious choice. 'Or do you think maybe I should ask him for help?' I said. 'I know he's a villain but he did seem quite friendly; helpful, almost. I mean, maybe—'

'Na, I don't really fink you should. I was kiddin. Just you keep your skinny white ass away from people like that.'

'You sure?'

'I'm sure, man.'

'Yeah, but he didn't seem *that* bad, I mean—'

'Listen. I'm gonna tell you sumfink about your Mr Merrial.'

'What?'

'It's a bit orrible, but I fink you need tellin.'

'What, then?'

'Right.' I heard Ed take a deep breath. Or possibly a toke. 'He's got this really big fucker works for him, right? Blond geezer built like a fuckin nuclear bunker.'

'I've seen him. He handed me Mr M's card this afternoon.'

'Right. Well, this is wot I heard from somebody wot was there when this appened once. When Mr Merrial wants to find sumfink out from somebody wot does not want to tell him, or if he's upset wif somebody, right, he has them tied to a chair wif their legs straight out an their feet tied to another chair, and then the big blond guy comes an sits on their legs an bounces up and down wif increasin force until either they talk or their knees bend the wrong way and their legs snap.'

'Oh for fuck's sake! Oh Jesus Christ, that's fucking *sick*.'

'An I eard this from a bruvver who is definitely wot you'd call a usually reliable source, too, mate, an not given to tellin milky whites. He was taken along to see wot would happen to him if he ever crossed Mr Merrial. Actually I fink the bruvver must have tried on sumfink very slightly dodgy himself an Mr M wanted to give him a ever so mild warning. So he got to see. And hear.'

'I feel ill.'

'This bruvver's a big fucker, too. An he can handle himself, but I swear when he was tellin me all this he fuckin went grey. Grey, Kennif.'

'Green,' I gulped. 'Me; now.'

'Yeah, well, I juss fot you ought to know, before you go gettin any more involved wif people like that.'

'Ken?' Jo yelled from below.

'That's my tea out, Ed. Though I do seem to have lost my appetite, for some reason. Anyway, thanks for the warning.'

'No probs.'

'I'll see you.'

'Yeah; you take care. Strenf, bruvver. Bye.'

I didn't look properly at Mr Merrial's card until the following morning, just before doing my under-vehicle bomb-check and heading for work. The Merrials lived in Ascot Square, Belgravia. I stopped at the side of the Landy and wondered about putting their home number into my phone, then decided I ought to. I placed it in Location 96, overwriting Celia's mobile number. I never had got round to removing it

216

– I still liked scrolling through to look at it sometimes – but entering her home phone there seemed fitting somehow.

I'd barely finished doing this when the phone buzzed in my hand; Phil, at the office. It was another dull December day and the rain had just started. I de-alarmed and unlocked the Landy and climbed in out of the rain as I said, 'Yup?'

'*Breaking News.*'

I put the keys in the ignition. 'What about it?'

'It's starting on Jan fourteenth.'

'What, *next* year? Kind of rushing things a bit, aren't they?'

'It's a month away. But it's definite, this time.'

'Of course it is, Philip.'

'No, it's firmly scheduled. And you're in it.'

'Not the world's most reassuring phraseology.'

'They've started doing publicity and everything.'

'Everything. Well.'

'The PR people are mentioning your name. There's a buzz.'

'A sound so often associated with dead, decaying things, don't you find?'

'Will you stop being so sodding cynical?'

'Probably shortly after I stop being so damn alive.'

'I thought you'd want to know.'

'You're right. It was the uncertainty that was killing me.'

'If all you can do is be sarcastic—'

'Then it should be a good show today.'

I heard him laugh. I went to start the Landy, then sat back again and waved my hands even though Phil couldn't see me. 'Oh, for Christ's sake,' I said. 'Why do TV people have to make such a big deal about everything? It's one fucking item on a minority interest telly show, not an unknown play by Shakespeare written on the back of the missing bit from the "Unfinished Symphony".' I put my hand on the keys again.

Phil said, 'You on your way in?'

'Better than being on the way out.'

'Save it for the show. Safe journey.'

'It's Chelsea to Soho, Phil, not the Paris–Dakar rally.'

'So we'll see you soon. Take care.'

'Yeah, bye.'

I put the phone away. I looked at my hand, resting on the Landy's keys, dangling from the ignition. People kept telling me to take care. I looked out across the Landy's battered bonnet, still not twisting the key in the ignition. It was raining quite hard now. I sighed, then got out and did the checking-for-bombs-under-the-vehicle bit. Nothing there.

'I'm all for globalism. I mean, if you're talking about the sort of globalisation that says, Stuff whatever you people voted for, you'll let us privatise your water and hike the prices five hundred per cent or else, then, no. Exclude me in. What I'm for is the globalism of the United Nations, imperfect though it may be, the globalism of arms treaties, the globalism of the Geneva Convention – possibly the next suspect piece of internationalism Dubya and his chums will want to withdraw from – the globalism of the International Court of Justice the US refuses to sign up for, the globalism of anti-pollution measures, and d'you know why, Phil? Because the winds know no boundaries. The globalism of the—'

'The ground.'

'What?'

'The ground, and the sea, and space. Those are boundaries, for the wind.'

I hit the FX of a lonely desert wind blowing through a long-abandoned ghost town, tumbleweed rolling across the dust between the creaking wooden ruins.

'What, like that?' I said, glaring at him.

'Possibly.' He was grinning back at me over his *Wall Street Journal*.

'I was, just possibly, on a roll there.'

'I've interrupted your flow, haven't I?'

'You are a veritable stopcock, Philip.'

'U-bend.'

'Beg pardon?'

'I thought I'd get that in before you did.'

'You're just a trust fund of straight lines this morning, aren't you?'

'It's a living.'

'Listen, Phil, if I may be allowed to put on my Serious Voice for a moment.'

'Oh no, not another Charity Announcement.'

'No. But, Philip, as you know, we don't tend to do requests.'

Phil looked surprised. 'Well, we can't; most of those you receive are anatomically impossible anyway.'

'I think you'll find there's a small private clinic in Tangier that would happily prove you wrong, for a price, Philsy-Willsy, but that's as maybe.'

'Keep going.'

'Na, yesterday I bumped into somebody I met at a party once and I said I'd play a request for his wife.'

Phil blinked at me. I raised the dead air stopwatch threateningly. 'Is that it?' he said.

'Sometimes, Phil, it's just banality all the way down.'

'Is this a new spot on the show? Guess The Relevance?'

'Nope. So, for the lovely Celia Jane, here's "Have a Nice Day", from the Stereophonics.'

I hit Play and swept the faders.

Phil looked nonplussed. He looked at the faders and listened to the song play in his headphones. 'You're not even talking up to the vocals,' he said, more to himself. He spread his arms. 'What's all this about?'

I eased my cans down round my neck to give my ears a rest. 'What you hear is what you get,' I told him. I nodded at the

219

unit spinning the CD. 'We were going to play it anyway. No extra paperwork involved.'

The skin around his eyes crinkled. 'You trying to get into this woman's knickers?'

'Phil! I told you; she's married.'

Phil laughed loudly. 'Since when has that ever stopped you?'

'You can be so cynical sometimes, Philip. You want to watch it; the wind'll change and you'll stay that way.'

'It's protective coloration around you, chum.'

'What's wrong with playing a request?'

'We never do it.'

'So it's a change.'

'There has to be an ulterior motive somewhere.'

'Will you just leave it? There's nothing going on.'

'I know the way your mind works, Ken. There has to be. You're more a creature of habit and ritual than you think you are.'

I shook my head. 'Okay, I confess I was put in a slightly awkward situation by a . . . a friend of Sir Jamie's,' I said, glancing at the track's run time on the play list and then at the studio clock.

'Ah-*hah*!'

'There's no bleedin Ah-hah! to it. Look; the guy's some sort of big shot, he knows the Dear Owner, we met unexpectedly yesterday and I sort of stumbled into promising I'd play a song for his missus.'

'Who is a looker, I bet,' Phil said.

'He's a big shot, like I say. They usually are. See people like that with a plain or ordinary-looking woman and you know it must be love. Will you *stop* looking at me like that?'

'Well, this was unexpected.'

'I wanted to say thank you.'

'Jesus, what sort of Christmas box do you tip your postman?'

220

Ceel smiled. 'Also, I won't be able to see you again until after the New Year. I'm sorry.'

'Ah well.'

'You had something planned this afternoon, didn't you?'

I shook my head. 'Nothing; appointment with some lawyers. They can wait.'

'You're not in trouble, are you?'

'No,' I said. 'It's not my own lawyers. Just a statement about an accident I witnessed a month or two back. So, what are you doing over the holidays?'

'Going home.'

'To the island?'

'Yes.'

'Mr M too?'

'Yes. And what about you?'

'Staying here in London.' Almost a year earlier it had been agreed I'd spend Xmas with Jo and her family in Manchester, but now Jo would be abroad over Christmas and New Year, dutifully helping Addicta strike while the iron of fame was hot. I couldn't even go back to see my own parents; they'd decided long ago they were fed up with Scottish winters and the whole seasonal rigmarole, and had spent the last few holidays – and would be spending the one up-coming – in Tenerife. 'Anyway, I'm glad we could meet up now.'

'It was just luck that John had to leave this morning. Amsterdam, again.' She looked at her watch, which was all she was wearing. A flicker of a frown had passed across her face as she'd pronounced the word 'Amsterdam'. 'However, we only have until two thirty.'

I levered myself up on one elbow and looked at her in the soft light spilling from the bathroom and a reading light above the scroll-top desk. She lay luxuriantly, legs spread, brown-gold hair strewn across the white sheets and one plump pillow like a fabulously braided river delta, one arm drawn up underneath her head, the fern-print of the long-ago lightning a fabulous marquetry on her dark honey skin. 'I had no idea you'd be there yesterday,' I told her. I shook my head. 'You looked so, so beautiful. I should have ducked away but I couldn't take my eyes off you.'

She stroked my arm. 'It's all right. I was worried, when I realised he'd seen me recognise you, but he thought he knew you already, from the party, or perhaps a photograph in the papers. He has a very good memory.'

'So he left early this morning and didn't hear me play your record?'

'Yes. But I heard it.'

I looked around. 'And decided on here.'

We were back at the Dorchester where our affair had begun. The big tree outside, the one we'd stared at from the suite a couple of floors above, in the mix of moon and flood light back in May, was leafless now. No silence this time. I said, 'I confess I had been wondering what you'd do when you ran out of posh hotels we hadn't already been to. One scenario I imagined had us going steadily down-market until we ended up sharing a bottom bunk in a dormitory in a back-packers' hostel in Earl's Court.'

She gave a small laugh. 'That would be an awful lot of assignations, even restricting ourselves to central London.'

'I'm an optimist. So, what did make you decide to come back here?'

'Well, I had thought to return on our first anniversary . . .'

'Really?' I said, smiling broadly. 'There *is* romance in your trim little soul after all, Celia Jane.'

She pinched my arm, making me yelp and have to rub the site. There might be a bruise. This was especially mean, of course, because I was not allowed to leave a mark on her.

'Ah,' she said, holding up one finger. 'But then I thought that that would be a kind of a pattern in itself, and so dangerous.'

'You would have made such a great spy.'

'And also it felt like something had changed, now that our different worlds have become entangled again.'

'A wee, cowering, terrified part of me imagined that it had changed utterly, and you would never want to see me again,' I confessed. 'Spell broken. You know.'

'Did you really imagine that?'

'Oh yes. I'm thankful I only had one night to lose sleep over it, but yes, I did. You have this thing about separation and entanglement, and a set of beliefs I find perfectly bizarre and that I can't comprehend or anticipate the results of . . . For all I knew, to you, yesterday was some sort of sign, a bolt from the heavens that absolutely meant – without argument or appeal, and according to a kind of faith I don't even begin to understand – we were over.'

She looked almost sleepy as she said, 'You think I'm irrational, don't you?'

'I think you behave like the most rational person I've ever met, but you claim to have this completely crackpot belief in your own half life/half death and a spookily entangled twin in another universe. Maybe that is profoundly rational in some deep sense that has eluded me until now, but I don't feel any nearer seeing it than I was when you sprang this frankly wacko ideology on me in the first place.'

She was silent for a moment. Those almond amber eyes gazed up at me, steady flames in a deep well. 'You are a globalist, aren't you?'

'Hey, you *were* listening.'

She smoothed her fingers through my chest hair, then gently took a fist of it and let her hand hang there, caught up. 'You make such a big thing,' she said, 'of developed countries, rich countries, not being allowed to impose their ways of life and their way of thinking and of doing business on smaller or poorer countries, and that extending to religions and customs and the

223

like, and yet you want to make everybody think the same way. You're like most people who have to . . . fulminate about things; you want everybody to think the same way you do.'

'Doesn't everybody?'

'But it is true, isn't it? You want the one way of thinking spread everywhere, throughout the world, replacing all the different ways of thinking that have grown up in all the different places and peoples and cultures. You are a colonialist of the mind. You believe in the justified imperialism of Western thought. Pax logica; that is what you believe in. You wish to see the flag of your rationalism planted firmly in every brain on the planet. You say you don't care what people believe in, that you respect their right to worship as they wish, but you don't really respect the people or their beliefs at all. You think that they are fools and what they believe in is worse than useless.'

I flopped onto my back. I let out a deep breath. 'Okay,' I said. 'Do I want people to think the way I do? I suppose I do. But I know it's never going to happen. Do I respect other people's beliefs? Shit, Ceel, I don't know. There's this saying about how you should respect a man's religious beliefs the same way you respect his belief that his wife is the most beautiful woman in the world. Casual – and hopefully non-malicious – sexism aside, I can see that. I do accept I could be wrong. Maybe the . . . the Abrahamists are right. Maybe their cruel, woman-hating, woman-fearing unholy trinity of mega-cultism is spot-on after all.

'Maybe, even, some tiny, tiny little strand of it, like, for example, the Wee Frees, who are part of the Presbyterian movement in Scotland, which is itself part of the Protestant franchise, which is part of the Christian faith, which is part of the Abrahamic belief-set, which is one of the mono-theistic religions . . . maybe they and only they – all few thousand of them – are absolutely bang on the money in what they believe and how they worship, and everybody else has been wrong-diddly-wrong-wrong all these centuries. Or maybe the One True Way has only ever been revealed to a one-man cult within the outer fringes of Guatemalan Highland Sufism, reformed. All I can say is, I've tried to prepare myself for being wrong, for waking up after I've died and finding that – uh-oh – my atheism was actually, like, a Really Big Mistake.'

I got up on one elbow again. 'And do I think reason should replace irrationality? Well, yes. Yes, I do. Guilty as charged. And, bless it, society really is to blame. Society and education and enquiry and doubt and argument and disputation and progress; all the schools and libraries and universities, all the scholars and monks and alchemists and teachers and scientists. Faith is fine for poetry, for images and metaphors and art and for telling us who we are, who we've been. But when faith tries to describe the world, describe the universe, it just plain gets it wrong. Which wouldn't matter if it admitted it was wrong, but it can't, because all it's got is its unwavering certainty in its own infallibility; the rest is smoke and mirrors, and admitting imperfection brings the whole lot tumbling down. There are no crystal spheres, and the planets are not the result of some sky god's wet-dream. If that is supposed to be taken literally, then it's a lie, plain and simple. If it's a metaphor, then it has bugger all to do with the way things really work. Reason works, the scientific method works. Technology works.

'If people want to respect their environment by believing that the fish they eat might have been an ancestor, or learn to lower toilet seats because their chi is leaking out, I'm happy to accept and even honour the results even if I think the root of their behaviour is basically barmy. I can live with that, and with them. I hope they can live with me.'

She spread her hand flat against my chest. I could feel my heart beating hard. I shouldn't let this sort of thing get to me like this, but I had no choice. This stuff was important to me; I couldn't help it.

'Sometimes,' she said quietly, looking at her own hand, or perhaps at my skin. 'Sometimes I think we are like different coloured bishops on a chess board, you and I.'

'Bishops? After all I've just said?'

She smiled, still spreading her hand on my chest, as though trying to span the distance between my nipples. 'Better to be a queen,' she agreed.

'You'll just have to take my word for it that I'd rather be a pawn than a bishop. At least they can transcend their origins.'

'I believe you.'

'Or a knight. I've always liked the fact a knight has what is basically a three-dimensional move on a two-dimensional surface. And the castle; there's something about the bluff, blunt power of the rook that attracts me as well. And it does do a potentially three-dimensional thing, too, just once, come to think of it, castling. Bishops are more devious, somehow, sliding in between pieces like a knife through ribs. The king, of course, is simply a liability.'

'I was thinking,' she said, 'of bishops on opposing sides, and of different colours as well. Just the two of them there on the chess board, with no other pieces present.'

I nodded. I saw, now, what she meant.

'They could never connect,' I said. 'They could slide past each other for ever, but never affect. They appear to inhabit the same board, but really they don't. Not at all.'

She looked up at me with heavy-lidded eyes, her head tipped fractionally to one side. 'Don't you think?'

'Perhaps. And is that us?'

'Maybe. Maybe all men and women. Maybe all people.'

'For ever? Without exception? Without hope?' I tried to say it lightly.

She took my cock in her hand, then brought her other hand

226

out from underneath her head and cupped her sex. 'We connect here . . .' She smiled. (A smile, it seemed to me just then, fit to light up the universe inside the skull; a smile, indeed, to light up two. A smile to illuminate infinities.) '. . . That will have to do for now.'

Seven

SEXUAL PIQUE

'Nikki! Oh my God! What have you *done?*'
　'Verhoeven? Underrated?' I thought about this. 'How?'
　'Hendrie. Aston Villa. Separated at birth.'
　'Wanking; why the bad press?'
　'Knock-knock.'
　'You know; all mouth and no trousers.'
　'The hell with you, grounded on Mount Arafat.'
　Craig was having a Hogmanay party at his place in Highgate.

'Ken, hi! What? Oh, I cut my hair. Like it?'
　'No! It's—'
　'Shorter. Easier to wash. Different.'
　'Yeah, and sort of browny-black. Are you mad?'
　'You sound like my dad.'
　'But you had beautiful hair!'
　'I still do, thanks.'

'Fink about the endin of *Total Recall.*'
　I sniggered.
　'Zactly.'

'What d'you mean "Zactly"? You can't just say "Zactly" and look all justified and smug like that. Explain yourself, man.'

'Wot was that reaction of yours there then, what was that all about?'

'It was about a totally preposterous ending featuring the Pyramid Mine – a biggish hill but still less than a pimple on a planetary scale – emplacing an entire Martian atmosphere at what appeared to be Standard Temperature and Pressure in about half a minute, complete with milky clouds and everything, in time to put Arnie and the ingenue's eyes back into their sockets about a minute after they started haemorrhaging, all with no lasting ill effects whatsoever to bodies either planetary or human.' I thought about what I'd just said. 'Or Arnie's, for that matter.'

Ed nodded. 'Zactly.'

'You're doing it again! Will you stop with the fucking "Zactly" shit already?'

'Hee hee hee.'

'Yeah, and the "Hee hee hee" thing is no great improvement.' I took Ed by the shoulders and through gritted teeth said, 'What the fuck do you *mean*?'

'Wot I mean is,' Ed said, giggling, 'right, is that it is basically so fuckin preposterous a endin that it can only mean, right, that Arnie, is character that is, must still be in a virtual reality dream. None of the endin's been real, azit?'

I opened my mouth. I took my hands off his shoulders. I wagged a finger at him. 'Hmm,' I said.

'An that therefore, like, that Verhoeven geezer is a subversive genius.'

I stood there, nodding, trying to recall more of the earlier parts of the film.

'Course,' Ed said, 'it's only a feery.'

'Hendrie who?'

'Hendrie; plays for Villa. You must have seen him.'

'No I mustn't. Why?'

'He looks like Robbie Williams.'

'. . . Craig, you need to get out more.'

'I *was* out. I went to the match. That's where I saw him.'

'Okay, you should stay in more.'

'Phil, "Wanking; why the bad press?" is not funny. Now, "Button pushers; why the bad press?"; that has a modicum of comedic value. Only a modicum, not enough to actually use in the show or anything, but I employ it purely as an example.'

'I was thinking of a new phone-in feature.'

'Right. Well, there are ladies on the end of premium-rate phone lines dedicated to ensuring this sort of thing is already well catered for. I'm told.'

'That wasn't what I was thinking of.'

'Well what, then? A sponsored wank-o-thon?'

'No no no. Right; it'll be called Get a Hold of Yourself.'

'Uh-huh. You've always been jealous Chris Evans had that *Breakfast Show* feature where a girl got her boyfriend's "lollipop" in her mouth and recited lyrics, haven't you?'

'Nooo; look—'

'Phil; no. Just leave it.'

'Really?'

'Yes.'

'You don't think—?'

'I think you should go and talk to Craig.'

'Who's There?'

'Tijuana.'

'Tijuana who?'

'Gary Glitter.'

'. . . *What?*'

'Tijuana be in my gang, my gang, my gang?'

* * *

'Oh, I understand the meaning it's meant to have,' I told Amy, leaning closer to her. We were on the decking in Craig's garden, near midnight. I'd just tried to talk to Jo, in Barcelona with Addicta, but without success. 'It's just not the meaning I took from it the first time I heard it. That's what I'm saying.'

'What, "Fur coat and no knickers"?'

'Yeah! I always thought, Damn, that sounds great! That sounds, like, *really sexy*!'

She laughed, putting her head back to show a long, winter-tanned neck and perfect teeth. Her blond hair glowed softly in the light falling from the lit windows of the house. 'Yes, well, you would.'

'Witty but unfair. Look, I—'

'You don't know what it feels like. You just have no idea. All you've got is your theory, just your precious one-man-party line, as usual. You have no concept what it's like. You haven't been there. You haven't felt the atmosphere. We're surrounded by people who hate us.'

'Ah, excuse me? This is me you're talking to here. I'm all too well acquainted with the tell-tale tingle on the temple that indicates the cross-hairs of antipathy have locked on to me once more. But just . . . just back up a bit, there; who's this "we"? When the hell did you become a Daughter of the Zionist Revolution?'

'When I realised it was them or us, Ken.'

'Oh, fuck, you mean you really *are*? Jeez, I was just—'

'They all hate us. Every nation on our borders would like to see us destroyed. Our only way out's the sea, and that's where they want us. Ken, just look at the map! We're tiny! And then, inside our own nation, these people murder and bomb and shoot us, inside our own borders, on our own streets, in the shops, on the buses, in our homes! We've got to stop them; we have no choice. And you, you have the gall to claim that we've become the Nazis, and can't see you've become just another bloody anti-Semite.'

'Oh, fuck, Jude, look, I know you feel really deeply about this—'

'No you *don't*! That's what I'm saying. You can't!'

'Well, I'm trying to! Look . . . please, please don't put words into my mouth or beliefs into my mind that aren't there.'

'They are there, Ken, you just won't accept it.'

'I am *not* anti-Semitic. Look, I *like* the Jews, I *admire* the Jews, I'm positively *pro*-Semitic for fuck's sake. I've told you this! Well, some of it! I've been this way since I was a kid, since I heard about the Holocaust and since I realised that the Scots and the Jews were so alike. The Scots are smart, but we get accused of being mean. Same with the Jews. It's culture, not race, but we've both punched way above our weight for civilisation; the Jews are the only people I ever put ahead of the Scots in terms of their influence on the world given the size of their population pool.'

'This is so bullshit.'

'I'm serious. I loved you guys from when I was a kid! So much I was embarrassed to tell *you* how much!'

'Don't bullshit me.'

'It's *true*. You were just so fearsomely far to the left I never dared.'

'Ken—'

'I'm serious. I used to love Israel.'

(This was true. When I was thirteen I'd fallen deeply in love with a girl called Hannah Gold. Her parents lived in Giffnock, one of the more leafy parts of Glasgow's suburban southern hinterland. They took a dim view of our friendship and my obvious infatuation with their daughter. But I charmed them, plus I did my research. Within six months Mr G was expressing his pleased surprise at how much I knew about Israel and the Jews. The Golds moved to London shortly after

235

Hannah's fourteenth birthday and we were pen pals for a while, but then they moved again and we lost touch. I'd been heartbroken when they left, but I recovered and went on, going from desolation to something shamingly close to indifference in about three weeks.

My new interest in Israel proved rather longer lasting. And at the time I didn't see how anybody could *not* love Israel. It was the world's most charismatic, brave, buccaneering nation, defying all these bullies around it. The Six Day War, Dayan and his eye-patch, a woman prime minister, the kibbutzim; when I was a kid I was so proud it was British-built tanks that had gone sailing across the Sinai with the Star of David flying from the whip aerials. I used to get books out the library about Israel. *Great Jewish Generals*; can you believe Trotsky was in there? I even knew that the Israeli army had improved their Centurions by putting petrol engines in place of the British diesels; I knew all that adolescent, war-geek stuff, I loved it. Yom Kippur; triumphing against the odds, nicking their own boats from under the noses of the French, the raid on Entebbe; it was breath-taking, cinematic! How could anyone not admire all that?)

'But that was before the invasion of Lebanon, before Sabra and Shatila—'

'That was done by *Christian* militias,' Jude protested.

'Oh, come on! It was Ariel Sharon who let them off the leash, and you know it. But that was the start; I began to wake up to what had happened to the Palestinians, to all the UN resolutions that Israel had just ignored, that it was uniquely *allowed* to ignore, then to the history – "The bride is beautiful, but she is already wed" – and to the illegal settlements, and the secret nukes. I heard what Rabbi Kehane believed, what his followers still believe, I saw the bodies lying bleeding in the mosque, and I felt sick. And now civilians are just killed without any legal process whatsoever, and I've heard Israelis as good as talk about a final solution for the Palestinian problem. I've listened to a cabinet minister say without irony that if they can just round up all the terrorists and get rid of them, there won't be any left, and I can't believe I'm hearing an educated person suggest anything as monumentally stupid, as psychologically obtuse as that.

'Look; I don't want anyone hurt. I don't believe in suicide bombings or attacking any civilians and of course you've every right to defend yourselves, but, oh, God, look, can we just agree on this? That the Holocaust wasn't evil and horrific and the single most obscene and concentrated act of human barbarism ever recorded because it happened to the Jews, it was all that because it happened to *anybody*, to *any* group, to *any* people. Because it did happen to the Jews, and there had been nowhere for them to escape to, I thought, Yes, of course, they did deserve a homeland. It was the least that could be done. The world felt that. Partly guilt, but at least it was there.

'But it wasn't a moral blank cheque. For fuck's sake, if any people should have known what it was to be demonised, victimised and oppressed and suffer under an arrogant, militaristic occupying regime, *and* possess the wit to see what was happening to them and what they were doing to others, *they* should have.

'So when Palestinian youths use sling-shots against tanks and the tanks put high explosive into tents where mothers are nursing, when every Arab village has its orchards razed, its houses dynamited and roads dug up – I mean can't you see what you're doing there? Those are ghettos you're creating! When the Israeli Army seriously claims that Mohammed Al-Durrah and his father were shot by Palestinian gunmen, as though this isn't the same shit in microcosm as claiming the death camps were built by the Allies after the War . . . I'm, I'm, I'm tearing my fucking *hair* out here, Jude! And *then* letters appear in the papers talking about appeasing the Palestinians and comparing Israel to Czechoslovakia just before the Second World War, and that's just absurd! Czechoslovakia was not the best armed state in Europe at the time, it was one of the weakest; it was not the only regional superpower with a monopoly on weapons of mass destruction, it was not the tooled-up victor of three earlier wars sitting on the occupied territory of others.'

'But *they* kill *us*! Step on a bus, go for a pizza, drive back from worship, walk down the wrong path in your own city—'

'And you've both got to stop! I know that! But *you* have the most control in this! You're the ones coming from a position of strength! It's always the one with the most power who has to give up the most, who has to exercise the most restraint, who has to take the final few blows before all the blows stop!'

Jude was shaking her tear-stained face at me. 'You are so full of shit. You'll never understand. You'll just never understand. So we're not perfect. Who is? We're fighting for our lives. All you do and all you say just gives succour to those who'd drive us into the waves. You're with the enemy, you're with the exterminators. *We* haven't become the Nazis; *you* have.'

I buried my face in my hands and when I surfaced, looking at Jude's angry, reddened face, all I could say was, 'I never said you had. And there is an Israeli Peace Movement, Jude. There are people, Jews, in Israel who oppose Sharon and what's been done, what's being done to the Palestinians. Who want peace. Peace for land if that's what it takes, but peace. Reservists who're refusing to fight in the Occupied territories. That's who I'm with. That's who I respect these days. I've escaped my adolescent crush on Israel but I'll never stop respecting, loving the Jewish people for all they've done . . . it's just that I can't stand to see what's being perpetrated in their name now by that fat, white-haired, war-criminal bastard.'

'Fuck you. Sharon was democratically elected. He's said he will trade land for peace. So fuck you. *Fuck* you!'

'Jude—'

'No! Goodbye, Ken. I won't bother to say I'll see you, because I hope I don't. And don't bother to call. In fact, don't ever bother again. Not ever.'

'Jude—'

'. . . I'm ashamed I ever let you so much as touch me.'

And with that, my ex-wife threw her drink over me, turned on her heel and walked off.

Happy New Year.

Bit later. Drunk and maudlin and time to go to bed. I was crashing at Craig's place, in the second spare bedroom. Some people had been using it as an unofficial cloakroom, dumping their coats and jackets on the bed; I gathered them up and took them next door to the box room, which was the official cloakroom.

'Oh, hi, Nikki.'

'Ken,' Nikki said, taking something from her jacket. She was dressed in a fluffy pink sweater and tight black jeans. 'How are you doing?'

'Tired,' I said, dumping the coats and jackets onto the pile on the bed. Music sounded pumping from downstairs and I could hear people whooping. The box room was devoid of furniture apart from an old desk – also piled with coats and stuff – and the narrow, mounded bed. Lots of shelves with books and assorted junk; a collapsible wallpaper table and a stepladder against one wall. The room's bulb was bare, unshielded. Nikki stood grinning at me. Even with the short hair she looked great.

She held up the slim silvery thing she'd taken from her jacket. Large orange lozenges. 'Got a cold,' she said through her smile, almost smugly. Under the direct light of the room's single bulb, her hair showed spiky highlights of glossy red and deep ochre.

I narrowed my eyes and looked at her as though over some glasses. 'What are you on?'

'Oh. Is it obvious? Uh-oh.' She giggled. She put her hands behind her back and stood there, staring up at the ceiling and swivelling back and forth. Her jaw was working from side to side, in time.

I shook my head. 'You young whipper-snapper; you're loved up, aren't you?'

'Fraid so, Uncle Ken.'

'Well, have fun, but remember Leah Betts; don't drink too much water.'

'I love you, Uncle Ken,' she said, leaning forward and smiling broadly.

I laughed. 'Yeah, I love you too, Nikki.'

She brandished the throat lozenges in my face like some sort of treat. 'Would you like a Strepsil?'

'Thanks. I'm trying to give them up.'

'Okay.'

I stepped to one side and grasped the handle of the door, which had swung shut. 'After you, ma'am,' I said, opening it.

'Thenk-yuh!' she said, stepping forward, then bumped into the edge of the door and thudded into my chest. 'Happy New Year, Ken.' She raised her face to mine, still grinning.

True enough, I thought, we'd managed to miss each other somehow in the hours since the bells. 'Happy New Y—' I said.

She pushed her mouth against mine and gave me a big wet sloppy kiss, then pulled away, smiling happily, then did a little side-to-side thing with her head, made a noise that might have been, *mm-hmm*, and came forward again and kissed me once more. With a certain amount of openness, it has to be said. Though no tongues.

Oh my God, oh shit, oh fuck, part of me was thinking. I mean, another part was thinking, Well, *Yesss*!, but most of me was thinking bad things of one sort or another. I put my arms around her and kissed back, tasting and smelling her, sucking in her sweet breath as though desperate for some transfusion

240

of youth. She squirmed in my arms, pressing herself against me and slipping her arms round my sides and back.

Something dropped to the floor; the lozenges.

Then she pushed back, blinking, and I had to let her go. The smile was gone for a moment. Then she shook her head and started laughing gently. She wiped her mouth delicately with the back of one hand.

'*What* am I doing?' she breathed, still shaking her head. I thought of the way her hair would have moved when she did that, if it had still been long.

'Well,' I said, swallowing. 'Making an old man very happy, obviously, but, um, I don't think . . .'

'No, I don't think either . . .' she said softly, then laughed loudly, then started coughing. She shook her head and looked down at the floor. I stooped and handed her the packet of throat lozenges.

Nikki's hoarse laugh echoed in the room. 'Oh, Uncle Ken, I'm sorry. I didn't mean to . . . I'm sorry.'

I held up one hand. 'No problem. And please stop apologising. It was fine for me, believe me. But, ah . . .'

Nikki coughed. The harsh sound echoed in the bare-walled room. She made a visible effort to pull herself together. 'Yes,' she said, and cleared her throat noisily. 'We probably better just pretend . . .'

'. . . that none of this happened, yeah.' I nodded.

She nodded too. 'Just until, you know, we die,' she suggested.

'Agree completely,' I said.

She shivered. 'Sorry, Ken, but this is all just a bit . . .'

'Weird?' I suggested.

'Yeah, weird.'

I'd opened the door again. 'Oh. Hi, Emma.'

'Mum! Hi!' Nikki waved, her smile broad across her face.

'What's weird?' Emma said, walking into the room and looking gloweringly suspicious. Little black number. Hair in

241

pearled black Alice band like a soft tiara, black pearls round her throat. Already holding a dark coat over her arm.

I waved one hand dismissively and nodded at the pack of throat lozenges in Nikki's hand. 'I was trying to proposition your daughter by offering her drugs, but she wasn't having it.' I smiled sadly and let my shoulders sag while Emma glared into my eyes. 'Just trying to get to bed, actually, Em; dog-tired. This you off too?'

Emma wavered, but then clearly decided I'd been just casual enough. Nothing going on. Nothing you'd want to think about, certainly. 'Yes,' she said, then looked at her daughter. 'Nikki; you ready?'

Nikki popped a lozenge, flicked it into the air and stepped forward with her mouth open, teeth clacking shut. She stepped back again with the throat sweet displayed between her teeth. 'Regy,' she said. She turned and rummaged in the pile of coats until she found her jacket. 'Night, Ken,' she said, pulling on her jacket and kissing me lightly on the cheek.

'Night, kid.'

'I'll be down in one minute,' Emma told Nikki.

'Okey-doke,' Nikki said as the door started to swing closed again. 'I'll say bye to Dad . . .'

Emma looked at me.

Oh-oh, I thought. Now what?

'Great kid,' I said to Emma, nodding towards the closing door. 'Love her to bits.'

'You all right?' Em said. She looked genuinely concerned. I relaxed.

'Tired,' I said, honestly.

'I heard Jude gave you a hard time.'

'It was mutual, but yes.' I sighed, yawned. 'Oh, dear. Sorry, sorry.'

'It's all right.'

'Jude and I agreed to disagree,' I said. 'Although, come to think of it, I'm not sure we even agreed that.'

Emma nodded, looked down at my chest briefly. She put one hand out and touched my arm, patting it. 'You get some sleep.'

'Best idea I've heard all night.' I held the door open for her.

'Night, Ken. You take care.' She kissed me lightly on the cheek, just like her daughter had. She turned at the top of the stairs as I was opening the door to my bedroom, and gave me a small, brave smile. She raised one hand hesitantly, then went quickly down the steps.

I stripped to my underpants and got into the bed. I went to sleep thinking about Celia, hoping she was well and safe with her family on Martinique. I did this quite often these days. Part of me hoped that by going to sleep thinking of her I'd see her in my dreams, but so far this hadn't happened.

I slept well for about half an hour until some people piled into the room, turning on the light and looking for their coats. I told them where they were, then once they'd gone I got up, pulled on my trousers and went through to the official cloak-room and pulled all the coats and jackets off the bed and hung them over the banister rail outside. This didn't stop another group of drunks coming into the room, turning on the light and looking for their coats.

I took the bulb out of the central light fixture and the next time somebody came in, muttering about coats and clicking the light switch about ten times, I snored very loudly until they went away.

When I wake up I'm dressed as an SS officer with my cock hanging out. I'm handcuffed to the bed and there's gaffer tape over my mouth and Jo's; they rape her, slit her throat and leave her lying on me. They've taken stuff to make it look like a robbery gone wrong and the boat's been holed so when the tide rises I'll drown.

243

'Ah!'

'Ken?'

'Fuck! Shit! Fuck! Fucking hell!'

'Ken! Come on! Just a dream. Whatever it was. Just a dream, a nightmare. Hey, come on . . .'

'Dear fucking Jesus Christ almighty.' I flopped back down onto the bed. My heart was hammering like an engine, I was breathing like I'd just run a marathon. 'Oh, God . . .'

Jo took me in her arms and cradled me. 'It's okay. Everything's all right. Calm down, calm down . . .'

'Oh . . .'

'That's not like you.'

'. . . Fuck . . .'

'Okay now?'

'Yeah. Okay. Okay now . . .'

Only I wasn't okay at all.

Jo fell quickly asleep again but I spent a long, long time looking round the darkened, slightly tilted bedroom, swallowing hard, catching the occasional whiff of sewage and decay coming from the mud outside, listening for ominous gurgling noises from the bilges, searching for heavies hiding in the shadows and shivering as the sheen of sweat dried on my skin.

I lay waiting for the dawn to come up and the tide to come in, waiting for the waters to raise us again, bring the *Temple Belle* level once more, smother the faint smell of death and restore balance.

'Hello?'

'Hey, Mrs C.'

'Ooh! Is that that man from the radio? Kennit, how are you doin, ma darlin?'

'Got a bit of a cold, but apart from that, fine. And all the better for talking to you, Mrs C. And how are you? Beautiful

244

and sexy as ever? Beautiful and sexy as the last time I saw you? On the big wheel, wasn't it?'

'Oh, hell, honey, I'm more so. More so! You a terrible man. I tell me son on you, you see if I don't do juss that.'

'Mrs C, you mustn't. My unbridled passion for you has to stay a deep and terrible secret, otherwise Ed would be terribly hurt. I mean, suppose you seduced me and then fell pregnant?'

'What? At my age? Oh, lissen to you, you rogue man! Ha!'

'I'd have to marry you; I'd be Ed's father. He'd never forgive me.'

'Stop! I'll bust meself. Where's me hanky? Oh, you surely are a terrible man. I'd get the boy himself to give you a serious talkin to but he's in France or Rome or some damn place like that, honey, so you'll have to call his mobile.'

'No problem, Mrs C. Actually I knew he was away; I just wanted an excuse to hear your voice.'

'There see now, you bein terrible again.'

'I just can't help myself. It's the power you have over me.'

'Terrible man, terrible, terrible rogue of a man.'

'Okay, Mrs C. I'll try Ed's mobile. It was good talking to you. Oh . . . I did want to have a word with a friend of his, too. Ah . . . Robe? Yeah; Robe. Would you have his number there at all?'

'Robe? What you want to talk to him for, hon?'

'. . . Sorry, just blowing my nose there, Mrs C. Excuse me.'

'You excused, hon. So, what's this you wantin to talk to Robe for?'

'Ah, yeah; I was talking to somebody. In a record company. Ice House? They're pretty big. Apparently the company, the record label, it's looking for security people; bodyguards, that sort of thing. For artists, rap artists, when they come over from the States. I just thought Robe could do that, maybe. I mean, these are often pretty serious people themselves, ex-gangsta, a lot of them; they wouldn't have any respect for the average

245

white kid with broad shoulders who's used to turning people away from clubs because they've got the wrong footwear. Robe, however, they'd relate to. But it's straight work, and well paid. I know he could do it. Could lead to, well, who knows?'

'Be a lot more respectable than what he usually gets up to, what I hear. Robe is Yardie, Kennit. He dangerous. Too many guns. He's not welcome in this house no more. Ed don't see him that I know of.'

'I realise that. Ed and I were talking about him, not long ago. That's why I thought maybe this could be a way to get him out of that sort of life. I thought maybe if I could have a word with him . . .'

'Well, I don't tink I got his number here, but I can get it, I suppose.'

'It'd be great if you could, Mrs C. Of course, I'd understand if you didn't want to say anything to Ed. Nothing might come of this, we have to accept that. But, you know; nothing ventured, and all that.'

'Well, you probably on a wild goose chase here, honey, but bless you for tinkin of it. I call you back, that okay?'

'You are a saint *and* sexy. I adore you.'

'Ah! Stop it now!'

I'd decided I might be developing a crush on my dentist. Of course I wasn't and I knew I wasn't, but the idea seemed nice; there was something oddly relaxing and carefree about it. Maybe it was some very mixed up Freudian thing, given that my dad was a dentist, maybe it was because Mary Fairley, BDS, was Scottish, from Nairn, and had the most wonderfully soft, burring accent I'd heard since I'd moved to London, maybe it was the whole thing about lying almost flat with my mouth open, entirely at this woman's mercy while some gentle music played and she and her almost as attractive assistant spoke quietly, professionally to each other, but whatever it was, I had almost convinced myself I felt something for her. Mary was chunky of build but delicate of movement and touch; she had sandy hair, grey-green eyes, a sprinkling of freckles across her nose, and breasts that got ever so slightly in her way sometimes, necessitating a quick, twisting movement – the bodily equivalent of a hair-flick – while she was leaning over me.

I gazed up into her eyes, wishing we didn't have to put these safety visor things on these days. Although, given that I seemed to have picked up Nikki's cold, that was probably no bad thing; I had to raise my hand and stop the dental work a couple of times to have a good sneeze.

Amazing how safe I felt in a dentist's surgery; always a little on edge, waiting for a twinge, but very safe. Mary was polite but not chatty, despite our Caledonian connection. Very professional. Having a crush on a disinterested dentist might appear frustrating and sad, but it also struck me as being innocent and pure, and even healthy. Certainly a lot healthier than falling hopelessly in love with a gangster's wife and planning to go tooled up into a telly studio.

Mary drilled through an old filling into decay, and the air in my mouth filled with a smell like death.

'Our client maintains strongly that he was not using his mobile at the time of the accident.'

'Then your client is lying.'

'Mr, ah, McNutt, with respect, you could only have gained the most fleeting of glimpses of our client's car when—'

'Tell you what . . . excuse . . . ah-choo!'

'Bless you.'

'Thank you. Excuse me. Yes, as I was saying; the young lady I was taking home made a phone call to report the accident to the police. That was about five, ten seconds, max, after the crash happened. Why don't we talk to her mobile network and your client's and compare the times when his call ended and hers began? Because, now I think about it, he was still holding the phone when he got out of the car, and I suspect he hadn't hung up. Let's see if that call and Ms Verrin's overlap, shall we?'

The lawyer and her articled clerk looked at each other.

'You lucky, lucky people. Not only has my cold gone into my throat so that I sound even huskier and sexier than ever, but we just played you the Hives, the White Stripes and the Strokes; three in a row with nary a syllable of nonsense to dilute the fun. *Damn*, we spoil you! Now then, Phil.'

'Yeah; you can't just leave an accusation hanging like that.'

'You mean my broad hint that a fully functioning brain might be a liability in a footballer?'

'Yes. So what are you saying; all football club changing rooms should have a sign saying, You don't have to be stupid to work here but it helps?'

'And how witty that would be if they did, Philip. But no.'

'But you're saying that footballers have to be stupid.'

'No, I'm just saying that it might help.'

'Why?'

'Think about it. You're playing tennis; what's the one shot that looks easy that people get wrong all the time? The one that even the professionals make an embarrassing mess of every now and again. Happened at least once that I saw this Wimbledon.'

'We may,' Phil said, 'have located the source of the footballer's seeming stupidity, if they think they're playing football but you've apparently changed sports to tennis.'

'You can see how having a single net in the middle instead of one at each end would be confusing, but that's not what I mean. Just stick with me here, Phil. In tennis, what looks like the easiest shot there could be, but people still get hopelessly wrong? Come on. Think. The good people of radio listenerland are depending on you.'

'Ah,' Phil said. 'The overhead smash when the ball's gone

248

way up in the sky and you seem to spend about half an hour at the net waiting for it to come down.'

'Correct. Now why do people get that shot so wrong when it looks so easy?'

'They're crap?'

'We've already established that even the best players in the world do this, so, no, not that.'

Phil shrugged. I was making a one-handed waving motion at him across the desk, as though trying to waft the aroma of a dish towards my nose. Sometimes we sort of half rehearsed these things, sometimes we didn't and I just landed stuff like this on him and trusted to luck and the fact we knew each other pretty well by now. Phil nodded. 'They have too much time to think.'

'Pre-flipping-cisely, Phil. Like most sports, tennis is a game of rapid movement, fast reactions, skilful hand-eye coordination – well, foot-eye coordination in the case of football, but you get the idea – and people often play their best when they've got no time to think. Think service returns against somebody like Sampras or Rusedski. Same in cricket; scientists reckon it shouldn't be possible for a batsman to hit the ball because there just isn't enough time between the ball leaving the hand of a good fast bowler and it getting to the bat. Of course, a decent batsman will have read the bowler's body language. Same applies to a tennis player who's good at returning against a big hitter; they can tell where the ball's going before the server hits it. The point is that it all happens too quick for the cerebral bit of the brain to get involved; there's no time to think, there's only time to react. Right?'

'Uh-huh.'

'Now, football.'

'Oh good, we're back.'

'In football you often have quite a lot of time to think. Certainly often you don't; a ball comes flying in, you raise your

249

leg and first-time it and it's away and you're already running down the touchline doing the shirt-over-the-head bit with your arms outstretched. But, if you're on a break-away, get the ball in midfield, there's only one defender to beat and nobody up to support, you've got what will seem like a long, long time to run and think, and I'm certainly not accusing footballers of not being able to do both at the same time. So; you beat the defender, there's only the goalie left, and now you've got time to think again. And this is where you see some guys, even at the very top, make a mess of it because they've had time to think. Their full frontal cortex or whatever it is has had time to go, Hmm, well, we could do it *this* way, or *this* way, or *that* way, or – but by that time it's too late, because the goalie's come out and you've hit it straight at him, or skied it to the ironic cheers of the opposing fans, or decided to go for a lob and hesitated and he's had time to dive at your feet and grab the ball off you. This happens to perfectly good, highly paid professional footballers, and in a way it's no disgrace, it's just being human.

'However. If you get a particularly thick footballer—'

'You're going to be horrible about that nice Gascoigne boy again, I can tell.'

'Oh, come on; this is a man so daft he couldn't even play air-flute without making a mess of it. But yes; Gazza is my best example. He is – well, was – a great, gifted footballer, but he was so intellectually challenged that even in all those seconds running in on the goalkeeper, he *still hasn't had time to think*. Or if he is thinking, he's thinking, Wuy-aye, that's a fit-lookin bird behind the goal there, man. And that's the difference; the longer you can go without really thinking, the better a footballer you'll be.'

Phil opened his mouth to speak, but I added, 'That's also why golf and snooker are so profoundly different; they're games of nerve and concentration, not reactive skill.'

Phil scratched his head. I hit the appropriate FX button.

'Well, that was a compendium rant,' he said. I'd already started the next track, playing the intro faded down. We had fifteen seconds to the vocals. 'We started on football,' Phil said, 'diverted to tennis, then on to cricket and finally came back to the beautiful game . . . but then body-swerved into golf and snooker at the last minute there. All very confusing.'

'Really?' I glanced at the seconds ticking away.

'Yes.'

'You sound a bit stupid. Have you thought of becoming a professional footballer?'

'So it's definite?' Debbie asked.

'Yes,' Phil said.

'How definite?'

'Well, definite,' Phil said awkwardly.

'Yes, but how definite is it? Is it fairly definite? Very definite? Totally one hundred per cent certainly definite?'

'Well, no, it's not that definite,' Phil conceded.

'Jesus Christ,' I said, 'I thought only films suffered from this on-off-stop-go-red-light/green-light/red-light bullshit. It's only a fucking telly programme, not Lord of the Fucking Rings parts one to three.'

'It's delicate,' Phil said.

'So's my head on a Saturday morning,' I muttered. 'I don't make this fucking song and dance about it.'

Debbie's new temporary office was almost as far down the light-well as ours. I gazed out at the white glazed bricks. It looked like it might be raining but it was hard to tell. This was Friday; the *Breaking News* thing was scheduled for Monday. Again. My great confrontation with the beastly Holocaust denier Larson Brogley, or whatever his name was, was back on again. In fact it had been on for over a month now without being cancelled, which was probably some sort of record. It might actually be going to happen. I felt nervous.

251

Of course I felt nervous, I thought, as Station Manager Debbie and Producer Phil argued the toss about how definite was definite like a pair of bishops trying to settle how many angels could dance on the head of a pin. It was okay for these guys; they thought the only danger was me making a fool of myself or bringing the station, or by extension Sir Jamie, into disrepute; they had no idea what I was planning to do (if they had, they would, of course, have been appalled and either tried to argue me out of it – and maybe warn the *Breaking News* production team – or just cancelled the whole deal and threatened me with the sack if I insisted on going ahead without their blessing. That's what I'd do if I was ever in a situation like this . . . if, that is, the talent concerned had been daft enough to tell me what he was thinking of doing).

Fucking typical; usually these TV things came up and happened really quickly. If I'd had my brilliant but dangerous idea for any other appearance or even proposed appearance it would all have been over months ago and I'd long since have been dealing with the consequences, whatever they'd turned out to be. For various reasons, but especially 11 September, this one was running and running, and so I was being given plenty of time to stew.

'. . . follow it up with a phone interview on the show?'

'Hmm. I don't think . . .'

Yeah, let the poor, deluded fools debate. They didn't know how lucky they were, not knowing. Only I knew about my great idea, my great, risky, probably mad, certainly criminal idea. I hadn't shared it with Jo, Craig, Ed; anybody. I'd started dreaming about it, though, and worried that I might say something in my sleep that Jo would hear. This was, certainly, better than dreaming about death squads raping Jo and leaving me dressed like a Nazi waiting to drown, but it still wasn't much fun. I'd got used to having pretty mundane, even boring dreams over the years, and the last run of nightmares I'd suffered had

252

been in the run-up to my last-year exams at school, so I wasn't psychologically prepared for having bad dreams about Nazis in TV studios and being tied to a chair and people waving guns about.

On the other hand, I'd probably crap out at the last minute. I'd do the planning, take the equipment, but fail to follow through. Some Imperial Guard of good sense, still loyal to the idea of keeping me in a job and out of court and prison or whatever, would storm the gates of the occupied Palace of Reason and effect a counter-revolution, a coup for common sense and decent standards of behaviour. That was, if I was being totally honest with myself, the most likely outcome. Not *by far* the most likely outcome, but still the most likely one all the same.

'Oh for God's sake,' I said, interrupting Debbie, who was faffing on about shared legal insurance against slander and who should pay what proportion. I almost wanted to tell her that me only *saying* something outrageous and criminal was the least of her worries, but I didn't. 'Let's just do it, can't we?'

'Okay,' Phil said. 'But we're holding out for an afternoon recording.'

'Whatever. I don't care. I just want it over and done with.' They both looked at me, as though surprised at something like this getting to me. Whoops, possible security breach here. I spread my hands slowly. 'Oh, I'm just getting fed up with the hanging around,' I explained calmly.

'Okay, then,' Debbie said. 'Monday it is.'

'Halle-blinkin-lujah.'

'Listen.'

And that's enough. Here we go . . .

'Jesus. Got enough wee funny lights in here?'

'Rough, innit?'

'Oh, totally rough.'

It was the Friday night. Ed and I were due to be limo'd to a gig in Bromley in an hour, but he'd wanted to show off his newly redecorated and refitted place, so I'd come to the family house; a much knocked-through and creatively mucked-about-with complex taking up two terraced houses in Brixton, one of them an end-terrace incorporating what had been a small supermarket on the ground floor. Ed could have afforded a mansion in Berkshire if he'd wanted, and I suspected he still kind of hankered after one, but I respected the fact he'd chosen to stay here with his mum and extended family, adapting the house he'd grown up in and buying the one next door too, plus the shop underneath, rather than get the hell out of his old 'hood the instant the money had started rolling in.

I'd been slightly worried that Ed had heard from his mum that I'd been trying to get hold of his Yardie pal Robe, guessed that I was still after a gun, and wanted to shout at me or something, but nothing like this had happened so far; we'd met up in the big main living-room on the ground floor and been suddenly surrounded by a chaotic, laughing crowd of Ed's aunts, cousins and sisters (several of them pretty damn attractive), and a couple of male relations and boyfriends. His mum hadn't been there because she was attending some night class, which had saved any potential embarrassment. Ed had made our apologies and we'd got away upstairs but he still hadn't said anything about Robe.

Ed's own place within the communal house ran the length of the two lofts. The big dormers just looked out onto other roofs but the views inside were more striking; a long, mostly open space in warm ochres and deep reds with splashes of yellow. Trust me; it was a lot more tasteful than it sounds. It all smelled very new. The only certifiable style-lapse was in Ed's moderately vast, impressively uncluttered bedroom.

'Mirrors, Edward?'

'Yeah! Wicked, eh?'

'Mirrors? I mean, on both sides—'

'They're wardrobes!'

'But on the ceiling? Oh dear. Oh dear, oh dear, oh dear.'

'Wot? Just cos nobody'd want to watch your sorry white ass when you're bangin some bird. Me, I'm a picture. If I wasn't straight as a bleedin die, I'd fall in love wif meself.'

I'd folded my arms, taken a step back and looked at him. Eventually I'd just shaken my head.

'Wot?'

'No,' I'd said, 'you got me; I'm lost for words.'

'Fuck me. Hold the showbiz page.'

'Come on; I'm off duty.'

Now we were in Ed's study/den/studio, and he'd turned on all his music gear. I gazed round the six stacked, angled keyboards, the three man-high, nineteen-inch racks and a mixing desk you'd struggle to touch both ends of even with your arms outstretched and your face jammed against the pots. There was a bunch of other bits and pieces too; much-be-buttoned units lying on desks, a set of drum pads, and at least three pieces the functions of which I could not even begin to guess at. Most of the gear was twinkling in the heavily curtained darkness; hundreds of little LEDs in broad constellations of red, green, yellow and blue, plus dozens of softly glowing pastel screens with dark, blocky writing on them. Two wide-screen monitors bigger than my TV flickered into life as Ed's Mac powered quietly up. Ed's monitors were giant Nautilus jobs, thirty grand's worth of gleaming, shoulder-high, spiked blue ammonites with bright yellow cones sitting on the far side of the room and aimed at the big, black, leather chair poised in the epicentre of all this cool-tech gizmology.

'What exactly does all this *do*, Ed?'

'Makes music, man.'

'I thought you just played the stuff.'

'Yeah, well, I'm branching out, inn-I?'

'You mean you're actually going to start composing?' I picked up a dark red A4-sized manual for something called a Virus and flicked through it, squinting in the low ambient light.

'Yeah. I fot it'd be a laugh. An anyway; just look at this stuff.'

I looked at it again. 'You know, you're absolutely right, Ed. It doesn't have to produce a fucking note to justify its total, glorious gorgeousness-hood-icity. Please don't tell me all you're going to produce on it will be N-chih N-chih music.'

'N-chih N-chih music?'

'Yeah, you know; the sort of music you hear from some brother's blacked-out Astra passing you in the street. It always goes N-chih N-chih N-chih.'

'Na, mate. Well, yeah, some, maybe. But, na; one day I'm gonna write a bleedin symphony.'

'A symphony?'

'Yeah. Why not?'

I looked him up and down again. 'You don't lack for ambition, do you, Edward?'

'Certainly fucking not; life's too short, mate.'

I leafed through the manual for the Virus thing. 'I mean, do you actually *understand* all this?'

'Course not. You don't need to to get good sounds out of it. But the deep stuff's there if you need it.'

'"Extended Panic functionality"!' I quoted. 'Ha! How can you not love something with Extended Panic functionality?'

'Uvverwise known as the All Notes Off command.'

'Brilliant,' I said, putting the manual back on its bookshelf with the others. My phone vibrated on my hip. I glanced at the screen. 'Jo,' I told Ed. 'Better answer it; she's in, I don't know, Berlin or Budapest or somewhere.'

'I'll fire up the software, let you hear some N-chih N-chih tunes.'

'Hello?' I said.

And, distantly, I heard, 'Yes, yes, yes, come on, fuck me, fuck me, do it, do it, there, yes there there there, fuck me, fuck me harder. Fuck me really hard. Right there, right there, yes, yes, yes!' This was accompanied by what sounded like clothing rubbing on clothing, a series of slaps, and then a man's voice saying, 'Oh yeah, oh yeah . . .'

It didn't stop, either. Went on for some time.

I stood there and listened for long enough to entirely convince myself that this was not a joke, not any sort of an attempt at humour at all, and also not in any way meant. This was about the time when Ed turned round from the bewilderingly complicated displays on his two giant monitors and looked at me; just a glance at first, then back again, frowning, eyebrows rising. I handed him the phone.

He listened for a while as well. The frown was replaced by a smile, even a leer for a moment or two, but then he must have read something from my face because the smile disappeared and he handed the phone back to me and looked down, clearing his throat and turning back to the screens. 'Sorry, bruv,' I heard him say.

I listened a little while longer, then Jo's phone must have fallen, because there was a loud but soft-sounding thump, and the noises became very muffled, incoherent. I folded the phone off. 'Well,' I said, 'I think the choice phrases involve sauces for ganders and geese; and petards, whatever the hell one of those is.' Ed knew well enough I wasn't faithful to Jo; blimey, we'd been able to watch each other at it with those two Argentinian girls that night on the beach at Brighton during early May.

Ed looked round, chewing his bottom lip. 'Fink that was a wind-up?'

'No.'

'Deliberate?'

I shook my head. 'I doubt it; I've had Jo's accidental calls jam my phone for hours at a time before. Usually her and her girlfriends in a bar or a club.' I released a deep breath. 'Plus, ah, that is the way she expresses herself, during the act. I don't think she's a good enough actress to fake that.'

'Woh. Right then. So. You two have one of them open relationships then, do ya?'

'Looks like it,' I said. 'Just neither of us ever bothered to tell the other.'

Ed looked concerned. 'You still want to hear some tunes, man, or would you ravver ave a drink or a smoke or sumfing?'

'Na, play some tunes, Ed. Bangin tunes, in fact; play some bangin tunes.' I gave a small, not funny laugh.

Jo said: 'Listen.'

And I said: 'Oh-oh.'

'What?'

'These days, people our age – okay, my age and also your age – don't say "listen" like that without it meaning something pretty fucking serious.'

Jo looked down. 'Yeah, well . . .'

Here we go, I thought.

We were in the London Aquarium, housed in the old GLC building on the South Bank of the Thames, beside the London Eye. Mouth Corp Records were having a bash and I'd been invited. So had Jo. She'd pretty much just arrived, coming straight from Heathrow off the flight from Budapest.

The aquarium was a slightly spooky place for a party, I thought. Especially a music industry party. Sharks in abundance; as above, so below. The light was kind of freaky too; apparently the fish wouldn't take kindly to lots of flashing disco-stylee lights, strobes and shit, so all you had was this bluey-green wash of underwater luminescence, making everybody look slightly sick. The light slid off Jo's facial metalwork, visual echoes of the green and blue diodes on Ed's music gear the night before.

I'd asked her how she was and been told, Okay. I'd thought

the better of asking her if she'd made any accidental phone calls twenty-four hours earlier, but now, with virtually no pre-amble, I was getting a 'listen'.

'Look,' Jo said. People passed on either side, somebody said, Hi, and great, sleek, grey bodies moved sinuously behind and above her.

'Oh,' I said. 'Now it's "look"? We're covering the senses one by one, are we? What'll your next exhortation be? "Sniff"?'

Jo sucked her lips in and looked at me. 'You don't want to make this easy on either of us, do you?'

'Make what easy, Jo? Why don't you tell me?'

'Ken, I think we should, ah, you know; split up.' She said this and drew herself straight, putting her shoulders back and her head up, as though defiant. I thought of the night we met, and the way her stance had shown off her nipples through her T-shirt. Now she wore a big, ribbed yellow jumper with a roll neck. Black jeans. Only the DMs were the same.

I stared at her. Of course I'd known that this was the most likely thing she was going to say after 'listen', but somehow it still came as a shock, and I was left temporarily speechless for the second time in two days, and this time not in a good way. I'd thought that maybe she was going to say she knew what had happened with the phone and she was sorry, or that she was pregnant (always a good stand-by, that one, if unlikely as we always, but always, used a condom) or maybe something else entirely, like she was taking a job in LA or Kuala Lumpur or had decided to become a nun or something, but I'd known, at least since last night, in Ed's studio, that maybe whatever it was we had had going was near the end.

Still, I found myself feeling kind of crushed, and surprised. I opened my mouth. She was still sucking in her lips, making her nose look longer. She had taken a sort of half-step away from me, almost bumping into people standing talking behind her, in front of the thick, distorting glass of the aquarium

259

windows. I wondered if she thought I was going to hit her. I never had. I'd never hit any woman; never would. Oh, well, apart from 'Raine', of course, but I reckoned I could claim massively extenuating circumstances there.

'Oh, well,' I said. I looked down at my bottle of Pils. I supposed I could throw that in her face, like Jude had thrown her G&T in my face at Craig's during the first hour of the New Year, but then Jude had had the forethought to arm herself with a nice wide tumbler; I had a narrow-necked bottle. To achieve a satisfactory soaking of my intended victim I'd have to ask Jo to wait a second or two while I jammed my thumb in the bottle and shook it up before emptying it in her face. That would be inelegant, somehow. Anyway, I didn't really want to do it.

So she'd cheated on me. Probably not the first time, but, well, so what to that, too; I'd done more than my own fair share of cheating.

'Is that all you can say?' she said. '"Oh, well"? Is that it?'

'I heard you fucking somebody last night, Jo,' I told her. 'On the phone. Your mobile; it did that thing again.'

She stood, blinking. 'I didn't know,' she said. She nodded. 'Found it on the floor this morning; batteries flat.' She took a deep breath. 'Woh.' She looked down at the floor, nodding, then up to me. She spread her arms. 'I'm sorry. I didn't want you to find out that way.'

'Well, I did.'

'Were you going to say anything?'

'Hadn't decided. I thought in the meantime you might have realised what had happened and whose mobile yours had rung, and when, and you'd be all contrite, or come up with some embarrassingly unlikely explanation.'

'Were you getting ready to dump me?'

'Not particularly, Jo. It had occurred to me in the past that, well, all those foreign trips, the nights away, the rock 'n' roll lifestyle, drugs and drink and stuff; I kind of suspected you might have had the occasional adventure and so—'

'And what about you?' she asked, raising her head again, the underwater lights glinting on the studs and bars barnacling her face.

'You mean,' I said, 'have I been playing away, too?'

'Yes. Well?'

'Wait a minute,' I said, starting to feel angry now. 'I'm being far too fucking reasonable here. *I* heard *you* fucking somebody else last night; you didn't hear me. And now you're dumping me and you're looking for some sort of justification after the fact? Well, no fucking way. You have no fucking right to start asking me questions. Yes; yes, I was going to dump you as a matter of fact. Actually, in my heart, in my head, I'd already dumped you, before you dumped me.'

'Don't be so childish.'

'Fuck off, Jo.'

'Don't you even want to know *why* I want out of this relationship?'

'I don't know and I don't care. Maybe your new guy's got a bigger cock than I have; who fucking gives a damn?'

'Oh, Ken, for fuck's sake.'

'Look, I hope you're both very fucking happy, okay? Now just get the hell away from me. And get your stuff off the *Belle*, as well.' This was more like it, I thought. This was taking the initiative. I deserved to, after all, dammit; I was the injured party here. 'I'll give you till Monday morning to clear your shit off my boat then it all goes over the side. Goodbye.' I turned and walked away, the effect barely spoiled by bumping into somebody and accidentally spilling a little Pils over their sleeve and having to mumble an apology as I stalked off.

I half expected Jo to follow me and remonstrate – and by golly this seemed to me to be a situation where a person could reasonably employ a word like 'remonstrate' or even 'inveigh' rather than just 'object' or 'argue' or something. But she didn't.

I spent the remainder of the party getting profoundly hammered on an exciting variety of alcoholic beverages and I didn't see Jo for the rest of the evening. This was probably because she'd taken me at my word about chucking her stuff in the drink and didn't trust me to wait as long as Monday morning, because when I did eventually roll home in the wee hours and poured myself out of the taxi and into the *Temple Belle*, she'd already been and gone; her clothes and bits and pieces had been cleared out and on the mat under the letter box lay her key.

I stared at it for a while, picked it up after only four or five attempts, took it out onto the deck and threw it wildly into the dark receding waters.

'It was always going to happen. You weren't right for each other.'

'Craig, Christ almighty, you sound like my mother.' We were sitting on a bench near the top of Parliament Hill, Hampstead Heath, looking out over the city, submerged beneath the watery sun and drifting showers of a cool January afternoon. Craig had walked here. I'd taken the tube.

I was probably still too hungover/drunk to drive, but I couldn't have even if I'd wanted to, at least not in the Landy; somebody had slashed a couple of its tyres and smashed both headlights last night. I'd reported it to the police and they said, Yes, they knew; they'd been round during the night after the trembler alarm in the Landy noticed the list to one side and informed the Mouth Corp security centre, which in turn had alerted the cops. They'd tried my door for ten minutes and my phone for half an hour before they gave up and left me to snore the sleep of the truly drunk. The CCTV tapes would be studied. Probably kids, that's all.

262

Yeah, right, I thought. Just when I'd been hoping that maybe whatever bad shit had been going on, it wasn't any more. Oh well.

'Aye,' Craig said, in response to my accusation of sounding like my mother. 'And what do mothers know? Best.'

I shook my head. 'People always give you this You weren't right for each other stuff *afterwards*.'

'Course they do; if anybody ever tells anybody before, when it could do some good, they get accused of being jealous or something, and then when the relationship does break up, they get accused of causing it. You can't win. Best just keep quiet until it's over.'

'Did you not like Jo?'

'I didn't dislike Jo. I thought she was all right. This wasn't one of those occasions where you're waiting for it to end so you can tell your friend what you thought of his or her ex. I just meant in theory. Jo was all right, but she was nearly as daft as you, and she's more ambitious. You need somebody who'll steady you a bit, not a fellow nutter you can fuck.'

'I don't think Jo was as crazy as you seem to think she was.'

Craig tipped his head once. 'Well, she was pretty off the rails at times. I'm amazed you lasted as long as you did.'

I sighed. 'Yeah, Kulwinder said he was surprised we'd lasted as long as we had at the nine-eleven party.' I watched the slow procession of big jets angling in around the distant scape of clouds, settling onto the gentle, invisible slope that would slide them west into Heathrow.

'She tried to get off with me you know, once,' Craig said.

I looked at him. 'You're kidding.' Now *this* could be awkward.

'Na; it was one time she'd lost you or something; during the summer. You'd had an argument and you'd stormed off and left your mobile behind and she assumed you'd come to mine, so she turned up on the doorstep. I invited the lass in; impolite to do anything else, specially as she was in tears. Offered her a drink, did the agony aunt thing . . .'

'. . . Agreed what a bastard I was.'

'Excuse me; I trod the fine line between masculine solidarity and lending a sympathetic ear to a distressed female.'

'So one thing led to another,' I said.

Oh shit, what if he had fucked her? Even if he wasn't going to admit to it here, what if he had? Think, Ken. Was I bothered? Well, was I?

Not particularly. I mean, I had no right to be jealous or upset, not with Craig, anyway, given what had happened with Emma, but that sort of logical, quid-pro-quo consideration wasn't the kind of argument that carried much weight with the set of instincts and part-programmed reactions that constitute the human heart.

'Well, no, not one thing leading to another,' Craig said. 'She just grabbed me. Out of the blue.'

'Jesus.'

'We'd had about a half-bottle each—'

'Wine?'

'Yeah, of course wine; I wasn't feeding the girl whisky.'

'Sorry.'

'I'd got up to uncork another—'

'Oh yeah?'

'Yes; I was still being polite and supportive. Fuck off with the suspicion and innuendo, will you?'

'Sorry, sorry.'

'Just wrapped herself around me. I turned round – surprised, you know – and she slapped her mouth over mine and grabbed my balls.'

'Fucking hell.' I looked up at the clouds, then back at Craig. 'You did the decent thing, though.'

'No, Kenneth,' he said, stretching his long legs out. He was wearing grey trackie bottoms under a jacket last fashionable

264

ten years ago. 'The decent thing would have been to have shown her how wonderful the act of love can be when you do it with a real man, but I didn't do that.'

'Bet you snogged her for a while, you bastard. She was a good kisser.'

Craig considered this. 'Hmm. I'd been putting that down to shock, but you're right.'

'You didn't fuck her, did you?'

'No. I did the self-sacrificing, You're beautiful and I'm flattered but if we do we'll both regret it in the morning thing. God help us, we even agreed it wouldn't be right to betray you; it was worth depriving ourselves of some pleasure for your sake.'

'Oh, fuck.'

'Now what?'

'Just had a terrible thought.'

'What? Who are you calling?'

'She went looking for me at Ed's once.'

'Wuh-oh.'

'Yeah.'

Craig made as if to get up off the bench. 'Want me to . . . ?'

'Na; if you're going to see me humiliated we might as well get it over with now.'

'You fucked her, didn't you?'

'No, I didn't!'

'Look, Ed, she told me she'd gone to yours, once. She went to Craig's once, too, and she threw herself at *him*.' ('Hey!' said Craig. 'I resent the implication.' I ignored him.) 'You trying to tell me Jo didn't try it on with you?'

'Ah . . .'

'Ah? *Ah*? Is that what you're fucking giving me? Fucking "*Ah*"?'

'Well . . .'

265

'You *did* fuck her! You *shite*!'

'She fuckin jumped me, man! It was practically rape!'

'Fuck off, Ed.'

'An anyway, she said she'd never done it wif a black guy; wot was I supposed to do? Deprive her?'

'Don't bring race into it, for fuck's sake! And don't give me this big black stud bullshit either!'

'I didn't bring race into it, man, *she* did!'

'Aw, Ed, fuck off; how could you?'

'I couldn't help it, man.'

'Well, fucking try learning, you overgrown adolescent!'

'Look, man, I am sorry; I felt terrible the next day an it never appened again.'

'Yeah, you'd had your fun, fucked your friend's girl and added another notch to your fucking ceiling mirrors; why bother?'

'Ken, listen; if I could go back in time an make it that it nevvir appened, believe me I would. I nevvir told you because I didn't want to hurt you or do anyfin against you an Jo. I wish it just adn't appened, I truly do. But it did, an I'm sorry, man. I really am sorry. I'm asking you to forgive me, right?'

'Well – just – I'm not –' I spluttered. 'Just let me fucking be angry at you a bit longer!' I said. 'You bastard!' I added, rather ineffectually.

'Sorry, man.'

And I thought, Yeah. We're all sorry. Everybody is so fucking sorry. It should be the fucking species' middle name; *Homo S. Sapiens*. Maybe we could change it by misdeed poll.

'. . . Listen,' Ed said.

Something cold seemed to land in my guts. Oh, good grief. A 'listen' from Ed; now what?

'What?' I said.

'You got this telly fing tomorrow, aven't you?'

Oh fuck, he'd heard about Robe after all and worked out that I might want a gun to take into the studio. 'Yes,' I said.

266

'Best of luck wif it, all right? Hope it goes well. You give this Nazi geezer wot-for, yeah?'

'Yeah,' I said.

'You can go back to bein mad at me now if you want, or you can wait till we meet up next weekend an shout at me then. If we're still meetin up. We still meetin up?'

'I suppose.'

'I'm sorry, man.'

'Yeah.'

'Still bruvvers?'

'Yeah, I suppose so. Still bruvvaz.'

Craig invited me to supper. I suspected it was a sympathy thing; Nikki was staying and Emma was coming round and I think what they really wanted was a quiet evening meal with just the three of them.

What I really wanted was to see Nikki again, just to be sure that we were okay, and that nothing had changed, at least not for the worse, after the New Year party, because that kiss – those two kisses – had left me worried. I'd let her kiss me, and I'd kissed her back, and the more I'd thought about this over the intervening period, the more ashamed I'd become, and I felt a terrible urge to tell her that it had changed nothing, and of course it would never happen again, and that I was sorry, too, for the time in the Land Rover in the rain, on the day of the crash, when I'd tried – in what now felt like a deeply sad and desperate way – to persuade her to have lunch with me, and that I'd always, always be a good friend and a good uncle for her, for the rest of her life . . . Though at the same time I also wanted not to have to say anything at all, and to have everything be just the same as it had always been between us, with no awkwardness or distance.

The trouble was that Emma would be there, too, and if Craig mentioned what had happened with Jo – I'd asked him not to say anything to Nikki or Emma, and especially not to mention Jo and Ed, but still – then it might get awkward, given the history I had with Emma. It was a very slim sliver of history, I kept on telling myself, but it was no less potentially lethal for my relationship with Craig for that.

I was in danger of losing one girlfriend, two best friends and – tomorrow – maybe my job, and liberty, all in one insane forty-eight-hour period.

Screw the nut, I thought. Batten down. Supper would have been nice, and I had such a bad hangover I'd probably not want to drink very much and so it would actually constitute quite a sensible, measured preparation for the big day tomorrow, but I decided to say no. Other plans.

'Ken, hi.'

'Amy, kid; how *are* you?'

'Brilliant. You?'

'Ah . . . kinda, you know.'

'Darling, no, I don't. What? Is there a problem?'

'Jo and I are . . . over.'

'Oh! I'm sorry to hear that. You seemed so close.'

'Well,' I said. *Did* we? I thought. I wouldn't have said so, but then maybe that was just the sort of thing you said when somebody told you something like this. 'Yeah,' I said. 'It's . . . it's, ah, very finished with. Kind of saw it coming, but . . . hit me a little harder than I'd expected, must confess.'

'Gosh. You poor thing.'

'Yeah. Nearly two years.'

'Really.'

'Yeah. Feels like longer.'

'Right.'

'Felt quite a lot for her, I have to say.'

'Well, of course.'

'. . . All gone now.'

'Oh dear.'

'. . . Anyway.'

'Hmm. Are you going to be all right?'

'Amy . . . I'll live.'

'Oh, dear; you sound so sad!'

'Ah, I'll get over it. One day.'

'Oh! Is there anything I can do?'

'Well, I suppose . . . You could let me take you out to dinner. Tonight, even. How does that sound?'

'That sounds like a totally bloody marvellous idea, Ken. I was at a bit of a loose end myself, actually.'

I looked at the mobile, thinking, Well, you might have got on-message a bit earlier there, woman.

'Amy, for goodness' sake. There are two lies here: one is that private management is automatically better than public—'

'But it is! Have you ever *dealt* with a local authority, Ken? Those useless bloody people wouldn't last two minutes in the real world!'

'Neither did Railtrack once the government subsidy was whipped away.'

'Ha! I bet they got their people from local government.'

'Oh, don't be . . . look. The other great lie is that private can be cheaper; it brings in extra money. But that's bullshit! Just Treasury accounting rules. Infrastructure costs no matter who builds it. You have to invest in it, so invest as cheaply as possible; pay the least you can in interest payments. And that's even before you factor in the profits a private investor expects, too; that comes on top. So, ask yourself: who or what can borrow money cheaper than any commercial concern? Answer: the state.'

'I think you'll find that depends on which state, actually, Ken.'

'Okay, the *British* state can borrow money cheaper, for a smaller interest rate, than any commercial concern.'

'Yes, because it doesn't go wasting it on things the private sector can do better.'

'Amy, that's ridiculous!'

'No, it isn't. And what about risk?'

'What risk? If it all goes wrong the poor bloody taxpayer ends up paying.'

'There's always a risk, Ken,' Amy said, smiling thinly at me. 'Life is full of risk.'

I sat back in my seat. We were in La Eateria, an achingly trendy new restaurant in Islington. Wooden garden furniture for tables and chairs, and walls lined with that perforated orange plastic stuff builders use to create instant fences. Menu pretentious, food barely adequate, staff surly. I was amazed it wasn't busier. Still, it was a Sunday night.

Amy looked great, with her fine, now straight blond hair glowing in the light of what looked like car headlights dangling from the ceiling. She was dressed in black tights and skirt, and a clingy black long-sleeved top with a gold chain lying on the tanned skin revealed by a square, low neck.

So she looked superb and she'd dressed up – if she'd appeared in paint-speckled jeans and an unironed T-shirt I'd have known there was no way anything was going to happen – and yet, suddenly, for the first time in all the times we'd met to eat, she'd turned into Little Miss Capitalist Lobby Girl.

Until now all our lunch and dinner dates-that-were-not-really-dates had consisted of eating, drinking and flirting. Dammit; they'd been great fun! Certainly no arguments about fucking PFI and PPPs. I mean, I knew that the lobbying firm she worked for was involved in promoting that sort of crap, but, Jeez, she'd never started pushing it at me. I'd made one off-hand remark about Railtrack and the forthcoming attractions of Postrack and Tubetrack, and she'd jumped down my throat feet first.

'You know what really gets me?' I said, putting my fork

down. I hadn't eaten much of my main course. The chef here seemed obsessed with height and apparently chose his ingredients and cooking methods to ensure the maximum altitude and stability of the towers of material the kitchen created, with edibility and taste coming way down the list of priorities. Probably somewhere between the grid of soggy rosti and the layer of glue-like mustard mash acting as a hold-fast.

'No, I don't know what really gets you, Ken,' Amy said, levering a forkful of her lamb and figs towards her mouth, 'but I have the awful feeling you're just dying to tell me.'

Dying to. Shit, I hadn't even told her about the whole 'Raine' thing, my inadvertent trip to the East End, the threatening phone call and the slashed tyres on the Landy yet. I'd told Craig, Ed and Jo, and sworn them all to secrecy, but with Amy I'd been holding it in reserve for later in the evening. Now I was starting to think there was no point.

'Yes,' I said. 'What I want to know is, why put what is basically greed above the urge to serve? What's wrong with wanting to help people? Isn't that what politicians say *they* want to do? They say they just want to serve society, they tell us that's why they became politicians in the first fucking place, so why don't they side with the nurses and the teachers and the fire brigade and the police and all the other people who really do serve?'

'They *do* side with the police, Kenneth.'

'Oh, so they do. But what about everybody else? So are they lying about wanting to serve, and just want power, or have they just not made the connection yet?'

Amy sat back too, breathing deeply and flexing her shoulders. I tried to keep eye contact and appreciate her breasts by peripheral vision only, but it was almost an insult to them. On the other hand, maybe I should make the most of the view, because it looked like what I was seeing now was all I was ever going to see. Amy shook her head and said, 'You really are quite naïve, aren't you, Ken?'

'Am I?'

'Yes. You seem so clued-up and clever but really you just scratch the surface of everything, don't you?'

'If you say so, Amy.'

She looked at me for a bit. Her eyes were greeny-blue and her irises had that over-defined look you get with contacts sometimes. She was still breathing fairly deeply and I just let my gaze fall to her chest, which was pleasant in a regretful sort of way. 'You're just Sir Jamie's little performing monkey, but you think you're some sort of cool radical type, isn't that right, Ken?'

I thought about this. 'On a good day,' I conceded. 'With a following.'

'I suppose you think you're Mouth Corp's conscience or something, don't you?'

'Oh, no. Jester, maybe; bladder, bit of string, that sort of thing, you know.'

Amy sat forward. 'Think about this, Ken,' she said. I sat forward too, eager to be given something to think about. 'You let Sir Jamie get away with *more*,' Amy told me. 'By employing you and allowing you to do your little rants and letting you criticise bits of the Mouth Corp empire and the people and the organisations it gets into bed with, Sir Jamie can give the impression of being even-handed and fair and able to tolerate criticism. What's *actually* going on is that the bad corporate stuff, which Mouth Corp does as much as anybody, gets a lot less publicity than it deserves, thanks to you.' She sat back. So did I. But she wasn't finished. 'You cost the radio station the occasional ad placement and Mouth Corp loses the odd contract, but Sir Jamie gets his money's worth out of you, Ken, don't think he doesn't. You're part of the system, too. You help make it work. We all do. It's just that some of us know it and some of us don't.'

She dabbed at the corner of her mouth with her napkin.

272

I looked at her for a moment. Her eyes were bright. She was smiling. I thought about Ceel and wondered suddenly what the hell I was doing here. 'So,' I said, 'do I get to fuck you or not?'

She laughed and leaned forward again, which was a good thing in itself. Voice lower this time. 'Have you got any drugs, Ken? Any E? Or Charlie?'

It actually occurred to me to lie and say no. Can you believe that? 'Not on me.'

'Get some.'

'Okay.'

So we did, but it wasn't very good. The drugs or the sex.

Eight

DENIAL

Maybe Jo's right; I hate so many things. I'm a media person and there's so much media stuff I just despise. From comics who make fun of their audience – ah, the masochism of paying good money to be insulted in public – to crap like *Big Brother*; hours and hours of boring, self-obsessed dimwits trying to be zany while performing pointless, stupid tasks that would be an insult to anyone with half a brain. Ali G, Dennis Pennis, Mrs Merton, *Trigger Happy TV*; shows that make me squirm with embarrassment and, sometimes, feel the beginnings of sympathy even for people who deserve nothing but my unalloyed hatred. God, I hated so much TV these days, and the terrifying thing was, it was this stuff that was popular, I who was out of step.

Numty TV, we called it on the show (part of our long-term and deeply insidious campaign to bring more Scottish words into day-to-day English usage). The only aspect of Numty TV I liked was the not-obviously-set-up entries on *You've Been Framed*, but part of me was ashamed of that, because I couldn't help feeling there was an edge of cruelty watching this stuff; you see a clip begin with some bozo on rollerblades wobbling towards the camcorder at high speed, or perched precariously on a still shiny mountain bike and tearing down a rutted path between the trees, or almost anything to do with jet skis, high winds, people on a rope swing over a muddy puddle, or weddings or wedding reception dances, and you could feel yourself thinking, Oh goody; this'll be a laugh. It was fun watching people making fools of themselves, but the question is, should it be?

Better to watch the truly despicable suffer, which was why I was here, I supposed.

Here was a Victorian warehouse in Clerkenwell converted into a TV studio and the place where Winsome Productions would be making their new, if much-delayed and re-scheduled, late-evening news magazine and analysis show *Breaking News*. Most of it would be live but the bit I'd be doing was being recorded. Sensibly. After I'd had my mad, bad idea for what to do here, I'd felt really deflated when I'd learned that the piece with the Holocaust denier would be taped rather than shown live; I'd wanted the buzz of it happening for real (but then I also started to feel relieved, thinking, Well, no point in doing it at all, then . . . before I caught myself, and thought, Oh yes there is; no chickening out).

Though I might still chicken out. There was a heavy metallic lump in the right pocket of my jacket reminding me that I had something to do here, something nobody was expecting, but I knew that when it came to the moment, I might still ignore it, play along, do what everybody expected me to do, and do nothing more than shoot my mouth off.

It was late afternoon. I felt over-briefed. Phil had gone through the obvious stuff with me, and so had yet another young, attractive, breathless, awfully well-spoken researcher.

Our presenter would be Cavan Lutton-James, a slim, darkly handsome and energetic guy with a quick, clipped but clear delivery and a natty interview style, which could veer from

278

emollient to biting in the turn of a phrase. He was Irish, so I'd already stockpiled one or two remarks about Ireland's inglorious part in the great war against Fascism, to keep in reserve just in case any misguided ideas about balance caused him to start siding with the bad guy. A bad guy I hadn't seen yet; they were keeping us apart.

The only person I'd met in the Green Room – apart from a couple of attractive but breathlessly awfully production assistants, at least one of whom was called Ravenna – was a young comedian called Preston Wynne, who came across as a bit of a fan boy and was supposed to record a topical, robust, cutting-edge, irreverent, yada-yada piece on something or other, after we'd done the big Holocaust denial discussion/confrontation. He was still working on his script while he sat in the Green Room, clattering quietly on his iBook, staring at a plate of gourmet sandwiches and drinking too much coffee. I almost felt like telling him to let the piece run longer than he'd been told, and even be prepared to pad a little, because the bit I was going to be on might not have quite the run-time the producer was expecting, but of course I didn't.

I didn't even have a drink in the Green Room. I really wanted one, but I kept myself sober because I wanted to be sharp and fully alert for what was going to happen.

Phil and I had spent a sober lunch in the corner of the Black Pig, another basic Soho boozer similar to the Bough. Phil was obviously worried I was going to make a mess of things, lose my rag, freeze, rant incoherently and start foaming at the mouth; whatever. He'd really wanted to come along with me but I'd told him weeks ago he wasn't going to. Partly this was for the stated reason, that he wasn't my dad and I didn't need my hand held, but partly also it was because he might, a) guess just from my look or behaviour closer to the event that I was going to get up to something seriously off-piste and so give the game away, and b) catch a little less flak from our mutual bosses after I'd done what I intended to do. If I had the guts to actually do it.

'Umm . . . what else. Oh, yeah, and obviously, the whole thing about the Second World War not happening, too; that's obviously a brilliant line to take. It's so basically ludicrous, yet it's not intrinsically any more so than claiming the Holocaust didn't happen.'

'I know, Phil,' I sighed. 'We have kind of been through this.'

'I know, I know, but you've got to get this rehearsed.'

'No, I don't. Actually rehearsed is the last thing I want it to be.'

'Too risky. What if you make a mess of it?'

'Look, I don't make a mess of it in front of a million radio listeners five days a week, why should I make a mess of it in front of a late-night Channel Four audience of probably fewer people . . . when it's taped, for fuck's sake?'

'Oh, yeah, and you won't swear, will you?'

'Phil, have I *ever* fucking sworn on air?'

Phil looked like a man with severe diarrhoea sitting in a Land Rover heading quickly down a bumpy jungle path towards extremely distant toilets. 'Well, no,' he admitted, 'but I still don't know how you do it. I mean, it doesn't seem possible you've managed to avoid it all these years.'

'Well, I have.'

'What, even on Inverclyde Sound?'

'StrathClyde Sound; the radio station where the creative's typist missed the space bar rather than accidentally hit the exclamation mark key, and no, not even there. It's because even though it might not sound like it, I do have a pretty accurate idea exactly what I'm going to say the instant before I say it, I never forget the context – am I in the pub or the studio? – and there's just sufficient time for my on-board censor to step in and make the relevant – if not always perfectly elegant or sometimes even grammatical – amendments.'

'Right. Well.'

'Anyway, it's late-night Channel Four, for Christ's sake, not *Blue Peter*. If they can say "fuck" on *Sex and the City* I don't see why I can't. Christ, I heard a "cunt" on *Larry Sanders* once.'

Phil's eyes went wide. 'Oh, no, I really don't think you should—'

'Look, will you just calm *down* a bit?' I told him. 'I'm not going on intending to swear, okay?'

He said, 'Okay,' but he still looked worried.

Of course, what I wanted to add was, Dammit, man, I won't have *time* to swear; it'll probably all be over in about five seconds and I really wouldn't worry your ugly big head about what I'm going to *say*.

Again, though, I didn't.

I was plumbed in. I'd half expected it would be radio mikes (always attached to you with a warning not to visit the loo with them switched on, in case you want to cause the sound engineers, ooh, seconds of hilarity), but they were using hard wire instead. What appeared to be a clone of one of the attractive but awfully assistants slipped the wire beneath my jacket, under the button of my shirt just above the waistband of my trousers and then – once I'd worked it upwards – attached it between the top two buttons of my shirt. I was going for the relaxed, casual, open-necked look. Besides, they take your tie off you in the nick, along with your belt and laces.

The awfully assistant smiled as we were negotiating the cool black wire up between my chest and the fabric of the shirt, and I smiled back, but while we'd been doing this her bare arm had swung against my jacket and made the pocket clunk off the seat and I was secretly terrified she was going to see the sweat prickling up underneath my make-up and ask, 'Hey, what's that hard, heavy, metallic thing in your jacket pocket?'

281

Paranoia. The terrible thing about paranoia is you always have the sneaking suspicion that the moment it passes is when you'll be at your most vulnerable.

They tested for sound and then the black microphone wire was taped to the arm of the plastic and chrome chair I was sitting in, below desk level and therefore out of sight for the cameras that would be trained on me. On the black-painted floor, the mike cable snaked away, almost invisible save for the lengths of silver gaffer tape securing it there.

I looked about the rest of the studio. Cavan would be in between us, a couple of metres away from me round the giant comma-shaped wooden desk; his seat was bigger and higher-backed than mine or the bad guy's, which was another two metres past Cavan's, round the curve. Lots of bright overhead lights kept the place very warm.

Somebody sat in the chair across the desk from mine and for a moment I wondered what was going on; it was one of the awfully assistants, not the scumbag Holocaust denier I was expecting. Then another assistant plonked herself in Cavan's seat in the middle and I realised they were just sitting in for the real people while they got the cameras sorted out.

In front of Cavan's position was a big camera with, on the front, the downward-angled hood and attached upward-facing monitor of an autocue; a little bearded guy looked almost lost behind the camera, minutely adjusting its position according to instructions through his headphones. There were two surprisingly small, unmanned cameras on heavy tripods, one for me and one for the bad guy, plus an umbilicalled handheld manned by a plump guy who at this point was muttering into his own head-mike as he crouched back and forth, rehearsing where he could go within the curve in front of the big desk without getting in shot from the other cameras.

Everybody was listening on their headphones and earpieces to the people in the production suite, and for a while it was actually very peaceful, sitting there in what was more or less silence, feeling pleasantly, politely ignored while everything else was sorted out. Somebody rolled a big monitor screen on a trolley to a position a couple of metres behind the cameras and turned it on; it showed a blue screen with a big white clock face on it and the programme ID. It sat, static, unchanging, in the midst of a semi-hush punctuated with murmurs.

I found myself thinking about Ceel. I remembered the feel of her body, the precise touch of her fingers, the satiny sensation of running my hand across her back, the deep, musky smell of her hair, the taste of her lips after a mouthful of champagne, the taste of her sweat from the hollow formed by her collar bone, and most of all the sound of her voice; that measured softness with the faint ghost of accent, a calmly sinuous stream of quiet amusement breaking into sudden rapids when she laughed.

The monitor flickered, the blue and white display replaced with a view of the assistant sitting in Cavan's chair. Then the clock and ident display flicked on again.

I was missing her. It had been a month now since I'd seen her, and a long month at that. I supposed time seemed to stretch over the Xmas/New Year holidays for everybody, but I felt I'd been particularly busy, which made the interval seem longer. I'd spent an unhealthy amount of time over the holidays checking that there had been no crashes of Air France flights bound for or coming back from Martinique, or sudden unseasonal hurricanes or fresh volcanic eruptions in the Eastern Caribbean.

Things were falling apart around me and it felt like it was all because Ceel wasn't here. There was no logic to this feeling whatsoever, and it wasn't as though Ceel and I spent very much time in each other's company when she was around – we saw each other for about half a day once a fortnight, so she shouldn't really have felt like any great influence on my life – but nevertheless with her away I felt adrift and disconnected, my life tumbling chaotically.

There wasn't even the promise, or at least the possibility, that we might meet up in a day or two, steadying me from a distance.

Coping with my break-up with Jo, with the ramifications of that touching Ed and Craig, with everything that had happened at the New Year party, with this continuing campaign of damage and threat some bastard was mounting against me – not to mention the chilly contemplation of what I was thinking of doing here – left me feeling dangerously exposed and at risk.

It was like trying to control a skid on a bike on a rainy street; that same feeling of cold, gut-clenching panic while wrestling desperately with something powerful but suddenly wild and out of control. I'd had a few skids like that in my courier days. I'd always managed to stay upright and I was proud of that, but I'd never kidded myself that on each occasion it had been anything other than luck, mostly, that had kept me out of the gutter or from under the wheels of a bus. At least those incidents were over in seconds; this was going on for weeks, months. Everything I might have hung onto for support seemed compromised. I needed Ceel. I needed to access her calmness, secure myself to that perverse rationality of hers.

I looked at the seat straight across from me, where the bad guy would be sitting. I glanced at my watch. I hated the way they kept you hanging around for TV.

I just wasn't cut out for this medium. Paul, my agent, despaired of me because I'd been offered TV stuff in the past plenty of times but the proposals always read like shit and I'd turned them down. They all seemed gimmicky, strained and overly elaborated, but that was almost not the point. On radio, you just go in and do it. You can talk about stuff in the pub or the office beforehand, effectively rehearsing bits, and you can script little exchanges and sketches, and there're always trailers and pre-recorded stuff to work painstakingly over until it's note perfect . . . but most of it, the best of it, I think, is just stuff that happens, words that come out of your mouth almost as you think (allowing for the on-board censor, which I was not bullshitting Phil about).

On radio, that fresh stuff is the norm. On TV it's very much the exception, and most of it's recorded, re-heated. So you sit there and make some really funny or cutting point and then discover there was a glitch on a camera feed, or somebody backed into a bit of the set and knocked it over, and they have to start again, and you have to either try to say something about the same thing, which is totally different but just as witty, or say the same again and pretend it's spontaneous. I hated that shit. Come to think of it, some of that had been the gist of Phil's little laid-back rant in the Capital Live! canteen a month or so earlier. I seemed to have appropriated it. Oh well, that wouldn't be the first time.

My mouth was dry. There was a very small plastic cup of still water in front of me, which I drained. I looked around, holding it out, and one of the awfully assistants came and topped it up with Evian. I wanted to sink the lot right there, but I put it back on the desk. I suspected they'd take it away before we started recording.

'Ken?' a very smooth Irish voice said from behind me. 'Nice to – ah, now, no; don't you get up. Cavan. Good to meet you.'

I couldn't have got up anyway, not with the mike wire securing me to the chair. I shook hands from a seated position. 'Cavan; hi.' I smoothed down the flap over my right jacket pocket, making sure he couldn't see into it.

Cavan perched one fawn, Armani-clad buttock on the desk between my seat and his. He looked tanned underneath the make-up and there was a hint of shadow where his beard would have been that probably no amount of shaving would remove.

His blue eyes were deep set, brows dark and full and shaped. A sharp ledge of black hair sat over his forehead. 'It's very good of you to come in.'

'My pleasure, Cavan.' A translucent wire coiled up from inside the rear collar of his jacket and ended in a discreet flesh-coloured earphone in his right ear. Where his soft beige jacket fell open against his hip, I could see the radio transmitter clipped to his belt. No hard-wiring for Cavan.

'You've been booked in for a while, Ken, is that right?'

'For what has on occasion felt like a significant part of my life, Cavan, yes.'

He laughed soundlessly. 'Yes, well, sorry about that.' He sighed and looked off into the shadows. 'We've all been kept hanging around while Winsome have been getting themselves sorted out.'

'I'm sure it's been a lot worse for you than it was for me.'

'Ah, yes. It's been a frustrating old time to have a current affairs show waiting in the wings while all this history's been happening, but hopefully we'll be making up for – ah. Excuse me, will you?'

'Sure.'

Lawson Brierley. That was the name of the man who walked out of the darkness, blinking in the light. My age. Green cords, fogey jacket, yellow waistcoat, farm manager's shirt and a cravat. I almost smiled. Tall, medium-heavy build, verging on beefy; hair like grey sand. Not a bad-looking face in a bland sort of way, except his nose was a little bulbous and he had the peering, scrunched look of a vain man on a date trying to do without his glasses. Ex-Federation of Conservative Students (one of the Hang Nelson Mandela brigade; later thrown out for being too right-wing), ex-National Front (quit when they moved too far to the left), and ex a few other extreme-right groups and parties. Claimed to be a libertarian racist now. I knew one or two people who'd come to libertarianism from

286

the left, and people like Lawson Brierley had them spitting blood.

Monetarist fundamentalist might be a more accurate description of his views, with the racist bit never very far away. According to Lawson, evolution was the ultimate free market in which the white races were proving their innate superiority through money, science and arms, threatened only by the perfidious guile of the Jews and the hordes of dark and dirty Untermenschen breeding like flies thanks to the misguided beneficence of the West.

We'd got all this off the man's own website; he ran – he basically was – something called the Freedom Research Institute.

Lawson genuinely didn't approve of democracy. He believed in getting rid of the state, and – in reply to the point that doing so would leave companies, corporations, multi-nationals (or whatever you would call multi-nationals when there were no more nations) in complete control of the world – he would have said, Yes, so? These corporations would be owned by shareholders, and money was the fairest way to exercise power, because as a rule stupid people would have less of it, and therefore less influence, than more intelligent people, and it was the more intelligent and successful people you wanted controlling things, not the great unwashed.

I'd decided my considered reply to all this would have been something on the lines of, Fuck the fucking shareholders, you ghastly fascist cunt.

I watched him sit down and get miked up. He was being wired in, taped to the seat like I'd been. Good. I couldn't make out what he was saying to the production assistant and the sound engineer as they helped him get settled in. He didn't look over at me. Cavan had spoken a few words to him and then nodded and gone to sit in his own big seat in the middle, getting its position just so, clearing his throat a few times, patting his tie down and running a hand over the air above his hair.

My heart was beating hard, now. Somebody came to take away the little cup of water, but I had them wait a moment while I drained it, my hand trembling. My bladder seemed to think I needed to pee but I knew I didn't really. It felt like I was listing to the right with the weight in my jacket pocket. To the right; how very, very inappropriate, I thought.

The monitor behind the cameras flicked to the head-on waist-up shot of Cavan coming from the big camera with the autocue.

The floor manager announced we were doing a taped rehearsal of the intro. Cavan cleared his throat a few more times.

'Okay; quiet in the studio,' the floor manager said, then, 'Turning over.' She did the 'Five, four, three . . .' thing, with the two and the one shown only on her fingers.

Cavan took a breath and said, 'The vexed issue of race, now, and the provenance – or not – of the Holocaust, in the first of a series of *Breaking News* special features pitching two people with profoundly different views against each other. I'm joined tonight by Lawson Brierley, a self-labelled libertarian racist from the Free Research Institute, and Ken Nott, from London's Capital Live!, doyen of the so-called . . . Sorry.'

'No problem,' the floor manager said. She was a tall gangly girl with close-cut brown hair; she wore big headphones and held a clipboard and a stopwatch. She listened to her phones again. 'Okay,' she said. 'You all right, Cavan?'

Cavan was squinting towards the camera ahead of him, shading his eyes from the overhead lights. 'Ah . . . Could you just move the autocue up a tiny little bit?' he asked.

The man with the big camera adjusted it fractionally.

Was I really a doyen? I wondered. That meant 'old', didn't it? More 'senior' rather than 'ancient', if I recalled the dictionary definition correctly, but still. I was sweating badly now. They'd probably notice and have to stop and bring one of the make-up girls in to touch up my face. I felt a pain in my guts and wondered if I was giving myself an ulcer.

Cavan nodded. 'Fine now.' He cleared his throat again.

'Okay,' said the floor manager. 'Everybody okay?' She looked around at us. Everybody seemed to be okay. I wasn't going to say anything about sweating. Lawson Brierley sat, blinking, looking from Cavan to the monitor, still avoiding my gaze. The little bearded guy with the big camera adjusted it back to where it had been before, but Cavan didn't notice. 'We're going again, quiet in the studio. Turning over,' said the floor manager. 'And: Five, four, three . . .'

'The vexed issue of race, now, and the provenance – or not – of the Holocaust, in the first of a series of *Breaking News* special features pitching two people with profoundly different views against each other. I'm joined tonight by Lawson Brierley, a self-labelled libertarian racist from the Freedom Research Institute, and Ken Nott, from London's Capital Live!, doyen of the so-called Shock Jocks and – as he's described himself – unrepentant post-lefty.' Cavan raised his eyebrows for effect. 'First, though, this report by Mara Engless, on the undeniable existence of deniers.'

I looked over to Lawson Brierley. He was smiling at Cavan.

'Good,' the floor manager said, nodding. 'Good. Perfect, Cavan.' (Cavan nodded gravely.) 'Okay, we're going for—'

'How long's the video bit?' Cavan asked.

The floor manager looked away for a moment, then said, 'Three twenty, Cavan.'

'Right, right. And we're just going straight into the interviews, the ah, discussion bit, now, right?'

'That's right, Cavan.'

'Fine. Fine.' Cavan cleared his throat a few more times. I found myself wanting to clear my own throat, too, as though in sympathy.

'Everybody ready to go?'

It looked like we were all ready to go.

'Okay. Quiet in the studio.'

I put my hand in my pocket.

'Turning over.'

In my pocket, the plastic coating the metal felt cold and slick in my right hand.

'And: Five, four, three . . .'

I leaned forward slightly, to hide my hand coming out of my pocket.

Two.

My other hand was at my belly, holding, steadying.

One.

Click.

Cavan took a breath and turned to me. 'Ken Nott, if I can turn to you first. You're on record as—'

I'd snipped the mike cable with the pliers.

I had tried to think all this through, weeks and weeks earlier, and I'd guessed they might wire us up; that was why I'd brought the pliers in my jacket pocket.

But that wasn't the clever bit.

I let the pliers fall as I kicked the seat back and jumped up on the big desk. I'd have settled for three seats in an arc, but the desk was better; I'd reckoned as long as I didn't take too long getting myself up there it would provide a highway. So far, so good; seat falling backwards out of the way and a clean leap up onto the wooden surface.

Though that wasn't the clever bit either.

Cavan had time to shut his mouth and jerk back. Lawson Brierley's eyes were going wide. I ran at him across the desk. I'd worn a pair of black trainers, for purchase, so I wouldn't slip, just for this.

That, too, was not the clever bit.

Lawson had his hands on the desk edge, tensing to push himself backwards. Cavan was falling off his seat as I passed him. From the corner of my other eye I thought I saw the big camera and the guy with the handheld both tracking me. From the shadows behind Cavan, somebody threw themself forward and grabbed at my feet, but missed. I threw myself down, too, my left hand out to grab Brierley's cravat if I could, my right hand coming back in a fist.

Lawson was moving backwards but he hadn't started pushing away in time, plus the mike wire would be slowing him down. I hit the desk on my belly and slid; my left hand missed his cravat, catching him by the padding in the left shoulder of his hacking jacket instead, but my right fist smacked satisfactorily – and painfully, for my fingers – into his left cheek, just below the eye.

My momentum, and his push, carried us both back over his seat, falling in a flailing tangle to the floor behind, where I landed another couple of lighter blows and he managed to thump me once on the side of the ribs and once on the back of the head with weak, painless punches before we were pulled apart by security guards and production people.

That, obviously, wasn't the clever bit either.

Brierley was ushered away shouting about communist violence and intimidation, surrounded by headphoned staff, while I was held, the backs of my thighs against the desk, by two uniformed security guards. I was smiling at Lawson, and not struggling at all. I was highly gratified to see that Lawson already looked like he was developing what we used to call, back where I came from, a keeker; a nice black eye. A door closed softly in the darkness and Brierley's shouts were silenced.

'It's okay, guys,' I told the security guards. 'Promise I won't run after him.'

They kept holding me, but their grip might have relaxed a little. I looked around. Cavan seemed to have disappeared as well. I grinned at each of the two security guards as the floor manager came over. She looked professional and unruffled. 'Ken; Mr Nott? Would you like to go back to the Green Room?'

'Fine,' I said. 'Though I'll want my pliers back, or a receipt.'
I smiled. 'I'll pay for a new mike cable.'
Still not the clever bit.

'Ken!' Cavan came into the Green Room. The two guards were in there with me, and two of the awfullies. I was watching News 24 on the room's TV and relaxing with a Scotch and soda. Not something I'd normally countenance, but, hey, it was only a blend, and besides, I felt a certain refreshing desire to get drunk quickly.

'Cavan!' I said.

He looked a little flushed. There was a smile on his face that looked unhappy to be there. 'Well, that was a bit of a surprise there, Ken. What was that all about?'

'What was what?' I asked.

Cavan sat on the edge of the table with all the sandwiches and drink. 'Bit of a rush to the head there, Ken?'

'Cavan,' I said. 'I have no idea what you're talking about.'

The door opened again and the exec producer came in; a small, bald, harassed, sullen-looking guy I'd met briefly earlier whose name I'd forgotten the instant I'd been told it. 'Ken,' he said throatily, '*Ken*; what, what, what was that . . . ? I mean we just can't allow, I mean, that was just, that was really just, I mean, what, what on earth—?'

'Cavan, old son,' I said.

'. . . I mean, I mean . . .'

'What?'

'. . . You can't, just can't . . .'

'Are you calling the police?'

'. . . no respect, professionalism . . .'

'Ah, the police?'

'. . . ashamed of yourself, quite, I mean, I don't . . .'

'Yes; are you calling the police?'

'. . . in my entire career . . .'

292

'Eh? Ah, now . . .'

'. . . disgrace, just a disgrace . . .'

'*Have* you called the police? Do you *intend* to call the police?'

'. . . what you could be thinking of . . .'

'I've no idea, Ken. Your man here might know. Mike; we calling the police?'

'What? I . . . Ah . . . I . . . I don't know? Should we?'

Mike looked at Cavan, who shrugged. He looked at me.

'Guys,' I laughed. 'I can't tell you!' I returned my attention to the telly and said, 'I think you should find out whether the feds are to be involved. Because, otherwise, I'm about to leave.'

'Ah . . . leave?' said Mike the exec producer.

'Mm-hmm,' I said, sipping my drink and watching shots of Camp X-Ray.

'But, well . . . we thought we could, maybe, still do the discussion. I mean, if you would agree . . .'

Cavan crossed his arms and appeared innocently bemused.

I was looking at the two of them, shaking my head. 'Listen, guys, I have no fucking intention of even beginning to take that nasty little right-wing shithead's diseased ideas seriously, to *debate* them, for fuck's sake.' I looked back at the TV. 'Never did,' I muttered. I looked back at the producer. He was standing with his mouth open. I frowned. 'You *did* get it all on tape, didn't you?'

'Yes. Of course we did.'

'Good,' I said. 'Very good.' I watched the TV a moment longer. 'So,' I said to him, when he still hadn't gone, 'if you could just find out if the boys in blue are going to be involved or not. Okay? Thanks.' I nodded at the door and then went back to watching the guys in orange shuffling between the cages in Guantanamo.

He shook his head at me, and left. I smiled at the two attractive awfullies, who grinned back nervously.

Cavan chuckled and got up to leave. 'Well,' he said, 'if I'm

293

not mistaken, Ken, you've totally fucked us.' He opened the door. 'But it was elegantly done.' He nodded as he left. 'Look after yourself.'

I just smiled at him.

Actually, at that point I'd quite happily have settled for whacking a fascist and getting away with it, but – in theory, according to the mad, bad plan at least – what had to happen next was that somebody did take the matter further, and the cops did become involved, and I was formally charged with assault.

Because then – despite all the witnesses, despite the cameras and the videotape and the thing being replayable in slow motion from two or three different angles, and certainly despite what I hoped would develop into a splendid black eye for Lawson Brierley – I had every intention, in front of the police, in front of the lawyers, in front of a judge and in front of a jury if it came to that, of denying it had ever happened.

And *that* was the fucking clever bit.

Nine

BIG GUNS

'I *knew* you were up to something.'

'Fuck off! You did not.'

'I did! Why do you think I was so nervous earlier in the Pig?'

'You're always nervous when I'm doing something you can't control.'

Phil made a noise you could only call a gasp. 'Now that's not true, Ken. That's unfair.' He seemed genuinely hurt.

I put a hand on his shoulder. It was still true, mind you, but I said, 'Sorry.'

'You didn't really hit him, did you?'

'Yup. Biffed the blighter on the phizog.'

'A proper punch?'

'A proper punch. Look at them bunch a fives.' I held my right hand out to show him the grazes on the knuckles. My hand still hurt.

'You're really proud of this, aren't you?'

I thought about it. 'Yes,' I said.

We were in the Bough. Phil had said he'd hang about Capital Live! until the recording for *Breaking News* was finished, expecting a debriefing; he'd been suitably surprised when I'd walked into the office barely ninety minutes after I'd left him for the studio in Clerkenwell.

'You attacked him?' Kayla had said, sitting back in her chair in her winter camos and chewing on a pen. I'd nodded, and she'd got up and kissed me. 'Brilliant, Ken.'

Phil and his assistant Andi had looked aghast at each other. Andi had said, 'Pub, now, I'd suggest.'

'But they didn't call the police.'

'Not so far. They spent most of their time trying to persuade me to stay and continue with the debate. I don't know what put them off eventually, me stonewalling or the make-up girls running out of foundation to cover up Lawson's black eye. Eventually I just walked out and got a taxi.'

'Do you think Brierley will press charges?'

'No idea.' I drank my London Pride and smiled widely at Phil. 'Don't fucking care.'

'You've been planning this for weeks, haven't you?'

'Months, actually. Since it was first brought up in Debbie's office, back in September. I had that classic dilemma thing going where you don't want to give these people a platform, but on the other hand you want to get them in public and grind the grisly fuckers into the dust – and I actually really thought I could do it, because I'm a fucking militant liberal, not the wishy-washy sort that would try to understand the bastard or just be appalled – but then I thought, na, just give the piece of shit a taste of his own medicine.'

Phil was silent for a while, so I looked at him; he was sitting side-on, looking at me.

'What?'

'Maybe I don't know you as well as I thought I did.'

'Yeah.' I grinned. 'Good, eh?'

'If he does press charges, though, you could be in serious trouble.'

'First offence? No weapon involved? I don't think I'll be going to prison. I did have a doomsday scenario going on in my head about getting carried away once I got my hands on the fuck and beating him to a pulp, leaving him paralysed or dead or something or with a Telefunken UB47 rammed up his arse, but in the end it played out pretty well. I can stand a fine and being bound over to keep the peace, or whatever.'

'I was thinking more about your job.'

I glanced at him. 'Yeah. In theory.'

'Not just in theory.'

'I thought I was pretty safe there. We haven't had a dressing down for, shit, weeks.'

'Ken, for goodness' sake; we exist on a knife-edge all the time whether or not we get a formal warning or even just a quiet word. I've had the ads department on to me about cancellations from American Airlines, the Israeli Tourist Board . . . and one or two others I've managed to repress, obviously. They're hurting. There are few enough big campaigns going as it is at the moment; losing those that are on offer is giving them sleepless nights, and I'm pretty sure news of the pain is being passed up the corporate structure.'

I frowned. 'Well, maybe the Israeli Tourist Board will come back now I've beaten up a horrible Holocaust denier.' I glanced at Phil.

He wore a suitably sceptical expression. 'Or maybe,' he said, 'this could be the bale of hay that breaks the camel's back. I'd check your contract. Never mind vague stuff about bringing the station into disrepute, I'll bet any criminal proceedings, even pending, threatened ones, means they can pull you off air without pay.'

'Shit.' I had a horrible feeling he was right. 'I'd better phone my agent.'

'So, Mr McNutt. Would you like to describe what happened

in the studio of Winsome Productions, in Clerkenwell, London, on the afternoon of Monday the fourteenth of January, 2002, in your own words?'

Oh shit, it was the same DS who'd interviewed me about the East End trip, when I'd broken the taxi's windscreen and punched 'Raine' in the face. I'd had the choice of coming to my local nick to give a statement, and I'd stupidly taken it. The DS was a young white guy, sharp-faced but a little jowly, with brown hair starting to recede at the temples. He smiled. 'In your own time, Mr McNutt.' He patted the big, clunky wooden cassette recorder sitting on the desk in the interview room.

I didn't like the relish with which he pronounced my name. For about the five hundredth time in my life to date, I cursed my parents for not having changed their name by deed poll before I was born.

'It never happened,' I said.

A pause. 'What, the entire afternoon?'

'No, whatever I'm being accused of,' I said.

'Assault, Mr McNutt.'

'Yes; that. It didn't happen. They made it all up.' I was starting to sweat. This had seemed like such a great plan right up until I had to start following through with it.

'They made it all up.'

'Yes.'

'So, what did happen, sir?'

'I went along to do an interview, and it was cancelled.'

'I see.' The Detective Sergeant thought for a moment. He looked at his notes. 'At what point was it cancelled?'

'I never left the Green Room,' I said, feeling suddenly inspired.

'The what, sir?'

'The Green Room, the hospitality suite; it's where they put you before they need you in the studio.'

'I see.'

'I never left it. They came and told me the interview, the discussion, was being cancelled.'

The DS looked at me through narrowed eyes. 'You are aware, sir, that you will be asked to repeat what you're saying, under oath, in court?'

Oh shit. Perjury. Why hadn't I thought of that? I'd been too busy congratulating myself on my own cleverness and blithely assuming that everybody would just play along once they saw what I was up to. I had thought this through a hundred times but somehow it always ended with me modestly accepting Man Of The Year awards, not being sent down for perjury.

I gulped. 'I may well choose to say nothing under oath.'

Now the DS was looking at me as though I was simply mad.

I cleared my throat. 'I think I should talk to my lawyer before I say anything else.'

'So I definitely get to be tried by a jury?'

'If you insist, Mr Nott, yes. However I'd strongly advise that you take the option of going before a magistrates' court instead.' The lawyer was called Maggie Sefton. She worked for the criminal department of my own lawyer's firm. She had deep brown skin and beautiful eyes behind the tiniest, most low-profile glasses I'd ever seen.

'But I need to plead Not Guilty!' I protested. 'I'm trying to make a political point here! This could make the news, dammit. Won't that mean it *has* to go to a higher court?'

'Not really, no. And it is usually best to avoid going before a judge.'

'But why?'

'Because magistrates can't impose custodial sentences.'

I frowned. Ms Sefton smiled the sympathetic, worldly-wise smile adults lay on children sometimes when the poor darlings just totally fail to understand the way things actually happen in the big bad world. 'They can't send you to jail, Kenneth. Whereas a High Court judge can.'

'Shit,' I said.

I'd sent Amy some flowers at her office, but she sent them back. After our rather unsatisfactory bout of going through the motions on the Sunday night she'd said she'd call me, but she hadn't, so after two days I'd headed for the nearest florist. I'd thought a dozen red roses would be just the right gesture for the sort of retro good-time semi-posh girl I'd had her characterised as – it certainly wasn't something I'd normally do – but obviously I'd got it completely wrong.

The dozen roses arrived back before I set off for work on the Thursday, three days after the *Breaking News* fracas. The note accompanying them said, 'Ken; interesting but hardly worth commemorating. See you sometime. A.'

'Bitch,' I said to myself, even though I had to admit she was right. I took the wrapping off the flowers and threw them into the river. It was a flood tide, so as they drifted slowly upstream, sped on their way by a stiff north-easterly, I reflected ruefully that if I came back at the right/wrong time this afternoon, I could watch them all come sailing back down again. Come to think of it, a timely combination of tides and winds could conceivably keep their bedraggled, distributed sorriness within sight of the *Temple Belle* for days; even weeks.

I shrugged, stuffed the wrapping paper into the bin and headed for the car park and the car Capital Live! had sent for me. The Landy was still in the garage; it had been fitted with its two new tyres – three, in fact, as the spare on the back door had been stabbed as well – but they hadn't replaced its headlights yet.

My phone went as soon as I turned it on, walking up the pontoon towards the car park.

'Debbie; you're up and running very early. How are you?'

'Come straight to my office when you get in, all right?'

I took a couple of steps. 'I'm fine too, Debs. Thanks for asking.'

'Just be there, okay?'

'Ah, okay,' I said. Oh-oh, I thought. 'Why? What's happening?'

'See you soon.' She hung up.

The Motorola vibrated again as I got to the Lexus waiting at the kerb. A Lexus; it had been a Mondeo yesterday. Good job something was looking up. I waved to the driver, who was reading the *Telegraph*. 'Nott?' I asked, unfolding the buzzing phone as he folded the paper. I thought it was best to ask; I'd once jumped into another houseboat dweller's limo waiting to take them to Heathrow. 'For Capital Live!'

'That's me, boss,' the driver said.

I got in, belted up and into the phone said, 'Yes, Phil?'

'The papers have got it.'

'What?' I asked as the car pulled smoothly away.

'Lawson Brierley's Institute for Fascist Studies, or whatever it's called, released a press statement this morning. Basically saying they can see what you're trying to do here, but . . . blah blah blah . . . the full majesty of English law, and common Anglo-Saxon justice, must take precedence over arrogant and theatrical pseudo-intellectual cosmopolitan political machinations.'

'You're not paraphrasing there, I hope.'

'No. We've just had the *Mail* on the phone. Followed by the *Sun*, followed by the *Standard* and then ITN, the *Eye* and the *Guardian*. I'm expecting to collect the rest of the set before the hour is out. Why is your land-line down?'

'I pulled it out last night; some fucker rang about one in the morning and kept ringing but not leaving a message on the machine, plus their identity was withheld, so I got annoyed and wheeched it.'

'Probably a journo favoured by Mr Brierley getting wind of it early. You weren't door-stepped this morning, were you?'

'No.'

'You were lucky. You in the car?'

'Yup.'

'Well, if you want to avoid questions at this end, have the driver take you down into the car park here and take the lift, okay?'

'Yeah. Shit. Okay,' I sighed. 'Oh, fuck, here we go . . .'

'Courage, mon brave.'

'Yeah. Right.'

'See you soon.'

'Yeah, in Debbie's office.'

'Damn, she's heard, has she?'

'Oh yes.'

'That'll be who's jamming my internal line here. Better talk to you when you get here; meet you down in the car park?'

'See you there.' I put the phone away.

The driver looked at me in the mirror, but didn't say anything.

I sat and watched the traffic go past. Shit. What if they were going to fire me? I'd taken heart, bizarrely, from the profoundly noxious Nina's remarks about publicity. I'd thought that no matter how messy everything got with the assault in the studio, at least it would be great publicity for me and the show and the station and that because of that everybody would be happy. Good grief, had I actually been insufficiently cynical? Maybe Amy was right. Maybe I was naïve. I thought back to the night in Soho during the summer with Ed and Craig, and me not dipping far enough down into the cess of human motivation with my imagination, being so innocent as to think that the worst reaction towards somebody who was helpless and vulnerable was indifference, not something worse.

How personally and professionally embarrassing.

I got lost in the traffic for a while, submerged in memories. A dispatch rider swept past on his panniered Bandit. Oh well, I thought, if I did get fired and I couldn't get in anywhere else, I could always get a job being a bike courier again. Or maybe Ed would take me seriously if I said I finally really really wanted to be a proper club-type DJ. Fuck, yeah; the money was good, and just because I'd been dismissive about it in the past and gone along for the fun, drugs and women didn't mean I couldn't try to make a go of it as a career now. Boy George could do it; why couldn't I?

We were drawing to a stop in the Mall, pulling in to the side near the ICA.

'What's the problem?' I asked.

The driver glanced in the mirror, pressed the hazard warning lights, killed the engine and turned round, handing the keys to me. I looked at them lying in my hand, wondering what the hell was going on. 'I'd like a word, Mr Nott,' he said (this was itself enough to have me tense up and check that the door-lock buttons were in the unlocked position), 'but I don't want to alarm you.' He nodded at the keys in my hand. 'That's why I've given you them. If you want to get out, you can.'

He was about fifty; a balding, slightly overweight guy with the sort of large-framed glasses last fashionable in the early nineties and a pinched, concerned-looking face; sad-looking eyes. Otherwise fairly nondescript. His accent sounded vaguely Midlands, like a Brummie born and raised who'd lived in London most of his life. He was neatly dressed in a light-grey suit that only now was starting to look a little too well cut to be that of your standard limo driver.

'Uh-huh?' I said. 'I'll just test the door, right?'

'Be my guest.'

The door opened easily enough and the sound of traffic and the chatter of a passing gaggle of Japanese tourists entered the cabin. I closed it again. 'I'll just keep my phone open here, too,' I said warily. The driver nodded.

He offered his hand. 'Chris. Chris Glatz.' We shook hands.

'So what's going on, Chris?' I asked him.

'Like I say, Mr Nott, I'd like a word.'

'About what?'

'A matter that has, umm, fallen to me to try to resolve.'

I screwed up my eyes. 'I'm kind of looking for specifics, here.'

He looked around. On the broad pavement under trees in front of the colonnaded white splendour of the ICA, a couple of cops were walking slowly along, eyeing us. 'Here isn't perfect, frankly,' he said apologetically. 'You suggest somewhere.'

I looked at my watch. An hour and ten before the last possible time I could get to the studio for the start of the show. 'Tell you what,' I said. 'I'll drive.'

If he'd taken too long, or said no, I'd have walked, but he just looked a little surprised, nodded and opened his door. I made sure the two cops got a really good look at us, waving at them and saying, 'Morning, officers!' They nodded, professionally.

I rang the office en route but the lines were busy. Instead I left a message with Debbie's secretary to say I'd be late.

I parked the Lexus behind the Imperial War Museum. We got some coffees from a mobile stall and walked round to the front, under the barrels of two colossal Naval guns. Mr Glatz pulled some gloves from his coat pocket and put them on. The air had an easterly tang to it and the clouds were grey as the paint on the giant artillery pieces above us.

'Nice car,' I said. 'Yours?'

'Yes, it is. Thanks.'

'Should have known I wouldn't rate a Lexus from the radio station.'

'Ha ha.'

'So, Mr Glatz; Chris.'

'Well, Mr Nott—'

'Call me Ken, please.'

'Right. Ken. Well, I'll come straight to the point. Oh; well, first, I'd better say, this is all off the record, right?'

'I'm not a journalist, Mr Glatz, but yes, all right.'

'Right. Good. Now then. You'll remember you witnessed a road traffic accident a few months back.'

'Mm-hmm. Guy in a blue Beemer Compact, talking on his mobile, came out—'

'That's the one, that's the one.' He sipped his coffee. 'See,' he said, 'Mark – the gentleman involved, Mr Southorne – is a, an occasional business partner of mine.'

'I see.'

'You haven't heard of him?'

'No, should I have?'

Glatz teeter-tottered one hand. 'He's fairly well known in the City. One of these flamboyant types, you know?'

Well, no, I thought, but I could imagine. He hadn't looked very fucking flamboyant standing holding his mobile in the rain looking down at a still stunned biker lying in the gutter, but maybe that had just been shock.

'Thing is, you see,' Glatz said, looking pained. 'He's sitting on ten points. On his licence.'

I nodded. 'The poor soul.'

'Twelve, and he's banned. Sure you know how it is.'

'Of course.'

'And, well, the thing is, Mark really needs his car. He loves his car; loves his cars. But he does a lot of driving, which he enjoys, and—'

I'd held up one hand. 'Hold on, Chris. That wa a bog-standard two-year-old Compact he was driving. If he loves cars so much—'

'Yeah, that was just a courtesy car. His M5 was being serviced.'

'Ah-hah,' I said. Ah-hah, indeed. Served me right, I thought. There I'd gone, making assumptions about the man just because he'd been driving the sort of car people bought because they wanted to say they'd got a BMW rather than because of what it actually did. In fact he had an M5. That was different. I'd test driven an M5 about a year ago; a sleek brute with four hundred horse-power. A brilliant motor, but wasted in London.

'Look, ah, Ken,' Glatz said, smiling awkwardly at me. 'Frankly, I think this has been mishandled. I think that the whole way this has been approached was pretty fucking stupid.' Another stilted smile. 'Excuse my vernacular.'

'Well, obviously I am shocked, but all right.'

He smiled. 'I'm going to level with you, Ken. Thing is, you see, we'd like you to retract your witness statement, especially the bit about Mark using the mobile at the time of the accident.'

'Oh?' I said. I sipped my coffee. Actually I hated this new coffee culture; people wandering around with these pint-sized cartons full of a mild, warm, watery drug it takes about twenty words and five questions just to fucking order, turning some streets in London into nothing but a procession of Starbuck's, Aromas, Coffee Republics, Costas and . . . but enough. Mr Glatz was making his point. 'We'll get a good brief, we'll suggest that the biker guy was going too fast, and with a bit of luck and a following wind, like they say, we'll get Mark off. But we do need you to retract that statement, you see, Ken, because that's the really damning bit. Without that there we might be able to swing it; with it the prosecution can walk all over us.'

I nodded. 'Right,' I said. A very strange, disturbing but oddly relieving idea had occurred to me. It seemed grotesquely unlikely, but then when had that ever proved a problem for

308

reality when it was determined to serve up a squid in your custard? 'This occasional business relationship you have with this guy Mark . . .'

'Yes, Ken?'

'In terms of above-boardness, whereabouts would we be talking here?'

Chris Glatz chuckled. 'You're catching on here, Ken. Frankly, pretty well below the waterline.'

'Right, and when you say,' I started slowly, 'that this has been mishandled, what exactly are you referring too?'

'Ah,' he said. 'Well. When – and I hasten to add here, Ken, that I was not personally involved at this point,' he said, holding up one hand. 'When it was decided that my colleagues might be able to help Mark with this problem, a – how's best to put this? – a rather extreme plan was formulated to, well, to attempt to impress upon you the fact we were serious in our commitment to aid our friend and colleague.'

We'd been strolling round the big circular path in front of the museum. Now I stepped round and stopped in front of him and said, 'Is this about my trip to the East End in a certain taxi, to fucking *Haggersley Street*?' I almost shouted the last bit.

My new pal Chris looked around and patted the air with one hand. 'Now, I can see why you might be upset about that, Ken, but—'

'You fuckers were trying to drug me and kidnap me because of a fucking *traffic violation*?' Again, I had trouble keeping my voice modulated for maximum mellifluousness.

Glatz did the air-patting thing again. He sighed and put a hand to one side of his face, then nodded forward and we set off again, walking slowly round the big circle. 'Ken, I'm not going to lie to you,' he said in a tired voice. 'That was an over-reaction. But,' he said, holding up one hand, before I could respond to this, 'the need was felt to impress on you that we are serious people, and that we have the necessary resources, and the will, to follow through with any – what's the best way to put this? – incentivisation framework we might wish to implement.'

'You can back up threats because you're crims.'

Chris actually laughed quite loudly at this. 'Well, basically, yes, if we're being frank with each other.'

'I see. And the threatening phone call? And the tyres on my Land Rover? And the headlights?'

He nodded. 'All a bit messy, a bit unrequired, frankly, Ken. That's why I'm here. That's why I'm approaching you as one reasonable man to another.'

I gave a small laugh. 'You obviously don't listen to my show.'

He smiled, sipped some more coffee. 'Ken, we'd like to compensate you for the damage and distress you've suffered.'

'I see. You mean bribe me.'

'Frankly, yes.'

'How much?'

'Two grand. And we'll settle the bill with the garage.'

'And what if I say no?'

He looked round at me. 'Frankly?'

'Frankly.'

'Then I go back to Mark and say that we've done our best; gone out on a limb for him, even, and it hasn't worked. We've tried money and that hasn't worked either, and unless he wants to raise the offer to something you'd accept—'

'I'm not poor, or greedy enough, Chris. And I am easily proud enough not to.' I smiled.

'Fair enough,' he said, dumping his coffee in a bin. I'd have followed his example except I'd remained just worried enough to be keeping the still-just-about-scaldingly-hot coffee to use as a weapon if things suddenly turned nasty again. 'So,' he said, 'I'd tell Mark that maybe he should just take his punishment like a man and take more care driving in future, and get a chauffeur for however long his ban lasts. And unless he does something very stupid, which I shall try to persuade him not to do, that'll be the end of the matter.'

'Really?' I looked into the man's eyes. I formed the distinct impression that actually Mr Glatz wouldn't be at all averse to his business associate having to swallow his pride and accept his punishment.

He shrugged. 'You have to have a sense of proportion about these things, Ken,' he said reasonably, 'otherwise people end up getting hurt. Which is messy. And messy, generally, is not good for business.'

'So,' I said. 'If I say I'm not going to retract my witness state-ment, that'll be that.'

'It should be.'

'I know it should be, but will it?'

'Ken,' Glatz sighed heavily. 'I am not here to threaten you. I am here to make you an offer, which I've done. You seem to be rejecting it. That's the end of the matter as far as I'm con-cerned and as far as my colleagues are concerned, in so far as you're concerned . . . if you see what I mean.'

'I think so. Go on.'

'I can't speak for Mark, who may wish to approach you him-self.'

'And what the fuck does that mean?'

'Ken, Ken,' he said, holding up both hands. 'Don't get upset. It means just what it says. It's not a threat.' He gave what was probably meant to be an encouraging smile. 'Mark is not . . . he's not the physical sort, know what I mean? That's why we make a good team. He's very good with money, and contacts, and charm, and . . . Well. But with us washing our hands of the case, the direct action side of things is pretty much off the agenda.'

'Good,' I said. I thought. I pointed a finger at Glatz. 'Just in case he does get any ideas, you tell him there's a man called John Merrial who owes me a favour, all right?'

Glatz looked very surprised for a vanishingly brief interval of time. Then he looked slightly surprised. 'Mr Merrial?' he asked. 'Really?'

'Really,' I said. 'And if he doesn't know who John is, I think maybe you ought to enlighten him. Don't you?'

Glatz was looking away from me, nodding. We were back almost under the big guns again, which felt like a shiveringly appropriate place to be when invoking the name of Mr M to another, palpably lesser, villain. 'I see, Ken,' he said, still nodding, glancing at me. 'Well, that is interesting. I'd no idea. A favour, eh?'

'That's what he said, last time I saw him,' I told Glatz.

He looked at me and nodded. 'I can rely on your discretion here, can't I, Ken? Off the record, as we agreed. Obviously all of this is strictly between you and me.'

'Obviously. Providing your friend Mark doesn't do anything stupid.'

'I'll have a word.'

'That'd be nice.'

He smiled. 'Right. Well, I think we're finished here, Ken, would you agree?'

I grinned. 'I think I would, Chris.'

'Okay.' He clapped his hands. 'Let's get you back to your radio station. Do you want to drive, or shall I?'

'Allow me,' I said. We started walking back to the car.

Mr Glatz nodded at my left wrist. 'By the way; nice watch.'

'Mm-hmm.'

Oh, the sheer bliss of it; when we arrived at Capital Live! I got to do the old Ronnie Reagan thing, cupping my hand to my ear, pretending I couldn't make out what the press were saying. Of course, rather than doing this across the White House lawn on the way to my helicopter with the press fifty metres away behind a rope, guarded by marines, I was about ten centimetres away from the journos, separated from them only by the thickness of a window I could have lowered with a single click of a button. This made it all the more fun.

'Ken! Ken! Is it true you kicked this guy?'

'Ken! What's the truth? Tell us what happened.'

'Ken, is it true he hit you first?'

'Ken! These pliers; did you throw them intending to hit him?'

It was *great* seeing so many journos here; I'd expected one or two, but this was real celeb stuff. Must be a quiet news day in the capital. I did the hand-ear thing, shook my head, smiled broadly and mouthed, I-can't-hear-you as I nudged the car slowly forward and angled it towards the car park ramp. They were trying the door handles but I'd locked all the doors some-where round Trafalgar Square. Two snappers were standing right in front of the car, aiming straight through the windscreen; I let the car trickle forward in Drive, brakes creaking, slowly forcing the photographers backwards.

In the passenger seat, Mr Glatz had looked puzzled when he'd seen the small crowd of reporters gathered round the office entrance. When they'd spotted me driving the car through the traffic towards the underground car park, and come run-ning over to hammer on the windows, tape recorders aimed, flashes flashing – heck, there was even a TV crew there – he'd been horrified, but by then it was too late. He'd picked up his newspaper and hid behind it. This was, of course, entirely the wrong thing to do, because now the ladies and gents of the press were starting to think, Hold on, who's Mr Shy in the passenger seat? A couple of the snapperistas took photos of Mr G's hands and the *Torygraph* they were clutching.

'Sorry about this, Chris,' I said.

'Jesus,' he said. 'What the fuck's all this about?'

'Oh, I was on a telly programme with this guy who deserved a good slap, so I duly whacked him one. Bit of a fuss about it for some reason.'

313

'Did I not need this,' Glatz breathed as I nodded at the security guy in the booth at the top of the ramp; the striped pole rose and we roared away down the slope. I stamped on the brakes and got a very satisfying squeal out of the tyres at the bottom.

Mr Glatz left looking unhappy, resigned to facing down the crowd of muttering rotters still milling at the top of the car park ramp.

I bumped into Timmy Mann in the lift.

'Timmy,' I said cheerfully. 'You're in early.'

'Uh, yeah, ah, hi, ah, Ken,' Timmy said, displaying the incisive wit that has made him such a hit on the lunchtime show. He looked down as the lift doors closed. Timmy was something of a throwback; older than me, an ex-Radio One *Breakfast Show* presenter, dark hair worn in a style dangerously close to being a mullet. He was short, even for a radio DJ.

I felt my good mood evaporate as the lift whined into action and my stomach seemed to drop. 'Oh, yeah, of course,' I said. 'You're here to do my show, aren't you?'

'Ah, just half,' he said. 'Maybe.'

'Well, don't forget to apply for overtime.'

'Um, yeah.'

'Where the *fuck* have you been?'

'Talking to a man about a fucking death threat,' I told Station Manager Debbie, throwing myself into a couch. The couch was on the far side of Debbie's redecorated office, a pale mauve oval carpet away from her new ash and chrome desk, where Producer Phil and Guy Boulen, Mouth Corp's legal geezer, were sitting. 'Hi, Phil, Guy.'

'I didn't say you could sit over there.'

'Good, Debbie, because I didn't fucking ask to.' The sofa was big and plump and cerise without actually looking like a pair of lips. It smelled very new.

'What's this about a death threat?' Phil asked quickly, while Debbie was still opening her mouth to say something.

'It's been resolved. It was all a hideous mistake; an over-reaction. I know what it was all about and it's *almost* certainly been taken care of.'

Phil and Boulen looked at each other. Boulen cleared his throat. 'You met whoever it was who's been behind all this?'

'It was an organisational thing, Guy; I met the guy whose desk this landed on after people below him didn't get the results they'd wanted. And arguably took it all too far.'

'Who was it? Who is it?' Phil asked.

'Can't tell you,' I said. 'Sworn to secrecy.'

'Is this—?' Boulen began.

'*Can* I just point out that we've a decision to make about a radio show due to start in twenty minutes?' Debbie said loudly, swinging our attention back to her.

'Debs,' I said. 'The *Breaking News*, Lawson Brierley thing; I'm denying everything. It didn't happen. It's all a lie. They made it up.' I looked at Boulen and smiled. 'That's the line I'm taking.' He nodded, then smiled too, uncertainly.

'But you've been charged,' Debbie said.

'Yup.'

'We can take you off air.'

'I know. So; going to?'

Debbie looked at me as though I'd just crapped on her new couch. Her desk phone warbled. She glared at it, grabbed it. 'Don't you fucking understand English? I said no—' Her eyes closed and she put a hand to her brow, making her glasses slip down her nose. She took them off and stared at the ceiling with tired eyes. 'Yes, of course. Sorry, Lena. Put him on.'

Each of us chaps looked at the other two.

Debbie drew herself up in her seat. 'Sir Jamie . . .'

'Chumbawumba and "Tubthumping". Good to hear the old

315

signature tune all the way through there, bit of comfort music in these trying times, don't you think, Phil?'

'Knock people down and they just jolly well get back up again,' Phil agreed.

'Ms Nutter, Mr Prescott and I would all agree. But what makes you mention knocking people down, Phil?'

'Oh, nothing,' Phil waved one hand airily. 'Just the lyrics of the song.'

'Splendid. Time for some vitally important advertisements. Back in a mo if we haven't been removed in the meantime for gross moral turpitude. Back, in fact, with Ian Dury and The Blockheads and "Hit Me With Your Rhythm Stick". Just kidding. It's actually Cornershop and "Lessons Learned From Rocky One to Rocky Three". Stop that, Phil.' I FX'd the squeaky noise for Phil's head shaking.

'What are you like?' he sighed.

'Just keeping things topical, Phil.'

'I despair.'

I laughed. 'Yeah, I know. It sounds pretty crap now but just you wait till later. It won't even be pretty.'

'Hit the ad cart, Ken.'

'It are hitted.'

We both sat back and put our cans round our necks as the ads played.

'So far so good,' Phil said.

'Getting away with it,' I agreed.

'All my life.' Phil glanced up at the portrait of Sir Jamie on the wall. 'Wonder if himself's listening in on the Internet feed.'

Sir Jamie had called Station Manager Debbie from the archipelago he owned in the Caribbean. He'd just heard about the press getting hold of the *Breaking News* story and called to say he thought it was vitally important that I should do my show unless the station had no legal choice but to pull it. I did believe it was the first time I'd actually felt a mild glow of affection

316

for the man. He'd even had Debbie pass me the phone and spoken a few words to me. He told me he was right behind me, right behind me, hundred and ten per cent.

'I can only hope and trust,' I told Phil, 'that I am living up to the faith placed in me by our Dear Owner.'

'Are we really going to take calls?'

'I think we must, Philip. We owe it to our public.'

'Yeah, right. Ken, what's this about you hitting some bloke on the telly then?'

'Sir, you have been grievously misinformed.'

'So it's not true then?'

'Actually I was just talking in general, Stan; you have the sound of a man who takes the tabloids, so you have undoubtably been grievously misinformed for, well, years, I imagine.'

'Come on, Ken. Did ya hit him or not?'

'At this point I have to resort to the old diplomatic service thing of saying that I can neither confirm nor deny whatever it is you may have heard.'

'But is it true?'

'What is truth, Stanley? One person's truth is another person's lie, one person's faith is another's heresy, one person's certainty is another's doubt, one person's boot-legs are another's flares, know what I'm saying?'

'You ain't gonna tell nobody, are ya?'

'Stan, I'm like the Egyptian fresh-water carp; I'm in denial.'

'What?'

'The matter I believe you might be referring to is *sub judice*, Stan, or soon will be; the exact technical legal status it holds at the moment is not entirely clear, but let's just say it's better to treat it as definitely not to be talked about.'

'All right. So, how's that rubbish football team of yours up there in Jockland going to do then?'

I laughed. 'Now we're talking, Stan. Which aspect of the

317

profound awfulness of the Bankies did you wish me to elaborate upon, Stanley? The choice is wide and the show is long.'

'Don't really give a toss, mate.'

'Ah; indifference. Good choice. Now . . . Stan? Stanley? Hello?' I'd cut him off. 'Ah, how oddly pointed was Stanley's casual but cutting dismissal just there. Though in fact I have to point out that actually the Bankies are currently doing remarkably well in the league and are strong promotion contenders. However, I'm sure normal service will be resumed in due course.'

I glanced at the callers' screen. The girls were doing their best to weed out journalists – the system was flagging numbers of newspapers and if Kayla or Andi were suspicious, they asterisked the name (though in Kayla's case, as well as * it could equally well be &, [, 7, 8, 9, U or I). One name and subject snagged my gaze instantly. Oh-oh.

Name: Ed. Subject: Robe.

'Ah . . . Toby; you've a beef about airport security.'

'Yeah. Hi, Ken. It's about glasses.'

'Glasses?'

'You can't take nail clippers onto a planc nowadays, not even little ones, but people wearing glasses; no probs.'

'Your point being?'

'Glass-lensed glasses, right? Not plastic, right? Break a glass lens and you've got two perfect blades, right? Really sharp. Take *them* on? No probs. But nail clippers? I mean, *nail clippers*? No way. What's all that about then?'

I saw Ed's entry on the screen disappear; he'd rung off. Point made, I guessed.

'What a fine point, Tobias,' I said. 'There should be a sin-bin for spectacles and a choice of soft contact lenses for these astigmatic miscreants at every airport security scanner.'

'Ed.'

'Wot. The fuck. Were you doin. Tryin to get old of Robe?'

318

'Oh, come on. Guess.'

'I told you not to. I told you to leave it.'

'I was desperate. But, listen; it's all right now.'

'It's not all right.'

'It is; he wouldn't sell me a . . . you know. Wouldn't even meet up. And—'

'Fot you were a cop, didn't he? Fot you was filf tryin to set im up.'

'I did kind of get that impression. But—'

'Now he's givin me grief cos you got is number froo me. Froo me mum, Kennif; froo me *mum*. I am not amused.'

'Ed, I'm sorry.' I was trying to hold off from saying something like, Come on, Ed it's not as bad as fucking your pal's girl. 'I was scared and I panicked, but I really am sorry.'

'So you should be.'

'But I don't need the . . . article in question any more. That's the good news.'

'You don't? Why not?'

'It turns out it was something of a misunderstanding. I met with somebody who's in the process of resolving the matter.'

'You're soundin like an accountant. As somebody got a gun to your ead now?'

'I think it's going to be all right. Almost certainly.'

'Right. So now you only got to worry about fascist boot boys comin round in the middle of the night an kickin your ead in in retaliation for fumpin this Holocaust geezer on telly.'

'Oh, you've heard.'

It had taken me most of the afternoon to get hold of Ed; his phone had been either off or engaged, and I hadn't wanted to leave a message. I'd started trying as soon as the show ended. We'd had yet another meeting with Debbie and Guy Boulen, got some sandwiches sent down from the canteen for lunch in the office and then got round to some routine but necessary work for the middle part of the afternoon.

When we were ready to leave Phil had walked round to a corridor with the appropriate view and seen that there were still some press waiting outside, so we'd called a taxi and a mini-cab to the underground car park; Phil, Kayla and Andi took the cab; they piled their coats and bags on the floor in a big mound that might just about have been big enough to hide a person and were duly followed. I left in the mini-cab's boot ten minutes later. I'd already cleared it with Craig to stay with him for a day or two until all the worst of the fuss died down. The mini-cab stopped as arranged on Park Road and I got out of the boot and into the front seat.

I finally got through to Ed after I'd settled in at Craig's.

'Course I've eard. You're in the *Standard*, mate.'

'Really, which page?'

'Wot, you aven't got one?'

'Not yet. I'll get one, I'll get one. Which page? Which page?'

'Um, five.'

'Above the fold or below?'

'The what?'

'The middle of the page. It doesn't matter so much on a tabloid, but—'

'You've got the whole page, mate. Well, part from a advert for cheap flights.'

'The whole page? Wow.'

'Says they reckon you did it cos you was under such stress from avin a def fret made against you an bein kidnapped an stuff.'

'*What?*'

Well, yuh.

I shook my head. 'Ridley Scott has a lot to answer for.'

'What?' asked Craig. 'Making *Black Hawk Down*?'

'Hell's teeth, yeah, but no; I was thinking more of introducing the concept of Gratuitous Steam.'

Craig glanced over at me. We were a bit drunk and a bit stoned, watching *Alien* on DVD after an early meal of a home-delivered pizza. We'd eaten it while watching the London local news programmes on the TV, in case I was mentioned, but I wasn't. I wondered who the camera team had been this morning outside the office in that case, then decided that probably they had been from one of the TV stations but they hadn't got enough good footage (maybe I should have got out, said something), or the story just hadn't been judged important enough by the TV news editors.

Craig was significantly less drunk and stoned than I was, plus he'd only eaten one slice of the pizza; he had a mystery date he wouldn't tell me about, at nine. In the meantime: *Alien*. Craig was exactly the sort of guy who would gradually replace all his treasured videos with DVDs. He was also exactly the sort of guy who'd ration himself, buying one old film on DVD whenever he bought a new one being released for the first time. *Alien* was the latest oldie.

Craig looked at me. 'Gratuitous Steam?'

'Yeah,' I said, gesturing at the screen. 'Look how fucking *steamy* it is in the old *Nostromo* there. Who the hell decreed space-ships dozens of generations after the shuttle – the Model-T of spacefaring craft as it will doubtless prove to be and not itself notoriously water-vapour-prone – would be so full of *steam*? I mean, why? And it's been grotesquely over-used in practically every SF film and no-brain thriller ever since.'

Craig sat and watched the film for a while. 'Designer.'

'What?'

'Set designer,' he said authoritatively. 'Because it looks good. Makes the place look lived in and industrial. And hides stuff, menacingly. Which is what you want in a horror movie, or a thriller. Plus it gives people like you something to complain about, which is patently an added bonus.'

'Do I complain a lot?'

'I didn't say that.'

'Yeah, but, come on; that's the implication. Do I?'

'You have all these problems with films, Ken.'

'I do?'

'Take Science Fiction. What, according to you, is the only technically credible SF film?'

'*2001*.'

Craig sighed. 'Why?'

'Because Kubrick doesn't allow noises in space. And because he was a genius, he knew how to use the no-sound thing, so you get the brilliant bit where what's-his-name blows himself out of the wee excursion pod thing and into the airlock and bounces around inside the open airlock until he hits the door-close and air-in controls and it's only then you get the sound feeding in; magnificent.'

'And every other space movie—'

'Is that bit less credible because you see an explosion in space and next thing you know there's a fucking teeth-rattling sound effect.'

'So—'

'Though it has to be said, virtually every movie with an explosion in it gets the time-delay thing wrong, anyway. Not only do film directors seem not to understand that sound doesn't travel in a vacuum, they also seem not to understand how it does travel in an atmosphere. You see an explosion half a fucking klick away, but the sound always happens at exactly the same time, not a second and a bit later, when you should hear it.'

'But—'

'Though there are signs of improvement. *Band of Brothers* had proper explosions. I mean, that was the least of its brilliance, but it was a sign they were taking the whole thing seriously, that the special effects people were making the explosions look like real high-explosive explosions look, with just maybe a single flash and stuff flying everywhere, rather than all this vaporised petrol or whatever it is; these great big rolling fiery clouds of burning gas, that's so bullshit.'

'Why?'

'*Why?*'

'Yeah. Why does all this matter? It's only the goddamn movies, Ken.'

'Because it isn't fucking *true*, that's why,' I said, waving my arms for emphasis.

'So,' Craig said, 'what happened in that TV studio?'

'I've told you.'

'Yeah, you have told me, and you've told me that what you told me is the truth. But it isn't what you've told other people, it isn't what you're putting in your sworn statement, is it?'

I turned on the couch to face him, ignoring Sigourney and her doomed chums. 'What the hell has that got to do with anything?'

'Ken, you're always banging on about truth and just sticking to the facts, but here you are telling lies in public.'

'But there's a *point* to all this! Haven't you understood *anything?*'

'I understand exactly what you're doing, Ken,' Craig said reasonably. 'I even applaud it. I think.' He stretched back in the couch, hands behind his neck. 'I mean, it's resorting to violence, which is more your bad person's stock-in-trade reaction, but I see what you're doing. All I'm saying is that in trying to make this point you're having to compromise this thing about telling the truth even when it hurts.'

'Craig, shit, come on; I'm no better than anybody else; I tell lies all the time. Mostly in the context of relationships. God, I'd love to be a dear, sweet, faithful, one-woman man, but I'm not. I've lied to . . . most of the women I've known. I've lied to my employers, to the press, to—'

'And me?'

That drew me up short. I sat back, thinking. 'Well, there

are . . . well, they used to be called white lies, didn't they? Relatively unimportant untruths necessary to . . . spare people's feelings, or to prevent people becoming complicit in . . . well, either complicit or—'

'I do kind of know what a white lie is, thanks, Ken.'

'Yeah; stuff that you need to tell people, even friends, if you're being untruthful to somebody else.' The on-board, on-line, on-message censor that was usually employed looking a few words or phrases ahead to make sure I didn't swear on air was here doing something similar so that I didn't actively lie to Craig, even as I was carefully not telling him the whole truth, which would have involved admitting I'd lied to him a lot about the night I'd spent with his wife. 'I wouldn't tell you the truth when I was off fucking somebody else if I thought that Jo might ask you if you knew where I was. Come on, man. You do it too; you're doing it now. Where are you going later? Who are you meeting?'

'That's not the same. I'm just not telling you. You can't compare refusing to tell at all with deliberately telling a lie.'

'Yeah, but it's still not being open, is it?'

'So fucking what? You don't have a right to know everything about my private life.'

'But I'm your best friend!' I looked at him. 'Amn't I?'

'Best male friend, definitely.'

'Who's your best female friend?'

'Well, what about Nikki?'

'*Nikki*?'

'Yeah; hey, I've known her all her life, for one thing.'

'Yeah, but—'

'We've had too many great times together to count, been through tough things too, plus she's great fun to be with, she's caring, funny, a great listener, understanding . . . What?'

I was shaking my head. 'You have to let the girl go, Craig. Okay, she's a great pal and all that, but—'

'I've *let* her go!' Craig protested. 'She's at Oxford. She's loving it; she hardly comes home any more, she's got more friends than she knows what to do with. For all I know she's already had more sexual partners than I've had in my fucking life. Ken, believe me, I'm pleased for her about all this and I don't want to smother her in affection or anything. But she'll always be a best friend.'

'Okay,' I said. 'Okay. But you have to be a bit funny about the sex thing.'

'Ken, I had umpteen years to prepare myself for the fact my child would have an independent sexual existence. Credit me with some forethought. And some . . . understanding. We've talked about this stuff, Ken; the three of us. Nikki takes precautions. We didn't raise her to be an idiot.' He prodded me on the knee with one finger. 'Anyway. That's all beside the point. The point being that I'm being truthful in telling you I'm not going to tell you something, I'm not—'

'All right already!' I said. 'Distinction taken.' And conversational direction subtly changed, you lying hypocritical dissembling louse, I told myself.

'Anyway, it's not just stuff like that,' I said, wanting to move swiftly on and away from all this lying and relationship stuff. 'Or stuff like using a parsec as a unit of time like they did in the original *Star Wars* and didn't even take it out in the new edition. It's the whole way movies, Hollywood movies, are put together. I've been thinking about this; imagine if paintings were produced the way Hollywood films are.'

Craig sighed, and I suspected he suspected there was a protorant coming up, which was true.

'The *Mona Lisa* as we know it would be just the first draft; in the second she'd be blond, in the third smiling happily and showing some cleavage, by the fourth there'd be her and her equally attractive and feisty sisters and the landscape behind would be a jolly seaside scene; the fifth draft would get rid of her and keep the sisters, lose the seaside for a misty mountain and make the girls both red-headed and a bit more, like, *ethnic* looking, and by the sixth or seventh the mountain would be replaced by a dark and mysterious jungle and there'd just be the one girl again, but she'd be a dusky maiden wearing a low-cut wrap and with a smouldering, alluring look and an exotic bloom in her long black tresses . . . Bingo – *La Giaconda* would look like something you were embarrassed your elderly uncle bought in Woolworths in the early seventies and never had the wit to get rid of in subsequent redecorations.'

'So what?' Craig asked. 'If films were all made the way paintings are every one would look like an Andy Warhol movie.' He gave a sort of stage shiver. 'Which, whatever it does for you, surely scares the hell out of me.' He looked at his watch. 'Anyway. I'd better get ready.' He stood up.

'You've nearly an hour,' I said.

'Yeah, but I need a shower and everything.' He headed for the door. 'Help yourself to stuff, okay?'

'Thanks,' I said. I tipped my head to one side in a way that I knew looked cute – and hard to resist – when Ceel did it. 'Who is she, Craig? Anyone I know?'

'Not telling you.'

'It is somebody I know. It's not *Emma*, is it?'

He just laughed.

'So it's somebody new?'

'Ken, this isn't any of your business.'

'Yeah, I know. But it is somebody new, isn't it?'

'Could be,' he said, the (in retrospect) bastard, with a small smile.

'Is she our age? Younger? Older? Children? How'd you meet?'

He shook his head as he opened the door. 'You're like a fucking journalist yourself, so you are.'

'Hope she's worth it!' I called as he left the living-room and headed upstairs.

I will freely confess that what I helped myself to while he was out – after a lonesome J and a bottle of Rioja – were the 1471 and last-number redial functions on his phone, but all I got was fucking Pronto Pizza.

Come on, now; I could have started rifling through his itemised telephone bill or something. The 1471/last-number thing was small beer . . . even if I did feel just the tiniest bit of guilt at abusing my host and Official Best Friend (Scottish)'s trust.

Like he was going to care; he still hadn't reappeared next morning when I left for work.

'Ms Boysert is working from home today.'

'Fine. Can you give me her home number?'

'I'm sorry. She doesn't want to be disturbed.'

'Not really work, then, is it?'

'I'm sorry?'

'Look, can I have her home number or not?'

'I'm sorry, Mr Nott. May I take a message?'

'Yes; tell her she's a bitch.'

'I see. Do you really want me to pass that on, Mr Nott? I shall if you insist, but . . .'

'Ah, forget it.'

Noon on the Friday of the week Celia was due back in town came and went, but there was no package and no phone call. I'd never felt so crushed at knowing I would have to wait longer to see her. I started to wish I'd done something a bit sad during one of our earlier afternoons, and asked her for a pair of her knickers or something. At least then I'd have something. I wondered if there was some Internet newsgroup or some website that would steer me to the old magazines and catalogues she'd appeared in as a model. There probably were, of course (I had long since hit the realisation, which comes to most users sometime, that there was almost nothing you

327

could imagine that was not on the Internet, somewhere), but almost as soon as I thought of this I decided that, on second and third thoughts, I really didn't want to know.

Craig spent the weekend away with his mystery woman. Ed was away, Emma was engaged all the time, Amy I'd given up on and Phil was busy decorating. I watched a lot of DVDs.

'Ken! What's your side of the story? Are you really claiming that none of it happened?'

'Ken! Ken! Did you send those death threats to yourself?'

'Would you say Lawson Brierley got what he deserved, Ken?'

'Ken, is it true them def frets were from someone wif a Muslim accent?'

'Ken, is this all about publicity? Is it true the show's being cancelled?'

'Ken! Straight to the point, straight to the point; we'll pay you for an exclusive. And you get approval. Pictures too!'

'Ken, is it true you punched and kicked two security guards *and* a girl production assistant as well?'

'Ken; they might get you for contempt of court; any thoughts?'

'Kenneth, would you say your actions last Monday and your position since constitute more of a context-challenging, meta-genristic art work rather than a simple act of political media violence?'

'Oy! Ken; didya biff the cant or not?'

'Hi, chaps! Chapesses! Fine morning, isn't it?'

(That was me.)

'Ken. Is your stance on this anything to do with your renowned antipathy towards Israel? Could you be said to be over-compensating?'

'Ken! Come on, Ken. You're one of us. Play ball for fuck's sake. Answer a fucking question, can't you? You know what'll happen if you don't. Did you thump this bloke or not?'

'Ken; is it true you have a conviction for assault already? In Scotland.'

'Mr Nott, you've frequently criticised politicians for refusing to answer straight questions from the media; don't you feel in any way or sense hypocritical here?'

'Love to answer all your questions, really would; just flippin well dying to, as a matter of fact, and you can quote me on that. But I can't. Ain't life a pain sometimes?'

(That would be me again.)

'Ken! Ken! Ere, Ken! Over ere! Come on, mate; give us a smoile.'

'Na, mate,' I said. 'That's not my best side.'

'Then wot the fuck is?'

'Whatever it was, I've put it behind me. See you, guys.'

Kenneth has entered the building.

I waved my pass at reception and the security guard and had the lift to myself to the second floor. In the lift, I let out a whoop, then relaxed, slumping briefly against the wall.

I'd decided to brave the press on the one-week anniversary of my now near-mythical tussle with the beastly fascist Holocaust denier and all-round rotten egg, Lawson Brierley. I'd walked, tubed and walked from Craig's to the Capital Live! offices and seen the waiting press pack ahead, on the broad pavement out-side the main Soho Square entrance. I'd squared my shoulders, reviewed one or two pre-prepared responses I'd thought might come in handy, and gone sailing in amongst the fuckers.

If they knew they weren't going to get anything out of you even when they could confront you face-to-face, they might give up a bit earlier than they would if you just plain avoided them, because if you just plain avoided them they could still hope that if they ever did get you alone you'd crumble and blab and basically come up with the goods they wanted. Not, of course, that that would stop them just making stuff up, including supposedly direct quotes – what the guy meant who'd said, You know what'll happen if you don't – but at least your own conscience would be clear.

The trick had nothing to do with not answering the sensible, reasonable questions; the trick was all about not responding to the ridiculous ones, the over-the-top ones: had I sent death threats to myself? Had I hit some girl assistant? Had I a conviction for assault already? (If I had, they'd have known all about it; they'd have had a photocopy of the fucking charge sheet.) These probably weren't even rumours the press had heard from anybody else; these would be questions the journos had made up themselves hoping that I'd react to at least one of them, saying, Of *course* not! . . . But the trouble was that answering one question would be like opening a vein while treading water in a pool full of sharks; it'd be a fucking feeding frenzy after that. Start answering – start denying – and it was very hard to stop.

But it had been very hard.

A Muslim accent, indeed. And, Was the show being cancelled? The devious, unprincipled fucks. (What the bampot who thought it was a work of art was on about, I had no fucking idea. Did the *Philosophical Review* have door-stepping rat-packers in these post-post-modern days? I had to suppose that there was every chance they did.)

Still, in a bizarre, leaving-morality-aside-for-a-moment sort of way, you couldn't help but be impressed by their ingenuity and dedication. I felt privileged to have been verbally roughed-up by such consummate experts. And I was doing well; those had to be the premier league newshounds out there, not cub reporters cutting their teeth.

Life and the show went on. Craig announced he would be out on the Monday night as well, so I thought I might as well move back to the *Temple Belle*. I did, and nothing bad happened. The Landy came back from the garage and spent a night outside in the car park without being attacked or set on fire or kid-napped or anything.

Having braved the journos once, it became easier and easier to keep on doing so. The trick was to respond to nothing at all. 'Ken; your dad says he's ashamed of you; what's your response?' (My response was to phone my mum and dad, who'd been door-stepped by the fucking *Mail on Sunday*. Of course they hadn't said they were ashamed of me at all; they'd responded to some hypothetical question the journalist had put to them about people hitting defenceless other people and this had somehow – spookily – been extrapolated into a direct quote.)

On the other hand, the *Guardian* had done some digging on Lawson Brierley and found that he *did* have convictions for assault; two, in fact, one with a racial element. Not to mention having done time for fraud and embezzlement. Some of the other papers were sounding just a little more sympathetic to me, though the *Telegraph* and the *Mail* still thought I ought to be hung up by the thumbs, and the *Mail* made a big thing about withdrawing its advertising from Capital Live!. Meanwhile I turned down a couple of TV appearances and several exclusive interviews; I think the offers topped out at eleven grand, which was mildly flattering without amounting to so much that I'd ever entertain actually succumbing.

'I suppose it must be a bit weird having to defend somebody you know is guilty,' I said to my lawyer.

Maggie Sefton looked at me with what looked like an, Are you serious? expression. I looked back at her and she obviously decided I was just as naïve as I appeared. 'Ken,' she said, shaking her head. 'Ask any defence lawyer; most of our clients are guilty.' She gave a soundless laugh. 'Civilians always seem to think it must be really hard defending somebody you know is guilty. It isn't; that's what you do practically all the time. Defending somebody you know is innocent; *that* is weird.' She hoisted one eyebrow and opened an already fairly stuffed box file. '*That* can cause you sleepless nights.'

'So, tell me straight, Maggie,' I said. 'Am I being really stupid here?'

She looked up sharply. 'You want my professional or personal opinion?'

'Both.'

'Professionally, you're entering a minefield. Riverdancing.'

I had to smile at that. She smiled too, then the smile went.

'Ken, you're risking charges of perjury and being in contempt of court. Happily – if it comes to it – your employers are able to afford a good brief, but I suspect he or she is going to spend a lot of their preparation time impressing upon you the fact that you'll have to be very, very controlled and careful in what you say. If you go shooting your mouth off – in court or out of it – you could be in serious trouble. The judge can send you down for contempt right there and then, without any extra procedure, and perjury is, rightly, regarded by judges as being a lot more serious an offence than simple unaggravated assault.'

'What about your personal opinion?'

Maggie smiled. 'Personally, Ken, I'd say, Bully for you. But then what I think personally doesn't matter a damn.'

'And the good news?'

She looked away for a while.

'. . . In your own time,' I said.

She clapped her hands. 'Let's crack on, shall we?'

Fending off journalists and ordinary callers interested in the matter during the phone-ins became a game for that week. The crowd of journos shrank rapidly until by the Thursday I got to work completely unmolested. I got it into my head that Ceel would be listening that day, and that there would be a package and a phone call from her when I finished the show, but – again – nothing.

That left Friday; there had to be something from Ceel on the Friday. Otherwise it would just be too long an interval. She'd forget what I looked like. She'd fall in love with her husband again. She'd find somebody else – Jeez, suppose she already had? Oh my God; suppose she was some sort of series-serial sexual adventurer and I was just one of a dozen or so guys she met up with for sex every couple of weeks? What if she was fucking a whole male harem of guys, one a day, even two a day! One in the morning, before me! Maybe she was never out of those five star hotels, maybe she practically lived in them, serviced by a steady stream of sadly deluded lovers. Maybe . . .

Shit, I was going crazy. I had to see her again, I had to talk to her.

'Hey; that's your old girlfriend, isn't it?'

We were in the office after the Thursday show. Kayla had grabbed our copy of the February edition of Q as soon as it had arrived. She was holding it up across the desk from me. Phil looked up from his computer screen.

I frowned. 'What? Who?'

'Jo,' Kayla said. 'Look.' She passed the magazine over.

It was in the News section. A small colour photograph and a couple of paragraphs. Brad Baker of Addicta pictured post-gig in Montreux with current squeeze Jo LePage. La LePage, part of Addicta's management team, has been spotted on stage helping to provide backing vocals for the band; definitely a better voice than Yoko Ono or Linda McCartney. Comparisons to Courtney Love not invited. Hate mail from female teenage Brad Baker fans probably in post already.

'She's fucking *that* bastard?' I said. 'She told me she hated him!'

'That old trick,' Kayla muttered. She was holding her hand out towards me. She clicked her fingers. 'Back, please.'

'And she was doing PR for Ice House,' I said. 'Not helping manage Addicta. Fucking useless fucking journalists. Bastards.'

'Ahem.' Kayla clicked her fingers again.

'Have it,' I said, shoving it into her hand.

'You're blushing!' Kayla said.

'Who's blushing?' Andi said, coming through the door with a tray of coffee and cakes.

'Ken is; look,' said Kayla. 'His old girlfriend's shagging Brad Baker.'

'What? The Addicta guy?'

'Yeah.'

'Lucky cow!'

'Yeah. It's in Q; see?'

'Oh, yeah.' Andi tutted, looking at the magazine as she put the tray down. She glanced at me. 'That's a shame.'

I looked at Phil. 'Am I really blushing?' I felt that I could have been. I certainly felt embarrassed. To still be so affected just because Jo was pictured with somebody else; pathetic.

Phil looked at me carefully. 'Ta,' he said absently as Andi handed him his cup and a doughnut. His eyes narrowed behind his glasses and he nodded. 'Maybe a little.'

'I think that's sweet,' Andi said, looking at me with a rueful, sympathetic smile. In return I managed a mouth-twitch that might, from a distance with the light behind it, have been interpretable as a smile by somebody partially sighted.

'Reminds me,' Phil said, clattering at his keyboard. 'Bit of gossip on the office e-mail.' He clattered some more. 'Yeah,' he said, nodding at the screen. 'Mouth Corp might be buying Ice House.'

'Ice Mouth!' Kayla said.

'Mouth House,' Andi suggested.

'Oh, fuck,' I said, eloquently.

The Friday show ended. No package. I felt utterly depressed. I was walking along the corridor to the office when my newly switched-on phone vibrated. Yes! I pulled the Motorola from its holster.

Shit; my lawyer, again.

'Maggie,' I said, sighing.

'Good news.'

I perked instantly; lawyers don't go bandying about phrases like that without very good reason. 'What? Lawson's been found in a child abuse ring?'

'Better. He's dropped the charges.'

'You're kidding!' I stopped in the corridor.

'No. He had some backers who were going to bankroll him in any resulting civil action and I think they decided if they saw it through they'd just give you a platform and let you make the point you're so obviously trying to make. So, they've pulled the plug. Mr Brierley has come to the same conclusion.'

That was rich; Lawson and his right-wing pals concerned about giving *me* a platform. 'So, is that it?'

'There's the matter of costs. We could go after them.'

'Right, well, you'd better talk to the money or the legal people here about that, but what about any sort of court case? I mean, is that it . . . for that?'

'As I say, a civil action appears to have been ruled out, and, given that the police didn't choose to suggest a prosecution themselves, yes. I think it's highly unlikely they'll change their minds now. Looks like you're in the clear.'

'Ya fucking beauty!' I said loudly. 'So we've won!'

'Well, you could put it that way, but technically we never fought, did we? Let's say they've withdrawn from the field and left it to your good self.'

'Brilliant. Maggie; thanks for everything you've done. I appreciate it. I really do. That's incredible.'

'Yes, well, the bill will be in the post, but for what it's worth, congratulations. It was nice to meet you, Ken.'

'Likewise, Mags. Superb job. Thanks again.'

'Okay. Enjoy the champagne.'

'Damn right! Hey; we're off soon, here. Do you want to come round for a drink?'

'Thank you, but I'm very busy. Some other time, maybe. Okay?'

'Yeah, okay. Thanks again. Cheers now. Bye.'

'Bye, Ken.'

I walked the last few steps and threw the office door open on a surprised-looking Phil, Kayla and Andi.

I threw my arms wide. 'Ta-fucking-*RA*!'

'Craig! Brilliant! I've been trying to get you!'

'Ken.'

I was standing outside the Bough, looking down the street. Behind me, the pub's CD box was playing Outkast's 'Ms. Jackson'. It was moderately loud in there; we'd persuaded Landlady Clara to turn the volume up to levels commensurate with serious celebration. It was about half six and the sky was as dark as it ever gets in London; the dark of a cloudless night after a clear day. An unseasonal smell of drains wafted in from some grating, briefly faecal before the light breeze flushed it away.

'I got off!' I yelled into the mobile. 'There isn't going to be a court case! Lawson Fucking Brierley caved in! Isn't that fucking *brilliant*?'

'Yeah. I'm very happy for you.'

His voice chilled me. 'Craig? What's wrong?' I asked, moving further out of the pub's doorway, further into the street, away from the noise and cheery, beery smell of the pub.

'Well,' Craig said. 'There's some good news and some bad news, Ken.'

'What? What is it? Is Nikki okay?'

'Nikki's fine. This is not about Nikki.'

That at least, was some sort of relief. 'Well, what, then?'

'The good news is that Emma and I are getting back together.'

336

'You are?' I stopped and thought. 'Well, that is fucking superb! Well done! That's great. I am so pleased for you. I am really so happy for the two of you. Honestly.'

'Yeah,' Craig said, and I could hear him take a deep breath.

'The bad news is that when we decided we were going to get back together we thought we ought to have a sort of clearing of the decks about other relationships.'

Oh-oh, I thought. 'Uh-huh,' I said.

'I had one or two . . . episodes to report.'

'Yeah,' I said, feeling suddenly cold. 'Good for you; glad to hear it.' I leaned back against the stonework by the side of one of the pub's windows.

'Emma had one or two little dalliances to put on the table too. And one – just a one-night thing – she didn't want to tell me about. We were supposed to tell each other everything, but she still didn't want to name names, or name the name. In fact, she never did tell me directly. But after a bit . . . well, eventually I just realised who it had to be, Ken.'

There was a long pause. 'Yes,' I said.

'It was you, wasn't it?'

Oh fuck. Oh fuck, fuck, fuck oh fuck.

'. . . You still there, Ken?'

'I'm still here, man.'

'So it was you, wasn't it?'

'Craig, I—'

'It was you.'

'Look, man, I—'

'It was you.'

'. . . Yes, it was me.'

Another long pause. I cleared my throat, shifted my position against the wall, smiled briefly, thinly at a guy walking past who glanced at me and seemed to recognise me.

'Well, come on, Ken,' Craig said softly. 'How do you think that makes me feel?'

I took a deep breath and released it. 'I love both you guys. I love Nikki, too.' I had to clear my throat again. 'It was just something that happened, Craig, not something we planned or, or meant in advance or anything. It was one of those comforting things, just got a bit, ah, just went on a bit beyond, well, you know . . . ?'

'No, I don't know, Ken,' Craig said. 'The only time I was in a remotely similar situation, like a mug I agreed with Jo that it wasn't worth jeopardising our relationships with you for a quick shag. I have to say I kind of regret that now. You must have been laughing your head off, inside, when I told you that, mustn't you?'

'Of course I wasn't, Craig; for fuck's sake, I was cringing. Look, for God's sake, man, I am sorry. I never wanted you to get hurt. I so did not want you or Emma to get hurt. It just happened, it was one of those things.' Oh Jesus, I thought. Listen to me. One of those things. Was that really the best I could do? 'I just thought we could . . .'

'Get away with it?'

'If you like. Just . . . just have it be a no-loss thing. God, man, it wasn't me getting one over on you or anything or any sort of macho shit, it was just, trying to be a friend to Em, to help her through what she was going through. It was all tears and, well, you know; drink had been taken, and, and so there were, like I say, a lot of . . . a lot of tears, and hugs, and, and—'

'And you fucked my wife, Ken.'

I closed my eyes, turned in towards the stonework of the pub. 'No,' I said.

'No?'

'No, that's not what happened. That just isn't what it was all about. Two people who'd known each other and been friends, and had somebody in common that they loved, or had loved and still loved, two people like that were together and one was very lonely and vulnerable and needed a shoulder to

338

cry on and the other was a bit lonely too, and weak the way most men are, and was so glad to be able to offer some support and flattered that the other person felt comforted being held and hugged and shushed by him, and . . . neither of them could stop just a sort of natural response happening when they held each other. And they both felt guilty, but they both felt . . . reassured, validated; no, not validated, that's such a crap word. They both had clung to another human being and though there was another person involved, another person they both loved, in the background, it was just that; it was not about—'

'Not about fucking my wife, Ken.'

I kept my eyes closed. 'No. It wasn't. That just wasn't it. If that's the way it feels, I'm sorry. I am so, so sorry, Craig. I did not want to hurt you, or her. I am so sorry I have.' I paused. 'I mean it.'

He was silent for a while. 'The sad thing is, Ken, you probably do mean it.'

'You are still getting back together? What I mean is, this isn't going to—'

'We're still getting back together, Ken,' Craig said. 'It's you who's the problem. Not me or Em.'

'Look, man, I—'

'Ken, Ken; Ken . . .'

'What?'

'Could you just leave us for a bit? Just the two of us. We need time to . . . to settle in together. Know what I mean?'

I wanted to be sick. I opened my mouth very wide. I swallowed. 'Sure. Yes. Of course. I . . . yeah, of course.'

'We'll maybe be . . . we'll need . . . we'll need time to think.'

'Yeah. Of course you will.' I found I'd bitten my lip. I could taste blood. 'I, ah, I hope you're both really happy. I hope it all works out. I really do.'

'Yeah. Well. Ah . . . thanks for being honest, at least. I'm glad your court thing came out well.'

'Yeah. Thanks. Yeah.'

'Goodbye, Ken.'

And, oh, Christ, just the way he said that, I felt tears on my cheeks as I said, 'Bye, Craig.'

The phone clicked off. I folded it, holstered it. I stood looking at the gutter for a while, listening to the sound of the music coming from the pub.

Eventually I pulled myself upright, wiped my nose and dabbed my cheeks, squared my shoulders and went back to the door of the Bough. I half thought of just walking away then, going home and crying into my pillow or something, but I still had a legal let-off to celebrate, and what better way to drown the pain of having hurt – and maybe lost for ever – my best pal than by getting disgustingly drunk?

Pints, whiskies, a cigar. Much pointed nattering and nonsense with Phil and Kayla and Andi, then the girls went and Phil and I were left alone for the last hour before chucking-out time. We talked about going to Clout or some other club, then settled on the Groucho. I bumped into an ad creative I knew usually carried excess gear and scored some reasonable quality coke off him, to sober myself up a little (mainly so I could get drunk all over again), but then I spilled most of it on the toilet floor just because I was so fucked on booze.

I didn't remember getting a taxi, or saying goodbye to Phil, or leaving the Groucho; all I remembered was getting home to the *Temple Belle* and standing on the deck looking out at the waters and having to close one eye so as not to see double and then deciding that it was absolutely necessary that I phoned Ceel. I hadn't seen her for far too long. I'd just escaped a court case and I might have lost one of my two best friends and I needed to talk to her, badly. I even considered, very briefly, going round to the Merrials' house and staring up at each window in turn, hoping she was in, hoping she was there, just so that I could feel I was close to her; maybe I could even ring the bell, and . . . No.

I'd phone her.

I had to use both hands on the phone and keep one eye closed but I found my way to Location 96 on the menu and immediately hit OK when it said Call Number? and then heard her voice. I heard her voice! It was recorded, but it was her! I found my eyes filling with tears.

A message. I could leave a message.

Ha; dirty, why not? Maybe she'd like that.

'Oh, lady, I want to fuck you *sooo* much,' I said, slurring. 'It's been far too long, Ceel . . . and that's not just my cock I'm talking about . . . Ha ha. Please get in touch. I need you. I miss you so much. I need to lick that lightning, yeah. Let's get together again, soon. Real soon. Love you. Night. Night, Ceel. Oh, oh, it's me; me, Ken. Ken the Naughty. Ha. Night night. Night night, Ceel. Love you. Want to fuck you. Night night. Love you. Night night.'

I got indoors and to bed somehow.

Some bit of my brain must still have been working, though, because when I woke to the light of morning it was not just to a total bastard of a hangover but to the full, awful, blood-draining, bowel-loosening, heart-constricting realisation of what I'd done.

Ten

LOCATION, LOCATION, LOCATION

Oh shit.

Eleven

EXTENDED PANIC FUNCTIONALITY

Oh dear holy fucking Christ almighty. Oh my fucking God. Oh fuck upon fuck upon total fuck to the power of fuck.

I hadn't, had I? Oh dear God, let it be a dream, let it be a nightmare, let it not have happened, let me have called a different number. Let it be anybody else's phone, anybody; my mum and dad's, Craig's, Ed's, the office, anybody anybody anybody just please please please not that one, not the number that I'd overwritten where Ceel's mobile number had been.

I fell off the bed, still fully clothed. The phone wasn't in its little holster on my hip. I looked around. Where the hell was it? Oh my God, oh my God. Where was it? I threw back the duvet, looked under the bed, searched the tops of the bedside cabinets, the dresser, the table in front of the couch. What had I done with it? I had to find the little fucker, had to check, had to make sure that what I was terrified I had done, I hadn't really done. Oh fucking hell, they could be on their way now, they might be parking, walking down the pontoon, treading on the gangplank, setting foot on the decking. They'd have the two seats set up, the big blond guy would be looking forward to the sound and feel of knees bending the wrong way

349

and snapping. Then they'd castrate me, then they'd torture me to death. Or maybe they'd be quick, merciful, and just put a bullet through my head. Oh but dear God, Ceel, What would Merrial do to her? What would he do to make her talk, then once she had, what would he do to her for what she'd done with me?

Oh no, no, no, this couldn't be happening. I stumbled through to the living-room. It had to be here. It had to be. Oh, fuck, this just could not be happening. This had to be a dream. This right now; I wasn't really awake at all. I was having the mother-fucking great-granddaddy of all nightmares. I had to be. I hadn't done that. I just hadn't. I could not be that drunk; nobody could. It was not physically possible to drink so much that any human being could forget that he'd overwritten his lover's mobile number with her home number, not when the home number was that of not just her but her husband, a major league fucking gangster notorious for having his giant body-guard bounce up and down on the legs of people he disliked until their knees cracked or their ankles snapped or their femurs popped out of their hip sockets or whatever fucking horrible thing or ghastly combination or succession of things happened when they did this to you.

I turned the living-room upside down. I threw cushions, lifted rugs, left drawers hanging open. This had to be a dream, this had to be a nightmare. I couldn't have done what I thought I had. There was not enough booze on the fucking planet to make a man do something so fucking stupid. There had never been, in the whole history of the species, sufficient drink fermented, distilled or brewed to make anybody, anybody, anybody at all no matter how stupid, how thoughtless, how much of a total fucking complete and utter fuckwit of the first water, do something that suicidally imbecilic. There were physical laws, immutable rules written into the very warp and woof of the fabric of reality itself, which would prevent any supposedly

350

sentient creature doing anything a tenth as cretinously, murderously insane as that.

A dream. A nightmare. The worst one ever; a new low-water mark in the sump of human fright and terror. I must still be asleep and my heart was probably about to stop out of sheer horror. I had to wake up. I really did.

I stumbled into the bathroom, turned on the cold tap and splashed my face, splashing and slapping my cheeks and staring at myself in the mirror, at the white, terror-struck face of a man who was not going to wake up from his nightmare because it was the worst sort of nightmare, the kind that's real, the kind you can die from but never wake from. The face of a man who'd killed the one woman he really loved in all the world, consigned her to a horrific, slow, painful, pitiful death because he'd got drunk and been stupid, because he just hadn't thought, because he'd selfishly wanted to talk to her, because he'd thought it would somehow be funny or sexy to leave a totally shite dirty message on her phone, because he couldn't read a fucking display and see that it was a different number, a land-line number, because he couldn't hear the difference between a mobile message service and a common-or-garden domestic answering machine.

Why had it been her? Why the fuck couldn't the fucking man of the house have recorded the fucking answering machine spiel? Why had that cunt Merrial made his wife record the message, the pathetic, useless, disgusting, inadequate piece of shit?

I looked down at the shelf above the sink. The phone was there. I grabbed it. But I must have left it on last night, because it was dead; no power.

I screamed at it. No words, just a scream. Yes, scream, I thought. Get in some practice for later, because you're probably going to be doing quite a lot of screaming in the very near future. Scream when you see the two chairs drawn up just a leg-length apart, when you see the big blond guy smiling at

351

you and bouncing up and down on his toes, scream when they tie you in, scream when they bring out the knives or the pliers or the blow torch. Yes, screaming now was a very good idea. Might even energise the phone in some spooky way, jar its battery into life. Because I had to check; I needed the fucking useless silvery little piece of shit on and working so I could hit the Last Calls Made list and find that – hey – of course I hadn't called Ceel (even though I could still hear her voice, still remember standing on the deck in the darkness and listening to her beautiful voice); no, I'd called somebody else. Any-fucking-body else.

Ceel. I had to phone her. I ran out, put the phone into the recharging unit on the living-room desk, and lifted the boat's own land-line phone.

Nothing. Oh, Jesus! They'd cut the phone line! They were – the dialling tone sounded. I hesitated. Right thing? Was I doing the right thing? Yes, of course. Right to check, just in case this was somehow as stupid as what I'd done last night, but the right thing. Definitely the right thing. I called her mobile number, the number I knew by heart. Oh please be there, please have it switched on. No; please don't be *there* at your house, please be somewhere else, anywhere else, some-where you can run, hide, get away from him.

Oh sweet Jesus Christ, answer, Ceel, answer. Please, please answer.

'Hello?'

Oh, Christ, yes!

'Celia. Hi. It's Ken. Kenneth. Ken Nott.' Oh God, I was going to have to tell her, going to have to admit I was an imbecile, that I'd put her in the most fucking awful danger, all through my sheer drunken stupidity.

'Yes?'

'Listen, I've done something really, unbelievably stupid. You need to get away, you need to run.'

352

'Yes,' she said calmly. 'I'm in Scotland.' Behind her voice I could hear what sounded like a car engine.

'Scotland?' I yelped. But then that was good. Anywhere away from London was good. Unless she was with him, unless she was with him and he was going to access their answering machine remotely, from wherever they were in Scotland. Oh, shit.

'Oh, you're breaking up, I'm afraid,' she lied. 'I'll call you back when I've got a clear . . . oh, no; gone. Well,' I heard her say to somebody else, 'that was unusua—'

And she was gone.

I picked up the mobile, hoping it had recharged sufficiently. No.

I sat down, shaking. Ceel was alive. In Scotland. She'd had a warning of sorts and she was going to call back when she wasn't with whomever she was with.

If I had done what I feared I had – and I had to accept I probably had because I could remember her voice and something of the words she'd used on the answering machine message – then what could I do? I looked at my watch. The massive Breitling said it was – shit – half ten. Had to give it back, I thought; go back to my more elegant Spoon . . . what was I thinking of? Fuck the watch, fucking thinking about the watch or anything else apart from the fucking suicidal, murderous position I'd put myself and Celia in. Think; maybe Merrial was with her. Maybe – probably – they were away for the whole weekend. That gave me a day and a half to do something.

What could I do? Burn their house down? Break in? Hope there was a maid or a butler or somebody (but then why the answering machine?) and try to impersonate a . . . I didn't know. Gas man? Cop? Jehovah's fucking Witness?

Could I access the tape or the chip from outside somehow? What if I rang again and just left an immensely long message, would it overwrite the one from last night? No. Of course not. No answering machine I'd ever encountered would do that. Nobody would design one like that. Well, nobody with any sense; a fuckwit like me would, obviously.

Set fire to the fucking place. Heave a petrol bomb through a window, pour lighter fluid through the letter box; when the fire brigade came – ring them first, ring them just beforehand, but not the police – let them break down the door and then go in with them, pretend to be a plain-clothes cop, or from special branch, or find a fancy dress shop and hire a police uniform . . .

Oh, please let it still not have happened. Please let it be a really vivid false memory syndrome thing. I'd imagined her voice on the answering machine message. It hadn't been her. I'd put the wrong number in from Merrial's card, misplaced a digit and it had been there all the time and the first time I used it I got some female who happened to live at the house that had the phone with the one-digit difference from the Merrials' and so I'd left this filthy, sexually abusive message on the answering machine of a total stranger. Oh, God, it had to be that. It had to be.

But if it wasn't, if I really had done it, what could I do?

I felt sick. I felt really sick. My head was spinning, I was getting the tunnel vision thing. Roaring in ears. I got up and stumbled to the loo.

Ten minutes later, still getting the occasional dry heave, my throat raw, my mouth vile despite the mouthwash, my teeth with that stripped stickiness that comes from having recently been bathed in stomach acid, I sat back at the living-room desk and tried the mobile again. My face had still been white in the mirror. My hands were shaking uncontrollably. I had to rest the mobile on my lap so that I could hit the right buttons. I started crying with the awkwardness and the hopelessness of it all.

354

The little phone buzzed awake on my thigh. It only had a single bar of battery capacity showing but that was all I'd need. Just keep going for a minute or two, you little piece of shit; you could have fucking died on me last night before I made the call that might get me tortured and killed and my beloved too, you silvery be-buttoned turd. Yes, I know you're fucking Searching . . . Just fucking stop it and get on with it. Menu; Phone Book, OK, Voice Dialling, Personal Numbers, Last Ten Calls. My mouth went dry. OK. Last Calls Made. Select? OK.

Here we go.

I stared at the number. I jumped up and got my wallet, where Merrial's card still was. I checked one number against the other. I checked again and again, willing one, just one, just one lousy single fucking little digit to be different. For fuck's sake, it wouldn't have been difficult to make a mistake; I made mistakes all the time. Even when I'm sober. Constantly. Just this one time let this be a mistake.

Call? said the little bit of script at the bottom of the screen. No. No, I don't fucking want to call it again, you worthless stupid piece of crap. I want to Undo. I want to press F1 or go to the relevant menu with a mouse arrow and Undo, totally fucking Undo what I did last night, rewind the tape, oh yes, wipe the chip, reformat the disk, rewind that fucking little deadly tape or whatever the hell it was sitting in a house less than a mile away from here, rewind and erase. Better still, take it out and fucking burn it and mash the ashes into a fine paste and flush it all down a waste disposal unit somewhere in Outer fucking Mongolia.

I read the numbers out from the phone's screen, comparing them to the numbers on Merrial's card. They were identical. They weren't going to change now. I closed the phone.

Maybe he wouldn't guess who it was. I'd said it was Ken, I remembered that – I thought – but maybe he wouldn't think to link that drunken Ken with the guy he'd met once in the courtyard of Somerset House . . . Oh, shit, what was I thinking of? I'd said Naughty Ken or something equally pathetic and incriminating, hadn't I? Or had I?

It didn't matter; I was a fucking radio DJ; I was proud I had a distinctive voice. Even if Merrial didn't ever listen to the show and had missed my high TV and radio presence over the last few weeks or never heard an ad with my voiceover, somebody he knew would recognise me. And anyway, I didn't bar my mobile number; his answering machine would have remembered the number, the way they all did, didn't they? Or maybe his didn't; maybe Merrial was one of those Early Adopters and he had a really old machine he'd never got round to replacing and it didn't keep a note of the incoming numbers.

Yeah, right.

But even if he had the number, how would he know it was mine? I hadn't given him my number, he couldn't . . . Yes, and of course as a big crime lord he'd have absolutely no way of finding who a mobile number belonged to. Of course he would.

I know! I thought. He owed me a favour. Merrial; he'd said to call him if there was ever a favour he could do for me. I'd phone and phone and phone until I got an answer, or go over there and slip a note through the door, ask him to just not listen to his messages, as a favour to me; just trust me. Heavens, yes, that was bound to work. And OJ was innocent and al-Megrahi was guilty.

Phone now! I thought. Of course! Phone now and find out if the fucking answering machine was still switched on. Why hadn't I thought of that first? Because I was still drunk, hungover and panicking under the influence of the most catastrophically fuckwittish mistake ever made in the long history of catastrophically fuckwittish mistakes.

I reached for the land-line. Oh fuck, what if he answered? What if he said something like, Ah, Kenneth, you again. I received your earlier message. Very interesting. I've just sent some of my colleagues round to your place to invite you for a little chat . . .

Oh fuck, oh fuck.

I took three attempts to press the number into the phone, my hands were shaking so much.

Ceel's voice, recorded. Her beautiful, clear, calm, perfect voice. Leave a message after the tone . . . then a series of beeps signifying the message or messages already left – mine! mine was there, that dirty, drunken, rambling shite being spooled past right now! – then the beep. I didn't leave another message. I put the phone down. So – probably – nobody had listened to the message. The worst had not yet happened. Unless, of course, Merrial was being clever and only pretending that he hadn't listened . . . but that was even more paranoid than reality demanded, and fuck knew that was bad enough.

Maybe I could sort of half own up. I could say I'd become obsessed with Celia after seeing her on the ice that day. I was living out this fantasy where we were lovers, stalking her . . . No. No, he'd still do something horrible to me, just for that, and more likely he'd want to check that nothing had been going on, so he'd still have me tortured to get at the truth. And I had no illusions about my ability to hold out under severe pain, not for Ceel, not for myself, not for anybody.

My palms were very sweaty. My mouth was so dry I couldn't swallow. I got up unsteadily and went to the kitchen for some bottled water. The land-line phone rang on the second swallow, and I sprayed water over the carpet.

'Yes?'

'Kenneth?' It was her. Thank fuck. Her; still alive, still not screaming in agony, still able to talk; now able to talk. 'What's wrong?'

I told her. In all my life – and there might not be much more of it to come – I had never known anybody stay so calm in the face of a disaster as utter and unmitigated. She had every

357

right to scream and cry and bawl, but she just asked a couple of sensible, measured questions to clear up some of the holes I'd left in my semi hysterical account of what had happened. Then I heard her sigh. 'Right,' she said. 'Well, I'm in Scotland, staying with some friends near Inverness. John is caving in the Peak District. He's due back tonight or tomorrow.'

'To*night*? Oh, Jesus Christ.'

'Depends on the weather; if there's been too much rain the system will be flooded and they won't be able to do much. It was touch and go, last I heard.'

I ran a hand over my face. 'Can you access the messages on your answering machine from outside, from a different phone?'

'No. John specifically did not want one which could do that, in case somebody else found out how to access it.'

'Okay, okay, well, that gives us until he gets home, at least.' I closed my eyes and stood there shaking my head. 'Oh, Ceel, I am so, so sorry. I can't, I just can't begin to tell you—'

'Kenneth, stop. We have to think. Right. *Bien*. I can claim an emergency and ask to be run straight back to the airport. I'll get on the next flight. I can get home before him, wipe the tape.'

'Oh, please, yes; please, please.'

'I'd better let my hosts know.' I heard her exhale. 'This should be interesting. I'll call you back as soon as I know what's happening.'

'Ceel?'

'What?'

'I love you.'

This time it was an in-taken breath. 'Yes,' she said. 'Well. Talk to you soon.'

And off.

I drank from the bottle of water, hands still shaking. I stared ahead, seeing nothing. Still alive. Both of us still alive. So far so good. So far no torture and painful death. She'd get back.

358

She'd return, in time. Brilliant, calm, resourceful Ceel would clear up the pig's diarrhoea of a mess her idiot lover had made. She'd make it all well again. Bless that smart, sexy, wonderful, gorgeous, fantastic woman. She might never talk to me again, she might write me out of her life forevermore and curse me ritually every night before she went to sleep for the rest of her hopefully long life for the ignorant scumbag dickhead that I so surely was, but at least she'd be alive to do it, at least we'd both live. We wouldn't suffer for my stupidity. I drank some more water and told myself that one day I'd see the funny side of all this.

Ceel rang back forty minutes later with the news that Inverness airport was out of action for the day, fog-bound.

'You have to run,' I said. My mouth had gone dry again. 'That's all we can do. Run. You have to get away. Further away. Oh, God, Ceel—'

'No-no,' she said crisply. 'I'll find out when there's a flight next to London from Aberdeen, Edinburgh or Glasgow, then hire a car to whichever one. I'll charter a plane or helicopter if I can. The timing will be tighter but it ought still to be possible. But there is another possibility.'

'What?'

'You could get into the house.'

'How? Does anybody else have a key? Is there anybody in the house?'

'No. There shouldn't be. The staff have the weekend off.'

'So, how—?'

'There's a key in the back garden, inside an artificial stone.'

'There *is*?' This sounded a bit low-rent and risky for such a posh address.

'Yes. Then once you're inside you'll have to switch the alarm off.'

'Okay, okay, right.'

'I'll give you the number for that. However, there is a problem.'

'Shit. What?'

'Getting into the back garden from the lane. There's a high wall.'

'So what's the point of—?'

'There's a garage off the lane; you're supposed to be able to get into the garage with the remote control in the car and then use the spare key. Or there's an ordinary door, but it's locked too.'

'Right. Okay.' I had an idea. 'How high is the wall exactly? Well, not ex—'

'Three metres, perhaps three and a half.'

'Any razor wire or anything?'

'No.'

'Not even broken bottles?'

'No.'

'Okay, I think I can get into the back garden. I suppose it's over-looked? By other—?'

'Yes. But it's usually quiet; it's a dead-end off the mews further down.'

'This artificial stone; how do I find it?'

'Counting from the rear wall of the garage there are two lanterns on the west garden wall, then the third one. The stone with the key inside is directly under the third lantern and two stones out from the wall. Once you see it it looks almost obvious.'

'West wall, garage rear wall, third lantern, two stones out.' I rubbed a hand over the back of my neck. All this was just what I needed in the condition I was in. 'What about the alarm? Is it linked to a security firm HQ or anything?'

'Yes, and to the local police station.'

'The local police station? *Really?*'

'You might be surprised at the arrangements John has with the Metropolitan Police, Kenneth.'

'Yeah, I dare say I might,' I agreed. 'What about surveillance cameras?'

'No. Well, none that I know of.'

'Right.'

'Here's the alarm code.'

'Shoot.'

'Write it down, will you?'

'Okay.' I lifted Merrial's card. 'Go.' I wrote the code down on the back of Merrial's card, then repeated it. 'And where is the answering machine?'

'It's in John's study. On the first floor. Oh.'

'Now what?'

'The study might be locked.'

'Locked? But—'

'It's a gun room, too; it's supposed to be locked.'

'A *gun* . . . ? Jeez. Right. So if it is, then what?'

'I have a key in my bedroom. That's on the second floor. John doesn't know about it. You'll have to go there first if the study door is locked.'

You couldn't just have the damn thing where people usually have answering machines, by the front door, could you? I thought. And, Ceel's bedroom; I'd fantasised about something like this for months, but not exactly in these circumstances.

'Okay. Where's the key?'

'In my bathroom. There is a cabinet above the sink. Inside the box of tampons.'

Smart thinking, I guessed. 'Right.'

'When you get to the answering machine, you wipe the tape by pressing Function and then Clear. Got that?'

'Function and Clear. I'd rather tear the whole tape out or take a big magnet and wipe it of everything, but that'll have to do. Maybe I'll do it twice.'

'Function and Clear should do it.'

'Okay.'

'Keep in touch.'

'Will do.'

'Please be careful, Kenneth.'

'Oh, I will. Best of luck getting a flight.'

'Thank you. Goodbye.'

'Bye.'

I put the phone down. I wasn't shaking so much now. I drank some more water. At least we had a plan of campaign. At least I had something I could do, rather than just wait for Celia to come and fix things. God, what sort of man was I? Of course I should be doing something. I'd got us both into this grisly mess; it should be me that got both of us out of it. Or even only her. If I could just save Ceel I'd have done something good, something to make up for my gross incompetence. My own miserable behind was patently not worth the saving, attached as it so obviously was to a spine with a lump of barely solidified porridge at the other end where a normal person would have a functioning brain, but hers . . . her glorious ass was entirely and utterly worth saving, even at the expense of my own.

Think. I'd have to park the Landy in the lane. What if people saw me going over the wall? They'd call the cops, or at the very least they might take the Land Rover's registration number.

How could I get new numbers for it? You could get rear number plates from any Halfords; people did all the time for trailers and there was no check on whether you really had a vehicle with that number, but you couldn't get white, front number plates that easily. Maybe I could make false ones using the computer. Print out a couple of sheets of A4 with the relevant sized numerals and then wrap them in cling-film or something and tape them over the real ones. Should fool the casual observer. Wouldn't even need exactly the right font because people had weird fonts on their plates sometimes; I'd seen them.

Better, I could phone the garage that had repaired the Landy and get some old plates off them. They were bound to have some; it would just be a short-term loan anyway. I had about three hundred quid in an emergency stash at the back of my sock drawer and I could pick up another two-fifty from a cash machine. That should hire a set of plates for an hour. Wouldn't it? How likely was I to find the only small London garage that would shake their heads at my proposed criminality and promptly phone the cops? Surely not.

On the other hand, it would take time, delay things. Supposing Merrial came back early? Detouring via the garage might make all the difference. And it would introduce another variable into the equation, one more source of potential leaking. Supposing the garage people knew people who knew Merrial? If the Landy was spotted and the false numbers were traced to them, who knew what might happen, what they'd do, what they'd be persuaded to say, how they'd jump?

So I couldn't risk it. But meanwhile I'd sat here slugging water and thinking about it and wasted a few minutes. Well done, Kenneth. Ten past eleven. Get going.

Traffic was relatively light. It was a pleasantly mild winter morning; high cloud and a watery sun. Breezy. Why the fuck couldn't it be breezy in fucking Inverness? And dry in the Peak fucking District? I could have gone faster, but I stuck to between thirty and thirty-five. This would be no time to be caught speeding, especially with God knew how much alcohol still sloshing about in my system.

Ascot Square was quiet. Bunches of silver balloons tied to railings indicated there'd been a party in one of the grand town-houses on the other side of the square from the Merrials'. Maybe a twenty-fifth anniversary or something. Lots of Mercs, Jags and BMWs, plus Range Rovers and a brace of Rollers or Bentleys; Audi A2s and a couple of Smarts, too. The Merrials lived in number eleven, near the centre of the imposing, four-storeys-plus-basement terrace. No obvious signs of life at number eleven.

Tall limes and beeches in the private gardens in the centre of the square. I drove on through into Eccleston Street then into Chester Square. I parked in a residents only space for a couple of minutes, climbing into the back of the Landy and pulling on my overalls. Brand new, basically; I'd got them when I bought the Landy, thinking I'd do my own repairs. And a size too small; my shirt sleeves and the bottom of my 501s protruded from the green overalls by a good two or three centimetres. Great; so now I looked stupid as well as villainous. I had an old Sony Music Awards baseball cap; I put that on too. Bit of a giveaway industry-wise, but what else was I supposed to do? Sunglasses from the cubby box between the front seats.

Gloves! Of course I needed gloves. I was going to break into a house, or make an illegal entry or whatever the legally nice definition was. I didn't want to go leaving fingerprints all over the fucking place. Gloves. I had some somewhere. I rummaged behind the bench seats on either side, feeling down between the seat cushions and the back rests. Blimey, you could hide a complete fucking tool kit along here . . . gloves. Got them. They were thick, padded things for pulling out bramble bushes or hauling on winch wires or some such manly shit as that, not at all the sort of fine, thin things you'd want for the delicate business of letting yourself into somebody else's house, but, shit, they'd just have to do.

I jumped back into the front and set off again, back past Ascot Square proper and round into the mews behind it on the south side. Lots of close-packed but very expensive mews properties with differing treatments of the old architecture; a jumbled variety of windows large and small, balconies, awnings and outside steps. Lots of plants, too; hanging baskets, big pot plants and trailing vines. Oh shit; and a family loading up their

Landy Discovery. Young couple and three kids getting their cool boxes and child seats sorted for a day out. Shit! What sort of time was this to be setting out for the day? It was practically noon! Best bit of the day gone, dammit! Couldn't the miserable fucking curs have got their shit together a bit closer to breakfast?

The man looked up when he saw my battered Short-Wheelbase approaching down the cobbles. Took a good look at me. Hmm, don't recognise that beaten-up old wreck, or the shifty looking weirdo with the sunglasses driving it. Not a resident I've ever seen before. And that's not a Power or Gas company van. You could practically see the thought bubbles.

I wound the window down and stopped by the Disco. 'Scuse me, mite. Zis Ascot Mews Norf?'

'Ah, na,' said the man. 'This is Siythe, actually.'

'*Sarf?*' I said. 'Ah, roight.' I looked over at the other seat, as though there was something there I was consulting. 'Roight. Ta, mite,' I said, and reversed out again.

I parked up near the corner of Eccleston Street and Eaton Square, pretending to study an *A to Z*. The Disco swung out into the traffic and headed for the river ten long, long minutes later. I pulled back into Ascot Mews South, drove on past the mews cottages into the last part of the lane where the garages and tall garden walls began. I counted my way along to number eleven, but I needn't have bothered; there was a number eleven on the gleaming green pedestrian door that gave out onto the lane beside the equally freshly painted garage doors.

I'd rehearsed this in my mind already. Best done quickly given it had to be done at all. Ignore the rear windows of the houses on the other side of the lane and those next door to number eleven. I killed the engine, got out, locked the door, climbed onto the roof via the front bumper and bonnet – the aluminium roof flexed under my feet, which I actually had the

365

reserve brain power to feel slightly disappointed by – then I jumped up onto the rounded top of the tall stone wall.

Japanese gardens raked gravel forming dry round lakelets with big smooth boulders forming islands in the frozen ripples of greyness. Small, tidily clipped bushes and shrubs; a still pool with another big boulder. Decking under green awnings. Something about its calm organisation told me this was Celia's garden more than her husband's. I looked down. I was going to have to drop the whole way, into more gravel. It was easily three and a half metres.

I swung one leg over, then the other, and let myself dangle as far to the ground as I could. In Scotland, as kids, we'd called this dreeping. I had no idea what it was called down here. I couldn't get any real hand-hold on the smooth round top of the wall so just had to keep as much friction as I could on my forearms and gloved hands until gravity took over and I dropped to the gravel bed. It was mercifully deep. I hit and rolled and didn't break anything. I'd have to do some remedial work on the gravel bed-work with a rake, though. I looked up at the wall. I'd worry about getting out again later. I smoothed the gravel out a bit now, while I thought of it, just in case I forgot later. It didn't look perfect but it might pass as the result of a cat coming into the garden. I checked the door in the garden wall. The lock was some sort of ruggedised outdoor Chubb; I tried to open it but it looked like you needed a key even from the inside.

My phone went as I was walking up the path towards the stone with the key inside. There was a sort of slit on each side of the overalls so you could get at the pockets of whatever you were wearing underneath. I hauled the Motorola out through one of those. Ceel.

'I'm in the back garden,' I said.

'Good. I've just had a thought. John should have the car. Use the keys just to the right of the back door, once you've got in, to open the garage and put your car in. It might look less suspicious.'

I hadn't paid much attention to the garage doors. I had the impression they were pretty tall, but I might have been wrong. 'It's a Land Rover,' I said. 'Two metres tall at least. Might not fit.'

'No, it should. It's an old coach house.'

'Okay, then. Good idea.' I stopped opposite the third lantern and looked down at a neat arrangement of smooth, varied stones. 'Hold on. What if he comes back? Seeing a Land Rover parked outside your back wall might be a little puzzling; finding the thing sitting inside his own garage . . .'

'Hmm, you're right. Also, I phoned the Weather Centre. The Peak District has had more rain than expected overnight. I think it's very likely he will be back later today.'

'Oh, shit. What about you? How are the flights looking?'

'Aberdeen is out. It's a three- or four-hour drive to Edinburgh or Glasgow. I'm trying to arrange a charter from a smaller airport closer to here but it's not proving easy.'

'Well, I'm in here already anyway. Hold on.' I stooped to the stones. The thick gloves meant I took a couple of attempts, but after a few seconds and some muttered curses I was able to announce, 'I've got the key.'

'You have the alarm number?'

'Memorised and written down. The door in the garden wall, back into the mews, into the lane; where would I find the key for that?'

'To the left of the back door in the utility room, looking out. It has a green plastic tag.'

'Can I lock the door without it? I'm trying to get out without having to climb the wall.'

'Let me think.' Ceel was silent for a couple of seconds. 'Yes. Use the key, open the door, put the key back, put the little button down on the lock and then close the door from outside.

367

That will do it. Don't forget to put the house back-door key back inside the stone first.'

'Christ,' I said, putting one hand over my eyes. 'Do I so not need all this with a serious fucking hangover.' I took a deep breath, straightened up. 'Okay. Never mind. Right. I've got all that. Thanks.'

'Good luck, Kenneth.'

'You too, kid.'

The back door swung closed and re-locked. I walked quickly through the utility room, the kitchen and along the hall; an insistent beeping noise was sounding from the far end, near the front door. I punched the code into the alarm unit but the thick gloves meant I must have pressed the wrong buttons. I felt sweat prick on my brow as I started again. The beeping went on. I was going to run out of time. I whipped my right glove off and entered the code properly. The noise stopped. My heart was thudding, my hands still shaking. I took a few deep breaths. I used a paper handkerchief to polish the keys I'd touched, then I put the glove back on. God, I was hot. I took off the stupid baseball cap and shoved it into a pocket. Something made me think that I should keep doing things while I thought of them, so I went to the back door, left it unlocked on the catch and wedged with a welly boot while I went out to the garden and replaced the key inside the artificial stone.

I closed the back door again. As I walked along to the foot of the stairs near the main door I realised I seriously needed to visit the toilet. This was ridiculous – for all I knew a suspicious neighbour was already on the phone to the local nick telling them she'd just seen a guy in badly fitting overalls jumping into a back garden – but I really was going to have to get to a loo in the next minute or so or basically I was going to soil myself. Partly, I guessed, it was the result of my colossal alcohol intake from the previous night, but partly it was simple fear. I recalled reading something about this, how burglars who left crap in the middle of their victim's carpets weren't necessarily just being shits themselves. They just couldn't help themselves. Breaking into somebody else's house was a scary thing to do; most people would be scared shitless. And – as a rule – *they* weren't invading the privacy of fucking London crime lords.

I ran up the stairs and started looking for a toilet, opening doors into a sitting-room, a library, a small cinema, another sitting-room, and a walk-in cupboard before finding one that wouldn't open, which must be the study where the answering machine was.

Oh my God, I was going to shit my pants. I could feel my bowels loosening, a muscle down there starting to spasm as I tried to hold things in. No loo here that I could see. Upstairs; I knew there was a toilet up there; that was where Celia's bedroom was with its en suite bathroom. I did a weird, knee-knocking sort of walk to the stairs leading up to the next storey, then minced up the steps, sucking in my belly as though this would stop the disaster I was expecting any second. Even as I got to the next floor I was thinking, What was I doing? Running up here had been stupid; there must be a loo downstairs, on the ground floor, where the kitchen and dining-room would be.

Too late now. I ran along to a door whose room probably looked to the rear of the house, overlooking the Japanese garden. I was sucking my cheeks in – I mean my cheeks on my face as well as the cheeks of my bum – as though in sympathy. My whole body was trembling now; I nearly fell as I stumbled through the door and into the room. Bedroom. Big. Dark behind dark-grey vertical blinds shielding two tall windows.

There was a door to each side of the wide, black and white bed. I pulled the left one open; a fucking *dressing*-room. Jesus fucking Christ, what *was* it with these rich fuckers? Couldn't they just have fucking wardrobes like fucking normal people, the self-indulgent sons of bitches? I hobbled round the bed, trying to keep my legs together and yet still walk, and actually putting my right hand to my backside, trying to press upwards, help keep things in. Oh Christ, oh Christ; if this door didn't lead to a loo, I was going to shit my fucking pants.

The door swung open and I was looking straight at a beautiful white china loo with a rich dark wooden seat and lid. I quickly pulled both gloves off.

My whimper of relief turned to a terrible keening of frustrated rage and despair as I had to waste a few seconds I hadn't been accounting for – and which I might not have to spare – as I had to tear at my stupid fucking under-size overalls before I could even get to my jeans and pants. I only just remembered to lift the lid of the loo before I turned round.

I started shitting even before my backside hit the wooden rim of the toilet. It was a ghastly, splattery and appallingly malodorous experience, but I believed I'd – just – succeeded in keeping within the bounds of social shitting behaviour.

Sitting back, I closed my eyes, breathing through my mouth to escape the putrid smell of what was going on down below, and – for a few, brief, fleeting moments – just let myself surf along the wave of animal relief surging through my body.

'Fucking hell,' I breathed.

Cleaning up took a while. I'd nearly finished when I realised that I'd just taken a seriously fucking rancid dump in what looked like John Merrial's own bathroom, not Ceel's. The toiletries spread about the shelves were all masculine and there was a shaving mirror and an electric razor on a shelf above one of the two big wash-handbasins. When I thought about it, I realised that the clothes in the dressing-room I'd looked in earlier had indeed been male clothes; in the wide-eyed terror of the moment, I hadn't even noticed.

Flushing a couple of times extra and using a loo brush to make sure there were no marks left seemed like a good idea.

I left the place as I'd found it, apart from the smell. I used an air-freshener, more in deference to my mother's early bathroom training than because it would make any difference; Alpine Glade would be every bit as suspicious as Fetid Faeces if Merrial happened to come home in the next hour or so and decided the first thing he needed was a nice shower to freshen up after a hard day's caving.

The perfectly folded towels in the bathroom intimidated me, so after I'd washed my hands I just wiped them dry on my overalls rather than sully those snowy white expanses. I did some more wiping down of touched surfaces with the paper hanky.

A few more deep breaths and a drink of water from the cold tap and I was just about steady and calm enough to continue. I found another large bedroom across the hall, also with a view to the rear. This bedroom was all pale greens and blues, from ceiling and walls and carpets to the furniture and fittings. Bursts of tropical colour on the walls were provided by paintings of riotous jungle scenes, all profuse abstractions of flowers, leaves, sky and rocks, shot through with what looked like squadrons of parrots or cockatiels racing across the scenes, caught in blurs of chromatic chaos.

Thick black Venetian blinds covered windows of a similar size to those in the room across the hall. Maybe everybody hereabouts kept their blinds closed all the time, I thought, allowing hope to blossom again. Maybe nobody would have seen me make the leap over the garden wall.

Pale furniture. A large dressing table with combs and bottles and a small ring tree with a few rings on it, all tidy, neatly arranged. It was very warm.

Definitely Ceel's room, I thought. The bathroom was on the opposite side to the room across the hall. I had to take the damn stupid big gloves off again. Why hadn't I thought of this? If I'd only taken a minute to look ahead I'd have realised back on the fucking *Temple Belle* that I'd need a good thin pair of gloves for this. Oh well. The Yale key was secured to the floor of the little box of tampons by a piece of double-sided tape. I confess I held a few of the tampons, looking at them, then, still holding them, looked round the bathroom; at her bath and, alongside it, a big steam-cabinet shower, with a seat. I found myself smiling as I looked at the loo.

Oh, God, what sort of poor pathetic loon was I, caressing the woman's tampons and staring fondly, love-struck, at her toilet seat, for fuck's sake? Get fucking real, Kenneth. And get fucking moving, fuckwit. I put the tampons back and replaced the box, then did the wiping-finger-touched-surfaces bit again.

I went down to the locked door on the first floor. I had a little more time to look around. The house was furnished in a slightly dated respectable style that was probably about right for the building. Actually it looked a lot like some of the slightly more modern hotel suites Ceel and I had been in. She must have felt at home. Not as stiflingly hot, though.

The study door opened with the key and I let it close behind me. The study was more old-fashioned than what I'd seen of the rest of the house. The big desk was un-ironic retro, with a gold-tooled burgundy leather top and a brass lamp with a green glass shade. The computer was a Hewlett Packard with a big plasma screen. Ha! I'd just known Merrial wouldn't be a Mac guy. I couldn't see any sign of a gun safe, but I guessed it might be hidden.

The answering machine was on its own little table near the door. I looked at it accusingly, as though this was all its fault. You see the trouble you've put me to, you nasty little piece of office-beige shite? I moved towards it.

That was when I heard the siren.

It must have been on the fringes of my hearing for a couple

of seconds. I'd been feeling a general unease, which seemed at odds with the fact I was now within sight of the thing I'd spent so much effort, angst and sweat getting to. Then I realised: a siren. The Emergency Services. You stop hearing the sound in a big city after a while.

If you're driving – and providing you're not the sort of cack-brained bozo who can have a fucking twenty-tonne fire engine right behind him with its lights flaring and its siren screaming and still not realise it's time to Get The Fuck Out Of The Way – then you do still take notice when you hear a siren; you start looking at side streets, checking the rear-view every few seconds, watching for people pulling out of the way or bumping up onto kerbs or swerving into bus stops to clear a path for the vehicle with the blue lights. Otherwise, you hear it but you pay no attention unless it signifies something you're waiting for, or it keeps getting louder all the time until it gets very loud and then stops.

I listened to the siren get closer and closer.

Doppler, you fuck, I thought. Fucking Doppler your fucking woop-wooping arse on past. Don't stop. Don't pull up here, in the mews or in the square outside. Keep on going. Let it be an emergency somewhere else. Let it be a cop car en route to a robbery on the King's Road or an ambulance heading for a boating accident on the river or a fire engine attending a false alarm at a shop; let it be anything at all but not a patrol car coming to check on a suspected break-in at the rear of Ascot Square.

I stood there, staring at the answering machine, knowing that I should keep going, knowing that the sensible, per cent-ages-wise course of action was to keep doing what I was doing, get at the tape, wipe the fucker, wipe the fucker twice, make sure it was clean and I and Celia were in the clear . . . but I couldn't. I had to hear what was going to happen with that damn siren. There would still be time to wipe the tape even if the sound did stop right outside anyway, but I just couldn't move, couldn't do anything until I knew. Closer, closer. Did they use a siren in such a situation? Would that not be like the stupidest thing to do if you were hoping to catch the crims in the act? Give the fuckers plenty of warning. Give them time to scarper with their bags of swag and their stripy jumpers and their eye masks, before the rozzers caught them bang to rights and they went to chokey so fast their feet didn't touch . . .

My own phone went, vibrating against my hip. I jumped as though zapped with a cattle prod then pulled my right-hand glove off and held it in my mouth while I withdrew the mobile from its holster. I was whimpering again. I was getting good at whimpering. My hands were shaking so much I almost dropped the phone. I flipped it open. Phil. I clicked, No, don't answer and put it away again, trembling fingers missing the holster three or four times. The siren was *still* coming closer. I put my glove back on.

Go past, go past. Oh, just fucking go past . . . Saint Doppler, I appeal to thee to intercede on my behalf . . . Oh, fuck off; what a load of fucking shite. Next I'd be appealing to the patron saint of atheists.

The siren's note started to deepen. I let out a breath I must have been holding for a minute or more. A roaring noise in my ears began to fade and the room took on more colour and stopped looking like the view down a pipe. Jeez, I must have been close to blacking out there.

Never mind. A candle would be lit at the shrine of Saint Doppler after all. Red shifted, of course.

I walked over to the skinny table and the answering machine. It had a little black-on-green LCD display which was in message counter mode at the moment. Five messages. I was still staring at the machine when it rang.

I jumped. 'Fuck!' I screamed. Then, 'You fucking bastarding little cunt!' At the time, this seemed only reasonable.

The machine clicked after four rings. 'There's nobody here right now,' Ceel's calm, beautiful voice said.

'Yes there fucking is!' I screamed hoarsely, shaking my fists in front of my chest.

'Please leave a message after the tone.'

'No!' I yelled. 'Don't fucking bother! Whoever the fuck you are, just fucking fuck off!'

Another click, and a hum as the machine's tape wound itself forward. Then, 'Aow hullo yes my name is Sam I'm calling on behalf of BT we would just like to check that you know of our latest offers for domestic customers I'll call again at a later time and hope to discuss these offers with you thank you goodbye.'

'Fuck off!' I screamed as the phone clicked again and the tape started to wind itself back to Ceel's announcement at the beginning. Fucking typical, I thought. Go ex-directory because you're fed up getting junk calls from fucking double-glazing salespeople and what happens? You get fucking junk calls from B fucking T. At least I ought to find it reassuring that even metropolitan crime lords weren't immune from that sort of shit.

When the machine had gone quiet again, I carefully identified the Function and Clear buttons. They were big enough to use with the heavy gloves still on. I pressed one – the black and green display asked Clear All Messages? – followed by the second button. Nothing happened.

I'd been stooping. Now I stood up.

Actually something had happened; the display now read No Messages. But there was no more clicking, no humming, no other sounds at all.

Was that it? It didn't seem right. Was that all there was to it? Shouldn't it wind forwards and wipe the tape after Ceel's introduction?

I guessed not. It would just forget about the messages sitting there already recorded and record over them when there was another incoming call.

Was that good enough? It should be. That was the way the machine worked. As far as it was concerned, there had been no messages. If you tried to play the tape, you'd get nothing, just No Messages.

But the message I'd left was still there. The words were still printed there in patterns of magnetised stripes on the little brown ribbon of oxide-coated plastic. If you took the micro-cassette out of the answering machine and put it in an ordinary dictation machine you'd still hear what I'd said.

I pressed Function again. Re-record Message? No. I pressed Function again a few times until I got to the No Messages screen again. I was sweating now. I couldn't decide what to do. In theory, it was all fixed now; mission accomplished. Definitely time to Get To Fuck.

But the message was still there. Was it worth the risk of leaving it there, even though it wasn't likely that anybody would take the necessary steps to access it? What if Merrial had called his own phone for some reason, and knew there was a message or messages there? Or somebody said they'd left a message? What would happen in that case if he came home and saw it said No Messages? Wouldn't he investigate, take the cassette out, try it in another machine?

Maybe Ceel would still beat him back and be able to say there was nothing on the tape, or only junk calls, but what if he was first back?

Jesus, what was I thinking of? I took off my glove again, got out my mobile and started walking to the door. I'd call the fucking answering machine myself and just leave a soundless call that would last long enough to overwrite my incriminating message from last night. Maybe not soundless; maybe the machine would sense that and switch off. I'd rub my hand over the microphone on the mobile so it would pick up some sound and lay that down on the tape.

First, though, I had to set up my mobile to ban its caller ID on the next outgoing call. I pressed Menu as I opened the door to the first-floor hall. I walked towards the stairs to the ground floor. Phone Book. OK. I got to the top of the stairs.

Oh, Jesus, I hadn't locked the fucking study. I turned back from the stairs. No, wait a minute; the study's Yale had locked itself; I didn't need to actively lock the damn thing. I got to the top of the stairs again. Call Related Features. OK.

Oh, fuck, I had to put the key back in Ceel's bathroom; I was going the wrong way. I turned round to head for the stairs leading up. Show Battery Meter. No; next. Restrict My Phone Number. OK. I walked upstairs.

This was stupid; I was trying to do two things at once when I was barely capable of doing one with any degree of competence. Restrict ID On Next Call.

At last! OK.

Crossing Ceel's bedroom, I clicked back until I could make a call then rang the number here. I still jumped when the land-line extension in the bedroom rang. The study key went back in the box of tampons and I listened to Ceel's voice inviting me to leave a message after the tone. There were no beeps in between, just the tone, immediately. I held the mobile clumsily in my gloved left hand and rubbed it with my thumb while I closed the cabinet and wiped it with the paper hanky again.

I was closing Ceel's bedroom door and still enthusiastically rubbing the phone's mike with the glove fabric (and thinking, Hey, this must sound a bit like when I got that unmeant call from Jo's mobile) when, distantly, down the stairwell, two storeys below, I heard the sound of the front door opening.

I froze. No. Not happen. Not to happen. No happening of such like thing. Just fucking, like, *no*.

Maybe I'd mistaken the sound. It went quiet. Was that a very quiet clicking I could hear from down there? Then a tiny beeping noise. Of course; the alarm that should have been on when somebody came into the house, the alarm they'd be expecting to be on but then discovered was not. Oh fuck.

'Celia?' said a voice. My bowels suddenly felt like they were up to their old tricks again, like there was unfinished business needing attention in there. Oh my God, it was him, back even earlier than we'd been expecting. Oh fucking hell, now what was I supposed to do? I looked down at the mobile phone in my gloved hand. My thumb was over the microphone. Shit, it wouldn't be picking all this up, would it? Re-transmitting it back to the answering machine in the study?

'Celia?' again. Louder. 'Maria?'

I took a couple of steps back, to Celia's bedroom door. I'd take sanctuary there. It was right. The natural place, the slim straw it was proper to clutch at, that of my love's inner sanctum . . . well, that was a load of bollocks. Assuming that was him, and he was looking for her, where would be the first place he'd try? Well, yes, Kenneth.

I stepped further back, to another door. I could hear footsteps down below. The door led to a shallow cupboard. Not enough room to hide in. That was it. There was his room, hers, and to access any others I'd have to walk past the stairwell and be visible from below for a certain amount of time. The footsteps were hard to make out. Was that somebody walking up the stairs to the floor below, the first floor? Or somebody walking along the hall on the ground floor?

I was quaking. I gripped the mobile so hard I was in danger of breaking it. My jaw was grinding like I'd taken twenty E an hour earlier. It felt like I was right slap bang on the verge of a heart attack. Sweat was trickling from my brows; I could taste it on my upper lip. Jesus Christ; I'd been on the piss from mid-afternoon yesterday, slept in my clothes, got up without changing or washing, suffered at least one full-on panic attack per hour since I woke up and now I was sweating like a paedophile in Mothercare; even if I found the perfect hiding place the fucker was going to *smell* me.

I walked as fast as possible past the stairwell towards the rooms at the front of the house. I did that walk where you step quickly but put each foot down very gently, trying not to cause any creaks or other noises. I stared wide-eyed down the stairwell. No obvious signs of anybody coming up to this floor or the one below. 'Maria?' More distantly this time. He must be through in the kitchen or thereabouts.

Three doors ahead. One to the side. That one led to another, narrower staircase heading steeply for what would have been the servants' or the children's rooms when the house was designed. I closed it. So far no comedy door-creaking noises from the well-maintained hinges. Thank fuck. Central door. Another cupboard. Not as shallow as the one along the landing, but nowhere to hide if he did look in.

Right-hand door. Jesus; was *this* his bedroom? Big enough. Grand enough. Masculine-looking enough (I thought). I'd vaguely assumed they both had their bedrooms at the rear because it would be quieter, but maybe the one opposite hers was somebody else's – the bodyguard, the big blond guy? – and this was Merrial's. It looked lived-in, somehow. I closed it. Maybe a little too quickly; there was a distinct click.

The third door revealed a gym. A very well-equipped gym with a polished blond-wood floor and lots of machines, some of which I recognised, a couple I didn't. Two more tall windows and translucent vertical blinds.

There were footsteps coming up the stairs. I was starting to hyperventilate. What did it feel like when you had a heart attack? Heart thrashing? Pains in chest? Headache? Sore arms? That would be (E) All of the above, then.

I slipped into the gym. Heck, the smell of stale sweat might even be less conspicuous in here. I still needed somewhere to hide. Two more doors; the first led to another en suite. The second belonged to a large, deep cupboard.

Oh shit; I could hear somebody on this floor now, out on the landing. The cupboard held old bits of fitness equipment plus various items of sports gear, including some scuba apparatus. This would have to do. I closed the door and made my way through the darkness as rapidly as I could, banging one shin and barking a hand on something hard and metallic. When I hit the rear wall I got into a corner and squatted down. The place smelled musty. I decided that was good.

A door opened. Was it the door to the gym?

Oh fuck. What the hell had I been thinking? If Merrial had just come back from caving, what was he likely to do? Put the gear away. Where was he likely to put it? Where would he come straight to? Right here. This cupboard, this door. Right here where mister fuckwit was hiding, squatting like a frightened schoolboy at the back of a hidey-hole.

Well done, Kenneth. Top fucking marks, son. Take a good feel of your knees while they still fold the same way as everybody else's.

Steps; a tread coming closer, shoes on polished wood. Oh, fucking hell. I wanted to cry. I was going to cry. I put my head down, bowing to the darkness. Hide your face, don't let the whites of the eyes show. Maybe the footsteps weren't coming this way. You couldn't always tell in unfamiliar houses. Maybe he was walking upstairs. Maybe – the door to the cupboard opened. Light sensed through the eyelids. I stopped breathing.

How long? What would happen? Would he smell me? Would he see me? How long? How long before I knew? Would he say something? Would he just look, squint, then shout, or take out a gun? Or go for a gun from his gun safe in the study? Or call the big blond guy? Light! There had to be a light fixture in a cupboard this size! I hadn't thought to look or feel for one, but there must be a switch. He'd turn on the light and see me hunched here. Fucking imbecile!

No light clicked on. Maybe he could see me without it. Anyway the smell was sure to do it. Animals could smell fear and we're all just animals, especially in situations like this. The oldest, basest, most deeply wired sense was going to betray me, and the more I panicked about it the more fear pheromones I'd be giving out and so the more likely it was to happen. Oh fuck, I was going to lose control of my bowels again. Something clattered, making the floor under my backside thump. I came very close to both jumping and yelping.

Then the door closed and the light went.

Steps sounded going away again.

I breathed again. Of course, Merrial might still have seen me but thought the best thing to do was to pretend he hadn't, so he could go and get a gun, or call the cops, or the blond guy.

'Yes, Celia?' I heard him say. 'I'm home . . . Yes, there was too much rain. But listen. The alarm wasn't on when I got in.' I heard a rhythmic metallic tapping noise as he spoke. Then, as I looked at the thin frame of light around the closed door, one edge of that glowing boundary started slowly to widen and enlarge. The fucking door was opening! 'The house alarm. It wasn't switched on.' The door opened silently and very slowly. Bits of gleaming fitness equipment came gradually into view. Then Merrial himself was revealed, standing by one of the polished chrome machines, looking out through the opened blinds of one tall window. He was dressed in jeans and a dark leather bomber jacket. 'Of course I'm sure,' he said. 'Don't ask stupid questions.' He was resting one hand on the fitness machine, tapping one of the wire-hung weights against the chrome metal support; that was the tapping noise I'd heard. He hadn't noticed the cupboard door still slowly opening. 'I don't even have Kaj here with me. I—' Now he must have noticed the door from the corner of his eye; he started and his head shot round as he jumped and made a small involuntary noise. 'Fucking door,' he said quietly. He was staring, it seemed, straight at me.

Oh fuck. If I shifted now he'd see the movement but if he kept looking at me he'd surely see my pasty white face in the darkness. I kept still but closed my eyes. Then opened them a touch because I could hear him walking towards me across the wooden floor of the gym.

'No, just the door to the cupboard in the gym. Swung open there. Gave me a . . . moment,' he said, putting one hand to the edge of the door and closing it. The light faded again. I took another breath. 'So were you last out, or what?' he said, voice muffled again by the closed door. 'Well, somebody forgot to set the fucking alarm, Celia.'

Oh, just fucking leave her alone, you fuck. It wasn't her. She's Ceel; she would never make a mistake like that. She's the calm, infallible one. Her only fault is a certain weakness for villains and idiots.

Maybe if I rushed the bastard and smacked him over the head with something heavy. Kill the fucker; murder the man. He was a fucking people-smuggling, life-ruining, knee-snapping crime lord, for fuck's sake; I'd be doing society a favour. Then Ceel and I could run away together.

Or, better still, say, just hide here in the darkness and hope.

'Well, I'm calling Kaj, get him to have a look at the alarm . . . Well, he helped install it. I'm going to take a look round, make sure there's nobody in here . . . It's not being paranoid, Celia. I'm not taking a shower thinking there could be some smack-head on the loose in here looking for your jewels or something. These types are unbalanced, capable of anything . . . Yes, that sort of remark is amusing around the dinner table, Celia. Standing here right now thinking there could be some junkie hiding behind a door with a knife, irony is the last thing on my mind . . . I'm not *suggesting* a junkie could defeat the alarm, I'm suggesting that *somebody* forgot to turn the alarm on and that therefore there could possibly be somebody in the house who got in without the alarm going off as it would have otherwise . . . I'm not discussing this with you. You seem in a very strange mood . . . No, I don't want to know how your weekend is going . . . Do what you want.' There was a soft snapping noise, like a phone being closed, perhaps. Then steps, a pause, more steps, a door opening off the room, then closing, then another door, and then silence.

My hand was getting sore. I was still gripping my mobile; it was still, I guessed, connected to the answering machine in the study on the floor below. I closed the phone then opened it again so that the back light would come on. Duration of call: 6:51, 6:52, 6:53 . . . End Call?

That had to cover the message I'd left last night. It must have been recorded over by now. I clicked OK to end the call. The phone vibrated almost immediately, making me panic again. I dropped the phone, grabbed at it while it was still in mid-air and succeeded only in batting it across the dark cupboard, off a wall with a loud thud and against some unidentified piece of metallic equipment with a resounding clang. Then it fell to the floor with another thump.

Fuck! Would he have heard that? And where was the phone? Lying on the floor somewhere. If I was lucky the fucker would have been smashed by the series of impacts, but if I wasn't then it was about to exhaust the three or four vibrations it went through in the mode I had it in and start ringing normally. I had to get to it before it did. Merrial was probably standing stopped in the hall outside, listening intently and thinking, Did I hear a couple of thuds with a clang in-between there? If he heard the piercing warble of an unfamiliar mobile phone coming from the room he'd just left, he'd be right back in here. Or more likely he'd dash down to his study, grab a gun and then come storming back.

I levered myself forward, feeling along the unseen floor for the little phone. Why did they have to make the damn things so fucking small nowadays? Old mobiles were the size of a brick; I'd have found the thing by now instead of whimpering as my hands fanned out across the wooden floor, banging into bits of gear and failing totally to find the phone, which I couldn't even hear now. The ringing would start any second. Not that that would matter, because thanks to my panic and subsequent whacking of the phone about the place like it was a fucking squash ball, Merrial had almost certainly realised there was somebody hiding in his gym store and probably already had his shotgun or whatever and was walking calmly upstairs, chambers full and hammers cocked.

Green glow to one side, quietly flicking off. The phone's screen. I found it, bashing my forehead off something metal as I did so. I closed then opened the phone again. The display looked normal; nothing wrong with the little fucker. So how come it hadn't gone from vibration to ring? Then I saw the little envelope symbol. Of course; it had registered an incoming text message and so had vibrated once only. I needn't have panicked; I certainly needn't have started bouncing it off the walls like a bluebottle in a fucking jam jar.

Still no sounds from outside. Maybe I'd got away with it. I squatted there in the darkness and accessed the message: OK 2 CALL? C.

I looked to the door of the cupboard. There was an old-fashioned keyhole there, halfway up one edge. I swivelled over to it to put my eye to the bright slit. My forehead banged off the door handle. I sat back, blinking through the tears. A door-knob just above a keyhole; who'd have thought that? Fucking, fucking idiot. It had hurt so much I hadn't really registered how loud the sound had been. Jesus H. For all the stealthiness I was showing here I might just as well march out singing a medley of Slipknot numbers and slide down the fucking banister rail yodelling.

I looked carefully through the keyhole. Most of the gym was visible, including the door to the hall outside. The door was closed. Nobody in the room. I wedged myself against the wall and dialled Celia's mobile number.

'Yes?'

'I'm in the cupboard in the gym,' I whispered. 'Can you hear me?'

'Yes. I just had a call from John.'

'I know. I heard. Who's this Kaj?'

'John's bodyguard. Swedish. You've met him, at Somerset House.'

The big blond guy. 'Oh, fuck.'

'Have you cleared the tape on the answering machine?'

'Thoroughly.'

'Get out. Quick as you can.'

'That was my intention.'

'He said he'd have a look round, and call Kaj to get him over. Also, he might have a shower. If he does shower you should hear it; it's a power shower and the pump is in a cupboard off the second-floor hall; it makes a fair amount of noise, on that floor at least.'

'Where will this Kaj person be coming from?'

'I don't know. I'm surprised he wasn't with him. Unless they were together and he gave him the rest of the day off. Wait; Kaj has a girlfriend who lives . . . somewhere off Regent's Park. He may be there. John could have dropped him on the way down from Derbyshire. He didn't say anything about seeing your Land Rover in the mews so he's probably parked out the front. But you must get out as soon as possible.'

'I *know*!' I hissed, glancing through the keyhole again. Regent's Park to Belgravia. How long would that take by car? Potentially several hours if you made the journey during a rainy weekday rush hour while there was a tube strike, but this was a sunny Saturday lunchtime. Ten minutes? No; maybe on a

Sunday. Twenty minutes? Longer? Always assuming that was where this Kaj guy was in the first place. Maybe the fucker was only five minutes' walk away, shoulders taking up half the pavement as he searched the King's Road for a trendy Outsize shop. 'I'll give it a couple of minutes more,' I told Ceel. 'If he's searching the place he probably reckons he needn't look in here because he's already taken care of it.'

'Why don't I phone him again?' Celia suggested. 'I can try to find out what he's going to do and how far away Kaj might be. I might even try to convince him he should go out until Kaj gets there, visit some friends or go to a café.'

I thought. 'Good idea,' I said. 'Call me back.'

'All right. Be ready to move.'

'Oh, I am,' I said. Ceel rang off. I was about to close the phone when the display faded of its own accord. Oh. No. I closed the phone and opened it, but the phone had turned itself off. I tried turning it back on again and it got as far as vibrating once and beginning its start-up procedure, showing zero bars out of three of available battery power before confirming this by going dark again. Out of power. I supposed I'd been lucky to get what I had out of it after such a short charge-up time on the *Temple Belle* this morning.

I sat there, breathing almost normally, with the little phone a dead lump in my hand, then I holstered it and sighed. So I was on my own now. Poor Ceel; she would worry, not being able to contact me. She'd guess the phone was out of juice, I hoped. The keyhole again. Still nothing happening in the gym. I supposed I ought to put on my other glove.

Ah; the other glove. Now then, where would that be?

I shook my head at the darkness. Swivelling and sliding back to where I'd been squatting earlier, in the rear corner of the store, I banged another shin on something very hard. At this rate it wouldn't need Kaj to jump up and down on my knees to wreck my fucking legs. I felt around on the floor. I felt the glove. And some relief. One more tiny hurdle accidentally set up but then cleared. Oh, Christ, I was getting very tired. I was going to spend the rest of my life in this fucking posh house, just trying to get the hell out of it.

Maybe I could just lie here and go to sleep and nobody would ever find me. I could squat here; stow away. Live secretly here in the house like a sort of soft hermit. Celia would discover me and bring me something to eat each evening, like a child sent to their room by a strict father brought food by a forgiving mother or younger sister.

My knees were getting sore from all this squatting. Sore knees. Think about that. Think of that pain, hold that image; Kaj's big face and short blond hair as he smiles at you and goes boingy-boingy on your fucking leg bones, man.

A surprisingly large part of my brain really did seem to want to do nothing. A significant and very vocal minority of my brain cells seemed to think that just resting here in the darkness was actually quite a good idea. It had proved all right so far; I hadn't been discovered, it was quiet and unthreatening; maybe if I stayed here everything would somehow be okay. I knew this was nonsense, obviously, but that was the temptation. Stay put. Leaving my dark, musty-smelling sanctuary meant going out into the light, braving the landings and stairs and floors and halls and doors of a house whose owner was present and suspicious and potentially – and very possibly by now – armed. And who was anyway a crime boss. And who had just ordered his personal Dolph Lundgren-on-steroids bodyguard here to investigate what was going on. Oh yes, staying here in the darkness and hiding quietly seemed like a seductively good idea. Or maybe I could go back to Ceel's bedroom and hide there, and our intense sexual karma would spookily protect me even from a determined and thorough search, until she got back and could smuggle me out when the coast was clear . . .

No. Out. Get the fuck out. Now. Get back to the door. Look

through the keyhole. Confirm nothing happening and nobody there. Take hold of the door handle. Twist handle and slowly open door. Rise. Feel knees complain, as though they're anticipating what might happen to them later if this all goes horribly wrong. Take deep breath. Close door again. Walk quietly to door of gym. No keyhole so can't look out to hall.

Stop and listen. Can you hear a power shower pump operating? No. So, what to do? Go back to the cupboard and wait there? Keep an ear to the keyhole so you could hear when the pump did start up? But then what if the pump couldn't be heard from inside the cupboard? Wait here, at the door leading to the hall? But then what if Merrial took another look inside the gym before taking his shower? He'd already been in here, but he might want to check again.

A house this size was probably well in excess of some mathematically provable topographical limit that defined when a space became too big for one person ever to search perfectly. You could confirm that there was nobody on a certain floor, but then while you were in the depths of one of these large rooms, checking in an en suite loo or whatever, the person doing the hiding could slip out of a not-yet-searched room and creep up to one of the already-searched rooms without the searcher being able to spot them. So checking a room twice would make some sort of sense.

Oh fuck, I didn't fucking know. I looked behind me. Opened blinds. The window Merrial had been standing at while he'd been talking to Ceel on his mobile. I could see the house on the far side of the square, visible through the leafless trees of winter. Probably too far away for it to be a problem. I wondered if there was any way to get out of the window and down to the ground without causing a fuss. Or making it to the upper storey, to the loft and then out onto the roof and then finding a way down. If I still had a working phone I could call 999 and ask for the fire brigade because there was a major fire in the place, and hope to get away in the confusion. No; all of these just led to more complications and more opportunities for things to go appallingly wrong.

Footsteps outside in the hall, coming closer. Oh shit. Did I have time to get back to the cupboard? Probably not, and certainly not quietly. I shrank back behind the door. If Merrial did open the door, and he was daft enough not to look behind it as soon as he'd opened it, then I might still escape.

The footsteps went past. A door closed. Closed and locked, I thought. I waited for the sound of a shower. I looked around the gym. If there was a phone extension in here, did I dare phone Ceel in case there was something vital she now knew that I needed to? But then what if Merrial was already on the landline? Bit of a giveaway, hearing that old other-extension click.

I waited. But how long did I have? Where was Kaj coming from? King's Road? Regent's Park? Somewhere else? And how fucking long did it take Merrial to get ready for a fucking shower, for fuck's sake? Come on, man; stop fucking about and get your fucking clothes off and jump into the fucking thing. Twist that dial and lather up.

Maybe Ceel had been exaggerating about how loud the pump was. Maybe she had more acute hearing than I did. Maybe some eccentricity of the way sound was transmitted through the house meant that right here where I was standing in the gym was the one place you couldn't hear the goddamn pump. I tried to listen really carefully. Was that the sound of a pump? Jesus, if my phone still had power I could phone Ceel and hold the phone up and ask her, Is that the sound of the pump, that barely audible hum way in the distance? Or is that the central heating, or the fucking drinks fridge in the study or something? Maybe Merrial was using a mains-pressure shower over his bath instead for some reason I could only guess at. Ha! Maybe he was showering as quietly as he could specifically because he didn't want to let his supposed junkie with a knife know where he was, even if he had locked the bedroom and presumably the bathroom door.

When the pump did start up I jumped again; it sounded like it was just through the wall from where I was standing. I thought about that phrase about somebody being as nervous as a kitten and thought what a load of crap it really was; I'd never *seen* a kitten as nervous as I'd been over the last couple of hours.

Okay. Signal to go. I put my hand on the door handle. But what if Merrial had started the shower going as a ruse, and was – no, no, no, fuck it; just fucking well fucking go for fuck's sake, you over-cautious fuck.

I went quickly but quietly out into the hall, gently closed the door and went along to the stairwell, treading on the sides of the steps as I descended to keep down any creaking noises. I did the same on the next set of stairs. I was right at the bottom stair, facing the front door and about to make the turn to head back along the long hall to the kitchen and the rear door, when I heard the sound of a key in the front door's lock.

I didn't freeze. I didn't even start to think that, Hey, maybe I can brazen it out, dressed in my incredibly convincing overalls. There was no time to dash back upstairs or get to the kitchen. There was maybe just enough time to get to the door to the right of the main door. I lunged for it, leaping from the bottom stair, grabbing the handle and pulling the door open to fall into a cloakroom as I hauled the door closed behind me, managing to damp its closing just enough to stop it slamming an instant before I heard the front door open.

Oh no, I was going to sneeze. I was panting, close to wheezing, worried that I was going to make so much noise that whoever it was – Kaj, probably – would hear me anyway, but now I felt the tingle in my nose that meant I was going to sneeze. I shoved my tongue up into the top of my mouth and forced the edge of a finger up into the base of my septum, under my nose. The urge to sneeze faded. I tried to work my way back into the coats and jackets – the smell of waxed material always did make me want to sneeze for some reason – and hoped that Kaj didn't need to put a coat in here. The front door closed.

'Boss?' a deep, male voice boomed. 'John?'

Then silence. I crouched down, behind and underneath the thickest clump of coats. It was winter; not exactly freezing but not exactly warm either, so there was every chance Kaj would have a coat he wanted to deposit in here. Oh no, don't. Oh no, please don't. Please be a really hard Swedish guy who just totally scorns the very idea of coats and jackets until the temperature is a good ten below and the wind chill doubles that.

The door opened.

Oh God, this is it. This must be. I didn't think I could be seen but my luck just had to run out sometime and I suspected it was long overdue for departure. All I could see, as I was buried under and behind the coats, were two very large Timberland boots and the broad shins of a pair of jeans. Could he see anything of me? There was a swishing noise, the sound of fabric on fabric, then the door closed.

I stayed where I was. Give the big blond bastard time to do a double-take; Yoost a meenoot, whose were those shoes that I saw yust there?

Then I heard heavy footsteps going rapidly upstairs.

My mouth had gone all dry once more. When I tried to stand up my legs collapsed under me and I had to sit down, breathing heavily. I levered myself up. I put my ear to the door. I was a metre from escape. I'd use the front door and the hell with getting out the way I came in. Thank *fuck* I'd replaced the key inside the stone earlier.

Silence. No keyhole here either. I risked cracking the door and looked out. Nobody about. The door opened and closed almost silently. Upstairs, I could still just hear the sound of the shower pump. A door closed up there, sounding faint. I turned to the wide front door. Please don't let there be a returning maid or an investigating copper standing outside. The front door was heavy but it too swung open without a sound and I went out. The fresh, cool air of a bright winter's afternoon hit my face as I skipped down the steps to the square, breathing deeply. It tasted like freedom.

Two left turns and I was in the mews. There was nobody at the Land Rover. I got in and reversed out. I whooped and hollered most of the way back to the *Temple Belle*. I parked on a double yellow by a phone box on Buckingham Palace Road to phone Ceel's mobile. Message service. I licked my lips, trying to think what to say.

'It's all okay,' I said.

I blew a kiss at a parking warden already starting to take the Landy's details.

Then when I got back to Chelsea Creek I could hardly move once I reached the car park. It felt like the front wheels were ploughing through half-melted tarmac, and my legs almost buckled underneath me as I got out. I had to support myself with both hands as I went down the narrow gangway to the boat. I got the door closed, half fell down the steps and – for the second time in twelve hours, and, in the overalls, even more fully clothed – collapsed onto the bed like a dead weight. I was asleep before the second bounce.

Twelve

DEAD CAT BOUNCE

There's this thing called the Dead Cat Bounce. It's a stock market term, I believe. What it's talking about is the fact that even a stock that is essentially worthless and really going nowhere but down for ever can register a slight upward movement, just for a bit, because there is generally a floor for almost everything. The comparison rests on the fact that even when a cat hits the pavement from forty storeys high and dies instantly, it'll still bounce back up a little.

Now may be a good time to think of something happy, inside here.

When I first came to London in '94 it wasn't as a DJ. I'd lost my job with StrathClyde Sound after a series of disputes (the last straw, absurdly, had been a campaign I'd called Don't Rubbish Our Stations, to bring back litter bins to Scottish railway stations, because the IRA had never carried out any terrorist attacks anywhere in Scotland and so there was no need to ape the English safety precaution of removing bins because they were potential places to leave a bomb). So I decided to make the move down south to the big smoke, like generations of Scots before me. In London, I'd got nowhere with the few contacts I had and the dozens of demo tapes I'd sent off, so I got a job as a bike courier, whizzing through the crowded streets on an already well-used Bandit that had cost me the last of my savings, weaving in and out between the cars and trucks and buses and going the wrong way round the occasional traffic island to get documents and disks and drawings from one office to another as quickly as possible.

Then I got a job with a firm of Motorcycle Chauffeurs, somehow convincing the manager that I was a good, responsible, and above all smooth driver (miraculously, I'd held on to a clean licence in all the mayhem of London dispatch biking, though I had been knocked down twice). The idea was that the London traffic had become so congested there was an almost literal gap in the market for getting people from one bit of the capital to the other quicker than a taxi or a limo could. A big bike was the answer; a Honda Pan European or a 1200 BMW tourer, complete with panniers to carry an extra helmet and an over-suit for the client and a tall enough screen so that the worst of any weather was kept off them (providing you were moving, though of course being on a bike, you should be able to, even in a serious jam).

The company did well enough but then ran into cashflow problems and was taken over by a limo firm; they lost half the drivers but I was one of the lucky ones.

One late spring morning, at the start of an early shift, I was called to an emergency job taking somebody from Islington to Langham Place. A car hadn't shown and I was nearest. I pulled up at a nice, semi-posh terraced house in Cloudesley Square, one of the district's leafier bits, and this elfin blonde in jeans and a rumpled T-shirt appeared, running down the steps pulling on a pretend biker's jacket and waving goodbye to a sleepy-looking guy standing in the doorway, wearing what looked like a very small woman's dressing-gown.

'Hi!' she said, pulling on the helmet I had held out to her.

She had a small, friendly looking face, profoundly unkempt short, curly hair and crinkly eyes that were about as wide-set as they could be in such a thin face. Cheeky-looking, somehow. I was sure I recognised her. Come to think of it, the guy in the too-small dressing-gown had rung a bell or two as well.

'Morning,' I said, helping her with the buckle under her chin. This wasn't as easy as it ought to have been because she was bouncing from one foot to the other all the time. 'You'll have to stop jumping up and down,' I told her gently.

'Sorry!' She waggled her eyebrows. The helmet was a bit big for her, but I did the strap up as tight as I could.

I got the buckle fastened and she swung her leg over and jumped on behind me. 'Broadcasting House! Langham Place!' she yelled, helmet banging against mine. 'Fast as you can! If that's okay.'

I nodded and we set off. It was about ten to six. We didn't quite make it in time but her producer filled for her and played a couple of records back to back and – parked up by a wee café on Cavendish Street and listening on my FM earpiece – I heard her start her show, and smiled when – breathless, giggling, apologising – she said thanks to the bike guy who'd helped her get there almost on time. 'Sorry I forgot to ask your name,' she said. 'But if you're listening, mate, well done. Right . . .'

Samantha Coghlan was something very close to being the nation's darling at the time. Sam had presented various shows on children's TV, been a big hit there, tried some more serious TV without any great success – one of those deals where they keep adding zeros to the money on offer until the talent has to say yes, then the execs stand around scratching their heads, wondering what exactly to do with the star they've bought – and then made the move to national radio in what at first looked like an act of desperation by both her and Radio One.

As it turned out, though, she was perfect for the *Breakfast*

Show. Well, perfect apart from sleeping in all too often with her celeb film-star boyfriend after showbiz parties and general late nights with their famous friends. Breezy and pally, but sharp and funny too, Sam added a million and a half listeners to the show and reinvigorated a career that might just have been starting to stutter. Within a year she was winning awards, fronting a TV rock and pop show to even more acclaim and helping a couple of major retailers lift their profile with a generation of customers they'd been losing touch with.

I became Biker Ken, her preferred mode of transport for most of that summer. I'd made a decision right at the start to keep quiet about my own dormant radio career. Sam started to mention me on air more often, and over a couple of months I became one of the disparate cloud of friends, acquaintances, hangers-on and, well, parasites she would mention – always funnily, never bitterly – during the course of her show; a cast of characters she built up apparently without thinking about it until we became part of a sort of real-life soap opera the listening public followed avidly five mornings out of seven.

After a while – once the bike hire company equipped us with two-way intercoms so that we could, if the client wanted to, communicate with each other – she started asking me, en route, about what I'd done before I'd become a bike chauffeur. Finally I couldn't keep my old career quiet without either being rude or lying, so I confessed all.

'Brilliant! Really?'

'Really.'

'Great! Come on the show!'

'Look,' I told her, 'I'm not going to say no, Sam, but you may want to recon—'

'Na; come on! It'll be fun!'

So I did. And found I hadn't lost my radio voice or my touch, and was suitably, humbly funny for a five-minute spot with her one morning when I was off duty. That afternoon, I got a call from one of the stations I'd sent a demo tape to a year earlier; would I like to come in and do an audition? So, Sam gave me my big break.

The lovely Samantha parted company with her listeners one tearful morning that autumn, leaving to go off and have babies in LA with her actor fiancé, whose career had taken off in serious style. We all missed her, but by then I had my own late-night show on a new commercial London station called M25. I sent her flowers; she sent a gracious, funny, affectionate note that I still had. She was a happily married mother of twin girls and a big hit on the Hollywood social scene, last I'd heard, but what I remembered most was not her leaving, or those five generous minutes on her show that kick-started my own stalled career, or even that morning when I first met her; what I remembered most, what I remembered now, was charging down the sleepy streets in the light of a new summer's morning, heading south for Langham Place through the sparse five-thirty traffic with the big bike humming beneath us. She held onto the grab handles at first, then, after a couple of weeks, asked if it would be okay to put her arms round my waist.

I'd said, Of course, and so, about three mornings out of five, and usually by the time we got to Caledonian Road, she'd clasp her gloved hands in front of my belly and put her helmet against mine and then fall comfortably asleep for the rest of the journey.

When we started wearing the intercom units, I could hear her snoring sometimes, ever so gently, as we thrummed smoothly down the quiet, side-lit streets towards the heart of the slowly waking city.

In all my life to that point, I had never been happier.

Since then, only when I'd been with Ceel.

And I'm thinking about her now, because now I'm in a box, all trussed, bound up, blind in the darkness and petrified that something gruesome is going to happen to me, because all that I did earlier, all the business with the getting into and getting out of Mental's house was somehow not enough, and the bad men have come for me and taken me away and I'm terrified for myself and for Celia, because I have the awful, gut-churning, bowel-chilling feeling that when they take me out of here I'm going to see her and she'll be in just as much trouble as I am.

They came in the depths of night and the bottom of the tide, when the whole ship was tilted, out of true and out of kilter, sloping away to one side on the dark slope of ancient mud where the smell of cold death rises from.

I woke up panicking again, but this time because I thought I'd heard something. I lay there across the bed in the darkness, not daring to move. Had I heard something? Sometimes I used to be sure I heard a great banging noise the instant before I woke, but Jo would always say that I must have been dreaming. Had that happened this time? I heard another noise, somewhere above me. I started to move my hand towards the head of the bed, where the big black Mag-Lite torch/club lay. Maybe I was dreaming. Or maybe it was Jo come back, shame-faced, unable to live without me. Maybe, better, it was Ceel; I'd left the door unlocked or she'd learned how to pick a lock from her husband's crim pals.

Another noise. Oh, sweet Jesus. Forget the Mag-Lite. Activate the fucking Breitling's emergency satellite signalling gizmo, dickhead. I started to bring my hands together.

The light clicked on. My eyes hurt. I spun round, turning over in the bed in time to see a tall, well-built white guy I didn't recognise standing above me; another big guy stood at the door to the bedroom, some sort of large box just behind him. They looked like I had; overalls and baseball caps. My right hand moved to my left wrist, where the big Breitling was, but it was all happening too slowly. The first guy punched me hard in the belly and the wind whooshed out of my lungs. He grabbed my wrist and tore the watch off my hand.

Released, I curled up, gasping and mewling, bunched round the pain and the wheezing vacuum formed by the punch, and they bound me in that position before I could do anything about it, quickly and efficiently sticking silver gaffer tape over my mouth and tying my hands and ankles all together with the same plastic ties the cops use. They both wore latex gloves, like surgeons. They frisked me quickly, efficiently, taking everything out of my pockets. Then they roped my neck to the same four-way knot securing my wrists and ankles so that I was trussed into a fetal position. That way I fitted into the foam-lined metal shell of a washing machine in the big cardboard box I'd glimpsed earlier, which they must have lifted down the stairs. They lowered me into it, sitting me on my buttocks and feet, and then secured the lid, cutting out all light. I heard the cardboard flaps slap down above me and the tearing noise of more gaffer tape being applied, then I felt myself being lifted up the steps.

I was on my side now, lying on and surrounded by what felt like thick expanded polystyrene. I tried to move, tried to scream down my nose, tried to kick or punch or do anything, but all that happened was I produced a pathetic keening noise through my snotty nostrils and got myself all hot in the tiny, insulated space. I felt myself carried up the gangway, along the pontoon, up the slope to the car park, and then heard the faint noise of what sounded like a pair of van rear doors opening. I was placed down, the doors closed with a muffled thud and a few seconds later the van, engine unheard within all the foam padding around me, started off, swinging into the main road and accelerating away.

Oh God, oh fuck, oh shit. The very, very best I could hope for now was that this was still something to do with that wanker and his dangerous driving case. Mark whatever he was called.

Maybe he was still trying to get away with a functioning driving licence; maybe he had persuaded my new pal Mr Glatz that, after all – and despite our little word outside the Imperial War Museum – I still needed to be leaned upon. Maybe he'd found new crim pals willing to do the job for him. Maybe he had more villainous resources of his own than Mr Glatz had credited him with. Maybe all this was just to get me utterly fucking petrified – if so; hey, mission accomplished, guys! – so I'd agree to change my witness statement.

Except I didn't think so.

It was all so fucking easy and efficient and well thought-out, somehow. Too practised. These fuckers had done this before. It was Merrial.

But maybe not. Maybe when we got to wherever we were going – and it was always possible we were going somewhere really terminally and immediately god-awful, like a crusher or an incinerator, or just the edge of an old dock – maybe I'd see this guy Southorne, not John Merrial. Maybe.

I started to cry. The pain in my abdomen was receding now, but I started to cry.

The van swung smoothly through the city's night-time streets, this way and that.

All the things I'll never get to say. All the rants I'll never get to rant. There was one shaping up about context, about blindness, about selectivity, about racism and our intense sucker-hood when it came to reacting to images and symbols, and our blank, glazed inability to accept and comprehend reality in the form of statistics.

It's because there was a reliable-sources statistic Phil discovered the other day; that every twenty-four hours about thirty-four thousand children die in the world from the effects of poverty; from malnutrition and disease, basically. Thirty-four thousand, from a world, a world-society, that could feed and

402

clothe and treat them all, with a workably different allocation of resources. Meanwhile, the latest estimate is that two thousand eight hundred people died in the Twin Towers, so it's like that image, that ghastly, grey-billowing, double-barrelled fall, repeated twelve times every single fucking day; twenty-four towers, one per hour, throughout each day and night. Full of children.

We feel for the people in the towers, we agree with almost any measure to stop it ever happening again, and so we should. But for the thirty-four thousand, each day? Given our behaviour, and despite the idea we're supposed to love our children, you could be forgiven for thinking that most of us just don't give a damn.

So, maybe not such a terrific world to be contemplating leaving, then (a straw caught in the undertow, heading downwards into the darkness, to clutch at). At least I said I loved Ceel. I told her, in the conventional three words. That's something. Not much, perhaps, and she never did return the sentiment, but it's something that I got to say, maybe the last unforced thing I'll ever say.

It seems like a long time before the van stops. Then it starts again, moving slowly. It jiggles over what feels like some roughish ground or badly pitted roadway, then angles down. One left corner, taken slowly, then a series of them, as though we're on a spiral ramp, heading downwards. Then we stop.

It feels like my heart is thrashing against my ribcage, desperate to escape; a rat in an already humming microwave. Sweat pours off me in the tightly insulated confines of the box. Then I'm lifted, set down, and there's the sound of tape being ripped from the cardboard above me. The lid comes off and a little light seeps in. I'm hoisted out easily by the two overalled guys who had put me into the box. They undo the rope holding my neck down to my ankles and wrists, then cut a plastic tie holding my wrists and ankles together. I'm opened out like a penknife and stand precariously between them, ankles still tied to each other and wrists the same. I'm in a big rectangular concrete tunnel. It's quite dark, lit only by a couple of armoured glass ceiling fixtures.

The van we came in was a white Astramax and a little part of my brain that doesn't believe all this is really happening to me thinks, Ah! Of *course* it's an Astramax; what else? Ahead there are two wire mesh gates and distant ceiling lights forming a grid in a larger space beyond. The air smells dank and filthy like rain-diluted sewage; it feels cold on my sweat-beaded skin.

They drag me to the mesh gates and push them open. We're on a slight slope. Beyond, the slope disappears into darkness black as night, the darkness of an infinite pit.

Lights come on across the black gulf. The mainbeams of a car, blinding. The blackness is water. We splash into it, raising a smell of something dead and rotten into the air. The water is only a couple of centimetres deep, barely more than a film. The toes of my shoes are dragged through the thin covering over old but still smooth concrete. About fifteen metres in from the shallow ramp we entered from, we get to the place where the car is. It's a big, dark, modern Bentley. By its off-side there is a little island of pallets; about two dozen squares of anaemic yellow-white undressed wood arranged to provide a sort of crude pontoon above the shallow sheet of dark water. The Bentley sits beside the pallet island for all the world like a liner tied up to a quayside.

In the centre of the pallets, a single metal column comes down from the roof. There are two piles of bricks on each side of the column, about sixty centimetres high, bound to the black iron column with thick black insulating tape. A metre away, facing this, there is a single big plain wooden seat, sturdy and armless, the sort of thing you might find at the head of a farmhouse table.

When I see it I try to struggle, but it's almost comically ineffective. I suspect the two guys holding me don't even notice. They put me in front of the seat. When I resist being sat in it the one who hit me before whacks me with one fist, crunching into my cheek. I lose it for a moment and when I'm fully aware again I'm already tied and taped into the seat and they're just finishing taping my feet to the iron column. My heels are resting on the piles of bricks, one on either side of the metal post.

I can't believe this. My head feels like it's revolving and somersaulting and vibrating, like it's a fairground waltzer and my brain's the single hapless, helpless passenger. When I'm quite secure and unable to move much beyond a twitch – my head is the only part of me I can really control at all – the driver's door of the Bentley opens and John Merrial gets out. He's dressed in a black three-piece suit with a high-necked waistcoat. Black gloves. The two guys, one to each side of me, straighten fractionally.

So there goes my last hope. It is him and not Mark Southorne. I am here because of yesterday, because of the message, because of Ceel, and not because of some idiotic points-dodging scam.

Mr Merrial looks small and dark and regretful, as though he isn't going to enjoy any of this either.

I lose control of my bowels and shit myself. I really can't help it. I'm a passenger in my own body now and I just sit there and listen and feel and then smell it all happen and I'm astonished how quickly and easily it takes place. Mr Merrial wrinkles his nose. The shit fills my underpants.

Nothing, I think. I'm to be spared nothing.

The guy who hasn't hit me goes to Merrial and offers him the stuff they've taken off me. Merrial takes a large pair of latex gloves from one pocket, puts them on over his black leather gloves and then accepts the big Breitling, hefting it. He smiles. 'Nice watch.' He hands it back to the guy. He tries to turn my phone on but of course it's dead. Then he looks in my wallet, taking out my various credit cards and bits and pieces and inspecting them. He pauses at his own white calling card, the one I'd written on.

From here, because I'm sitting down and so looking from a lower perspective, I can see the back of the card, where I wrote down the code Celia told me over the phone, the code that turns off the burglar alarm in the Merrials' house. I've been sitting here desperately trying to work out what to say and I do have an idea, but it all depends on the fucker not looking at the back of that little white card. If he does, there's nothing I can think of that might save Celia, let alone me. If he doesn't, then the slenderest of chances remains.

The moment seems to freeze. In that instant I'm suddenly with Ceel and her absurd entanglement theory. In one universe, Merrial flips the card over in his fingers and sees the alarm code written there. In the other, he just looks at the one already printed side and that's all.

Maybe I deserve what might happen here. I know I'm not a particularly good person; I've lied and I've cheated and it's no consolation that little of it was illegal. It's not illegal to lie to your best friend, to fuck his wife, to lie to your partner, to cheat on her. Smashing car windows, hitting somebody in the face, smoking dope, burglary; that sort of thing's illegal and I've done all that too, but none of that means very much compared to betraying the people you're closest to; that's the stuff really to be ashamed of. So maybe I'd have no real cause to complain if I'm made to suffer here.

But nothing I've done deserves the death penalty, or even having my legs broken, does it? I've told lies on a small scale but I've tried to tell the truth on a larger scale. I've tried to be true to what I believe in rather than make as much money as I could have. Doesn't that count for something? And who the fuck are these people to judge me anyway? I'm a liar and I'm weak and I'm certainly no hero because I've filled my fucking pants, but – even sitting here in my own stench, in greasy, sweat-stained two-hard-days'-living clothes – I'm a fucking better man than these vindictive shitheads, for all their crisply ironed shirts.

If only deserving something was all there was to it.

Actually it doesn't matter a damn. I am in the realm of pure luck here, even if Ceel's crazy ideas are true (which they just damn well aren't). So roll the dice; let the universe do the fucking maths.

Merrial slips the card back into my wallet, without looking at the other side. He hands everything back to the man in the overalls, then slowly removes his latex gloves and gives those to the guy, who comes and stands behind my shoulder again.

Merrial says, 'Take the tape off his mouth, would you, Alex?'

The guy who's hit me twice so far does that, tearing it off casually. It hurts a bit. I swallow. Cold sweat trickles down my face and into my mouth.

'Good evening, Kenneth,' Merrial says.

For a while I just breathe, unwilling to trust myself to come out with anything coherent.

Merrial hoists himself a little and sits on the wing of the Bentley. 'Well,' he says with a hint of a smile. 'Thank you for coming. I expect you're wondering why I've invited you here this evening.'

This is probably meant to be funny. I keep on breathing, not willing to say anything. I stare into his eyes, dark under his brows and the shadows of the small overhead lights. I keep swallowing, trying to get some saliva into my mouth. I look about the place, squint into the Bentley. At least there's no sign of Celia. Maybe she got away in time. Maybe she's not been linked to this. Oh, Lord, a straw to grasp at; a still-floating one.

'Do you like being underground, Kenneth?' Merrial asks. I don't think he really wants an answer so I don't give him one.

'I do,' he says, smiling, looking around at the darkness. 'I don't know . . . just makes me feel . . .' He stares up. 'Safe, I suppose.'

I'm a single nerve-firing away from hysterical laughter at this point, at that particular word, but I don't think that laughing in Mr Merrial's face right now would be a very good idea at all, and sense prevails. A series of small, horrible, bubbly farts announce my bowels have completed their evolutionary duty and prepared me for fight or flight by getting rid of the excess matter they'd been holding inside my body. Very helpful, I think, sat here, immobile and helpless.

'Yes,' Merrial says, looking round too. 'I like it here. Useful old place, this.' He gestures down at the floor, where the water has already stopped rippling and gone back to its impression of pure blackness again. 'Flooding, now.' He shakes his head, lips pursed. 'Won't be able to use it in a year or two.' He looks at me. 'Water table, you see, Kenneth. Water table of the whole of London is rising again. It was going down for years; centuries, apparently, while they were taking water out for industry; tanning, breweries, that sort of thing. Now it's rising again. They have to keep pumps going all the time in the deep tube lines and some multi-storey underground car parks.' He smiles thinly. 'You'd think they could use some of it as drinking water instead of flooding nice valleys in the Home Counties, but apparently it's too polluted. Shame, really, don't you think?'

'Mr Merrial,' I say, voice quivering, 'I honestly don't know why—'

Merrial raises one hand to me and looks towards the ramp I was brought down. Lights, and the sound of a big car engine. A Range Rover trundles down the slope. It edges between the opened V of the wire mesh gates and into the water. It comes hissing slowly towards us on small, inky bow-waves, then loops away into the darkness and curves back in again, stopping on the other side of the little pallet-island from the Bentley, a series of miniature wakes rippling and gurgling against the wood beneath us. The Range Rover kills its lights. The air smells of exhaust.

On the far side, the driver's door opens and Kaj gets out. He comes splashing round, steps up onto the pallets and puts one hand to the passenger door's handle.

I know it might be her. I know who's probably going to be there behind the smoked glass. Merrial is watching me intently; I can feel it. I stare at the Range Rover's door. For as long as I can, I'm going to do what I can to protect her. That might not be very long, but it's all I can do, the only control over anything I have here. When the door opens and I see it's Celia, I look surprised, no more. I stare at her, then look round briefly at Merrial.

Ceel appears uninjured. She looks at Merrial, then Kaj, still holding the door open for her. She steps out, wrinkling her nose at the smell. She's dressed in blue jeans, a thick red shirt and a yellow and black hiking jacket. Hair down, spread. Hiking boots. She looks calmly angry.

'*What* do you think—?' she starts to ask Merrial, then she seems to see me properly for the first time. Oh, Jesus, don't blow it so soon, kid. She frowns at me. 'That's . . . that's Ken Nott. The DJ.' She glares accusingly at Merrial. 'What the hell's *he* supposed to have done?' The question ends on what is almost a laugh.

Merrial stays where he is, sitting on the wing of the Bentley. Kaj quietly closes the door of the Range Rover and stands beside Celia with his hands folded over his crotch, bouncer style, eyes flicking about the scene. The two guys who kidnapped me stand still, one at each of my shoulders.

'Let's ask him, shall we?' Merrial said pleasantly. He looks at me. 'So, Ken, why do you think you're here?'

'Mr Merrial,' I say, 'I don't know. I don't know what you think I've done, but—'

Merrial shakes his head. 'Ah, no, Ken. You see you've started lying already now, haven't you?' He looks genuinely disappointed in me. 'I thought you were always saying on your show how people had to be truthful, how they had to be truthful even when it hurt, but there you go, you see, the first proper answer we've had from you so far and it's a flat lie, isn't it?'

'If, if, if,' I stammer, for the first time since I was four. I suck in a deep breath. 'If I've done something you don't like, I'm sorry, Mr Merrial. I really am.'

Merrial shrugs, raising his eyebrows and making a pouting motion with his lower lip. 'Well, everybody's sorry when they get caught, Kenneth,' he says reasonably. 'But I think you do know why you're here.' His voice is quite soft.

Nothing useful I can say at this point, I suspect. I stick to swallowing. The shit is starting to go cold around my backside on the front of the seat I'm tied to. Jesus, I stink. Oh, Celia, I wish you didn't have to see, smell, experience all this. I wish you'd run, got away, just kept on heading north or anywhere as long as it was away from this man.

'Kaj?' Merrial says. 'You have exhibit A, do you?'

Kaj nods and opens the Range Rover's rear door.

'John,' Celia says. 'I don't know what's going on here, but I don't want to be part of it. I want to go home. Now.' She sounds composed, unflustered, but still distinctly pissed off.

'I'd like you to stay a while yet, Celia,' Merrial says.

'I don't *want* to stay,' she says through clenched teeth.

'I'm sure you don't,' Merrial tells her. He swings one foot a couple of times, gently tapping the flank of the Bentley with his heel. 'But I insist.'

Kaj is holding an opened laptop computer.

Celia narrows her eyes. She takes a breath. 'There had better,' she says slowly, 'be a very good reason for this, John.' She looks about the place, sparing me a brief, pitying, slightly disgusted look. 'You've kept me away from . . . this sort of thing until now. I always assumed that was because you knew how I might react if I was brought into contact with it.' Her gaze snaps back to Merrial. 'This changes things between us, John,' she tells him. 'You can't go back from this. I hope you realise what you're doing.'

Merrial just smiles. 'Show Kenneth the evidence, would you, Kaj?'

The big blond guy holds the laptop open a metre away from me. From this angle, Celia can see the screen too. Kaj presses Return and a big grey-blue window already open on the desk-top flickers into life.

Oh shit. If I hadn't already crapped myself, I would now.

It's the interior of the Merrials' house; one of the landings. Daylight. First floor; I can see down the stairwell to the front door and the loo I hid in later. Only the first quarter metre of each door is visible. The alarm controls aren't visible. There's me, coming up the stairs in jerky every-few-seconds lo-fi slo-mo, the sort of thing you see on TV real-life crime programmes when they're showing a recording of a raid on a bank or building society or a sub-post office. No sound. Looks like the shot is taken from the ceiling.

'The cameras are inside smoke sensors,' Merrial tells me casu-ally. 'In case you were wondering.' He glances at his wife. Celia takes in a deep breath, puffing herself up. 'I had, ah,' Merrial says quickly, 'one or two suspicions about things; this was a way of—'

'You put surveillance in my *home*?' Celia says, rage over-flowing. 'You didn't even think to *ask* me, *tell* me?'

Merrial looks almost awkward. 'Security is my concern, Celia, not yours,' he says, not looking at her but at me. 'It's only in the hall and landings, not anywhere else.'

'Have you lost your senses, man?' Celia breathes, almost more to herself than to her husband. 'How could you? How *could* you?'

Merrial doesn't answer.

Meanwhile, on screen, in living grainy Rubbish Colour, I try various doors then disappear upstairs. The clip switches to the next floor up, and me ascending the stairs. I go into the bedroom across from Celia's. Not exactly good portrait-quality pictures, but good enough; easily sufficient to convince a jury that that was me, all right. Especially as I'm still wearing the same fucking clothes now as I was then.

'Okay, Kaj,' Merrial says softly. Kaj closes the laptop and puts it back in the Range Rover. 'So, Kenneth,' Merrial says. 'What were you doing in my house?'

I look at him. Swallow. I say, 'I was wiping the tape on your answering machine.'

He tips his head. He looks mildly surprised. 'Were you, now? And why would you want to do that?'

'Because I left a message on it that I regretted the instant I woke up the next morning, a message I thought would get me into trouble if you heard it.' I look around at the two gleaming cars, the pallet island, the black, unseen waters. I gulp. 'This sort of trouble.'

Merrial nods for a moment. 'What did the message say, Kenneth?'

'It was insulting to you, Mr Merrial.'

'What exactly did it say, Kenneth?'

'I honestly can't remember the exact words,' I say, closing my eyes for a few seconds. 'I swear I can't. I was . . . I was very drunk when I made the call. Very drunk indeed. I'd had a bit of an emotional sort of day, to be honest.' I attempt a hopefully infectious smile, but it seems Mr M's empathic immune system is proof against this. 'A friend found out that I'd been, ah, seeing his estranged wife,' I tell him, struggling manfully on. 'But I also discovered I'd just got out of a court case I hadn't exactly been looking forward to. So there was, ah, a sorrow to be drowned and something to be celebrated as well. I did both, and got very drunk indeed. Obviously I wouldn't have been stupid enough to have made the call if I hadn't been extremely drunk. But I was, ah . . .' I lick my cold, dry lips. I clear my throat. 'Listen,' I say, trying to look appealing. 'I don't suppose I could have some water, could I?'

Mr Merrial nods his head. 'You suppose correctly, Kenneth. Go on.'

I swallow on my dry throat, grimacing. 'What happened was that I'd found out from another of my friends what you . . . what you were involved in,' I tell Merrial. 'What your, ah, profession was, what it involved.' I shrug, look away. 'I felt angry that I'd played you, your wife a record. I felt, um, complicit, dirtied up, you might say. I called you to tell you this and got, ah, a little carried away, you might say. I called you things I would not call you to your face now, Mr Merrial. I, ah, I'm sure you can fill in the blanks yourself.'

Mr Merrial nods slowly. 'And my wife?'

I let my brows tremble. I glance at Celia, who is looking aghast at her husband. In a small voice I say, 'I, ah, may have referred to her as . . . a gangster's moll, or something.'

I have half a hope this might get a laugh, or at least a smile, but Merrial looks quite serious. 'And so you thought you'd burgle my house?' he says, not sounding completely convinced. Not sounding at all convinced, in fact.

'I realised what I'd done when I woke up,' I tell him. 'So I called your house again. The answering machine was still on so I guessed you were away for the weekend. I drove to your place, climbed into the garden from the roof of my Land Rover, found a key to the back door in one of those artificial stone things, realised the alarm wasn't switched on and thought, Hey, the Gods are with me here.' I shift in my seat. This is a mistake. The shit feels like some disgusting jelly inside my pants and jeans, and is already seeping through to my overalls. 'Then I really, really needed to take a dump, so I started looking for

413

a toilet. I finally found one. Then I went back down to the study, wiped the tape and—'

'You're leaving my wife's bedroom out of all this,' Merrial said. He glanced at Celia, then smiled. 'I can't help noticing.'

Celia glared at me and crossed her arms.

'I'd thought earlier that if there was any sign I'd – anybody had – been in then I should try to make it look like a robbery,' I tell him. 'So I took a couple of rings from Mrs Merrial's dressing table. Then, after I'd got the tape cleared, I realised taking the rings would just draw attention to the fact that somebody had been in the house, so I went back to her room and put them back where I'd found them.' I look at Merrial. He looks sceptical. I shrug as best I can. 'I'd never done this sort of thing before, Mr Merrial. I'd talked to people; I knew about artificial stones and fake Campbell's Soup tins and pretend mains sockets for hiding valuables in and stuff like that, but I didn't think I'd get in and out without an alarm going. But it didn't matter. I was going to get in no matter what it took; smash a window, break down a door; anything, because even if I was caught by the cops, whatever sentence I got, whatever fine I was hit with or time I had to serve, it had to be less . . . less unpleasant than what would happen to me if you heard that answering machine tape.'

'And if my friends in the Met had caught you, what were you going to claim was your purpose in breaking into my house?'

I shrug again. 'My, ah, first thought was to claim that I'd become obsessed with your wife, but then I thought you'd probably be pretty upset about that, too, so I decided I'd claim that I'd become a . . . vigilante or something, that I was looking for evidence of your criminality, or just wanted to give you a taste of your own medicine, subjecting you to crime. It didn't matter how stupid it sounded, how lame, as long as I got that tape wiped.'

'But the study was locked, Kenneth,' Merrial says reasonably. 'How did you get in there?'

I frown. Just lie, I think. Deny the video, the recorded evidence. Pretend it's Lawson Brierley we're dealing with here. Trust to the graininess of the image, the awkward angle the camera has of that door and the big gloves I was wearing to obscure the fact I used a key. 'No it wasn't,' I tell him. 'The study was open.'

'Kenneth,' Merrial says gently. He nods at the Range Rover where Kaj put the laptop. 'We can see it was locked.'

'It wasn't!' I protest. 'I stuck my head in, saw it wasn't a bedroom, caught a glimpse of the answering machine and kept going!' I look at Kaj. 'I did! It took about two seconds; I was desperate. I was about to . . .' I let my voice fall away and look down at my lap. 'I was about to do what I've just done, for Christ's sake. I took a very quick look, closed the door and kept on going.' I'm breathing deep and hard. There are tears in my eyes. I look at Merrial. 'God, man, what I'm telling you is bad enough; what more could make it worse?'

Merrial looks slowly from me to Celia. He looks thoughtful. 'That's what I've been asking myself, Kenneth.' He switches his gaze to Kaj. 'That possible? What he just said?' he asks.

Kaj shrugs massively. 'Perhaps,' he says. His voice is deep but not as Swedish as I'd been expecting. 'The frame capture rate is about one per three seconds. He might have had time to open and close the door between frames.'

Merrial looks at me. 'The study was locked when I got back yesterday,' he says.

I shrug again. 'Well, I don't know!' I say, almost wailing. 'Maybe I put the sneck down.'

Merrial looks puzzled. 'The what?'

'Scottish word,' I say desperately. 'The, the, the catch thing down, on the lock inside the door. Anyway, I was about to leave when you came back, so I hid in the cupboard in the gym. I heard you on the phone to your wife saying you were calling somebody called Sky or Kyle or something. Then when you were showering I almost made it to the front door when, when –' I gesture at Kaj '– when he came in, so I hid in the cloakroom by the front door. Once he'd gone upstairs I just walked out.' I let out a deep, juddering breath. 'That's it. Whole truth. Nothing but.'

Mr Merrial purses his lips. He looks at me for a few moments, and I grit my teeth and return his stare. He nods.

And I realise then that there is – just – the hint of a chance. There's a hint of a chance because, complicit in the conspiracy Ceel and I are involved in here, attempting to deceive Mr Merrial, there is, surprisingly, a third person, and that third person is Merrial himself.

The man doesn't really want to find out he's been cuckolded. He knows he has to be suspicious – suspicion is sensible, suspicion is safe, suspicion is how he lives his entire professional life – but, ultimately, he'd rather not discover his wife and another man have made a fool of him. He will go so far to make sure it looks like nothing's happened – as far as is reasonable, as far as he must to establish the truth beyond something like reasonable doubt – but he won't pursue the matter as doggedly and as determinedly as he might a debt, or an insult from another crook.

His own pride puts him on the same side as Ceel and me; none of us wants him to know the truth.

Merrial makes a sort of huffing noise that might be a laugh and gets down from the Bentley, walking slowly over to me, his hands raised in front of his chin as though in prayer. He stops and looks at Celia. 'Maria was last out, apparently,' he says. 'I think we need a new maid.' Celia's frown deepens. Merrial comes up to me. He sits down, gently, on my right knee. Oh shit, oh shit, oh shit. Totally fucking wrong about all the above. Oh fuck. Here it comes.

416

He smiles at me. 'This is on account, Kenneth,' he says easily, in a pleasant voice. 'Nothing compared to what'll follow, I should think, but this is personal, from me, for invading my privacy.'

He takes a good back swing and punches me hard in the balls.

I'd forgotten how much it hurt. School playground, last time this happened. I'd forgotten the lights, the nausea, the waves and waves of subtly differing types of pain that course through your body when this is done to you. Not being able to double up properly just makes it worse. It was as though your brain had stored up all the orgasms you'd ever had in your whole life to that point, then paid them back, all in one go, with the polarity reversed so that what had been ecstasy became agony and what had been over in seconds each day was lumped together over five or ten consecutive minutes of pure, grisly, pulsating pain.

I screamed, loud and high and shrill, then sucked and wheezed and gasped in the slowly, slowly ebbing aftermath.

Merrial had gone back to the Bentley.

'How fucking dare you,' Celia said. Her voice sounded more menacing and cold than Merrial's had at any point so far. I blinked through the tears and looked at her. She was looking levelly, gravely at Merrial.

Merrial looked back. 'Yes, dear?' he said. But it already sounded weak. Something in the way Ceel had spoken had given her the initiative here.

'How fucking *dare* you do that to him and make me watch it,' she breathed. She walked across the pallets towards Merrial. Kaj followed a step behind, looking wary. Celia stopped a metre from her husband. 'You have no right to do that,' she said. Her voice was shaking with controlled fury. 'You have no right to make me witness it, no right to make me part of it, no right to make yourself the law and me no better than one of your fucking *thugs*.' She spat the last word out like a broken tooth.

Merrial looked down briefly. 'You know I don't like you using that sort of language, Celia,' he said calmly.

'I am *not* one of your fucking gang!' she shouted at him

He looked up, blinking. 'Oh, for Christ's sake!' he yelled back. 'What do you think buys your jewellery, your dresses, the holidays?'

'I'm not stupid!' Celia exploded. 'I'm not a *fool*! I know damn well! *Mon dieu!* I thought, I stupidly *thought* until tonight that I didn't get involved in *this* sort of thing –' she gestured behind, towards me '– in return for me staying with you, even though I know what you do, what you've become!'

Merrial shook his head and pulled down his cuffs, looking awkward but recovering his composure. 'It was always like this, Ceel.'

(And, as some further little part of me died along with hope, I thought, Oh, no. Oh, no; he calls her Ceel, he uses the same name for her that I do.)

She clenched her fists in front of her, shaking her head. 'I did not marry *this*!' she said, a sort of tumultuous control infecting her voice. 'I married *you*. I married a man who took me from a bad place and bad people and a bad thing inside myself, a man who made me feel protected as well as desired.' She stood back and straightened up. She looked down at him. 'I will not stand for this, John.'

He looked down again. 'You've been having an affair,' he told her quietly.

'*What?*' she said, and, with that one word, somehow, and for only about the third or fourth time since I'd met her, sounded like a French-speaker speaking English.

'We have photographs, more video,' he said, looking down again. He glanced to me, then Kaj.

She stared at him. She shook her head slowly. 'You have nothing,' she said quietly. A silence followed. I realised that somewhere in the black, hollow distance, somewhere through the ambient smell of decay, there was a slow drip-drip-drip noise. 'Nothing,' she repeated. 'Except paranoia.'

He looked up at her. She shook her head again. 'My girlfriends,' she said slowly, 'have boyfriends, husbands, brothers; sometimes when we meet up one of them will get there just before or just after me, before the others do. Don't think that a photograph of me sitting in Harvey Nics with a man you don't know constitutes an affair. Leave those people out of your sordid imaginings.'

Merrial looked from her to me.

Celia frowned, then glanced back at me. 'With *him*?' she said, and laughed. She turned to look at me, and stopped laughing, looked serious. 'Mr Nott; no offence, but I could do better.'

'None taken,' I managed to wheeze round the pain.

Celia whirled round to face her husband again. 'Show me, then. Show me what this evidence is!'

Merrial just smiled at her, but the smile was strained, and by then even I could see what she'd sensed instantly; he really didn't have any evidence on her, he'd been hoping to force a confession out of her with the accusation alone, if a confession had been due.

Celia fixed her gaze upon her husband then and took on a frosty look. Actually, frosty didn't even start to cover it; it was more of a shaving-of-a-degree-above-absolute-zero look. It put the fear of God into me and I was only caught in the backwash of its baleful focus. Merrial withstood it somehow – must have built up some sort of immunity over the years they'd been married, I supposed – but you could see he was affected. Some fuckwit part of me, patently not in any way connected to my horribly bruised and still jangling testes, almost felt sorry for the bastard.

'I have been a faithful wife to you,' Celia said in a measured, contained, utterly sure and certain voice. 'I have always been *faithful* to you!' she said, her voice breaking.

And sitting there, right then, goddammit, even *I* believed her. I'd have stood up in court or on any field of honour to insist with my last breath that this woman had been an utterly faithful wife and was being sorely, grievously wronged and defamed by being accused of being anything else.

Part of me found the time to wonder how the hell she was *doing* this, and that was when it occurred to me that – just possibly – Ceel's patently lunatic ideas about entanglement were making a real and crucial difference here. Maybe at this moment she genuinely believed that she had been a faithful wife, because, in that other reality she claimed to be linked to, she actually was. She was speaking not so much for herself but for the Celia on the other side of that divide; the Celia who was a perfectly, unimpeachably good wife who had never cheated; the Celia who could rightly claim, as she just had, that she had always been faithful to her husband.

'Can you say the same to me, John?' Her voice was hollow as a vast canyon, and as sad as the sound of earth hitting a tiny coffin.

Merrial met her gaze.

Drip, drip, drip, in the distance. I was breathing hard, swallowing on a dry, parched throat. The smell of death and shit didn't seem quite so bad in the air around us now, but maybe it was just something you got used to. Eventually Merrial said, 'Of course I can say it, Celia.'

That last shaving above Zero Kelvin vanished with a whimper into the darkness surrounding us.

'Do not treat me like a fool, John,' Celia said, and her voice was like the voice a glacier would have if it could speak, the voice of the oldest, steepest, widest, most powerful mountain-grinding-up glacier in all the fucking world, after it had thought good and hard in glacier terms about precisely what it wanted to articulate.

Merrial cleared his throat. I didn't realise he must have

looked away until he brought his gaze up to meet hers again
with what looked like an appalling, abysmally draining amount
of effort. 'You—'

'I want a divorce, John,' she said.

Fucking bombshell. Just like that. Merrial blinked. The two
of them stayed that way for a few moments, him swinging one
foot without realising it, thunking against the trailing edge of
the Bentley's wheel arch, her glaring down at him, perfectly,
savagely still.

Merrial glanced at Kaj, me and the other two guys before
looking back to her. 'I don't think here is really—'

'We talk about it here, now,' Celia said quickly. 'You brought
me here to see this, you changed our rules. You put cameras
in my *home*.' Her voice almost broke, and she took a quick,
controlling breath. 'So business and marriage are the same,
now,' she told him. 'They are in the same arena. I said: I want
a divorce.'

Merrial ground his teeth. 'No,' he said.

She didn't react. Dear God, this woman had perfected
threatening stillness to a high art indeed. Merrial might be
good, but Ceel would have made a brilliant crime boss.

Merrial cleared his throat and lifted his head up to her again.
'Actually, *I* want a divorce, Celia.'

She tilted her head a little. 'You do, do you?' Her voice was
neutral now, but sounded ready to slip into menace or accusation at any moment.

'Yes, I need a divorce.' Merrial gave an unhealthy looking
little smile. 'I don't like the term "widower", Celia, so I hope
you'll be as accommodating as I require you to be.'

She laughed a quick, convulsive laugh. 'And what does *that*
mean?'

Merrial looked just plain nasty now. 'It means don't expect
any money.'

She gasped. Really gasped, genuinely astonished. 'I don't

421

want your *money*, John,' she told him. There was a hint in her tone as though she had just realised she had been dealing with a child all along. 'I didn't marry you for money I didn't want it then and I don't now. Keep the money. Have your divorce.' She was breathing hard now, shoulders rising and falling in the yellow and black jacket. Her voice had quivered over the last few sentences, barely under control. 'So,' she said, shaking her head once, regaining command. 'Has one of them insisted you make an honest woman of her?'

'You might say that,' Merrial said. You could see he was having to force himself to keep looking at her, battling against the pressure of that remorselessly self-possessed gaze.

'The one in Amsterdam?' she asked evenly.

'The one in Amsterdam.' There was a strange sort of defiance in his tone.

'And is she younger than I am, John?' Celia asked quietly. 'Is she more beautiful? Is she as young as I was when you met me? Or younger? Is she as exotic, is she as foreign? Is she better connected? Has she a famous name? Has she money? Is she fertile?'

Merrial's gaze might have flickered a little.

Ceel relaxed her stance. She stood back, her weight went more on one foot than the other as she nodded. 'Ah,' she said. 'She is pregnant, is she?'

Merrial's eyes went wide just for a moment, then he gave a small laugh. 'You always were good like that, weren't you, Celia?' He looked past his wife to the big blond guy. 'Isn't she, Kaj?'

Kaj just looked awkward, and nodded.

'Well, congratulations,' Celia said bitterly.

She seemed suddenly to collapse inside then, looking quickly away and putting one hand up to her eyes. Silently, her shoulders – wide inside the thick yellow and black hiking jacket – shook; spasming once, twice, three times. Merrial looked even

422

more awkward and uncertain. He seemed to be about to go to her and hug her, but he didn't. He tried to find something to do with his hands and then folded his arms and looked at Kaj and did a sort of pathetic, Women, eh? look and gesture at the bigger man. Kaj sort of twitched, which was probably as close as he was going to come to waxing eloquent on the matter.

You beautiful, brave, intelligent, fabulous woman, I thought, staring at her with tears in my eyes. I had to look away, in case Merrial saw the way I was gazing at his wife. I was still having to remind myself that the extraordinary, exquisite, immaculately righteous ire she was displaying here was all in fact a complete fake, that she was lying through her perfect, delicious teeth when she told Merrial she'd been a faithful wife, but she had successfully, so far, anyway, shifted the focus of all that was going on here away from me and onto herself, onto her marriage. She'd gone nuclear with the big D word and duly been nuked in return, but it looked like she was actually getting away with it.

This was a woman fighting for her own life and that of her lover, but she wasn't settling for just the result, she seemed determined to accomplish the task with audacity, bravura and style. I didn't think I'd seen a more resourceful and courageous piece of acting in all my life, in person, on stage or on screen. Even if it still all went horribly, painfully, lethally wrong from here on in, at least I could suffer and die knowing I had been in the presence of genius.

Celia dried her eyes with one hand, then fetched a handkerchief from one of the pockets in her jeans and dabbed at her nose and cheeks. She sniffed and put the hanky away again. She drew herself up. 'I don't want any money. And I won't say anything, to the press, the police, to anybody. I never have, I never will. But I want to be left alone, afterwards. I want to live my own life. You live yours. I live mine. And nothing must happen to any of my family, any of my loved ones.' She raised her chin to him after she said this, as though defying him to object to any of it.

Merrial nodded, then said softly, 'Fair enough.' He made a small gesture with his hands. 'I'm sorry it had to end like this, Celia.'

'I'm sorry it had to be so bloody undignified, in front of Kaj and these guys and –' she gestured vaguely in my direction '– this poor clown.'

Merrial looked at me like he'd forgotten I was there. He sighed. 'I thought . . .' he began. Then he shrugged. He fixed me with a stare I shrank back from. 'One word on your show about this, Mr Nott, one word to anybody at all; friends or family or police or public, and I'll make sure you die slowly, do you understand?'

I swallowed, nodded. I didn't trust myself to say anything sensible. The fuckwit bit of me with its thumb seemingly superglued to my personal Self-Destruct button wanted to say something like, Yeah yeah yeah, fucking *omertà* or I die in drawn-out agony, yada yada yada big man, but your wife's just worked you over and we both fucking know it and this compensatory macho threat stuff isn't convincing anybody . . . Eventually, though, under that gaze, I had to give way and croak, 'Yeah. Yes, I understand. Nothing. Nobody.'

Merrial kept looking at me for a moment longer, then nodded to the two guys standing at my shoulders. 'Give him back his stuff and take him back to where you found him.'

'In the box, Mr M?' said the guy who'd hit me.

Merrial looked upset. 'No, not in the fucking box. In the back of the van; put some tape over his eyes, that'll do.'

I thought, Yes! . . . but just a tad too soon. Kaj stepped past Celia, lowered his mouth to his boss's ear and muttered something. Merrial smiled that thin, thin smile of his and quietly said, 'All right. One little one.' Then, as I thought, No, no, no!

424

We got *away* with it! This isn't supposed to happen! Please, no! Merrial looked at Celia and sighed and said, 'Maybe you'd best look away.' Celia rolled her eyes and did so.

Kaj stood in front of me.

'This is for crapping in my loo,' he said.

I had just enough time to think, *Now* the cunt sounds vaguely Swedish, then he punched me so hard across the face I didn't wake up until I was in the back of the Astramax again, eyes taped over and hands tied together but otherwise unrestricted. My head and my balls hurt like fuck, blood was bubbling from my nose, my pants were full of chilled shit and I was very cold indeed; a bitter winter breeze was whipping through the van from the open front windows.

I didn't blame the guys; it was reeking in here.

Thirteen

THE SCOTTISH
VERDICT

'What the fucking hell happened to you?'

'I walked into a door.'

'. . . Right. Would some stairs be involved at any point?'

'That's right; then I fell down some stairs.'

'And after that?'

'Then somebody beat the shit out of me, Craig.'

'That must have taken a while. Were they working shifts?'

'. . . Now that has got to smart.'

'Philip, if I live for a thousand years, "smart" is not a word I will ever choose to associate with how I came to acquire this little lot.'

'Good, your brain and tongue are still working. Debbie wants to see us after the show and the first record up is Addicta's new one with Jo on joint lead vocals . . . Na, looking for sympathy doesn't get any more efficient with a black eye. Good try, though.'

'Oh, my good Lord almighty, get yourself in here, Kennit, you need tendin to.'

'Fackin ell, man, you white guys go *brilliant* colours!'

Anonymous. 'Yes?'

'Don't forget to wipe your phone's Last Calls Made and Received memories, just in case. I've tidied everything at this end.'

'Already done.' I'd destroyed the calling card with the incriminating code number on it, too. 'Though now I'll have to do this one, of course. Celia?'

'What, Kenneth?'

'Thank you. You were brilliant. You saved my miserable life.'

'It was my pleasure.'

'I love you.'

'Still? Are you sure?'

'I do. I mean it.'

'Well. Thank you, Kenneth.'

'. . . What happens now?'

'I have to pay the woman who was our maid some money to compensate her for her dismissal.'

'That's not what I meant.'

'I know.'

'So.'

'So. Well, wait.'

'For what?'

'For a package, and a phone call?'

'So I'll see you again.'

'I can hear you are smiling as you say that. Yes.'

'Ditto, kid. And will I see you again, after this next time?'

'I would hope so. You know it will not be the same, though, don't you? It can never be the same again.'

'I know. But maybe it can be better.'

'John has started divorce proceedings. He is in Amsterdam most of the time now.'

'So can we meet up soon?'

'I need to be very careful, still, but I hope so, soon. I must go.'

'I'm sorry, Ceel. About getting us both into that mess.'

'Good came of it. Never do its like again.'

'I pro—'

'I must go, my love.'

'—mise. Hey, wait; did you say—?'

'. . .'

There is this verdict, which is unique, as far as I know, to the Scottish legal system, and remained distinct from the English one even for the three centuries of the full Union with the rest of the UK. It's called Not Proven.

It means that the jury isn't going to go as far as pronouncing the defendant Not Guilty, but that the prosecuting authorities simply have not proved their case. It's a funny verdict, because you still leave the court a free man or woman, with no criminal record (well, unless you had one before, of course), though people – friends and family, the community at large – may remember, and the implications of that neither-one-thing-nor-the-other verdict might well live with you for the rest of your life.

There have been moves to get rid of it, to adopt the binary choice of Guilty or Not Guilty, but I think that's a mistake. If I was on a jury I would never agree to a Not Proven verdict for somebody I basically thought was Guilty, but I would go as far as Not Proven for somebody I would otherwise have found just plain Not Guilty and who I thought ought not to be punished beyond the implications of that debatable verdict itself. Because that's what it is: a semi-punishment, a sort of warning, a conditional discharge that is, remarkably, in the gift of the jury, not the judge. I think it's worth keeping for that alone.

I've wondered for many months now if that was the

judgement John Merrial recorded in the personal courtroom he kept in his head, if he still suspected there was something more going on somewhere, just with me, or even between me and Celia.

I don't know. I can't decide.

Not Proven. It would do.

It's one of those odd concepts that, the more you think about it, the more it seems applicable within all sorts of other contexts besides the one it originated in. My whole radio career, for example, feels like it has been Not Proven (actually it's been Guilty loads of times, whenever I got fired again, but – overall – I'm still claiming the Not Proven thing). Scotland; the UK, devolution. More British? More European? Not Proven.

And Celia and me. Not Proven.

I never did get that package and that phone call. Instead she decided we ought to start meeting in public. She suggested the British Museum, the first time; the room that held the Nereid Monument. This was in March. In front of that pale and towering edifice of Imperial plunder, we met, nodded, shook hands, then went for coffee in the museum's café. She asked how I was and I said I was recovering. She apologised for her husband's behaviour, hurting me as he had, and I apologised for mine, entering her home without permission. We talked as though playing parts, then parted with another handshake. I slipped the folded piece of paper she'd passed during the handshake into my pocket and met her in the Sanderson the next afternoon. The sex hurt. Me; not her, obviously. But it was still great.

We started to meet up more often, through the spring and into the summer, while Mr M set up his operating base in Amsterdam and the divorce proceedings slid smoothly along and his new fiancée blossomed.

We met in public as friends. In private, less often, as the lovers we had always been.

One day in June she kissed me on the cheek as she left the bar, and the following week brushed her lips with mine as she got out of the taxi, after dinner. A fortnight later we went to Clout, dancing, and kissed on the dance floor and later in a shady booth in the Retox bar. It was late July before she came to the *Temple Belle* and stayed overnight, so that I finally got to spend a whole night with her, and wake up with her. We never did discover if anybody had been watching. But the risk had not been worth taking.

I still worry that one day Merrial will wake up and just somehow know that of course Celia and I had been lovers back then, when it seemed he had suspected we might be, and still take his revenge, but Ceel seems quite sanguine about this.

'John thinks I am too proper and too concerned with fairness,' she told me. 'Paying off Maria and meeting you to apologise for all that happened appear like symptoms of an amusing obsession to him. He thinks that I am going out with you to spite him, that I am deliberately or subconsciously taking what he suspected wrongly and making it true, just to punish him. So he believes that what you and I have together is about him, not us, which pleases his ego, and he thinks that I am deceiving myself over my motives in seeing you in the first place, which he also finds a comfort.'

I frowned. 'You sure about this?'

'But of course. I can see what he thinks, and I know how to make him think certain things.'

I thought about this, and an appalling thought occurred to me. 'You can't do the same with me, can you?'

Celia laughed lightly, squeezed my hand and said, 'What could possibly make you think that?'

I had no real answer.

So, anyway, I think we're safe, but still; Not Proven.

Another of my worries was that what we had between us would all have changed too much, that we had only ever existed as the fervently coupled entity we had been as a sort of two-person sexual freak; exquisite and fine in the rarefied, hot-house atmosphere of those episodically connected, lily-scented hotel rooms, but utterly unsuited to the rest of life, to the day-to-dayness of mundane existence, where such a delicate bloom would shrivel and die in the light of the commonplace. Maybe we had nothing more to say to each other than what we had already said, with our minds and our bodies, in those intense darknesses. Perhaps we both had habits, idiosyncrasies, that the other had never experienced because until then – in the erratically dispersed and limited intervals we'd been able to claim, inside those tropically lush, reality-divorced suites – we'd been too busy having sex to exhibit any other behaviours.

So she discovered that I snored if I'd been drinking and then slept on my back (I'm sure there's a *lot* more, but I trust her to tell me). What I found was that, try as she might, she could not resist slipping into rapid-fire Martinique-style French patois whenever she was with her relations or talked to them over the phone. Oh, and when she had a cold once, she was a *rotten* patient; she whined and over-dramatised like a man. She claims this is because she practically never gets ill and so has had no practice. That's about it. Well, that and the craziness about being entangled. Her twenty-eighth birthday had come and gone without incident or appreciable change, and she had seemed vaguely, distractedly disappointed for a day or so, then had shrugged it off and got on with things.

'How can you just give up on all that?' I'd protested. 'How can you just let it drop? I thought you really believed in all that crap!'

Ceel had shrugged. 'I think perhaps that the cross-over point came earlier than it was meant to,' she'd said, frowning. 'In that underground car park. It was meant to happen on my birthday, but it happened then instead. That was a strong event.

434

It pulled matters towards it, distorting things sufficiently.' She'd nodded, as if coming to a decision, and smiled at me, radiantly. 'Yes.'

I'd shaken my head.

The ironic thing was that now sometimes I had dreams and nightmares in which I was the entangled one, and caught terrifying glimpses into another reality where I hobbled round on crutches, a broken man, and never saw Celia again; or I'd wake panting from images of my own decaying body, a space of rotting flesh curled fetal within a concrete mould inside a waterlogged packing case resting on the bottom of the Thames, downstream.

And in any case Celia still thought she was entangled, provisional. So: one of us? Both of us? Neither?

Me, I'd tick Option C there, but who the hell really knew? Not Proven, if you liked.

I never went back to the house in Ascot Square. Celia slept aboard the *Temple Belle* maybe once a week. Craig and I became friends again, though we were kind of starting from scratch. Emma was probably the most okay about it. Nikki found out about me and her mum and gave me a glare I will remember to the end of my days. 'Ken,' she said, relenting and shaking her head ruefully. 'What are you like?'

They all think Ceel's wonderful. Ed does too. The first time he laid eyes on her he immediately said, 'Leave im. Be mine. I'll give up all the uvvers. An I mean for ever. Plob'ly.'

Celia smiled and said, 'You must be Edward. How do you do?'

Later that evening, when she was out of earshot, I asked him, 'You like her, then? Think I should stick with this one?'

I was trying to be funny but he looked at me pityingly and said, 'Mate, I don't fink it's a question of *you* decidin to stick wif *er*.' Even now sometimes he'll just stare at the two of us and shake his head and look at me and say, '*Ow?*'

435

I suppose he's right.

I don't make a big thing of it, but I have told Ceel I love her, while she doesn't so much tell me as let it slip, rarely. About the only time I ever see her get flustered or embarrassed is when she says something like she said that first time over the phone, and calls me 'my love', or something similar. I asked her about this one night when we were particularly relaxed and easy with things, and she just smiled and suggested that love was a word that had become cheapened. 'Where love is concerned,' she told me, 'you must be a behaviourist.' I thought about this and decided, Well, I feel loved.

So, Not Proven. Maybe no relationship that is not over is ever really proven, one way or the other. Perhaps that's all we can ever hope for, in this fractured, fallen world we've constructed for ourselves, and our heirs.

Addicta became very big indeed and Jo's face seemed to be everywhere, but thankfully then they or their management decided they had to crack the States, and they did the rising-without-trace thing and effectively disappeared off most people's near-space radar screens.

I kept my job, amazingly.

The month before we were due to go to Martinique, we flew to Glasgow. All Celia had really seen of Scotland was this fucking bleak estate and draughty castle near Inverness and close-ups of the heads of stags and hinds through a telescope before some other bugger shot them, and I wanted to start showing her the rest of the place, in all its late-summer glory. We had a week, would hire a car, stay in B&Bs. We spent some time shopping and wandering around Glasgow during that first day, before we went back to my parents' place for dinner, and – in a sudden shower, dodging traffic – we ran across Renfield Street, holding hands.

If you have enjoyed this book, you can find out more about Iain Banks' other titles on his website

www.iain-banks.net

Or for more books by Iain Banks, Abacus or Little, Brown books go to our website

www.littlebrown.co.uk

To order any Abacus titles p & p free in the UK, please contact our mail order supplier on:

+ 44 (0)1832 737525

Customers not based in the UK should contact the same number for appropriate postage and packing costs.